FAR AWAY
Run the Roads

MARGARITA BORKAEV

Zeta Publishing, Inc
P.O. Box 953
Silver Springs, FL 34489
www.zetapublishing.com

This is a work of fiction. All of the characters, names, incidents, organizations, and dialogue in this novel are either the products of the author's imagination or are used fictitiously.

Ordering Information:
Quantity sales. Special discounts are available on quantity purchases by corporations, associations, and others. For details, contact the publisher at the address above.
Orders by U.S. trade bookstores and wholesalers. Please contact Zeta Publishing: Tel: (352) 694-2553; Fax: (352) 694-1791 or visit www.zetapublishing.com

First published by Xlibris in 2012

Rev. Date: October 2019

ISBN: 978-1-950340-20-0 (sc)
ISBN: 978-1-950340-21-7 (e)

Library of Congress: 2019915754
Printed in the United States of America

INTRODUCTION

Margarita Borkaev (Borukaeva) has a romantic profession. She is a "microbe hunter," and she pursued her prey with great ardor in some of the most prestigious laboratories of the Soviet Union. Then fate willed her to the front lines of microbiology in the United States of America. Undoubtedly, the riddles of this science seemed to her fantastically fascinating in light of the romantic nature of her soul, which, from her earliest adolescence manifested itself in its pull to find self-expression in poetry.

Thus arose her first collection of poems (published in Moscow). Poems – from those giving a lyric voice to important social issues, to poems that chronicled the joys, the vicissitudes, and the sorrows of love and sought to embody the beauty of nature – were written throughout the entire duration of her life. These poems appear regularly in the Russian-speaking American newspapers.

I am certain that the readers not only value them but also find themes that are personally close to themselves.

Margarita took a great interest in prose too. Her essays, stories, short novels have been published in American (in English) and Russian-American (in Russian) magazines and newspapers.

Recently she has published this book in Russia. The book based on autobiographical events, but it includes stories about people, involved in Margarita's life, and reflects conflicts the author experienced in the Soviet Union. . The content of some stories of this book is dramatic, but their style is so lyrical that it reminds one of verse in prose form. This especially apparent as each section ends with an emotional final chord. The book was instantly absorbed and disseminated by her readers

I had found effortless to read this book анд entirely engrossing since in it is reflected all of the facets of Margarita's character, her openness towards new people and new experiences, her friendliness, her near-unlimited capacity for compassion and understanding. Margarita has a remarkable ability to come to an innate understanding of the core of a person and then to describe it with such affection and sympathy that as a reader I felt that I shared not just her adventures, but also her friendships.

I advise you to read this book as a long time friend and an old admirer of Margarita's talent. I am certain, that like me, once you begin, this book will capture your imagination until you reach the final paragraph. And, like me, long after you close the cover you will still reflect on the extraordinary events you will have find there, and the unpredictable twist of fate that can be expected of us all.

-Roy Medvedev.

For English readers: **Roy Medvedev** is a Russian historian renowned as the author of the dissident history of Stalinism, *Let History Judge*, first published in English in 1972. He is the author of numerous well-respected works. Medvedev became a prominent Russian writer, politician, and Member of Parliament. He served as a consultant to Mikhail Gorbachev.

PART I.
Discern where the light is.

Discern where the light is,
And you'll know where the darkness is,
What in this world is sacred and what is sinful...
-Alexander Blok

DISTURBING PUZZLE

How old was she when we talked the last time? It's hard to tell. During all her life Leah never seemed to change. Was it that her age did not affect her, or, possibly, she had been "an older woman" all her life? Stiff, stern, wearing pince-nez, her face in long wrinkles, she kept herself straight and her voice was a little squeaky. She had neither family nor children, and everybody assumed her incapable of tender feelings. When I was a kid I didn't like her. She constantly lectured my mother about how children are not to be spoiled, and I hated that. I turned away my contemptuous little face even when Leah threw her backpack under my and my sister's feet, to spare us from stepping barefoot on the cold-asphalted floor of the train station. It was during the war (we always say *the war* referring to World War II) when family members of those working at research institutes, had to take trains and go to work in our vegetable gardens out in the countryside to supplement our meager food ration.

But then, twenty years later, at our last meeting, we were sitting on a wooden bench in front of a big flower bed at the Flower Square. It was a wonderful idea: demolish the terrible barracks of wartime and fill this space with flowers. I was sorry to see some pompous building erected there later.

The evening was warm and soft: spring had gone but it was not summer yet; smells of flowers were coming from all over. Leah closed her eyes; I thought she was dozing off, so I sat quietly enjoying this peaceful rest. I was even disappointed when she started talking, but the next minute I was listening to her, rapt with attention.

Now, as an adult, I appreciated Leah, loved her. Time and circumstances neither changed her looks nor her iron principals. She remained a faithful and constant friend of our family, although she had never said a single affectionate word to our parents or to us children. Maybe that was the reason why it was so amazing for me to hear her now. The way she was talking was different; her voice sounded sad and thoughtful, so unusual for her, even without that squeaking.

"They were beautiful, your parents, oh, how beautiful they were... I always admired them." She smiled, "There was such a sparkle in your father's eyes that I thought, if I put a piece of paper close to them, the paper would flare up. The fire; this is a very precise word to describe your father. He was always full of fire; whatever he was doing he was always burning with excitement. And he had a great talent, an almost magical geological vision. Everything about him was so very bright, so different. I enjoyed working with him."

She stopped for a minute and continued: "There was one thing, though, I could not understand: he had a penetrating mind, but he could not recognize his enemies. Your father trusted people too much. Once we had a fight; I told him straight to his face who had denounced him. He became terribly angry with me; he didn't even talk to me for a month. I decided then to prove, whatever it takes, that I was right, that I was not bad-mouthing that man, his enemy, just because I did not like him, as your father accused me of doing".

Leah became silent. I got impatient; it was difficult for me to wait.

"So, Leah, did you find the proof?"

"I did, but it was too late. Who knows, maybe it was for the better because your father trusted this man and loved him. I don't know why he liked him and never saw what a villain he was."

I had a hard time holding my emotions. As a child, I remembered my mother telling us how our father escaped arrest three times, by some miracle. Denunciation and slander followed him all his life. I absolutely had to find out the name of this person, who followed my father like a black shadow.

"Leah, who was it?"

"Wait, don't rush. I could tell you now, but I'd better give you all my papers. These are not a diary, but I had always written down everything that was of interest to me, everything that was beyond the usual. There you'll find the answer to your question.

This delay annoyed me, but I understood she wanted to give a proper foundation to her accusations. We agreed that the next morning she would organize all her records and I would come to get them at noon.

I couldn't sleep that night. In my mind I was going through all the familiar names, but I could not think of any one who could be that person. At three o'clock in the morning I got up, turned on the light and tried to read the book I which was very interesting for me the day before. But I was looking at a page, reading and rereading the same sentence without understanding. My thoughts kept going back to the same question: who was he, this enemy, who played the fateful role in my father's life so many times? Finally fatigue took over; I fell asleep in my chair, the book in my hands. My sleep was unpleasant, with bad dreams. A dark scary figure was threatening my father. I wanted to scream and warn him, but I had no voice. I strained every nerve trying to run for help; my feet were too heavy, I could not pull them off the floor. The dark figure was coming closer and closer to my father, and I despaired because of my helplessness; I was in terror feeling something awful was about to happen.

I woke with my heart beating rapidly, but a friendly Asian sun poured into the room. Through my open window I could hear melodious calls of small Indian pigeons, introduced recently to the area to save poplars from voracious caterpillars. Feeling enormous relief, I stuck my head out of the window and deeply inhaled the bitterish smell of young poplar leaves. Leah would be digging through her papers right at this moment; I still had two or three more hours before going to see her. I tried to find something to occupy myself but I couldn't concentrate on anything. I finally decided that eleven o'clock is almost noon, and I hurried out to Leah's.

At the entrance of her four-story apartment building, I saw a small group of people and an ambulance. A pang stabbed my heart as I rushed in. Emergency personnel carrying a stretcher were coming toward me.

At the hospital I was told it was a heart attack. Leah had called the emergency number; "A heart pain..." she said. She gave her address and the telephone fell from her hands. When the medical help arrived, she was unconscious. "The voice on the telephone sounded so calm, as though she was talking not about herself, but about a perfect stranger," a nurse told me in amazement. As for me, I knew Leah, and I understood: even in this extreme situation she kept her self-control.

Leah passed away, and another connection with my childhood and my parents was gone. I felt bitterness and pain of losing this last old friend of my family. Leah's apartment was sealed until one of her relatives could arrive. My vacation was over, and I had to be back at my job in Moscow. Sadly, I parted from my sister at the airport and she promised to contact Leah's relative as soon as she arrived, and to get the papers Leah promised me. When I told my sister about my last conversation with Leah, she got excited, no less than I.

My sister did everything possible to get the papers, and in less than three months, I received the big package. Leah's notes were short and dry, but she described all the important events having to do with my father with great accuracy, and she even had some supporting documents. My sister also sent me another folder. It held my mother's recollections; notes she made of what my father told her, and also of what his friends and colleagues remembered. These papers, as opposed to Leah's, were very vivid, written in good language, and easy to read.

Of course I also remembered things, but my childhood memories were disjointed; isolated pictures would flash in my head.

It is a night in the boundless steppe; our car is moving fast, somewhere in total darkness. Giant shadows of monsters jump in our headlights, and I refuse to believe that they are just the jerboas. Phosphorescent eyes of mysterious creatures flare up along the sides of the car. My sister and I feel our mother's worry, and I am afraid when she asks, "Raslan, you can't see the road, where are we going?" I hear the voice of our father sitting next to the driver, "We are going in the right direction, Elena, I know it, I feel it." He turns toward us, and immediately I am calm: his look is so confident and full of joy.

Another picture; again we are on an expedition, and again it is a boundless steppe at night. This time our old American willys (left after WW11) drives in the pouring rain. It is cold, uncomfortable and very late at night. I am tired, but it is impossible to sleep in sleeping bags under the rain, but our geological camp is still too far. We come to a small, made from clay lonely hut, walk in through a squeaking door and ask if we can stay overnight. A weak old woman's voice answers from her sleeping nook on top of the high *Russian stove,* *

"Don't even think about it. There is no food, you cannot stay here. I have been dying for three days; I am too weak to get down from the stove."

My father approaches the stove; "Are you dying, grandma? But I have a medicine. It is from the Kremlin Hospital; it will cure anybody from anything at once. Do you see this pill? Take it and look at me, look straight into my eyes. I'll be counting. All your ailments will be gone by the time I count to ten, as if you were never sick."

With some distrust the old woman swallows the pill, and father begins to count very slowly, clearly, loudly, his eyes fixed on her. We stay very–very quiet; I am holding my breath. At the count ten the old woman says in amazement; "I am really better now. From Kremlin, it is a miracle. Well, help me down from the stove."

Then we drink tea and eat homemade bread. We sleep in our sleeping bags spread on the floor. In the morning we continue our journey.

"That pill, it worked so fast. It is magic! Is it really from the Kremlin?" our driver asks.

My father laughs. "This was just an aspirin. I cured her by hypnosis. This, my friend, is stronger than any Kremlin pill."

---

* The Russian stove was not only a heater and a cooker, but also it provided a perfect sleeping nook. The plank bed, arranged on the very top of the stove just beneath the ceiling, gained plenty of warm air.

* * *

I read the papers my sister sent. The image of my father came to life – lively, with his remarkable shining eyes; and my mother beside him. They were always together, tender loving, with deep respect for each other. Both of them were beautiful, stately, and to us children, they looked like Olympic Gods. They were like-minded in their understanding of life, colleagues at work. They supplemented each other harmoniously. Our well organized, calm, dignified mother was the family authority when it came to art, and our father -- ardent, emotional, passionately loving life, fearless in front of the high and mighty or any danger, with an iron will and firm principals... and at the same time kind, thoughtful and very vulnerable. He burned himself out, putting his passionate soul into everything he did.

In the very beginning of the nineteen thirties my father was assigned to go from Leningrad (St. Petersburg) to Kazakhstan in order to organize a geological survey. I pictured him sitting at the Research Institute Director's Office, with a big geological map on the wall behind him, the map he made. A boy, born in a remote mountain village, he came a long way to become the head of geological science in faraway Kazakhstan.

As I was reading, striking pictures of my father's life arose in front of me.

A BOY FROM CAUCASUS RIDGE.

The enemy cavalry was in retreat. Wind whistled in Raslan's ears, the excitement of a pursuit intoxicated him, and his black stallion pulled ahead of all the others. Closer, closer! His blood boiling with excitement, Raslan took aim ready to shoot. He put his finger on the trigger, but at this very moment, *the White* (2) he was about to kill looked back. Raslan recognized him right away, he was his friend, a neighbor. They had grown up together, playing, learning to ride horses and to be a brave warrior – *djigit*. The hand with the rifle fell; Raslan sharply drew the reins. The horse stood still from a full gallop, bent his hind legs, fell to one side, and jumped back up again, shaking nervously. Raslan jumped down before the stallion dropped to the ground, and at the moment the horse was up again he was already back in the saddle trying to catch up with his troupe rushing past. Only a few seconds were lost; these very seconds gave *the Whites* a chance to disappear from view. *The Reds* (2) stopped. Their commander, furious, turned his horse to Raslan.

"You did not want to shoot!" he yelled, his face distorted with anger, "You made your horse fall down on purpose!"

Raslan looked straight at him without a word.

"It means you are one of them! You yourself deserve to be shot!" The commander grabbed his gun and turned it onto Raslan. "Our Revolution has no pity for enemies!"

At this very moment, a grenade exploded nearby. The commander's horse jumped aside, and the bullet whined past Raslan's ear. The troupe turned around and rushed again to chase the

Whites. Everybody but Raslan. His horse danced impatiently under him; he did not know which way to turn. He anguished, "If I have to kill my friend for the sake of happiness, I do not want such happiness. But what about the fight for brotherhood and justice? It is worth dying for, but not to kill a friend! Who am I? A traitor or savior?"

---

(2) The Russian Civil War (1917–1921) occurred after the Russian provisional government collapsed and the Soviets under the domination of the Bolshevik party assumed power. The principal fighting occurred between the Bolshevik Red Army, and the White Army, the anti-Bolshevik forces.

Everything got so complicated, perplexing, and so difficult to grasp. In a single moment Raslan found himself all alone against the whole world, rejecting *the Whites*, and being rejected by *the Reds*. He had only his horse, his faithful friend. Raslan gratefully touched him with his spurs, and the stallion took off in a quick pace carrying the rider up to the mountains.

Clatter of horses' hoofs echoed from the rock over a steep mountain path. A silhouette of the rider and the horse moved along a granite wall as a single unit. Only a man from the Caucasus Mountains could ride this way. A felt cloak, *Burka* rose above Raslan's shoulders like big black wings. The path twisted, hidden in brushwood of juniper, and at times disappeared completely, but Raslan rushed ahead until a gorge opened in front of him. It was enclosed by rocky Caucasus Mountains on all four sides. Here the rider stopped the horse, as if he didn't want to break the absolute silence of this amazing place. He was motionless for a minute. Then, by a light touch of the spurs, he directed his black stallion to the center of the gorge. The horse began to move down slowly and almost noiselessly.

The sun was already low; it caressed the mountain ridge and touched the glacier which sparkled like an altar in a temple where the deity was nature itself. Shrubs, bright red from cold autumn nights, covered surrounding rocks like a red cardinal mantle. It intensified the impression of the sanctity of this place . An old, low wooden structure made out of logs darkened by time, was set in the middle of the almost-round gorge. Two birch trees had dropped autumn leaves on the roof, making it look golden. Carved ornaments reminiscent of aurochs horns decorated every corner of the roof. Skulls of mountain goats and aurochs lay on the ground around the house in a strict order. They were white and partially destroyed, but nevertheless held their twisted shapes. It was an old pagan chapel, erected here before Christianity and Islam came to break this country into two separate parts. The secret of the pagan chapel's existence was passed from one generation to the next. Here, warriors joined the spirit of their ancestors, meditated or hid. This entire gorge was inundated by golden light of the approaching evening. There was a solemn silence of a splendid cathedral created by magnificent Caucasus nature.

Raslan jumped off the horse. He was tall, slim, but strong and looked older than his eighteen years. His face was intelligent, with regular features and black eyes which had an amazing sparkle, as if he was full of an internal fire. But now there was anxiety in them and perplexity caused by an insoluble problem.

The bullet's whine still sounded in Raslan's ears, his blood had not cooled down yet from the heat of a battle, but suddenly his entire world turned upside down, became repulsive and incomprehensible. Two hours earlier he was a part of a revolutionary light cavalry detachment, and he knew who he was to fight and, more importantly, why. Liberty, brotherhood, equality and truth promised by the revolution were worth fighting for. But now everything was mixed up.

Raslan stood for a long time in front of the old pagan chapel in deep thoughts, with the reins of his patiently waiting stallion in his hands. When he finally raised his head, there were calm and resolve in his eyes. He knew the war was over for him.

The sun had hidden behind the ridge, and the magic radiance of the glacier died out. The night descended to the mountains. The rider went down slowly, quietly, like a shadow, toward the village, where the air itself was still full of memories of his childhood and youth.

* * *

The arrival of Raslan in this world was both a happy and a worrisome event in the large family of Aslanbek. The Inhabitants of the mountain village were not in a hurry with their congratulations. The reason was a sad event that happened several years earlier.

Six times Aslanbek swallowed his disappointment learning that another daughter was born. Six times, with courage proper to a man of the mountains, he pronounced; "We will wait for a son." Six times his hopes didn't materialize, until a great day finally came, and a son was born. Happiness of the father was limitless, the news swept across the village. Aslanbek spared nothing to celebrate the birth of the heir, his future helper in difficult peasants' work and a warrior-defender from the village's hostile neighbors.

The entire village gathered at the feast called *kouvd*. It was organized at a scale the village had not seen for a long time. Whole rams roasted on big spits and home made beer were in abundance. The mother, still weak, together with sisters bustled around large kettles; people sitting at long tables under the bright Caucasus sun pronounced long slow toasts. During this hot July day, an unusually quiet baby lay in a cradle in a small stuffy room while visitors crowded to take a look at a tiny little warrior, *djigit*. By the evening the baby died.

The joyous celebration changed to women's sobbing and men's mournful silence. The hero of the occasion was dead! He, who was expected to be their hope, their joy and happiness, had died, not even having time to acquire a name.

The grief of the father, mother and sisters was immeasurable. They believed the explanation of this sad event was that gods were angry with Aslanbek for boasting about his son, and they took away the object of his pride.

Four more times Aslanbek swallowed his disappointment, when his wife, quiet, loving Gaze gave him another daughter, and the next. Four more times he pronounced with the courage of a man of the mountains the same, "We will wait for a son." Two years after the birth of the tenth daughter, vivid black-eyed Hazidaz, Gace got pregnant again without any hope for a son, and then... Raslan was born! Aslanbek hid his joy when he was told the long awaited news. The fellow-villagers whispered the happy news, not to irritate the gods. Every time they met Aslanbek they asked, "So, how is it?" He answered just by nodding, confirming that everything was fine. Who blessed this boy? Was it a divine intent, a fate, or his mother trembling for his life? Nobody knew, but the boy was growing robust and healthy; he showed his character right away by protesting against the crib and swaddling. And he won; there were many loving arms to hold him, for his sisters had already grown.

A year later, the Elders gathered in Aslanbek's house, but not for a celebration and pronouncing great toasts. They came to learn the boy's destiny. Thin, straight old men, wearing belts with silver inlays, each with a dagger on his waist, ceremoniously entered a special room intended for guests only, *kunatskaia*. Aslanbek greeted each one by lowering his head and placing his hand on his chest. Guests solemnly seated themselves on the benches along a wall. Slow laconic speech was considered virtues of a man. The Elders sat quietly and spoke rarely, with those special expressions of dignity characteristic for people from the Caucasus Mountains, especially to Ossetians, or Allans, as they called themselves. After a while, the eldest of the Elders gave a sign, and Gace brought in the one-year-old Raslan. She put him on one side of a big floor rug. A dagger, a sickle, a book, and a rosary were put on the other side of the rug. The boy quickly crawled toward the book and began to rumple it with a happy enthusiasm. Aslanbek was a wise man; he gained respect from his countrymen for his wisdom, while quiet Gace knew secrets of herbs and folk medicine. And now learning and education were foretold for their son.

The Elders clicked their tongues and nodded their heads. The destiny for the boy was clear: at the proper time, the village community would send him to study.

* * *

A group of dark-eyed barefoot boys gathered in a little flock, balanced on broad horses' backs, leading those four-legged beauties to watering them. The day in the mountains was bright, sunny, and fresh as usual. Five and six-year old riders sat on the horses confidently, using their bare heels to control the horses. It was so natural for them, they were taught to ride a horse before they knew how to walk. Training boys to be men was very serious business in the mountains. From their time in the cradle they were trained to ignore pain and to fight fear. From the very early years all boys studied Caucasian *Djigitovka*, or riding a horse while shooting a target or fighting with daggers. So, sitting on a horse without a saddle five-year-old Raslan felt as a brave warrior, a *djigit*.

Life in the village followed patriarchal traditions and laws passed down through generations, which were not to be violated. It was a special world, separated from city innovations and intrusions by mountain ridges. The young inhabitants of this mountain village, rocking on horseback, did not know and did not suspect that they were the "last Mohicans" of a disappearing world, like Atlantis, to be swallowed by the waves of modern civilization. Everything in these mountain people's lives followed old traditions and laws, the backbone of which was strict respect for each other. The unwritten motto of this small country was "respect yourself by respecting your neighbor". The older a person became the more respect he gained, and any request from an elder was a law for a younger one. The Elders were judges and they also dealt with all matters and problems of the community. Women, who had reached an especially respected age, could participate in this counsel too. All men worked in the fields in a valley, and every one of them was a warrior, ready at any moment to defend the village against encroachments from a multitude of foreigners. The dagger on a leather belt was considered as necessary for a man as a heart in his chest. But nobody was allowed to unsheathe this symbol of courage and bravery without a reason; it was a disgrace to use the dagger as a threat. If a dagger was drawn it was to be stained with blood – that was a strict rule, and this is why it was used only under exceptional circumstances.

Women bustled around the house, and the old laws defined a respected role for them in the solid life structure of the village. Islam was brought to this country relatively recently; it limited their social life to some degree, but it could not destroy all the old traditions. Women did not cover their faces, and the way it used to be in earlier ages, they accepted with dignity signs of respect when men met them on the street. Insult of a wife, sister or daughter was punished severely and mercilessly. Raslan was four years old when his father took him to a mill, hidden in the gorge, in the middle of a rapid river. The miller's face was horribly disfigured by an enormous mouth and a scar from ear- to-ear. Responding to a question from the terrified boy, Aslanbek briefly explained: many years ago, when the miller lived in the village, he insulted his neighbor's daughter, and he had his mouth cut by a dagger as a sign of eternal disgrace.

Raslan's childhood was happy and pleasant despite the strict studies of farming and military art. There were many animals in their household, and he was their best friend. Dogs adored him, even chickens cackled happily as they crowded around him; it was Raslan's responsibility to feed them. Together with the other boys he drove enormous buffalos to a mountain river with murmuring, clear icy water coming from glaciers. After plunging into the ice-cold water the boys enjoyed lying on hot rocks. It was a pleasure to warm up their thin small bodies and watch the lazy giants suck clean water for such a long time, as if they wanted to dry the river to the bottom.

But the best pleasure for Raslan was to ride a stallion. He was too small for a saddle and rode without it, clinging to the hot steel muscles of the horse. He was not yet allowed to gallop, but once he could not resist the temptation to show his boldness; and he let the stallion gallop at full speed. Neither the little rider nor the horse noticed a big ditch. The stallion stopped abruptly in front of the unexpected obstacle, and the little rider somersaulted over the horse's head. The horse jumped to the side, smashing Raslan's face with a huge hoof. He ran home, covered with blood, to the complete horror of his mother. She cleaned Raslan's wounds and covered them with her own healing ointment made from herbs and honey. Neither the pain nor the blood saved little Raslan from the punishment for his disobedience. His father was strict and stern in spite of tender love for his little boy. Raslan was put on the big stone in the middle of the village and stood on this Golgotha until nightfall when Aslanbek finally took him from it. Of course, Raslan did not cry, he could not allow himself such shame.

At home Raslan's sisters spoiled him secretly with honey from household beehives. They had a special name for him *Kroshka*, a tiny one. This was a Russian word; they did not know this language, but the word sounded especially tender to them. The father could not show his soft feelings to his son. By the unwritten traditions this was exclusively a woman's privilege. From time to time however Aslanbek put his hand on Raslan's shoulder; and this simple sign of his father's love filled the boy's heart with joy and pride. Aslanbek was strict but fair. He treated his son as if he were a little man. It was Raslan's duty from his early days to help his father with the household, especially in the stable.

One day Aslanbek had to go to another village. The night before, when the twilight dissolved the outlines of familiar objects, making them mysterious, he asked Raslan to bring a saddle and reins from the shed, which was in the farthest corner of the yard.

"Prepare everything and check it, I am going to Beslan at the first light."

"It is very dark in the shed already, I can not see anything"

"But you know very well where everything is."

The southern night was falling quickly, dropping a black veil over everything and causing sweet horror to a small boy who was only five years old. Imagination sketched strange and terrifying monsters about which Raslan's older sister, Hasidaz, liked to tell him hair–raising stories. With his eyes closed tight, he ran through the big yard and opened the stable door. There was gloomy darkness inside, but the familiar smell of the horses crunching corn gave the boy some courage. He pulled a bridle from a wall; and at this very moment a devil looked at him from the darkness, a real devil with a pointed muzzle and fiery eyes. With a loud and sinister laugh he came crashing down on the boy. The devil was as real as life itself and terribly frightening. Raslan dashed out of the stable toward the illuminated windows of the house, but the devil ran after him and breathed loudly on the boy's neck. The little boy burst through the door horror-stricken and almost fainting.

"There is a devil, a real devil... I saw him... He ran after me! "

"O Allah bismillah, devils do not exist, my little silly boy. Let us go and we will chase away your devil."

It was much more comfortable to walk holding dad's hand; and the night was not frightening anymore.

"So, where is your devil? Look, the harness is on the floor; it fell down when you pulled the bridle; that was the noise!"

"What about the eyes? That awful laugh?"

"That was a horse. It neighed, turned its head towards you, and it's green eye sparkled! Here, hang everything back, and do it accurately, don't rush! And don't worry, there is no devil."

"But who was chasing me? And b-breathing?"

"It was your own fear; and it was you who breathed hard from being afraid. Kill your fear, and all devils will be afraid of you! "

So, everything became understandable and clear. Raslan sighed, it was so good when his father was by his side. But the devil's image remained in the depth of the boy's soul, it was too alive, too real. Maybe it was simply hiding from adults?

* * *

In the fall Raslan's father, who kept in mind the boy's destiny, decided it was time for him to study. Even if it was not foretold, Aslanbek was ready to do anything in his power to make sure his only son would be an educated man. He was sure the first step should be to learn the Russian language. An opportunity presented itself. A relative of Aslanbek, Tokh, was a brave, cheerful and carefree officer of the Russian army. He was traveling to a place he had been assigned, and he stopped for a short break in his travel at their village. His big and friendly family accompanied him. Aslanbek asked Tokh to take Raslan with them, to teach the little boy Russian and prepare him for school. Tokh readily agreed.

In the open summer kitchen Raslan helped his older sister Fatima pump honey from beehives. He and Fatima had a great time chatting and sucking the empty honeycombs when Raslan heard his father calling him.

"Raslan, your uncle will take you with him. You will live with his family in a big town and you will study Russian. Go and tell your sisters about it."

The boy was not ready for such a decision from his father; he didn't want to leave his home, but he was not supposed to object or ask questions.

Gaze's heart was aching, she did not want her little son, her favorite, to go away; but she knew she didn't have to worry. Tokh and his lovely wife Khangi would take good care of Raslan; he would be treated the same as their own children. Tamara, Firka, Kosha, Raisa, a baby Beybulat, and now Raslan; it was a noisy and happy bunch of kids. New shirts and pants were sewn, little city shoes were bought, and the big family left for Timerkhan-Shura, the place Tokh had been assigned.

This first faraway trip was interesting for the little boy; he looked around with curiosity. But soon he felt sad, he missed his father, his loving mother and sisters. These feelings were stronger than the novelty of the trip, and Raslan had a hard time to hold back his tears.

Tokh grabbed him from his seat in the cart and put him in front of himself on the horse. "Hey, *djigit*, why are you down in the dumps?"

Raslan took a deep breath and swallowed a bitter lump, knowing that father would not like to see him whining. It was much better to be sitting on horseback with his uncle than in the cart, and he cheered up.

Following Aslanbek request, all members of this new family talked with Raslan in Russian; this was very confusing to the boy. On top of that Tokh found a teacher for him who agreed to give a boy lessons for a reasonable price. Now, every day after dinner Raslan, with a pen and a notebook would go for the lessons. Oh, how difficult it was! Just unbearable! He went there very sad; he didn't understand why they made him do that, if he knew very well how to talk with his father, his sisters, and his friends. His teacher, a young Russian woman, put an inkpot on the clean white tablecloth and drew strange signs on paper. Raslan tried very hard, but despite all his efforts, his scribbles were not even close to the neat teacher's writings. The big glass inkpot drew the interest of the five-year-old boy. He wanted to draw something familiar, something that would be close to his heart, like a little house or a little man, but he didn't dare ask about it.

One time the teacher left him alone in the room. His little hand, by itself, reached out to that magnetic item, the inkpot, and quickly dipping the pen into it, he started drawing. Raslan was thrilled to see on the paper something resembling a horse, when, oh, what a nightmare! A big blue spot crawled on the snow-white tablecloth. The inkpot tipped over. Raslan froze in despair; terrified, he stood there for several seconds, then dashed to the window, jumped out and ran.

Nothing could persuade the poor boy to return to his studies. In the spring they brought Raslan back home to his village.

"Listen, Aslanbek, he is too small to study, let the *djigit* grow up a little, maybe another year", explained Tokh about their early return.

Raslan was absolutely happy. Everybody was glad to see him back, his father, mother, sisters. Even their huge dogs who were almost as tall as he was, gathered around him, expressing their delight. The boy could swim again in the little river, to drive buffalo and horses to give them cold water from a turbulent river, feed chickens, and clean the harness for his father's horse.

A year later, when he was six, this time with pleasure and pride, Raslan went to the two-year local village school. There were children of different ages in his class; some kids were twice as old and twice as tall as he was. Rules were extremely strict. Hitting hands with a ruler immediately punished bad behavior. Those who were lazy or not smart were subject to lashing. Raslan turned out to be quick and sharp, especially with addition and subtraction. Little by little he was gaining knowledge of Russian, though their teacher was not the best. By that time he already knew that besides his village there was a huge unknown Russia and even other amazing countries where people spoke different languages, having nothing in common with his own. The most important thing he understood was that his village needed an educated man, and that he must learn to speak, read and write in Russian. That was what the Elders and his father wanted.

"This is a pencil", the students repeated after the teacher. *"She sells seashells by the seashore."* He dictated trying and failing to pronounce hard Russian "s" because this sound does not exist in the Ossetian language. The poor students heard, *"She shells sheashells by the sheashore"* and wrote it in earnest in their notebooks. "Ay-ya-yay!" The teacher was outraged. "You have the heads of rams! Why are you writing *"sh"* instead of... *"sh"*?! A Russian person would never say, *"She shells sheashells by the sheashore!"*. Now, listen! And everything repeated again and again simply because all of them (including the teacher) could not help it, and made soft Ossetian *"sh"* from Russian *"s"*.

Two years later Raslan's sisters were amazed and proud to listen to Raslan reading in Russian, slowly but confidently from a book that he received as an award for his success in school. They were proud of their little brother, but Aslanbek dreams were even bigger. He hoped for the impossible, to send Raslan to study in the city. He put on his best *cherkeska* (the native attire) and went to talk to the Elders.

The council of the Elders decided to ask The Ossetian Mountain Society to pay for Raslan's education at the Vladikavkaz Natural Sciences School. They agreed under one condition, he had to pass difficult entrance exams.

Raslan couldn't sleep the night before going to the city. He worried he wouldn't justify his father's hopes. He also wanted to study in the *big school* the way his dad called it. Luckily, the test started with math. He solved all the problems and, trying to put off the scary part, the test of his mastery of the Russian language, he asked for more math problems. The examiner smiled. "No, my friend, I see you're good in math. Now you write what I dictate". This part was much more difficult. Raslan wrote slowly, carefully drawing every letter, the sweat stood out on his forehead.

He was admitted and his proud father brought him to their rich relative, a retired army general, to stay with his family. In return

Aslanbek brought honey, corn, fruit, vegetables and live indignantly cackling chickens.

Raslan's uncle twice removed was a very important man; the whole of Aslanbek clan was proud of him. He reached almost impossible for the Ossetian man having achieved the rank of general in the Russian army.

Again Raslan lived without his large loving family. Now he was older and stronger in spirit. But the atmosphere in the uncle's house was not as warm and cheerful as in the Tokh's family. The house, like the general himself, was big and somber; the household was large, including a cook, a maid and a stableman serving an equipage with three beautiful horses. There was an addition to the house where nobody lived. It was a tiny cubicle with a separate entrance. That was where they settled Raslan, far away from the so called "clean" rooms. Eight-year-old Raslan felt very uncomfortable; he was not treated as a part of the family, he remained a relative living at their expense. His uncle had a sour look because he could not say "no" to his village relatives, but at the same time Raslan's presence was burdensome for him. He was a little stingy. At this age Raslan had already acquired a strong feeling of Ossetian pride, and this pride made him often hungry. He didn't want to be a burden for his famous relative.

There was a big kitchen where a fat Russian woman cooked and baked for the whole family. Bringing water from a nearby well was Raslan's responsibility. He tried as hard as he could to be of use; early in the morning, before going to school he ran with a bucket to the well until the cook told him it was too much water. She was a kind woman and, understanding how empty the little guy's stomach was, she frequently gave him some bread, sometimes even with jam. Raslan proudly refused; she kindly tousled his hair saying, "Eat, you are not gonna last long on your pride." He ate, and he was thankful to her not only for the bread but also for kindness, which he needed so much in that cold and strange house.

Inside the large rooms of the house Raslan felt unbearably uncomfortable. The general's Russian wife was a woman of the world, and the Raslan's two cousins were raised in the same spirit; they studied music and dance. They were lively and sharp girls, and Raslan felt constrained and clumsy in rooms with a shiny parquet floor. He didn't know what to do with his hands, he felt out of place sitting with everybody at a big table with European rules.

To help Raslan feel more at ease and for their own fun, the girls talked their mother into including Raslan in their dance class. This added one more torture for him. To his immense relief, the teacher found him not capable to learn French *pas*, and they left him alone.

The cousins attended a gymnasium. Every morning they were presented with elegant little baskets with their lunch; Raslan received one kopeck for a boublik (little bagel). Despite their different status, the girls treated fairly their relative from a mountain village. First the merry, laugh-loving girls acted ceremoniously, as was appropriate for nice "general's daughters" and they looked at Raslan with some caution, but soon they became very friendly. They made fun of him when he pronounced *"sh"y* instead of *"sigh"*, or made a *"shock"* out of *"sock"*. Raslan blushed but he was not upset very much, because the girls were good-humored, and also because they were just girls. By the end of the first year he was able to say fluently, without stumbling: "Silly Sally swiftly shooed seven silly sheep" and his Ossetian pride didn't suffer any more.

Early one morning, when the spring sun poured over the yard and the street, and the time was approaching to go back home, Raslan heard his uncle's angry voice summoning him. The uncle stood on the verandah staring at a broken window.

"Did you break the window?"

"No"

"Then who did it?"

"I don't know… It wasn't me"

"Not you? You're lying. Nobody could have done it but you! Get out of here, and I don't want to see you until you confess!"

The boy grew pale and nervously bit his lip. Never in his entire life had anybody accused him of lying. He felt an unbearable bitter resentment; he wanted to say something bold and harsh and to run away from this cold house... He closed the door of his cubicle and retreated into his textbooks.

The next morning there was no breakfast, not even one kopeck for a boublik. There was no dinner at the big table, no supper – just a starving empty stomach and difficult homework. The kind woman-cook tried to feed him at the kitchen but he refused. Before bedtime his aunt came:

"Confess, Raslan, and the uncle will forgive you."

"I have never lied and I am not lying now, I did not break the glass!" The boy's voice was breaking from feeling deeply insulted.

"Oh, calm down. Come for breakfast tomorrow, we'll clear it up"

Raslan was dizzy with hunger; he had a sinking sensation in the pit of his stomach, but he didn't come. He didn't show up for dinner either, nor for supper. They sent the cook for him. The uncle, looking morose, pointed at a chair. The girls, quiet like little mice, sat with guilty looks on their faces.

***

At the Natural Sciences school Raslan felt like a stranger. In winter and in summer he wore only a part of the uniform, the same lightweight gray shirt with a narrow belt. His father could not pay for a summer and winter uniform jacket. Other students wore warm broadcloth coats during cold month. As for Raslan, he had the same cheap shirt in any weather; in winter he had to run fast to the school and back home in order not to freeze. His classmates were mostly Russians, and mainly from well-to-do families. Ruslan was an Ossetian, the son of a peasant, whose wealth consisted of a cornfield, a pair of horses and a dozen sheep. But his classmates did not dare laugh at him. Ossetian pride not allowing any humiliation was well known. Not being Russian and rich, he nevertheless had one big advantage: the main subject at the school – math – was easy for him, like a fun game; logic of physics and chemistry was as natural for him as breathing. Teachers appreciated this and praised him. The Russian language was for him that fortress that he had to storm every day and every year. In the fall, when he came back after spending summer vacations at his village, Raslan felt he was again thrown back in his progress. His classmates traveled, read, rested, and Raslan worked in fields. He liked this work, his muscles became like iron, his body was strong and flexible, but he had no time to read, and he envied those who talked about books they had read during vacation months.

Raslan anxiously waited for summer to come. Summers brought the long-awaited return home, full of mother and sisters' love, of absolute, though somewhat reserved adoration on the part of his father. Going home! To the dear village! He had sweet sleep there; in the morning an egg pancake made by his mom and a freshly baked *churek*, local flat bread, were waiting for him on the table. It was a sheer delight, after that gloomy hated general's house, to ride a horse, to swim in the mountain river, where freezing cold water burned his body, to work tirelessly in corn fields with his father and sisters! When he worked in the fields he felt a man; he didn't want to reveal that all his body was hurting, because during winter months he got out of the habit of working physically. But his muscles got stronger fast and a week later his slender body turned into a well-tuned mechanism. His moves were precise, well organized and he enjoyed the work the way a dancer enjoys being on a dance floor. It was hard work, but it was accompanied by jokes and laughter, with family love and caring, and this made him happy.

Summer was the time when his father taught him the art of *djigitovka*, a spatial horse–riding, so important for a man of the mountains. In a large backyard, a fast and strong stallion made circle after circle pulling a long rope Aslanbek held tight in his hand. When Aslanbek let out a guttural sound, Raslan ran to head off the horse, trying to jump up on the saddle. First he couldn't even seize the saddle. He repeated the move again and again until he easily flew up on the running stallion. Then he learned how to shoot a target while riding a horse at full gallop and even jump from one horse to another.

Every Fall Raslan's mother fixed and mended his clothes quietly shedding a tear or two. It was the time of the new harvest, and the family gathered honey and fruit to bring to the general's house as a sign of their gratitude. Neither the family, nor Raslan ever thought of quitting his education; everybody understood the importance of it. And his studies went on.

* * *

Years passed. Time turned its wheel slowly but surely. The little boy grew taller and he almost got over the difficulties of the Russian language; only some accent and slowness of speech remained. During winter months he read all the books he could get his hands on, though without any logical order. There were Dostoyevsky, Tolstoy, Senkevich, Turgenev and also some writers who were forgotten with time. All of these books must be put aside at summers when the field job kept Raslan busy from dawn to sunset.

Once it was a warm July evening; the sun already hid behind the white mountain tops and grass smells flowed over the warm ground. Fourteen-year-old Raslan and his father rode home after a long day of work at a cornfield. The narrow road rose; their horses' sides almost touched. It felt nice to ride together with his father, slowly, relaxing, talking, and feeling the strong horse's body following the slightest move of the rider. Suddenly Aslanbek pricked up his ears, and at that very moment Raslan saw a group of horsemen galloping to head them off. Chechens! The father whipped Raslan's horse, it rushed ahead; Aslanbek followed right behind. The road was open and both riders presented a good target. Chechens started shooting and the distance was getting shorter. Raslan and Aslanbek horses galloped at full speed. They needed to get to a turn of the road, to get out of sight behind rocks. Then they would have an advantage, the Chechens wouldn't dare to follow them there. The turn was still too far, the road was too steep. They heard bullets whining, the horses sped ahead as if they understood the danger. Finally, father and son turned behind the rock. Raslan grabbed his rifle ready to shoot and at this moment he turned to Aslanbek and saw him almost lying on his horse, his shirt soaked with blood.

"Father!"

"Don't worry, it's not so bad," Aslanbek answered with difficulty. "Let's go!"

The Chechens had already turned back, not wanting to be shot from behind the rock. Raslan and his father rode side by side, Raslan supporting him in his saddle.

When they came home, Gace didn't start wailing, groaning; she only grew white, helping Raslan put her husband on the trestle-bed. Aslanbek lost a lot of blood, but Gaze's herbs and herbal extracts helped heal the wound. In two weeks he was already back on his feet; but he lost some of his internal strength and became weaker and weaker. He tried to hide it, to cheer up. Every morning before dawn, father and son went as usual to the cornfields. But Aslanbek couldn't beat his illness, it soon took full possession of his weakening body, and the whole burden of man's work more and more fell on the son's shoulders.

Raslan turned fifteen years old, and it sickened him already to feel he was still dependant on his rich relative's handouts. During the past years the uncle didn't get attached to him and didn't get kinder; and thought his aunt treated him much better and the cousins were very cordial, Raslan dreamed of an independent life. The problem was that all jobs he could find conflicted with his school schedule. Fortunately, his math teacher helped him.

"Raslan, I heard you were looking for a job. Why don't you work as a tutor for younger kids and those who have difficulties with math? I can recommend a couple of those right now, and you can see how it works."

It worked well; he started giving private lessons. Math was like a song for him, and he explained its harmony to his students. His earnings were enough for him and two of his friends to rent a room, where they had three beds, a table and a pile of books in a corner. Their regular food was bread and tea, but every once in a while they could go on a spree. There was *"Obzhorka"* ("A Gobbling Place") in a basement of a big building downtown where, for modest money they could get a big bowl of steaming giblet soup. Life became much better and more interesting.

Time was flying fast, busy with classes and work. Winter changed into summer, and again Raslan worked in the cornfields. The old house, the sheds, the horse stable, and the well - everything needed a man's hands. Summer nights were short it seemed. As soon as the young man closed his eyes and fell into a sound sleep – it was already time for Raslan's mother and his sisters to wake him up. He was still very young; you could almost put your hands around his slender waist, and it was almost too much for him to do the difficult work with a pitchfork, a scythe, and heavy bags of corn. From now on Raslan completely devoted his vacations to running the household.

* * *

It was during a dark cold December evening. After a class he had taught to one of his students Raslan was going home. His hungry imagination pictured a nice cup of hot tea and a crispy piece of bread he would enjoy sitting cozily at his table and reading a book. He wore an old uniform coat, not too warm but bought with the money he made himself. In his pocket there was a thick booklet he borrowed for one night. He had already had a chance to page through the book. It promised freedom, fraternity, and good life for everybody. It was about equal rights, democracy, and freedom of choice. Every line was exciting and stimulating, breathing air of a new time. He had heard that the author was in exile.

Right at the door of his house he bumped into his friends.

"We're waiting for you! Let's go, we're late!"

"Where? Why?"

"You'll see"

They went to an apartment packed with people, unfamiliar faces, most of them students judging by their uniforms. It seemed everybody talked loudly, at the same time, not hearing each other. In the room full of cigarette smoke the atmosphere was electrified by strange and happy excitement. In the middle of the room there was a table and some older people sat around it. It was hard to understand who they were. But there was still some order in this meeting, because suddenly everybody got quiet; one of those people sitting at the table got up and started talking, not loudly but enunciating clearly every word. He said that a revolution was approaching and that it was necessary to support it here, at the Caucasus.

"What specifically we can do now?" he asked, but at this moment a man who first stood at the door and then quickly approached the speaker. Right away he commanded quickly and without pathos, "Break up! Fast, no panic, through the back exit, we've been spotted by police!" Everybody rushed to the door at the same time, and a terrible jam started. Raslan and his friends squeezed between people to a window; their undernourishment helped them and their slim bodies slipped through out through the narrow openings. They found themselves on a roof of the next building, and then they had to get over to another one and then another.

The booklet in Raslan's pocket impeded his movements and he had to hold on to it not to lose it. They ended up descending to a backyard by a fire escape. Then everything was simple and they jumped over a fence. The thick booklet fell finally out of Raslan's pocket and plopped down on the ground. He bent down and at the moment he had it in his hand a policeman appeared right in front of him. "Who are you? Where are you from? Where are you going?" One of the friends, a cheery joker, laughed and pointed to a lighted window. "We're from there, but the father kicked us out!" He giggled again.

The policeman looked at them with some doubt but the school uniform reassured him. "Ok, don't cause any trouble!" he grumbled and left. Raslan stuffed the dangerous booklet back in his pocket; his heart pounded, but with some mischievous feeling, as if he had just dodged a bullet.

After this first gathering there were others; they had to run from police, but they managed to get away again and again. Raslan was all ears listening to calls for justice, fraternity and equal rights. He was in a festive mood thinking of great upcoming changes.

And in October 1917 the changes arrived. Revolution! There were red ribbons on chests, red flags everywhere. Everything turned upside down, everything got mixed up. Crowds of people, banners, proclamations. Freedom! No czar and there won't be anymore. But what will there be? How will it be? Nobody knew. The huge crowd was rejoicing and it was not a time for questions. A volunteer speaker stood on a high porch, calling for something and soon was pulled off. Another man with a ribbon on his chest took his place, started campaigning, yelling, proving something; it was impossible to hear what exactly. One thing was clear – equality and fraternity for all people of Russia became a reality. It made everybody excited and happy!

When these stormy days were over the school opened again. At the end of this year Raslan got his graduation diploma with all excellent grades.

Proud and happy Aslanbek presented his son with a gift this youth could not even dream of. It was a black Arab stallion, a fast runner, and a real beauty. It nervously danced on thin long legs and squinted at his new master. Only a man from the Caucasus Mountain could understand the rapture Raslan felt, jumping easily on this wonder of nature. Already very ill, Aslanbek admired this graceful young rider wearing a new *cherkeska*, national attire for a warrior, and a dagger on a leather belt with silver ornamentation. This was his son who met all of Aslanbek's expectations, a warrior full of courage and dignity.

Pride, courage, and dignity – these were the cores of a small country lost between the Caucasus ridges. These were the cores of the Ossetians, to whom Raslan belonged. A free wind of mountains and radiant white snow gave them freedom of spirit. Rumbling waterfalls, rapid rivers and flying over a deep abyss on a horse taught them to despise danger and even death itself. These representatives of a disappearing civilization never put themselves down by drunkenness or using foul language, never offended themselves by fistfights. Peasant–warriors, they were noble lords of the spirit and preferred death to an insult and never knew slavery. Proud men of the Caucasus Mountains – humiliation or cowardice were unacceptable to them. They stayed with raised heads even in front of God and built high doorways so God would not think they bowed to Him.

Civil war covered a wide front. Horses trampled fields of corn and wheat; chaos reigned everywhere and in everything. Age–old traditions were lost, new rules confused everybody and complicated life. Village people became gloomy, preoccupied, and Raslan was perplexed. In the speeches he had heard, in the pamphlets he had read, the life portrayed was shockingly different from what he saw around him. Everything turned out harsh and unsightly. A new low was declared, called *Prodrasvertka*, Food Ruling, by which all peasant holdings – wheat, potato, corn, meat, dairy products were forcibly taken away to support starving cities and the army. This made peasants furious and hostile to *the Reds*. Raslan was between a rock and hard place. He understood peasant's irritation and at the same time appreciated the necessity for the revolution to succeed and not to be suffocated by the hunger of the army and the cities.

The capital of Ossetia, *Vladikavkaz* (in English it means Own the Caucasus) was in the hands of the *White* army, and the Revolutionary Center went underground and moved from the city to the small town of Beslan. The chair of this Revolutionary Center, Kazbek was Raslan's relative, and he sent to his young cousin a note, asking him to come, because the Center desperately needed more members. Raslan had not seen Kazbek, a smart and experienced revolutionary, for five years since he had left Ossetia for Saint Petersburg. The young man was glad to receive this invitation. It was a great opportunity for him to solve, with the help of his 32-years-old cousin, everything tormenting him about the current turmoil. He remembered Kazbek as good-natured and a very knowledgeable man and was sure he would get the right answer from him.

Beslan was a familiar town for Raslan and he found Center without a problem. An orderly at the door was prepared for his arrival and took him immediately into the big room where Kazbek sat at a desk engulfed by piles of papers. He jumped from the chair to hug Raslan affectionately.

"You are a real man now; it is difficult to recognize you! Let me have a better look at you. Good lad! Just what we need, yes, we need you now very much!"

"And you did not change at all, Kazbek, I am happy to see you, I have so many questions to ask, I hope you can help ease my mind."

Kazbek offered a stool to Raslan. "Sit down, take hot tea; we have some good flat bread. I am sure you are hungry after your trip. Relax till I finish this paper, and then you can ask any question."

They talked until the evening. It was easy for the experienced and smart propagandist to dispel all doubts and distrust of a confused youngster, and the very next day Raslan began to work at Revolutionary Center.

* * *

Raslan and a young Russian man Andrey were the only two persons in the Center on this particular day. They were absorbed in their job of printing leaflets, when the silence outside the tightly shuttered windows changed suddenly to the noise and shouting of a furious crowd pouring into the yard. There were loud thumps on the door, and malicious threats of many voices amid the general hubbub.

"Hey, Red Commander, come out, we'll show you our own Court and Justice!"

"Where are our horses? Where are our wheat and corn?"

"Come out to talk with our daggers!"

The shouting became louder and more aggressive every minute. Raslan peered through a fissure in the shutter, the yard was filled with a vicious crowd. He moved to the door. Andrey tried to hold him:

"Stay! Where are you going?! They'll shred you to pieces!"

"I need to talk with them."

Raslan took off his dagger, tightened his belt and went straight out to the furious crowd. He stayed unarmed, calmly keeping both thumbs under his belt. The men moved aside making a semicircle with Raslan standing in the center.

"Listen to me, good people! You can kill me now, but it will not make your life better..."

He talked with them using clear simple words about what he believed and what he learned from Kazbek. How did he manage to conquer this mad crowd ready for mob rule? Did the courage of this unarmed young lad or the words from the heart break their anger? Who could tell, but a miracle happened, the crowd ready to tear Raslan apart calmed down. People shifted from one foot to the other and spoke brusquely with gloomy eyes under the frowning eyebrows. And then they began to disperse, one after another very slowly and grudgingly till the yard became empty. And Raslan stood still quietly, straight and taut in the black Caucasian shirt, his face resolute and calm.

A few weeks later Aslanbek died. In less than half a year his devoted wife Gaze took to her bed never to rise from it again. Raslan was crushed by the death of his father; the death of his mother was another blow for him. Three sisters from ten lived to adulthood, and now they all had their own families. Raslan remained alone in his home, which was still full of memories of a big, loving happy family. The youngster was deeply shocked by the early death of his parents, and did not want to be a master of his empty house. He did not want to return to Beslan either. "If everything you told me is true, I want to fight for this truth," he wrote to Kazbek and together with his strong black stallion joined a squad of the Red Army Light Cavalry.

For six month Raslan fought fearlessly for the victory of the revolution with death hard on his heels, believing that the dream of universal brotherhood, liberty and justice was coming closer and closer. It was worth dying for. In the end the *White Army* ceased to exist, pressing against the Black sea. It was a victory, but some small squads of White Army still tried to resist. Angry and embittered by new orders, Caucasian peasant-warriors joined them.

* * *

The enemy cavalry was in retreat. Horses and riders were like flying arrows. The wind whistled in Raslan's ears; the ardor of pursuit intoxicated him, and his black stallion pulled ahead of the others. Closer, closer! Blood boiling with excitement, Raslan took aim, ready to shoot. He put his finger on the trigger, but in this very moment, the *White* he was going to kill turned back. Raslan recognized him immediately. He was his friend, a neighbor; they had grown up together, playing and going to the horse-pond. The hand with the gun lowered. He could not shoot his people, his brothers even in the name of the noblest ideas.

The war was over for Raslan.

MY FRIEND – MY ENEMY

Reading Leah's notes I wanted to learn more not only about my father's life, but also to find the name of the person who constantly poisoned his life by denunciation. And I found it out. I understood then why Leah didn't want to tell me his name before I had read all her notes. It seemed impossible to believe that his closest friend would be capable of such slander and betrayal.

But today I am looking at documents supporting this; every page talks about how during the whole life of this man his friendship and betrayal walked hand in hand. I knew him since I was born and I loved him because my father treated him as his own brother. What forces could have warped this old friend's soul? How could it have happened?

* * *

There were three of them, Murat, Raslan and Googa. Murat was the tallest of all, with light-reddish hair, and light–blue eyes. He was a good-natured youth with a nice open face and unhurried moves.

Raslan was slender, nicely built, possessing that natural grace of a man of the Caucasus; his moves quick but not hurried. The face of this young man with regular features and pitch-black sparkling intelligent eyes was easy to remember. He radiated decisiveness and will power; at the same time he was kind, and sometimes even sentimental.

The third one, Googa, with his big round head and round bulging eyes, was a shorty. His soft, sloping shoulders, too wide for his height, made him look like a square with truncated corners. Since childhood he suffered because of his shortness, which is rare among people of the mountains. Trying to hide his hurt self-esteem, he was a jester, acting sometimes like a clown. He found comfort in a secret confidence in his mental superiority to his peers. He had his reasons to think this way because while he was in school, and later in college, teachers also praised his intellectual abilities. While Murat was not talkative and Raslan reserved, Googa was constantly fooling around. His abundant jokes were eccentric, but amusing and often witty. Strangely, his big bulging eyes always stayed grave. All three of them were Ossetians. They were sent as gifted young men after a severe competitive selection from the Vladikavkaz Polytechnic College to study in the Petrograd (3) College of Mines.

* * *

After the fratricidal Civil War, society degenerated, the moral and immoral exchanged places. Mass demobilization of the hungry army led to "red" banditry. The executions of the "bourgeois" were carried out on the spot, and no one figured out how justified they were and who, in fact, was being shot. Under the slogan "expropriation of expropriators" there was an outright robbery, and the streets of Petrograd became dangerous not only at night, but also during the day: people seemed to be brutalized by hunger and incomprehensible to them freedom.

The "Red Terror" proclaimed by the decree of September 5, 1918, like a giant cannibal devoured the remnants of "enemies of the revolution" and parallel decimate all the best in Russia. Two million bearers of the cultural wealth of this unfortunate country managed to leave it, and most of the idealists-intellectuals who believed in the revolution were killed. Because of the catastrophe of 1917, millions of the most talented people, the pride of Russia, saved their lives in other countries. These geniuses were an involuntary "revolutionary gift" of the Bolsheviks to other countries and continents. As a result, foreign countries received a whole cohort of brilliant engineers, inventors, scientists, thinkers, artists, musicians. They greatly advanced the science, technology and culture in countries where they managed to escape from the revolution.

***Trotsky and Lenin are the two leaders of the Red Terror and the
Military Dictatorship, announced by 1922.***

What is the military dictatorship? Nothing else but lawless violence against disenfranchised citizens

Meanwhile, the enthusiasm of the masses, who were sure that they were "building a new fair state with their own hands" (sic a powerful propaganda of the Bolsheviks represented this massacre), reached fanaticism. The head were spinning in the heat of events even among those unfortunates who were soon destined to lose their heads in the KGB dungeon.Euphoria and horror mixed in what can be called a revolutionary mood.

Against this background, classes began at the Petrograd Mining Institute, where Raslan became a student.

A huge country lay in ruins. Hunger reigned everywhere, and especially in the beautiful capital. It's strange that in this terrible year of 1921 someone at all could think of such luxury as study. It seemed that every sensible person had to run away from the frozen and hungry Petrograd. Nevertheless, and contrary to all logic, Raslan dreamed of becoming a geologist at the famous Mining Institute.

---

(3) St. Petersburg was renamed Petrograd (during World War I), than Leningrad (after Revolution) and back to St. Petersburg (in 1991).

---

* * *

Petrograd! Magnificent, regal, and austere. Once the sublime capital of Russia it plunged in 1921 into total economic ruin. The amazing beauty of this metropolis aroused admiration and some pity, like a charming dead Princess, who has not lost its wonderful features but her body was touched by the decomposition. The three young men in black Caucasian shirts and thin European coats instead of familiar heavy felt cloaks *burkas* got off the train and were stunned by the beauty of the straight and spacious Nevsky Prospect. Instead of taking a tram, without discussion they started walking along the Prospect, across the Palace Bridgeand along the riverfront. They didn't talk, being overwhelmed by the surrounding beauty; they only stopped every now and then before another architectural masterpiece.

Raslan was so captivated looking at an unusual building with huge stained-glass windows that he accidentally stumbled upon an old man wrapped over the shabby coat by a female shawl. Embarrassed, the young man began to apologize, but the old man stopped him.

- It is nothing, nothing, quite forgivable accident. You're a stranger, are not you? Give me pleasure, let me tell you about this building, which you are staring at.

He with unexpected credulity put his hand on Raslan shoulder.

- What do you see now through these beautiful stained glass windows? Well, of course, crystal cascade still luxurious, but dead chandeliers. They can not illuminate the inside of the building. But, who needs to look at the empty and dusty shelves? You see it, but if I would close my eyes I can see quite a different picture. Just recently, only a few years ago you could see an incredible abundance of products, everything you would able imagine or you could wish for. Sparkling crystal "Baccarat" contained the best French products catering for all tastes. Selection of cheeses seemed limitless, the variety of sausages and their quality immediately aroused the appetite. Head could begin to spin of the number of colonial goods, groceries and most varied and sometimes unknown fruit. And wine! Ah, what a wine!

"Wooden butter" (as was called olive oil) was delivered directly from Provence. This store had its own bakery: large and small cakes or small "ladies cakes" ...

The old man paused, then murmured:

- As the poet said, "And I was there, drinking honey-beer...". In the fairy tale is always a happy ending. The evil is punished, the enemy is destroyed ... But here it's not a fairy tale but our reality ...

He stood with his eyes closed and with a sad smile on his face. And suddenly, as if frightened, ingratiating he muttered apologetically:

- Ah, forgive an old man, I chattered nonsense. And all this to the fact you are standing in front of the once famous Yeliseyev Grocery Store. -

And then he added quite wretchedly

- Maybe you have a little piece of dried bread?

Raslan regretfully shrugged. The old man nodded with an understanding of:

- The bread became the only desire... Frozen water in the cranes, drainage is not working, broken windows are sealed with plywood... So we are living. But your whole life is ahead of you. I hope, you will see the better times ... Farewell, and do not blame an old man...

The majestic building of the College of Mines at the Neva riverfront with two antique sculptures at the entrance looked proud and aloof. A huge marble vestibule, study rooms and halls, everything was astounding and made the friends feel deeply aware of their provincialism. But in spite of their involuntary shyness caused by this splendor, all of them were determined to continue their studies here and to become part of this new life. They didn't know then, in 1921, at the time of complete economic dislocation, what kind of arduous trials this once regal capital had in store for them.

The Caucasians were met at the dean's office with an indifferent politeness. After all their papers were completed, they were directed to a student union where they were told that there was no place for them to live because the dormitory was filled to capacity.

They took this first blow courageously. The situation was not nice but not hopeless. Somebody gave them good advice to check around many cold half-empty apartments where lonely old and abandoned residents lived as remnants of the bygone regime, all forgotten during revolutionary skirmishes. The friends started looking right away and on the very first day they found what they wanted. An old Germans couple that lived in St. Petersburg from time immemorial were completely knocked out of the familiar tracks of life by a new revolutionary regime. The apartment was huge; the couple used to live in grand style in Tsarist times. Now it was empty and cold, with beautiful stucco ceilings too high to warm up the spacious rooms in this time of scarcity of firewood. There were several big, luxurious marble fireplaces, once blazing, but now gaping mockingly with black emptiness, where ash was packed in the bottom as a dead gray knot.

The old couple, kind of archaic Philemon and Baucis, huddled together in one room, the smallest room for servants, heated by a very primitive hand made stove which was called in this post–revolutionary time by a mocking name, *bourgeois*. When they heard somebody knocking insistently at their door, they slightly opened it keeping the chain lock on. "Who is there? Who sent you? A room? Yes, we have a room, but it is cold, the windows are broken, there is no heat and we have no firewood."

The young men seemed nice to the little old couple. They were glad to give them a room hoping that it wouldn't be so lonely and scary in this broken world with them. And they were right. Within the first week the friends, with the help of the same student union, managed to get some plywood, closed up the broken windows in all the rooms, built from an old tin container a stove *bourgeois*, found some firewood and even shared it with the old couple. They slept on luxurious sofas with golden fringes, covered with their thin coats. It was difficult for three friends to get used to Petrograd. Every morning instead of bright Caucasian sun there was dense white fog in the windows, which were similar to big, blind, and depressing cataractous eyes. In October drizzling rain showers turned into snow and a severe northern winter came.

The three Ossetians were inseparable. This alien, regal, hostile city strengthened their friendship into a real brotherhood. Besides being constantly cold they were constantly hungry. A meager students' scholarship was not enough to live on, but it was very difficult to find a job to earn a little extra money. The boys accepted anything, just to feed themselves somehow. They were happy to find a job at the navy yard carrying wood barrels, bags, and packs on their backs. All workers had to be very careful not to destroy their irreplaceable clothes and shoes when a hoop fell off of a barrel filled with tar, and the tar would spill a big black puddle. Sometimes there was an unexpected feast, a broken barrel might contain herring. In this case the whole crowd of yard laborers would devour the salty fish, including heads and tails. The days at the navy yard did not pass without tragedies. Time after time somebody could be hurt or even killed by a heavy load, or a hungry loader could die after eating something bad, spoiled or poisoned. Even a broken bag of cocoa was a danger; it caused a horrible pain of twisted bowels and took a few lives after workers had eaten this wonderful smelling powder by handfuls.

Hunger, hunger. Once after classes the three friends passed by a big food store. Suddenly a poor gourmet, Googa, stopped spellbound at a dusty storefront. There were big pink slices of ham behind the glass window.

"Hey guys, how much money do we have? Let's buy at least a little piece!"

He almost sensed this long forgotten tender taste in his mouth as he hurried to the counter:

"A hundred grams of ham, please!"

He even unbuttoned his coat and stuck out his big lower lip to make this hundred grams sound more significant.

"We don't have ham."

"But, what is in the window? Get it from there!" He made an authoritative gesture.

"Dear comrade, it is a *mulage* (a display model at the window.)"

Googa shrug his shoulders.

"Ok, it is even better! A hundred grams of this *mulage*, I am paying!"

Raslan and Murat pulled him out of the store.

"Don't make a fool out of yourself, you stupid! This *mulage* is made out of cardboard. Are you going to chew cardboard? "

Googa suffered from hunger more than his slender friends. He lost weight, his skin sagged, and his brain worked constantly trying to find all possible ways to silence the piteous moans of his empty stomach. Once, after school, while putting his books in his rucksack, he came up with an unexpected and almost impossible suggestion.

"Guys, I have great news, my uncle sent me money. Let's go to a restaurant and eat as much as we want!" Googa was rubbing his hands with pleasure.

"Where did you get the uncle, and a rich one?" asked Murat.

"Oh, I have always had the uncle. Do you want me to name all my relatives? He just sent money to his nephew! Do you think, I am lying?"

"But why waste money at a restaurant? We can buy food; it will be enough for ten days!"

"Oh, no!" It is better to quench your thirst with real blood once than to feed yourself with carrion all your life!" he quoted from famous *Maxim Gorky.* "Let's go, I am inviting you, I'm paying!"

They walked into a small little restaurant in a semi-basement. The smell was heavenly.

"Ok, order whatever you like guys; let's go on a spree, I'll pay for everything!"

It felt so nice to finally fill their hungry stomachs! The friends felt dizzy from hot food. Googa got up from the table.

"Wait for me; I need to use a bathroom."

A minute passed, then another one when Murat and Raslan heard a knock on the nearby window they were sitting by. It was Googa. He waved to them nonchalantly and disappeared around a corner. The friends pulled out their monthly scholarship money they had just received. They had to pay everything they had, to the last kopeck. They didn't beat Googa, but they had to go to the navy yard right after school and work till late night. Googa's scholarship money alone was not enough for a month for three of them. It was a difficult and hungry time for the friends, but for once they were lucky.

These inseparable boys were going home after their regular work at the port. They were very tired, cold, their hands were thrust in their pockets and their collars were raised . Freezing, piercing wind from the sea blew in the narrow alleyways squeezed by high walls of houses with dark patches of sleeping windows. The time was close to midnight, but the friends had not eaten since morning. It was not a good day. Before lectures they ate only two potatoes for the three of them. In the port they loaded some heavy equipment, but did not get anything to chew. Their shoulders and backs smarted from heavy boxes, fatigue blunted their hunger, and the friends were in a hurry to warm themselves at the hot *bourgeois* stove. They were not far from their home when they were stopped by a sudden sharp whistle. Some very strange white spots dashed at them from both sides of the alleyway, changing their shapes in the draft of the lane and giving the impression of the creatures from the hell. A horrifying wonder took place at twilight on the gloomy streets of Petersburg soon after the Revolution. Ghosts attacked passers-by. Flying with howls from one place to another they froze the victims with fear and terror, frightened them to death and despoiled them completely.

This time however the effect was unexpected for the ghost themselves. It was pure joy for the friends to warm-up after a long gray, gloomy day. They fought with cheerful ardor, and in no time the ghosts skedaddled, losing their long white overalls, springs which allowed them to give the impression of the flight, and all the loot from the previous victims. The trophies were big; a small bag of potatoes, two apples, three half–loaves of bread and a quite rotten piece of meat. In addition they gathered all the white rags which also could be useful in their beggarly household. Their little old hostess smelled out the rotten meat through all the rooms. She came, washed it thoroughly with permanganate and boiled it for a long time to be sure the young men would not be poisoned. The poor old host and hostess were very kind and sympathetic, feeding time by time from their frugal supply their three always hungry lodgers. On this happy night the students gave them as a present two apples and one half-loaf of bread.

In spite of all the difficulties, their study was underway. In this hungry, cold Petrograd the starving professors required the same knowledge from the students of the College of Mines as always.

Raslan was quicker than two of his friends to enter into the rhythm of student life. He was modest, but his brilliant ability, unfailing honesty and straightforwardness created around him a halo of deep respect among his co-students and even professors. Murat felt bewildered at the beginning, but his natural grip when it came to knowledge, and his persistent desire to study returned him the confidence and reconciled with the novelty of the situation. Googa also was dispirited at first, but over time he got used to a new life, and his jokes and bywords found a new audience and even gained popularity.

The students of 1920 represented a very diverse tribe. There was a small quota for the intellectuals entering any university, College of

Mine included; and they were a minority among the students. The door was open wide for the proletarians, the poorest class of woking people, who was announced at this time of the ruling class and proud to call proletariat. Many of them came straight from the army, and navy Mauser pistols hanging from their belts were impressive evidence of it. This new type of student looked at the well–groomed beards of professors with some gloom and suspicion, saber-rattling occasionally. It was difficult for them to study, and you could not say they were fools, because , later on many of them became good and even talented geologists. They were not sufficiently prepared, and the wheels in their brains rusted during the years in the army. One of them, a former sailor, listened gloomy to a lecture and after twice asking the professor the same question, got up and in despair and exclaimed: "No, guys, we will never understand this!" But one way or another they were forced to understand, and they plowed a difficult field of science very slowly, but faithfully.

In 1920 a strictly men-only-student-body was replenished by women, to the complete wrath of the old professoriate, convinced that geology was a men's and only men's kingdom. There were not many of them in the College of Mines, but they were forced to affirm their rights every day. Only three young women were in the group where the Ossetian friends were studying. "Mademoiselle," – croaked old mineralogist Petrovsky puffing in his combed beard during the examination of smart and assiduous Natasha, "Mademoiselle, you can't distinguish quartz from fluorite." Puff . "Study more and come another time." Natasha lightly touched his sleeve trying with womanly suavity to appeal to his justice. The old misogynist rumbled, "Me! An old man! You try to tempt! Get out!!"

The second girl, Tatiana, was tall, broad-shouldered with a stentorian voice and seemed to wear a skirt by misunderstanding. She was a plain straightforward fellow. The professors cringed from her mannish commissar like behavior and they not dare to contradict her, because her strong waist was tightened by a belt holding a Mauzer.

The third student was a short little blond-haired girl who reminded one of a tender flower. She watered by her abundant tears the professorial carping. It was so much harder on her than on Natasha and Tatiana because she was way too far from the common image of an engineer-geologist. Her last name was *Krolik* (Rabbit) and it fit her gentle appearance so well.

Old professors were deeply convinced that women introduce a romantic atmosphere in a serious college environment and they were partially right. The fair-haired Rabbit warmed up Raslan's heart from the first day. He looked at her tender face and felt a little warm spark that appeared in their otherwise difficult life in Petrograd. Raslan tried hard not to show his feelings, but it was difficult to trick his friends and they mercilessly poked fun at him.

"Raslan," Googa would laugh, "it looks like you're going to work on rabbit-breeding".

Raslan was blushing profusely because Rabbit was really squeezing his ascetic heart with her soft little paws. But that unvoiced romance didn't last long because before the end of the third college semester Rabbit unexpectedly got married to a young assistant professor and all her fights with woman-hater professors ended. She flitted away into a nice solid marriage without even suspecting what her smiles meant for the young man who came from the Caucasus mountains. For him these smiles were assurances of her returned affection, of her fidelity; and her sudden betrayal shook his belief in love so profoundly, that he thought at that time, it dashed his hopes on the possibility of love in his life forever.

That winter was dragging endlessly, but at last a spring sun, shy, not too warm, but still cheerful, pierced heavy leaden clouds. The most important thing was that they would soon go back home to the Caucasus, for the whole two months of vacations. Murat and Googa were going to a city, to their parents; as far as Ruslan was concerned, his older sister was waiting for him in their village.

These two happy months went exactly the way the friends were hoping for during that cold Petrograd winter. There was a hearty welcome, there was warmth all around, there was sunshine, green valleys, and plenty of hot corn pancakes with homemade cheese.

Tanned after working in corn fields, Raslan was now going back to Petrograd in an overcrowded train. He hid a priceless gift his sister prepared for him, a covered wicker basket packed with baked goods and homemade cheese under his seat. To make sure that nobody would steals his treasure he tied the basket to his leg with a rope. All night long he dozed on and off frequently checking his basket by pulling on the rope. The basket was there. In the morning Raslan got the basket from under the seat and found it unexpectedly light, everything from the basket was stolen through a cleverly cut hole.

This year passed by, and then the next one. Petrograd was awakening after famine and economic devastation. Life was slowly getting back to normal. For the three friends who were in their senior years, classes became more interesting and their life got easier. The College of Mines offered them some jobs and they were getting paid, which was very decent for those times. They all lived together now in a student's dormitory. The nice old German couple was saddened by their departure.

After the fourth year in school Raslan unexpectedly received an offer to spend the next winter at a distant copper and gold mine, to work there as a chief engineer-geologist, and organize a mining exploration. Actually, this assignment was not so surprising, since geologists were in demand, and Raslan's exceptional abilities were noticed since his first years in college. Murat was sincerely and openly happy for his friend. For Googa it was a very hard blow since his candidacy was not even considered. It was not the first time when his being a friend was challenged by feeling envious. Usually friendship would win but not this time; now Googa was upset and irritated. His love for Raslan was yielding to a feeling that Googa himself couldn't understand and couldn't suppress. "What was it, envy? Nonsense!," Googa thought, "How can I be envious? He is like a brother to me. But, on the other hand, it would have been so easy to love him if he was weaker, if I could patronize him," Googa grinned recalling Raslan's eyes sparkling with enthusiasm. No patronizing here! Nasty thoughts kept running through his head giving him some comfort; maybe Raslan won't be able to handle his task, maybe he will be recalled, and somebody else will replace him. It would be easy to feel friendship if he would fail. But Raslan was not recalled; he finished the job, calculated deposits of the mine and came back. He was full of happy energy; he brought boxes of geological samples and a well-written report. Googa became depressed, but Raslan didn't notice it; he was glad to see his friends;

and, happy and excited, he was talking about the severe winter at the mine. And then he got absorbed in his studies getting ready for his college exams.

* * *

In the last autumn of their study at the College of Mines both Ruslan's friends came back from Ossetia with their young wives. Their little close-knit circle broke up. Raslan stayed at the dormitory and his friends rented rooms in communal apartments.

Murat's wife Lisa was as tall as his shoulder; otherwise she was very much like him – light-eyed, red-haired, with a nice and friendly personality, as if they were created for each other. Ruslan felt at ease with them and stopped by frequently for no reason.

Googa married an astonishing beauty. Her name was Zarema. She was elegant, with big dark velvety eyes and thick long eyelashes, fine-shaped nose and porcelain white skin. When, in her light step, she moved along Nevsky Prospect, her wavy black hair covered with a little beret, passers-by stopped and followed her with their eyes. She never looked around as if she didn't even see those admiring glances. But she was very aware of her beauty, and one could always see in her velvety eyes an expression of regret being surrounded by those who were so unworthy.

Murat and Lisa knew each other before they got married, while Zarema, according to old Ossetian custom, saw her husband only after she became his wife. She didn't find him attractive at all. The only one thought comforted her, shy knew that she would follow him to Petrograd where he would make a good career . But when they came to Petrograd Googa lost all his exclusiveness as a big metropolitan student. He turned out to be the same as all his colleagues; the worst part though was that he was physically the most unattractive. Zarema, this exceptional beauty Zarema, with her pride so badly hurt, never allowed herself to be seen with her husband. Thus she was doomed to complete seclusion. She tried to take some beginners classes at the University but soon she dropped out, giving as a reason the fact that Googa was going crazy with jealousy. So, she remained a beautiful little bird in a house cage and only once did she make an attempt to fly out.

Googa's two bosom friends, Murat and Raslan, would frequently visit their little room in a Petrograd communal apartment. They were among the not too numerous guests there. Murat was not to Zarema taste, and he was married. As far as Raslan was concerned, at the first sight at him she understood he was exactly the kind of man she wanted for a husband. He possessed everything; he had good looks, he was smart, kind and had a great career in front of him. She started designing a love net for him. Raslan never thought of Zarema, and he didn't even notice her amorous plot. Meanwhile her imagination grew wild day after day; pictures of her wonderful victory were running through her head; she imagined Raslan's declaration of love and was dreaming of a punishment for Googa, the ugly one who dared to make her, Zarema, having no equal, make her his wife! She decided all she needed was just to give him a little push, to encourage him. And she decided to move ahead with her plan.

An opportunity was soon presented. One evening, right at the time when Raslan was going to stop by at the young couple's, Googa had to leave. He asked Zarema to keep Raslan waiting until he returns. Zarema, all excited and happy, was waiting for Raslan. She believed that evening would change everything for her.

When she opened the door she was a dazzling beauty. She removed her hairpins and her silky wavy hair covered her shoulders; a black lacy shawl emphasized her white neck and arms, and there was an expression of almost childlike defenselessness in her big velvety eyes. When Raslan learned that Googa wasn't there he wanted to leave and promised to stop by some other time. Zarema was sure he was just afraid to stay with her tête-à-tête not to reveal his feelings. She threw her shawl behind Raslan's back like a fishing net and pulled him in. "Come in, come in for a minute". Pulled by the net and feeling very uneasy he stepped in. And at this very moment Zarema fell to his chest begging, "Save me Raslan, please save me". Feeling completely lost he lightly pushed her back.

"What happened?"

Her eyes were begging and full of suffering.

"I cannot , I can't live with this ugly creature anymore. You don't understand how terrible it is. I am suffering, suffering! Please take me from him, I want to be with you, only with you!"

"Zarema, you're talking nonsense! I am Googa's friend and I will never betray him! And he is not ugly, he loves you, what else do you need? You are and you will always be my friend's wife for me, and that is it! Please remember this once and for all! Pull yourself together and forget about this conversation as if it never happened."

Zarema was frozen in shock. She did not expect such an outcome. Tone of Raslan's voice, firm and irritated, even seemed rude to her, unreal, unthinkable; she was so sure he was in love with her, was dreaming of her, and now, instead of a declaration of love she was getting this insulting rebuff.

Raslan turned to leave and here he saw the black shawl still on his shoulder. Deeply annoyed, he threw it off and shut the door leaving behind a bitter enemy for all his life.

* * *

By the twenty-fifth year, Stalin had seized power and clearly strove for autocracy. Repressions increased; The accused were shot without trial. On the night of 9 to 10 June, 9,000 people were arrested. So far, it was thousands, later there would be millions, but no one else knew about it. The people were horrified by the number of "enemies of the people", but all-powerful propaganda - the all-encompassing instrument of power - was launched in full force, the newspapers called for "rallying together", to which the masses responded with enthusiastic enthusiasm ... until many themselves fell under the ruthless, insatiable force, which deman incessant human victims.

Raslan, like most, did not want to believe that those noble ideas, the passionate calls for freedom, equality, and brotherhood for which he fought only a few years ago, were now replaced by terror for. The thought of this was unbearable, and he tried to believe that "internal enemies" really threaten the new people's state in such incredible proportions.

Years passed, and "better days" still remained the faraway dream.

Nevertheless the friends graduated from the College of Mines and were assigned to a research institute. During summer months they traveled to different parts of the country to meet again in winter when they worked on analyzing material they collected.

Raslan's group traveled by train to faraway boundless expanses of Kirghiz steppe named Kazakhstan not long before that time. There was plenty of work to be done there. A base where they were getting their equipment, hiring workers, buying horses, was located in a small town on the bank of Irtysh River. The group could get there in a roundabout way; first by train to Omsk, then by the river on a small ship constantly hitting uncharted sandbanks, where they had to spend time under a scorching sun to be freed.

Loaded camels looked grand as they walked with measured steps through the flat, gray, sandy little town; small Kirghiz horses were running around pulling a wicker cart, *treshpankas*. Windy, dusty gray adobe little houses, some leafless vegetation reflected enormous efforts by local authorities to make this place livable. That was the city of Pavlodar of those times.

A small little adobe house at Trotsky Street (named in the honor of famous leader) served as a geological base. Here the people, equipment, and sheep that resentfully and frightenedly baa, were loaded on the wooden carriages called "brichkas". The brichkas dragging by horses were going to those boundless yellowing steppes. A compass and an old topographical map with little crosses that marked places of their future stop sites were their only guiding tools in that flat boundless ocean. The brichkas would pass, native-grasses would straighten up their drying stalks, the wind would spiral over the dust, and no traces of an expedition would be left there to see.

Hired workers – Kazakhs were leading the group. Sometimes along the way they would see a nomad's *yurta*, a tent made from camels felt, where they were welcomed with mare's milk, *kumiss*. Hosts were cordial and curious. "Where are you going? Why? Looking for gold?" When they heard that the boss's name was Raslan they were getting excited. "You're Muslim!" Raslan diplomatically responded, "I am from Muslim area". Then they would get especially hospitable, "Oh, drink kumiss as much as you like".

They would usually set up their camp near water by a small river, or a little lake, or an old abandoned well if it was still possible to get to precious water. Tents were small, one could hold four people. The body could fit inside, and legs were outside. A pit in the ground with walls faced by stones served as a kitchen. In the morning Raslan, who would get up at dawn would wake up the sleepy camp. "Get up enlightened proletariat!"

Morning breeze was caressing, there was not a single cloud in the clear sky that looked like a bright blue canopy. After a quick breakfast full of jokes and laughter they were all ready to start their long day, afoot or on horseback, until sunset, with no weekends, holidays or days off. On a rare rainy day they would work on their reports or drawing maps. Every once in a while the geologists would get up even earlier with the first signs of daylight, just to enjoy hunting for wild ducks or turkeys in the rushes by a little lake.

Sometimes annoying delays happened in their work caused by the necessity to get new equipment, replenish food supplies or horse fodder. Then they would be waiting for hours or even days at the site because there was no regular schedule for any kind of deliveries. There was absolutely nothing to keep a person occupied in the dismal little town under scorching sun. And once, in one of those painful days of waiting something extraordinary happened, bright circus posters decorated the little town.

Magic, Miracles and Illusions!
Famous and World Renowned Magician – Emil Renard

Our geologist from Leningrad, that is how Petrograd was now called, had never heard the name of that world renowned magician, but it was a chance to kill time and together they went to watch Miracles and Magic. The mystery performance was in a little adobe house, which was sometimes used to show movies and thus was called a movie theater.

There were few spectators and all the geologists took comfortable seats in the first row of a little hall smelling of wet clay. The magician looked splendid in a white turban and a black tuxedo, and the performance unexpectedly turned out interesting. The most impressive part was a moment when a charming houri, dressed as an oriental beauty was put into hypnotic sleep by a wave of his magic wand and then started floating in the air in the same position. The ovation was ecstatic. The houri flitted out on the stage, dropped a curtsey and all of a sudden waved to somebody in the audience. Everybody turned to the lucky one. It was Raslan. His friends knew how strict, even ascetic

Raslan was about women and they amused themselves, by making fun of embarrassed Raslan. During intermission an attendant came to him.

"You are asked to come backstage."

"What for?"

"Please, it is very important."

Confused, Raslan followed the attendant, and his friends' happy hooting accompanied him all the way. At the moment he stepped backstage the oriental beauty fell on his neck.

"Raslan, what a surprise. I am so happy!"

"Kosha, that's you? What are you doing here?"

Kosha, Raslan's first cousin, said laughing, "You've just seen what I do here, I work with my husband. Let's go, I'll introduce you!"

She pulled Raslan toward the magician who was approaching them. The men's handshake was not too cordial. Despite the fact that Raslan was very glad to see his cousin, his friend since their childhood, he was not too happy about her new role as a circus houri. It was obvious he was bewildered and upset. He was disappointed long ago, when she first decided to be an actress, and now it was the circus. They spent the evening together, but that was the first and the last time Raslan met her husband who later became the world-renowned magician, as that little poster predicted. Even much later, when the magician was honored by being invited to visit Queen Elizabeth herself, Raslan didn't warm up to him. He had never forgiven him for his cousin's career as a performer of his magic tricks and her dress as a personage grom "Thousand and One Night."

In the fall when blowing winds were toppling the tents, sleet appeared, and water in buckets started freezing at nights, the time came to take a winter break. The geologists dismissed the workers, sold their horses and returned to Leningrad until spring when they were to go back and continue the work.

* * *

A year passed, then the next, then another one and every time as soon as winter was just letting up, another expedition was ready to go and to continue the job.

In the rush of a railroad station Raslan was giving his final instructions. Everybody was already there except one student, a trainee from Moscow with a German sounding last name. Raslan looked around. Where is this E. Muller?

A slender grey-eyed brown-haired young girl, all out of breath, was rushing to their railroad car.

"Would you tell me please, are you with a geologist group?" she asked.

"Yes, who are you looking for?"

"For the leader, I am assigned to the group."

"I am the leader, but it must be a mistake, you are not on my list!"

"Not on the list? Would you check please? My name is Elena Muller."

"Elena? I was expecting a Eugene!"

"Elena, Elena Muller," - she was getting impatient. – "So, may I get in?"

"Y-y-es, " he answered hesitantly, picked up her backpack and asked dumbfounded, "But why Elena?"

"Because that's the name my parents gave me."

She seemed annoyed when she glanced at him and jumped in.

The reason for Raslan's confusion was the fact that his strict rule was no women in the group. Conditions were difficult, dangerous sometimes, and it would be very bothersome to deal with a representative of the weaker sex, and it was also bad for the general moral. He himself checked the list of participants and he never expected E. Muller to be a grey-eyed Elena.

Meanwhile Elena was making her way through the railroad car thinking ''such a queer fellow this guy is. My name is not good for him. His eyes, they are so piercing. And he is wearing some stupid galoshes in this sunny day. Such an unpleasant encounter I don't even want to go".

She sat aside, by the window, watching the streets of Leningrad floating by. It was a beautiful springtime. She didn't look at her boss and other members of the group, healthy young guys who were arranging their bags, knapsacks, and boxes on upper berths. She felt alone and sad, she was hungry and drowsy. A conductor brought some tea and the boss became more animated. Suddenly his piercing eyes turned kind and smiley and not biting at all. As he unpacked his bag he invited the whole group to the table. Everyone felt a little shy and was politely refusing, but he was so hospitable and insisting that soon all the group got around a little table shoveling up chicken and bread and washing it down with hot tea. All that feeling shy and awkwardness was gone, everybody talked, asked questions. During the long trip people got used to each other, and by the time they arrived at the Irtysh River they were all friends.

Now there was a woman in their group, and not just a woman but also a beautiful one, smart, with self-esteem. Raslan was the first one to fall victim to his own misunderstanding of the name on his list. He tried very hard to avoid being obsessed by her big gray eyes, but he felt he was struck.

And then their daily from daybreak to sunset trips, called *route*, started .

For Raslan the whole world changed when Elena joined the group. No matter how deep he would be involved in everyday problems, he was always thinking about her. She created a happy spot in his heart and soul. Everything he was doing turned out well, he never felt tired. He was waiting for the evening work in a tent on material gathered during the day because Elena was there, and it made Raslan entirely happy. That happiness caused by her presence was so pungent that sometimes he couldn't catch his breath. Raslan felt thankful to her for the mere fact that she existed and was around. He couldn't hide his love even if he wanted, his eyes flared when she showed up. Everybody saw this but nobody would make fun of it, maybe because they respected their leader, maybe because everybody liked Elena, or maybe all of them understood that Raslan's feeling was a real thing, very deep and genuine, and there was no room for any jokes there. Of course they were a little envious.

When Raslan was assigning members of the group to a specific route for making geological maps and looking for possible deposits, he always chose the most difficult and long ones for himself. When it came to Elena, he tried to protect her and despite her resentment, he forbid her to travel by herself since it could have been unsafe at those times. Recently general collectivization had been announced; and Kazakh's nomads responded by slaughtering all their livestock. Soon after this, human bones would appear right by sheep, horse, and camel bones – as a result of a famine over the whole steppe area. It became necessary to protect the group's food supply, and all geologists were armed. Horses, their only means of transportation, were also guarded to prevent them from being stolen and eaten. They tried their best to be vigilant, but in spite of it a strong gelding was stolen, then a little white mare, Masha, Elena's favorite, the one she used for her routes, also disappeared.

Searches ended when they found Masha's white tail in one of an *urta*, a coarse felt tent, of native people. Elena couldn't hold her tears, but Raslan didn't punish those who were at fault; he knew too well what a famine was all about. The real danger were ruthless Basmach (bandits) troops of devastated and hungry nomad, who, along with the ready help of neighbors from nearby Uzbekistan and Afganistanian, were protesting against collectivization and drastic change brought to their lives.

Sometimes geologists passed a lonely campfire. They grabbed their arms, getting ready to fight a basmach troop; but there were starving women and children staring at the fire with their empty starving eyes. Raslan and his little group were shocked when they found all eighteen local nomad Kazakhs whom they had hired to dig excavation dead. These people were famished and had died of twisted bowels after eating a dinner.

To live and work in this gloomy and frightening atmosphere overstrained the geologists' nerves. They tried to help the poor starving Kazakhs, but it was impossible to feed the whole steppe region. Those abandoned adobe huts with white bones inside stayed for many more years as grim reminders of what happened when collectivization took place in Kazakhstan.

By the twenty-fifth year, Stalin had seized power and clearly strove for autocracy. Repressions increased; The accused were shot without trial. On the night of 9 to 10 June, 9,000 people were arrested. So far, it was thousands, later there would be millions, but no one else knew about it. The people were horrified by the number of "enemies of the people", but all-powerful propaganda - the all-encompassing instrument of power - was launched in full force, the newspapers called for "rallying together", to which the masses responded with enthusiastic enthusiasm ... until many themselves fell under the ruthless, insatiable force, which deman incessant human victims.

Raslan, like most, did not want to believe that those noble ideas, the passionate calls for freedom, equality, and brotherhood for which he fought only a few years ago, were now replaced by terror for. The thought of this was unbearable, and he tried to believe that "internal enemies" really threaten the new people's state in such incredible proportions.

Years passed, and "better days" still remained the faraway dream.

* * *

A workday ended, and the geologists and student-trainees were returning to the site. After dusk everybody was there except Raslan. When night fell, the sky was covered with storm clouds and a severe thunderstorm started. Lightning flared in the pitch-dark night; thunder deafened like huge metal sheets torn across the sky. The small group inside their joint tent– canteen were worried. Their leader had ridden off in the morning on a red stallion and he was supposed to be back long ago. Elena didn't even bother to hide her frustration. She waited tensely for the sound of a running horse. But it was useless peering into the darkness of the night listening for the clatter of horses' hoofs because of the rattling downpour.

It was almost midnight when Raslan arrived. He was soaked; but his eyes were beaming with such excitement and enthusiasm that it took everybody's breath away.

"Elena,…guys,…I saw,…I found something huge! A field, a deposit, copper, maybe gold, it stretches for many kilometers! I didn't have enough time. Tomorrow we're going there, we have to start exploring it as soon as we can!"

Everybody in the group was affected by Raslan's excitement. An event of importance and significance was about to enter their lives. For geologists a discovery of a deposit is like the discovery of a new land for sailors. They gathered around a map assigning routes. A festive mood was in the air; and nobody wanted to sleep, but after a while Raslan commanded, "It's time to go to bed. We will have a busy tomorrow!"

Elena, in her little tent, knelt on a large felt mat on the floor, and lit a small candle. Beads of moisture sparkled on the heavy canvas tent. A dampened letter was on the box she used as a writing table. She had already read it , and now this little white square with ink running off took her back from the excitement and joy of the last moment to a different world, faraway and faded. Elena was surprised that this man whom she had met only recently meant so much to her. She thought about what the letter said and felt sorry for her former boyfriend, the one she had almost forgotten, and who was patiently waiting for her in Moscow.

"How different they are," she thought. "One is like a fire, the other like a calm stream of water. One is full of action, of striving force; the other is an unhurried discussion. I used to feel so peaceful and cozy by those streams. Everything was simple and clear, like when I was a child – music, books, long quiet conversations, and walks in the park. And here, life is a flame of emotions, a tornado of events. This is real life, it is thrilling." Elena recalled how Raslan, soaking wet and excited entered the tent, "Elena,…guys…". He wanted to share the important news with her first! It made her happy, she knew she was loved, and she was in love too .

During today's long wait for Raslan, she had experienced such worry, such fear for his life, that now Moscow and the one who was there waiting for her, completely receded into the background and faded. That night Elena didn't sleep; rolls of thunder moved faraway while she was writing a letter to Moscow: "It is hard for me to tell you the truth…"

* * *

After that memorable thunderstorm the geologists' work moved full speed ahead. They were hiring new people and the whole steppe heard the news. Nomad Kazakhs were coming from all over, from nearby and faraway places, young and old, even women with children. They were pitching their *urtas* and settling down. Newly hired people affected by the enthusiasm of the leader, were digging, shoveling, drilling, rushing to show green copper samples to Raslan. Everybody was getting up before dawn, trying to be ahead of others, to get deeper and deeper into the ground. It was an outburst of enthusiasm involving the leader, the geologists, students-trainees, and hired workers, even a stableman and a cook. Reports and requests for financing Bochekul, as Raslan called this deposit, had already been sent out. Raslan was overwhelmed; he had to be at dozens of places at the same time. Elena tried hard to help him as much as she could and was busy selecting and packing samples of copper ore. The spiritual closeness formed between the two of them was almost tangible. One glance was enough for them to understand each other. Because of that life was beautiful, and they enjoyed their work with all their hearts .

One unexpected event interrupted this harmony. It would not have happened if not for Elena's city dweller naivety. The steppe around her was not as harmless as it looked. The vipers were abundant there and very dangerous. Unfortunately Elena did not realize their bite could be fatal. Long ago, sometime in early adolescence she read about taming snakes, and would never have remembered this book if not for these numerous voiceless and quiet mystical inhabitants of the boundless steppe. There were many vipers around, basking in the sun and not worrying much about the scurrying people nearby.

While going together with Raslan to the next dig hole, Elena watched with amazement and curiosity the gray thick live coils enjoying themselves in the sun-heated stones. Was it tricks of eastern snake tamers or just young bravado that encouraged her? She came closer to one of these vipers and reached out her hand. In one moment Raslan shoved Elena aside, and she fell down. He wanted to help her to her feet, but Elena, bemused, pushed him off, leaped up like a spring and began walk away, wiping the tears of resentment.

"Elena, darling, please understand; I didn't have a choice but to save you this way. One second and the snake would bite you! This is a steppe viper. The viper! Its bite can be fatal! Why did you reach for it?"

"It is just the way snakes tamers catch the snakes," Elena answered in a muffled voice, "gripping them at the head."

"Let me show you something."

Raslan searched and found a long stick. He cleaned it and sharpened the end of it with a folding knife. He brought the sharp end of the stick to the viper while tightly holding Elena's hand.

"Did you notice anything?"

"Of course I did, you frightened the snake, and it immediately crawled away."

"That is all? But look here."

Two dots were very well visible on the white surface of the sharp wood slice.

"Before crawling away the viper bit the stick so swiftly you were not able to notice it. You did not even notice it, and you wanted to catch its head! Do you understand what danger was waiting for you, what was going to happen? Please, promise me, this experiment with taming the vipers is the very first and the very last one!"

Elena looked at these two sinister dots with amazement and admiration.

"Yes," answered Elena reluctantly. "I promise. But anyway you should not have shoved me aside so vigorously!"

Raslan hugged Elena and kissed her still wet eyes.

"I had to" he replied.

An old and experienced geologist arrived. He was Raslan's teacher and a good friend, and Raslan was glad to see him and to show him the discovered deposit. They walked from sunrise to sunset, studying the area, descending down into pits and shafts. The tent was full of samples.

The new Bochekul deposit became the center of all their thoughts, hopes, and expectations.

In the late fall, the winds and sleet became ferocious. It was time for Raslan's group to roll up their tents and let the hired workers go. The steppe became empty again.

It was the last year in college for Elena and she went to Leningrad together with Raslan to work on her thesis. It was unthinkable for them to live apart. The independent gray-eyed Elena, with whom everybody in the group was a little in love, that very Elena lost her independence.

* * *

Lisa and Murat met Elena with open arms and right away became her friends. Zarema, like a scared doe, shied away from young Raslan's wife. Elena was not upset by it at all, it even amused her, but any friendship with Zarema was out-of-question. Googa always stopped by to visit the newlyweds without Zarema. He talked far too long with some unclear and mysterious significance, shaking his round head, which grew bald very early. His ramblings were not understandable to Elena, and she actually didn't try to pay much attention to them. She was so incredibly happy and her life was so interesting and full of love that she didn't see any shadows around.

Googa had heart-to-heart talk with Raslan.

"Raslan, dear, I am your best friend, the friend who loves you. I must tell you that you are breaking my heart. You forget our customs and traditions. Elena is a beautiful woman, she is a smart woman, but for us, Caucasians, she is a stranger. Her concepts of life are different from ours. What are you going to tell your sister, your relatives? Your father would spin in his grave. Elders will curse you. How are you going to live with this? Elena is a European woman; she has no idea how to respect her husband. She can spend an evening with her friends, without you, with other men. How will you know what might happen there? For a European woman to cheat on her husband is as easy as to eat a piece of flat bread for us. Think well what you're doing, dear."

Raslan frowned. Googa's unpleasant suggestions were disturbing. Nothing in the whole world, not even their mountain customs, which he deeply respected, could make him give up Elena; but as every Caucasian, he was jealous. He couldn't bear even the thought that Elena could be unfaithful to him. Googa knew how to touch a sore spot.

As for Elena, she had no idea about all the Caucasian problems and macho feelings. She grew up in an educated, well–cultured family, where the Russian language was used along with German, and French, where music, poetry, and philosophy were attributes of everyday life. Her father, Baron von Muller, taught history in the old and famous University of Derpt until the First World War started. At that time he and his family had to run secretly to a small provincial town. This dangerous escape, "dissolution in the thin air", saved him and his family from imprisonment and unavoidable execution in this horrible revolutionary time. Baron von Muller came from Russian-German aristocracy, and that fact should have been forgotten once and for all, because the title "Baron" could mean death. After escaping from the city, where many knew him, Bernard Muller worked at a small high school and tried to make himself as inconspicuous as possible. By some intricate manipulations with documents he managed to get rid of his title and the treacherous prefix *von* before his last name.

By a twist of fate, Raslan could not have found a more European girl in the whole of Russia. Ironically, he probably didn't even realize that this high culture and finesse that were Elena's very essence were for him her most attractive features.

It had never even come to Elena's mind to behave according to Googa's standards of a modest Ossetian wife; she, of course, felt equal with men; she liked friends gathering, clever jokes and (oh, how terrible!) even dances.

One day Elena came back home later than usual and said she had been at a restaurant with friends who came from Moscow for a visit. Raslan was in shock, blood rushed to his head.

"Elena, you cannot do this, you have no right to go to restaurants without me! Even during the day, even with your best friends. It is an insult to me! If you ever turn unfaithful, yes, if you ever turn unfaithful," he grabbed a hunting rifle from the wall, "I'll kill you and I'll kill myself!"

Some other time Elena would have laughed at this medieval explosion of passion. But at that moment there was such fury in Raslan's eyes that it threw her into confusion and fear. She had never seen him act like this. It was serious; it was past laughter and jokes. She understood that her beloved Raslan was capable of killing her and himself.

They didn't talk for two days, but after a happy reconciliation Elena realized that her husband was an Ossetian, and nothing could be done about it. His jealousy could be scary. It looked like Othello could live in real life, not only in Shakespeare's play.

* * *

In the spring, work at the new copper and gold deposit site was in full swing. Equipment roared as they began work on a new borehole. Hundreds of workers, students and young graduates arrived. A reporter was running around and soon an article in a local paper appeared with an announcement:

A stubborn Ossetian came and said, "Here, right here there will be gold and copper!" And he found them!"

Elena laughed and Raslan made a wry smile. A tent camp developed into new settlement, adobe structures, apartment buildings, dormitories, warehouses, a bathhouse, and a club. Not little horses but big trucks were crossing the steppe. Boring rigs were rattling, forges were clinking, and axes were knocking, promising a good development.

All of a sudden everything stopped. The Bochekul ore deposit closed down, all the works suspended, and nobody knew why. All events connected with Raslan discovery was like fireworks that brighten up the sky for a short time.

* * *

Googa paced the small room of his Leningrad apartment. He couldn't sleep. He was terrified by the betrayal he had committed and at the same time was happy with the result, which surpassed all his expectations.

"I didn't really write anything bad", he tried to console himself, "I only said that a young and inexperienced geologist became fascinated by some copper ore samples. I said there could not be significant mineral deposits in that region, and that there was no reason to spend big money for this project. It would be just a waste; it should be checked more thoroughly. Yes, I actually didn't recommend to the government to close it, but just to check it! It is true, Raslan is young and inexperienced, and it is very possible that he is mistaken. It doesn't work like this, "come, saw, conquered!" Googa tried to convince himself that he was right, but he still was conscience-stricken and couldn't sleep. He had always been envious of his friend, when they still were students; then this feeling grew to some kind of disease constantly haunting him. As for Zarema, it looked as if they shared these sentiments, they were one. She was literally seething with rage, feeling mad about Raslan's success, the one who so rudely rejected her. She couldn't stand the thought that it was he who got so much ahead of her husband. And it was her idea to write, *to "give a signal"*, as the NKVD (later changed to the KGB, Committee of State Security) called it.

Besides his conscience, Googa was also tormented by fear. "What if the NKVD want to find out who sent this letter? What if Raslan finds out?" He of course didn't write his name, he signed this *"signal"* as "a group of concerned geologists." But if the NKVD decided to investigate, they will know. But why would they want to know? A signal is a signal.

It is hard to know if Googa's letter to the NKVD alone caused the freezing of the development of this rich mineral deposit, or there were other undercurrents working against Raslan; everything was possible. But this very letter had a special somber meaning, it detected Googa's personality distraction, and it worked itself as rust corroding his soul. The Rubicon was crossed, he did something that seemed impossible, unthinkable, he denounced his friend to the NKVD (KGB), and it was the end of his decency.

* * *

The development of Bochekul ore deposit was suspended. The settlement was dead but every year Raslan's group of geologists was growing. Maps of the region were getting more detailed. The brilliance of Raslan's mind and his amazing intuition, he seemed to have a mystical talent for seeing through the ground, together with his energy and deep love for everything he was doing were all bringing great results. The geological picture of that remote area was getting clear and definite.

In the years when our planet had not yet been made small by cars and planes, when distances were measured by days, weeks and months, instead of hours, as it is now, the life of geologists demanded a deep devotion to the profession, sometimes even self–sacrifices. They walked many miles, galloped on horseback, jogged in carts, rocked on camels, and cooked monotonous and poor food on campfires. They were baked in the heat, shivering with cold, and suffering from swarms of mosquitoes. Under a scorching sun, beautiful clean blue lakes with birds and animal traces along the shores turned into alkali soils. Attractive water ripples were just a mirage. From time to time thunder and lightning rent the steppe air, the grass blazed up like gunpowder, and a fiery stream rushed to the horizon turning the yellow steppe into a black desert. And still every morning geologists woke up, astounded by the boundless expanse of the steppe, by its calm and serenity. This very freedom and the explorer's passion were the best rewards for their trying work.

* * *

Again, goodbye to Leningrad, the long train ride, ferryboat, and horseback ride. Again, boundless steppes where short green spring gave way to a scorching summer, and low yellow hills parched by the sun were rolling to the horizon.

It was late evening, almost night. Dry hot air was electrified, and one could see sheet lightning across the sky. Everybody was back in their small tents, and only four people sat at the table in the general tent to plan routes for the next day, Raslan, Elena and two young geologists, Alex and Vasya.

The door of the tent was made out of a coarse felt mat. They rolled this door up to the ceiling to let some air blow through the tent. Suddenly Raslan stopped in the middle of a sentence when a round fiery mass floated in through the open doorway. It was ball lightning – a frequent guest in those steppe regions. Everybody froze motionless following the ball of fire with their eyes; only Alex managed to dive under a deck with geological samples. The fiery ball slowly floated above these three people's heads making their hair stand on end with a crackling sound. Quietly it floated out through an open tent window, turning it to a round hole with charred edges and exploded with a deafening sound at a distance of about two feet from the tent, after hitting a big rock. Alex, embarrassed, crept out from under the deck.

"You climbed into the most dangerous place!" Raslan told Alex laughing, "There is a dynamite box there!"

Nobody suffered any injury. A fire at a food supply tent was put out quickly, the bread was toasted but still eatable, only all boxes with matches were burned. The next morning Raslan left for three days to research some faraway area. Elena offered to travel to their base, which was not too far. The main purpose of her trip was to get matches, but salt and the mail were also important. She got a camel and a little cart; the trip was supposed to take three to four days. Elena got to the base with no problem; she slept in a sleeping bag under the cart, while the camel was grazing around. She didn't waste any time at the base either and at dawn, she started on her way back.

When the adobe houses disappeared out of sight she suddenly felt terribly alone. A vast steppe, boundless like a sea was all around her, and nobody, not a soul anywhere. Her camel cheerfully jogged along and Elena didn't hurry him up. Still she joggled in the cart, while the sun made it's usual round, and dark night enveloped the steppe. Suddenly, as happens in open spaces, a thunderstorm broke out. She should have unharnessed the camel before dark and hidden under the cart but the camp was not too far, only two or three hours away; and it was so tempting to get to where everybody was, to the safety of the tents, where Raslan would be waiting for her. How could she suspect that the hot and lazy steppe would suddenly turn into a whistling hurricane of cold torrential downpours?

Elena pulled on a canvas windbreaker. It was already wet, it didn't protect her from the rain, and cold water was streaming down from her head. The Ship of the Desert obviously didn't like to play the role of Noah's Ark; he dragged himself along for some time ignoring Elena's urging, and then he just lay down, his head high up. Pushing him, talking to him and even whipping were of no avail. A camel is not a dog that is in love with its master; he is not a horse understanding his master's wishes; he is not even a donkey who demonstrates emotions by his stubbornness. The Ship of the Desert ignored Elena's presence in his imperturbable haughtiness. But it looked like that two-humped misanthrope was right when he decided not to move. In the darkness they could easily lose their way, because a road did not exist. It was impossible to see anything on a map because of the pouring rain, and a compass without a map was useless. Elena was in despair. She didn't know if it was tears or rain or both streaming down her face. But she had to do something. She jumped out of the cart, kicked the stubborn animal once more and stooping under the wind, began walking in the direction she thought straight towards the camp. The camel and the cart disappeared in the darkness of the night. In about half an hour she didn't know if she was following the course or going in circles.

It was as if the sky had fallen onto the ground. Water was everywhere, up and down, over her head, under the windbreaker. She couldn't breathe because of the wind. The sky was torn by lightning every several seconds, deafening rolls of thunder made her want to press herself to the ground. She didn't know where to go, but she could not stay in place. Now she panicked. A fiery lightning again, and in this short blinding moment she saw a horseman who rushed along at full speed. It was Raslan with his superhuman ability not to know, but feel, where he should look for Elena to rescue her in the midst of this rattling thunderstorm.

* * *

The summer flew by, the expedition moved to a winter camp, using small aabundaned adobe huts, which remained there after people died as a result of collectivization of the numerous Kazakh nomadic economy. In November it started snowing; sleet and ground winds were whirling across the steppe. The geologists lit candles long after it was dark. They had to economize.

"Brr! How bleak it is!", Elena thought. "It make me feel creepy to hear wolves howling every night. It will be good to go back to Leningrad."

Everybody was busy preparing for the departure. Raslan was putting the final marks on a map; Elena along with other geologists was packing samples. It was a long and monotonous job; and she thought of how nice it would be to get out of the sad adobe hut, to take a breath of fresh air, and say goodbye to the steppe for the last time. She easily found an excuse to go out because it was necessary to get some water. They usually brought it from a stream that was not yet frozen and not too far away, at the place where their summer camp used to be. They harnessed an ox and put a keg in a cart. Elena, wrapped in a sheepskin coat, set off. There was a rule at the camp, when winter starts never leave the camp without a gun. But Elena felt it was not too far to go, and it was unlikely that wolves would be that bold, so she didn't take a gun. Elena was still very close to the camp when she saw some gray mass moving toward her. This mass quickly became a pack of wolves drawing nearer and nearer, noiselessly and ominously, like in a silent movie. Elena grew cold with terror when she saw those long soft beast's jumps. She swiftly turned back, the horrified ox running as fast as he could. The huts were very close, Elena yelled at the top of her lungs; Raslan jumped out of the hut, dashed to Elena's cart shooting in the air; the rest of the group followed him. It was too late!

61

The wolves surrounded Elena and in a split second she was in the middle of a gray cloud of wolf hair and snow. Growling, chattering of teeth, and the ox dropped on the bloody snow. The next moment the pack was running away under the gunfire.

Elena, shaking, was still curled up in the cart; wolf footprints churned up the snow around her. Raslan threw his arms around her, hugged her tightly and led her to the hut. Bloody guts of the poor ox left a red trace behind the disappearing pack. Yes, definitely it was time to leave this wild country, such a lazy and peaceful place during summer and so scary in winter!

* * *

The group finally wrapped up their work, packed boxes with samples and got ready to leave.

Elena embraced Akkyz, a slim-legged graceful foxhound for the last time. She tenderly called it Akkyz meaning white girl in Kazakh language. The dog had to be returned to a shepherd who had brought her to the camp at the beginning of the season when she was still a puppy. It was too long a trip to Leningrad, and a small communal apartment was no place for a dog. Horses set off; Akyz pulled her lead trying to follow the sleigh. Elena heard her bark, yelp, almost cry as long as she could see the dog's white back.

After a long ride to a little train station, they stayed for two days in a poor shanty proudly called a hotel, waiting for a train. In the morning Elena heard an impatient cry and yelp at the door – it was Akkyz, skinny, shaking but terribly happy. Not only her tail, her whole little body was wagging and spinning, expressing all her love and devotion.

"Akkyz, darling, how did you get here? How did it happen that wolves didn't kill you? What do I do now? I can't even think of taking you in the train; they will throw you out from an overcrowded car, even before a train stop. At this difficult time who will feel sorry for you when there are not enough kind hearts even for children?"

Elena begged a woman attendant to take the dog, offering her money. The woman didn't understand Elena's emotions. "Oh, come on, such a fuss about just a beast." But she took the money and promised to take care of the dog.

A year later Elena found out that poor Akkyz died; the little dog's heart couldn't bear the separation. "She just laid here at the door and didn't eat until her last breath. It looked like she was waiting and waiting for you to came."

* * *

When Raslan and Elena arrived back in Leningrad, it was already covered with snow. After six months wandering in the steppe, the city looked especially impressive and beautiful. Every day they enjoyed walking from their tiny apartment along magnificent streets to the Geological Research Institute where they spent long hours working on the materials they had gathered during the summer. One night they were, as usual, going home tired, but content. It was a very pleasant walk. The cold was not yet strong in November, the wind died, and light, soft snowflakes whirled quietly. Elena put her face under the fallen snow feeling its tender touch instead of biting steppe sleet. They walked slowly; Elena didn't want to rush enjoying the peace and calm of that clear northern night, which did not hide anything from view. The streets were not yet sleeping, but already quiet with the warm light of numerous windows. It was pure delight to see the noble and grand beauty of Leningrad. She snuggled up to Raslan and looked at his face to see if he was sharing her feeling of peace and joy. She was surprised to see how very concerned he looked.

"What are you thinking about? What worries you?"

" I know how much you love this city, its theaters, concert halles, all this beauty. "

" So? What's wrong with that?"

"No, nothing is wrong, but it hurts me to know that I will tear you away from all this, that I am pulling you into desert expeditions, into the remotest depth of the Asian provincial towns."

"Why are you saying that you are pulling me away? I chose this nomad profession myself."

"No, Elena, you never intended to live far away from Leningrad or Moscow. It is one thing to go away for a summer and then come back, but this is totally different to live there all year around, to really live there, to make it your home."

"I don't understand what you are talking about."

"I was waiting for a moment when we are alone to tell you

63

everything." He stopped, turned to her, took her hands into his as if he wanted to emphasize the importance of what he was going to tell her. "Elena, the Head of Geology of the USR Academy of Science himself called me. He suggested that I reorganize and revive a small office on the Irtysh River, which is dying, and transform it into a powerful Geological Survey, a big exploration center.

"So?"

"Try to imagine how important and how much needed it is! I was already thinking of what could be done there."

With excitement and enthusiasm he started telling her in length about his plans. Elena saw and felt that all of him, all his soul, his thoughts, his big plans, everything was already there, in that little provincial town. "Goodbye Leningrad", she thought, "goodbye my dear city with all your beauty, music, theaters, libraries. Goodbye boulevards, canals, little bridges, magnificent Nevsky Prospect and bright river-fronts."

Elena's heart sank, but she tried to shake down the bitterness of losing this magic city. She tried to look at things through Raslan's eyes. "It is really his life", she tried convincing herself, "it will happen again. He will inspire everybody around him with his enthusiasm, everybody, geologists, workmen, even the cook. There will be such freedom for his work, such wide opportunities. A geological center in the heart of huge open fields! Yes, this project is designed for him, he is already living it." Elena listened to Raslan and began to feel his happiness. "It is a wonderful idea to start this project the way he is planning. The important thing now is to convince others." She pressed herself against him, whispering, "I will follow you to the end of the world."

Raslan was anxious to put his plan into practice. He wanted to persuade a group of young and talented Leningrad geologists to move together with their families from this bright metropolis to a tiny poor town somewhere in a steppe, five thousand versts (about 3,000 miles) away. It was not an easy task.

The very next morning Raslan, with all his passion, started talking with each of fifteen geologists he had selected, trying to convince them, first one-by-one, then all together, that the real happiness would be to build a big new geological center, with their own hands, the one that might be even more developed than this one, in the capital. There would be tons of work and unlimited opportunities for the young and talented! And he succeeded, he did convince them. Twelve families followed him and Elena to the miles-and-miles-away place. With this move, the poor small Organization turned into a strong Center with a body of well-educated and excellently prepared geologists. There was no need to persuade Murat, he readily followed. Googa decided against joining the new Center for the time being.

The work was in full swing, geological exploration started all over Kazakhstan. Discovery after discovery, deposits of chromites, phosphoresces, stibium, polymetals, and coal. These were the triumphs of their work, their energy and inspiration. The desert region was transformed beyond recognition. Newly found underground rivers and lakes could bring a new life to towns and industries.

Geologists worked intensely, putting in long hours, with the enthusiasm and energy of the young. The atmosphere was friendly and warm. Raslan conducted himself modestly and with friendliness, while being very demanding, especially of himself. A strong willpower and purposefulness blended together wonderfully with his kindness and his love of the people around him. And people loved him back.

"Raslan, dear", an older woman-secretary, one of those "remnant of the bygone Tsar's regime" whom he highly valued for her high grammatical competence, would ask him, "Tell me please what does C.P.S.U stand for and this sm-a-a-a-ll little *b* in parenthesis?"

Raslan would laugh heartily. "Aglaya, where, in what century, in what country do you live, my dear? C.P.S.U. means Communist Party of the Soviet Union, and small *b* means Bolsheviks! Please don't tell anybody you don't know it!"

Once there was a meeting about the nomination of candidates for the Supreme Soviet. It was enough to simply raise a hand but at one moment a Kazakh worker suddenly got up and looking embarrassed, kneading his cap in his hands, said, " I want to vote for our Raslan!"

In geological circles people had already been talking about a *Mighty Handful* in Kazakhstan and its leader. There were articles about the newly developed Center in local and central magazines and newspapers; there were congratulations and awards to Raslan and his group from the USR Academy of Science and Ministry of Geology.

* * *

Who knows whether it was a pure coincidence or the NKVD (KGB) deduced who had written *the signal*, but when in the middle of one night Googa, still half asleep, heard a loud knock at the door he felt in his bones *THEY* had come, and *THEY* had come for him. Googa was not a coward but a ride under escort across the city, a long walk through a brightly lit hallway with bare white walls, a long wait sitting on a hard chair at a distance from a large heavy desk, a bright light directed right to his face – all this strained his every nerve. He wanted to conduct himself calmly and independently, and he gathered all his will power for that, but when a man dressed in a half-military uniform abruptly opened the door, he jumped up from the chair. "An investigator!" he thought and he grew cold with terror.

"Sit down."

He sat down, his mouth dry, his body tense. He tried to make himself say that he didn't understand why he had been brought here, or even to express his resentment to the fact that he was treated with such disrespect. But he couldn't pronounce a word; his tongue was glued to the roof of his mouth, and he kept silent. As if he was under hypnosis, he followed with his eyes the long white fingers paging through some papers. Because of the blinding light Googa couldn't see the investigator's face. Finally, the man looked at him and asked an unexpected and even confusing question: "What is your attitude toward the Soviet regime?"

Googa could hardly move his tongue and trying to sound as sincere as he could, he said, "I… I support … I mean, I support it and I salute it with all my heart."

"We are surrounded by enemies who would like to pay a high price for our defeat. You are saying that you support and salute the Soviet regime. And what have you done for it? How can you prove that you are with us and not against us?"

"I am ready to prove it. If there is a war I am ready to fight."

"The war is already going on, a cruel war. We have to fight today, right now, every minute!"

"I am ready to fight right now."

The man's metallic voice went on asking questions. Some of the questions were short, others lengthy; Googa tried to respond clearly but he was getting confused, repeating himself and all the time referring to the fact that he, Googa, was Soviet with all his heart. Then there was a pause. The investigator got up, walked around the room, sat casually on a corner of the desk and suddenly changed his tone to become almost trusting. It felt now as if this tone transformed Googa from a suspect or even an enemy to a confidant.

"It is easy to talk about being devoted to the Soviet regime; it is so much harder to protect it from enemies. We need people we can trust, we need soldiers of the revolution who fight in difficult conditions of everyday life."

Googa made a movement forward. Yes, it is true, he, Googa, was for the Soviet regime with all his soul and the fact that the investigator started talking with him as if he was one of *their own*; this fact filled him with happy excitement.

"I am ready to help in every way I can."

"Wherever you are, whoever you talk to, be on the lookout. Listen and analyze. Inform us of any suspicion. Don't try to figure out yourself if you're right or wrong; we'll find it out. Remember, you are protecting your Motherland from enemies, you're protecting your wife and your son."

The investigator emphasized the words *wife and son* as he looked closely in Googa's eyes. Googa felt uneasy.

"We'll be waiting to hear from you. And don't remain silent.

The investigator extended his hand to Googa:

"The one who is not with us, is against us, right?"

Googa was overwhelmed with a hot wave of devotion. He did not realized yet that he was hooked and hooked' for life.

This was the way the NKVD (KGB) got their informants: appeal to patriotism, make casual hints about vulnerability of loved ones (and Googa adored his son and wife), show trust and frighten. And how not to be frightened? Numerous people were disappearing every day without a trace, millions of them suffered beyond comprehension.

* * *

The winter ended, and summer came right away. Tender and

delicate spring flashed, flew by quickly, waving goodbye with its flowering feather grass and leaving behind a yellow sun-scorched steppe.

It was peaceful and calm at a small country house by a little river. Three little girls luxuriated in the sun and played on the straw mat on a small terrace. Cute two-year-old May didn't have a doll, so she poured all her motherly instincts over her baby sister. The baby wasn't actually the sweet doll May dreamed about. She had a black forelock instead of golden curls and a loud voice, but May was nonetheless very caring with her. The oldest sister, half sleeping in the heat, watched the two little ones while lying on the same mat. They waited for their Mom who, tired but happy, was usually home from the Center while it was still daylight. But seeing their father and playing with him was a rare treat. He was busy getting a new expedition ready. All the equipment was loaded on carts, maps were done, and the whole caravan was prepared to leave.

This particular day was in its wane; this time it was not their Mom but a nanny who put the girls to bed. They fell asleep not knowing that the horizon of their life had begun to darken, and that danger hung over their happy life, threatening to make them orphans and outcasts as *children of the enemies of the people.*

* * *

Elena entered an overcrowded assembly hall of the Geological Center. Everybody was there today. There was confusion, embarrassment and fear on people's faces. Raslan didn't sit at his usual place at the table but in a chair a distance from the presidium, as if intentionally distanced and detached from everybody. His posture was tense but his shoulders were straight; his eyes under close-knit brows had that special sparkle they always had at moments of danger. This sparkle was a sign of his resolve.

Four years had passed since that wonderful happy moment when Elena entered this assembly hall for the first time. She remembered it so well. Raslan sat at the presidium table; his posture, the way he moved, and especially his sparkly eyes were full of happy energy, which was transmitted to everybody; the audience was animated and cheerful. Elena stood at the door, watching familiar and unfamiliar faces; for a second she looked at her husband. He turned away from papers and responded with a bright smile. His attention was so open and prolonged that everybody turned and looked at Elena curiously. She felt embarrassed, and slipped into a vacant seat trying to be unnoticed, but Raslan's bright and happy eyes followed her until she hid behind people's backs.

This time everything was completely different. An unfamiliar person dressed in the half military uniform of NKVD (KGB) strapped by belts, opened the meeting with a lengthy description of the country progress. Suddenly he changed the tone of his voice to almost falsetto and attacked traitors:

"They stand in the way of the country, preventing it from moving forward. These sneaky enemies pretend to be friends; meanwhile trying to destroy our factories, dams and bridges, our collective farmers. They are involved in subversive activities, trying to shed the blood of proletarians, the blood of the worker– peasant class." After the traditional, "but the Party and people are watchful," he turned to Raslan.

It was absolutely stunning how absurd his accusations were. One of the most significant accusations was Raslan's refusal to give a list of enemies of the people among those working in the Center, which he headed. Raslan insisted he knew every coworker personally and he was ready to guarantee his or her loyalty. This explanation was not convincing and very suspicious to the NKVD (KGB).

"If he covers up for enemies of the people, he must be an enemy himself. It is clear, fish goes bad from the head," the NKVD representative accused.

Elena felt she couldn't stop shaking, she got dizzy, blood hammered in her temple. "They're killing him, they're killing him!" Right now, right here a wild force was killing her strong, full of life husband. This wild force doesn't know and doesn't want to know any truth or any justice. She knew a paralyzing fear of NKVD would make everybody present vote for this killing. Everybody was sure, "If it is not Raslan, then it will be me". Terrified by what was going on, Elena stood up.

"Give me the floor, I want to say something." She approached the table for the presidium and turned her burning face to the audience.

Elena was a good speaker, and at that moment her appeal was full of passion, her powerful protest against the unthinkable monstrosity of the accusations. Her voice rang with outrage, and her words fell straight on the target, to the very heart of the people.

"Comrades, you have been working with Raslan for many years. You are not just his coworkers and subordinates; you are his close friends. Don't you know how much effort and energy he has given to our common cause? You came here with him and you literally moved mountains under his guidance. You discovered many deposits; you covered huge territories with geological maps! How can you believe these absurd accusations?! Raslan refused to name the enemies of the people. These are your names they want to get from him! He doesn't want to give them you names, because he cannot betray you! He won't betray you even though it means risking his own life; so now, are you going to betray him knowing full well that all these accusations are false, that they are lies, that they are slanderous?"

She spoke and people around her were reviving from the icy lethargy of fear. All of them came with Raslan to this deserted area from Leningrad, trusting him as their new boss. They covered thousands of kilometers under a scorching sun and in bitter cold to build, in Raslan's words, their own country with their own hands. And they were really building it. If Raslan is accused of being a traitor, it means they are accused too. One after another they stood to refute the accusations. The first one to stand up was Murat.

Then an impossible, incredible thing happened; the NKVD (KGB) lost its iron grip on these people. How did it happen? They hadn't expected that Raslan's wife love and devotion would be stronger than fear. Did they miscalculate? They did not think that a bunch of geologists, three thousand kilometers from Moscow, would be so strongly united. But an order for arrest had already been prepared. Officials of the NKVD planned to arrest Raslan right here, at this meeting. What happened was a blow to them, but it did not change a thing. They could not arrest him on the spot, so they would do it at night. They would also arrest the wife as an accomplice. The daughters would be sent to a special orphanage for children of enemies of the people to live with harsh discipline. All their life they would be ashamed of their parents and suffer as outcasts of the Society.

The NKVD swayed the destinies of thousands of people according to their own laws. This punitive authority could never be mistaken. Everybody had been forced to believe in it. Those who had a different opinion were fated to regret it bitterly.

It was a late, pitch dark night, as dark as it could be only in Middle Asia with bright stars on a velvety sky and little sparks of tiny fireflies. Screeching noise of the brakes of an oncoming car broke the quiet of the night and a chirr of cicadas. A flicker from a flashlight fell on a narrow path to a small country house. Four men in half military uniforms stepped on the porch, a loud commanding knock at the door. The house remained dark; no sounds. Only dogs barked from nearby houses. Another loud knock and a harsh, imperious voice. No reply. All was quiet inside. A strong blow broke a hinge of the door. The house was empty.

In the cool of the night the horses ran easily taking the geologists away to the vast expanse of the steppe. It was in vain for authorities to try to find them now with only a desert and wilderness all around.

In that time, the nineteen thirties, geological expeditions were similar to American pioneers. Horsemen convoyed wagons with women, children and all the geologists' belongings. Murat and Raslan's horses leisurely ran side-by-side heading the procession.

"It looks, Raslan, like you've got some enemies. Somebody threw a stone in an anthill."

"Who? Why? What did I do to make an enemy?"

"It's hard to tell, you are too visible at this point; you are an easy target now. One thing is clear , it isn't anybody from our group. You saw how everybody, together stood up for you."

"I won't give up alive. I am only afraid for Elena and the kids."

"While I am alive, Raslan, I will not abandon them."

"While you're alive! If I am arrested, Murat, it means you're the next."

"We have to let Googa know. Maybe he will find something out."

"No, not now. Let's see what happens when we return. And we aren't going back soon."

It was absolutely impossible for anybody to hide from the NKVD. But there, in the middle of nowhere, in this limitless desert there was at least one way to disappear, if only for awhile. During that time of the crazy Stalinist repression, people's roles changed quickly. The ones, who used to be the leading legates, could be announced criminals. So, during the eight months of the expedition Raslan's accusers from the NKVD themselves got under the wheels of the repression and disappeared, who knows where; either they died, were sentenced to be shot or were sent into exile somewhere in Siberia. A short little letter, *the signal* which initiated the case, got lost in the bureaucratic spider web and disappeared while those spiders fought with each other. Meanwhile the life of the lucky family of geologists kept rolling on in horse driven wagons.

* * *

Now Googa didn't suffer as he had five years ago. During those years strange changes occurred in his soul. Thinking about his betrayal of a friend didn't make him panic. He accepted the uncontrollable envy, which possessed him like a disease. And Zarema was always ready to stir up Googa's grudge as his conscience kept finding all kinds of loopholes and excuses. Googa's desire to stop Raslan became an obsession; an irritation caused by the successes of his friend was like a thorn in his side and this made him play a double role as the best friend and the worst secret enemy. Zarema used every chance to hurt Googa's wounded pride. And it worked.

Googa's information letter was very cautious. It said that Raslan demonstrated a political imprudence by gathering a group of geologists without checking their social background and their ideological orientation. It may be possible that there were enemies of the state in the group. There were two lines, only two lines there. Googa tried to convince himself that he acted properly; that he didn't betray his friend and maybe even helped him. "*THEY*" will figure everything out, he thought. "I didn't even write that Raslan himself was an enemy; I just pointed out that he had made a mistake." Googa tried to justify his actions to himself, but he knew full well how little was needed to cause a person to disappear forever.

The black clouds over the heads of the citizens of the USSR more and more thickened. One unflattering phrase about Stalin and his policy or a political anecdote lead to a sentence of 10 to 25 years.

Murder of Kirov

The popularity among the people of leader Kirov did not give rest to the envious Stalin. The murder of this leader was fabricated by Stalin in December 1934. In addition to getting rid of Kirov, Stalin received a pretext for the start of mass political repressions under the pretext of seeking political conspiracies threatening the life of the country leaders.

Stalin, who finished with his main comrade-in-arms, competitor Kirov, began to get rid of all others. The names of the former heroes of the revolution were forever erased together with their lives. Stalin cynically eliminated the democratic principles of justice, and justice has become a fiction. Powerful propaganda has earned its full force, loudly screamed radio and newspapers, and the fooled, as always, people "rallied and demanded to clear the country of traitors."

NKVD (KGB) shot "on the right and on the left", killing thousand and thousand.

Raslan, like everyone else, could not know the true cause of these criminal events. Ironically, his life was filled with joy when the tragic shots thundered in the cellars of the NKVD: Elena gave birth to a daughter, a healthy, charming girl.

In the same year, one more event brought joy to the family: soon after Stalin announced "cadres decide everything," Raslan, along with 19 other young geologists, was ordered to go to America to upgrade his skills.

America! A distant, amazing country far ahead of all the world in the development of science and technology. One can imagine the enormous excitement engulfing all members of the family, excluding, perhaps, only the three-month May.

Everything was ready for departure, all formalities were met, clothes and other things were packed in a suitcase ... but on the eve of an exciting event, Raslan fell ill with typhus. Nineteen young geologists left for America without him.

Two years later, in the terrible 1937, known as the Great Terror, all nineteen young talented geologists were shot on charges of espionage. No evidence of this was found, and they were not required.

Who could have guessed that Raslan's deadly disease - typhus - would save his life? The news of the shooting of his young and talented colleagues was like a bomb exploding, he could not believe that all nineteen recruited by "American bourgeois" into spies.

"Big Terror" has become an ominous symbol of the system of massacres.

The enormous scale of repression with mass torture and executions has swept the entire country and all layers of society without exception.

During the Stalinist repression, **39 million people were killed -** shot, exiled and dead in the camps.

Vlad Milushkin - In exile

* * *

That summer was hot and dry; the blowing wind felt as if it came from an oven, and the air current rising from the hot burned ground created deceptive mirages. The fall started suddenly, almost in one day. Cold rains came down in torrents; wind from the north began to howl. In one of those dank October days, Raslan soaked to the skin, worked long hours on his rounds of exploring shafts. The next morning he started coughing, but he paid no attention. When he returned to the city, he had pleurisy. By next spring he started coughing blood – the sign of tuberculosis.

"I am afraid your husband cannot be out in the fields anymore. It would be suicide for him; he will not come back alive. He needs to follow a gentle regimen, then a quiet lifestyle will help him survive for a couple more years", a doctor said to Elena.

Raslan fiercely refused to live by the doctor's advice. Elena begged him in vain to be careful. He was barely back on his feet when he began to relocate the Geological Center to the capital of the Kazakh Republic, the city of Alma-Ata with its lush greenery and gurgling streams (irrigation ditches) running along all the streets from the surrounding mountains.

Елена had to go to Alma-Ata before Раслан, because she was offered a teaching position at the newly established Mining College. With the school year starting in September, she had to hurry.

By that time, Googa had already been working at the college where Elena was about to start teaching, but in a different department. He had moved there about a year earlier from Semipalatinsk where he taught at a technical school. Now he had a much higher position.

From the train station Elena and the children went directly to the college. She was given a small classroom as their temporary living quarters. The long travel with the girls exhausted her; the new dwelling was bleak and comfortless. In a hurry Elena tried to clean up and organize the room, make beds, get food on the table and put the tired girls to sleep. She was loaded with work.

Even before Elena had a chance to finished unpacking she noticed to her horror that the youngest daughter had difficulties breathing. She took the girl into her arms. The child was hot; her fevered eyes looked very sick. At this late hour, nobody was around the collage to ask for help. There were no phones; an emergency service did not exist there at that time. Elena needed to find a doctor. But where? Who could help? She remembered that right before she left, Raslan gave her Googa's address and explained how to find him. It was the only hope. Surrounded by an apple orchard the house where Googa's family lived was not far from the College. Elena rushed to their house with the little girl in her arms. Zarema open the door.

"Zarema, my baby is sick..." Elena didn't even finish her words. The door slammed in front of her face. She became numb, frozen realizing that nobody in that house was going to help her. Now the only possible thing in her situation was just to knock at any nearby house, and that was what she did. A pleasant young woman opened the door. Elena started telling her what happened. The woman understood everything immediately; she picked up the girl, put her on a bed, opened a drawer of her desk and got a stethoscope. It was a miracle, the woman was doctor; though she was not a pediatrician, she recognized the danger right away.

"It looks like pneumonia; we have to get her to a hospital immediately."

Elena clasped the daughter to her bosom and ran after the young doctor through unfamiliar streets.

Two weeks passed and the girl was still between life and death. The fever would not subside, every breath was accompanied by wheezing; her little lips were swollen. She didn't recognize anybody. With every passing day the hope of keeping her alive was vanishing. When Elena fell into despair, a sudden turn for the better happened. The girl's forehead became covered by tiny beads of sweat, her eyes became alive, the fever dropped. Three weeks later she was running along the College corridor, chasing around her very pretty older sister. Around them busy students hurried up to their classes. One of them picked up the little girl: "Tell your Mommy to give me an A." But she couldn't tell it to her Mommy because she didn't even know how to talk yet.

* * *

In December the Geological Center moved to the Kazakh Republic's capital. Raslan, who had become stronger, healthier and was full of energy, was happy to hug Elena and their two little girls. The life in their classroom dwelling became joyous and happy, and soon they moved to an apartment with a balcony and a breathtaking view of the magnificent snow-capped mountains. Nobody cared about furniture, they had their necessities. The most important fact was that they had running water; the big brick stove worked fine, and the very first evening Raslan fixed all electrical outlets.

Elena told Raslan about what happened during recent weeks; Raslan got very upset and angry. He asked Googa for an explanation.

"What can you do about the crazy mother? I am sorry, dear, but try to understand Zarema too. She trembles for our six years old son; she doesn't take her eyes off him. She got panicky that he might get infected from your baby. Of course she didn't act right. And I wasn't at home, I didn't know anything."

Raslan and Elena didn't hold a grudge but the contacts with Googa's family still didn't work. Zarema kept on hiding like a touch-me-not queen, deep in their spacious cottage surrounded by an apple orchard. She never appeared anywhere and never invited anybody in. Zarema oddities were taken as a matter of course, while Googa was always a welcome guest in Raslan's and Murat's families.

When Googa became a teaching professor at the School of Mining he felt he was at the right place. He was a man of great erudition, he liked lecturing and, more important, he finally found an outlet for his ambition. He rose above the crowd of students; he taught them good lessons, while they listened to him spellbound. His lectures were like shows; and he acted like an absolute autocrat. When a group didn't do a good job with their homework, he walked into a class very slowly making scary rounds with his big goggled eyes and repeated with quiet fury, "Saxauls, saxauls, saxauls!"*(Saxaul is a small tree of a desert, which is a living picture of stupidity)* Then he roared: "you are saxauls, with the intelligence of a log!" When Googa explained what tectonic was and how mountain layers crush, he would approach a student and mercilessly crumple his jacket. Then he would pull out his snow white starched handkerchief and thoroughly dust off the poor lad's jacket with it. If a student mumbled during a test, Googa would throw this fellow's record-book out the window or toss it under a cabinet producing the same famous roar. Some students were afraid of him and at the same time they adored him. Others called him a clown, and didn't like him. But nevertheless he became a legendary person at the College of Mining. People told all kinds of funny stories about him, some of them true, some absurd. Googa liked all of it; it satisfied his ambition.

* * *

In the winter Raslan became gravely ill again; he started coughing up blood. The diagnosis was gloomy. "I can't hide it from you" the doctor said to Elena after examining Raslan. "The situation is serious, if not critical. Be prepared that the spring waters will take him with them to the other world."

"Elena," Raslan took her hand. "Don't worry, don't listen to the doctors, I am not going to die. I will get better, I'll go to an expedition and everything will be all right." His pale face on a white pillow was weak, but there was complete confidence and determination in his black eyes, and no fear of death. Tears welled up in Elena's eyes. "Yes, yes, this is the way it will be! I believe you, you will get better, everything will be fine, and this is the only way!"

Raglan kept his word, and he went to an expedition again in spite of doctors' objections. He came back joyous and full of energy and strength, and with his inherent passion started working on organizing a Scientific Research Institute with the Kazakh branch of the Academy of Science. By this time the republic had grown to the level of having its own branch of the Academy. The illness was again forgotten.

* * *

The World War II started when Raslan was out in the fields, on the expedition. He rushed back to the city and went to an enlistment office. He was not subject to draft, and they would not take him as a volunteer. He went back to become completely absorbed in his work.

Now Raslan was under terrible pressure, he forgot what it was to sleep or to relax. There was no time to eat and almost nothing to eat. All food reserves were going to the front; those who stayed on the home front were starving. Raslan didn't want and didn't ask for any special privileges. Nobody in the family complained, it was wartime. Their apartment looked like a dormitory or a shelter for refugees. People they knew, some people they didn't really know or just total strangers slept in a hallway. The girls lived in the kitchen, which was the only heated place; at night they were afraid to go to the bathroom for fear they would stumble over somebody's body. The refugees were a different lot, and soon all warm clothes and some valuables disappeared. Elena who had always been beautiful and well dressed now wore a vatnik, a shapeless country jacket with cotton filling, and old worn down valenki, handmade crude felt boots. The girls felt sorry for her. "Mommy dear, when the war ends we will buy you golden shoes!" Elena laughed: "And I will buy strawberry ice cream for you!" Her laugh was so wonderful, clear and melodious, it always cheered the girls up.

Once, in the late fall, Elena got sick. She had contacted malaria, working in a vegetable garden out in the countryside. Raslan sat by her bed holding her hand. She was semi-conscious, shivering, tossing restlessly. Suddenly she calmed down, stretched and yawned. "Elena!" – cried Raslan in horror. She opened her eyes, looked at him and burst into laughter, it was like silver bells rolling all over the room. "Why are you laughing?" Raslan asked happily, straightening fondly and with relief the wet hair on her forehead. "I am laughing because I have never seen such a terrified expression on your face!" The girls who had been sad and quiet also laughed. The little one jumped, clapping her hands without understanding why everybody was suddenly so happy.

During winter months they heated the kitchen burning saxaul, small trees, growing in the deserts of Kazakhstan. These trees lack leaves, their branches instead covered by scales and their deep roots allowing them to thrive in dry, saline, and sandy land. The war brought these exotic plants to the city apartments. It was impossible to cut or saw them; hitting them against a stone could only break the fibrous trunks. Saxaul was also subject to rationing. There was still not enough of it, and Elena and Raslan together with their colleagues had to go at nighttime to a train station to help unload coal. It was a backbreaking job, but the dirty–black yet happy couple took home two full buckets of the most precious fuel, the coal. The girls tried their best to help and gathered every single little twig they could find on their way home from kindergarten. The kitchen was warm, but the rooms were icy cold.

As a rule, Raslan never was home from his job as a head of Geological Research Institute earlier than nine o'clock at night and continued to work at his desk by the bed for another few hours. It made Elena worry about Raslan's health, and she was right in her concern. When spring came he started coughing blood again and was forced to stay in a hospital. Patients at this tuberculosis center were fed according to special food supply rules. They received buckwheat porridge and small white buns. Raslan could not eat these luxurious items, the very thought of his hungry daughters repressed his appetite. When Elena came to visit Raslan he had saved more than a half of his food for the girls. "You must not do this, Raslan! You must eat everything to keep yourself alive for us!" "Elena, if you don't take it to the girls, I will get sick from the thought that they are hungry. I have enough, I know how much I need!"

Elena brought home these fabulous treats. Once she warmed up a little bowl with the porridge and approaching the table she stumbled and fell. She hurt herself but while she lay on the floor she still held the bowl up in her hand. Not a single tiny grain of the porridge fell. She later laughed, "One more year of this war and I will be ready to perform circus tricks!"

Once again doctors sentenced Raslan to death, and once again they were wrong. His will to live was stronger than his disease. "You are sitting on a gunpowder barrel, on a tinderbox" his doctor would say.

"Such a way of life is not for you, you must not go out in the fields!" But Raslan kept on working with such passion and such energy that it looked as if death itself was stunned by this and backed down.

* * *

Meanwhile, Googa kept on writing a monograph, dreaming of getting a professorship. He tried hard, but never finished it. With all his erudition and excellent memory, poor Googa completely lacked that precious spark of talent called creativity, the very spark of talent that turns an ordinary employee in the field of science into a real scientist.

From time to time he dropped by into Raslan and Elena house, and they welcomed him as a good friend. If it happened that Raslan was not home, and it did happen frequently, Googa talked for a long time. He made a monolog in his strange manner of mysterious mumbling about the great achievements of Raslan, his importance now and absolute need in the good care of him. It looked like the welfare of Raslan was the biggest concern for Googa, and Elena was always deeply moved by his kindness.

Googa's family was a strange one. Instead of the traditional Ossetian hospitality, a spirit of suspicion prevailed in it. Zarema almost never left her house. She was now in her forties, but she still was preoccupied by the thoughts about her incomparable beauty, general envy of it and intrigue around her. This strange woman doomed herself to complete seclusion, eagerly hearing from Googa everything about friends and acquaintances, and making comments, monstrously misinterpreting facts and suspecting malicious intent in everything. She never forgave Raslan for having preferred to her "that half-Russian half-German". During all her life with Googa she fomented his jealousy of Raslan by stirring up his hurt pride and whispering all kinds of absurdities in his ear. Being neurotic and narrow-minded, she nevertheless knew very well how to manipulate her husband, and he listened to all her nonsense while looking with devotion into her still beautiful, velvety eyes.

* * *

After the war was over, the big deposits of copper and gold at the Bochekul District at the center of Kazakhstan discovered by Raslan and closed down by the Government for almost thirteen years, finally opened again. Raslan was happy to see how the steppe woke up with all kinds of machine noises. The settlement came alive afresh. Once again Raslan made calculations of the capacity of Bochekul deposits and sent them to the Moscow center. He could not imagine that behind his back his closest friend acted too. Googa turned even bolder than before; his signal to the KGB was more spiteful. He accused Raslan of malicious overstatement of capacity of deposits, and trying to hurt the country's weakened budget by expensive drilling. Actually it was an accusation of treason.

In the middle of the summer, at the height of the working season, Raslan received an order from the KGB to return immediately from Bochekul to the Kazakh branch of the Academy of Science, which Raslan led as a director. He felt with heavy heart somebody had evil intentions, and he was right. On arrival Raslan was told there was "a signal" regarding some wrong calculation of the deposit capacity. He was required to stay in the city to provide necessary additional information while the matter was being investigated.

At night the sound of screeching brakes woke up Elena. She saw Raslan staring through the window out at the dark street. "It is from KGB. Tell them I am not here, tell them I had to go urgently back to the mine". Quickly and quietly with the exceptional ease of a man from the mountains, he slipped out almost under the noses of these ominous night guests and disappeared in the dark. An hour later, after turning everything in the apartment upside down and finding nothing that could compromise Raslan, NKVD officers left taking with them all the papers from his desk. Meanwhile Raslan was already on a train going to Moscow to search for the truth.

For the next three months nobody heard anything about Raslan. All this time he hid in the house of his old teacher, the one who had come down to the steppe at the time of deposit discovery. This wise friend urged Raslan to sit tight and wait, until everything quieted down, without trying to search for the truth; because this search could finish with arrest and quick execution before any justice could come. Meanwhile a well-known scientist, a member of the Academy, who knew Raslan well, called for a big commission to do independent calculations of the capacity of the deposit. The commission confirmed Raslan's calculations to within one hundredth of one percent. Now, when the danger was over Raslan went from Moscow directly to the mine.

Six years after this passed quite normally. There was a demanding but exciting job, good times with the family, and periodical fights with some bureaucrats. Yes, they would be good years if not counting the return of Raslan's tuberculosis when he had to spend time in hospitals until the disease subsided. When he managed to convince his doctor to let him stay at home, his little bedroom would become a hospital; a nurse would come and boil syringes to sterilize them for countless injections. Once she brought in an infection. Raslan's arm swelled up all the way from the elbow to the shoulder, and it was terribly painful.

A doctor came. "We must cut it open and the sooner the better. Tomorrow we are taking you to a hospital," he said. "If the sooner the better, then why not now?" "Are you kidding? I don't have any anesthetics with me!" "Do you have a lancet?" "Of course I do." "Then cut it now!" "Without anesthesia?"

"Do you think you'll be able to endure this?"

"Yes, I will survive; don't worry, go ahead and cut it."

Raslan sat on the bed holding on the back of a chair with his inflamed arm.

The lancet made a deep cut; the edges of the wound pulled apart like two big lips. Nica, the youngest of Raslan's daughters, who helped the doctor, collapsed; but her father kept holding on to the chair without letting out a sound.

As soon as the TB subsided, Raslan immediately began living his life to the fullest, as if he didn't want to lose a single minute to his disease. He ignored it until it would again put him in bed. During periods between relapses it was hard to believe he was sick because he was so full of life and energy.

Raslan and Elena always kept an open house. Raslan liked people and always brought some friends for dinner; and Elena was happy to see guests, especially Murat and Lisa.

* * *

It was very late when the telephone rang. Lisa's voice sounded very worried, almost crying: "Raslan, I don't know where Murat is. He went to check on a group of geologists; I expected him back the day before yesterday, and now they called and said he never got there."

"But where is the car they sent to meet him at the station?"

"They didn't send the car. Something was mixed up and they didn't expect him until next week."

"But did he get to the station of destination?"

"I don't know. I saw him off at the train and since then nobody's seen him."

"Lisa, I will fly there and I will organize a search. It is no use to call anybody now; we have to wait until morning."

The night was sleepless. Raslan knew Murat well enough to understand that something was terribly wrong.

The search went on all day. They found Murat within only five kilometers of the camp. He was dead. It looked like he waited and waited for a car and then decided to walk the thirty kilometers,18.6 miles to the camp. It was an intolerably hot day and his heart was not strong enough. Raslan took the loss of the close friend very hard. It looked like Googa was also shocked. At the funeral Raslan embraced him. "Take care of yourself, Googa. You are now my only brother left."

A month later Elena and Raslan said goodbye to poor Lisa and her son who went home to Ossetia.

* * *

By the time Raslan turned fifty he really became a big man, as Googa would say. Making a geological survey still remained a labor of love for him. Every summer he traveled the endless steppe, followed by a pack of automobiles, not a caravan of horses anymore. Sometimes he took Elena and the daughters along. During winter months there were a lot of things to do – some interesting and necessary, some annoying and useless, like endless meetings with government bureaucrats. But then summers brought a pure joy of just geology. His beloved students always surrounded Raslan; they called themselves his musketeers. He promoted a friendly, family atmosphere in the camps. In the tents serving as cantinas jokes and laughter were always present around big tables. But there was never any foul language or drunkenness. Everybody followed prohibition, even those laborers who were decorated by maudlin words, "I will always remember my dear mother" on their arms and chests, a notorious tattoo of criminals.

Once when the weather was unpleasant and dark, and the whole camp was impatiently waiting for the long rain to stop, Raslan heard some drunken profanities behind his tent. It sounded like somebody found booze somewhere and "celebrated". Raslan stopped working on the map, threw open the tent door and walked out. A young recently hired worker, completely drunk, was walking towards him swearing. In one second Raslan threw the man to the wet ground in an angry outburst. "I will crush you like a snake!" And here he stopped. Not even touching the drunkard he returned to his tent. Still frowning, Raslan went back to work on his map. The man got up and silently stumbled to his tent. One could have expected some kind of a rage or even revenge; but the next day, after night sleep, he apologized awkwardly and for the rest of the time he was utterly respectful of Raslan and his rules.

This busy and exciting life stopped unexpectedly and unpredictably. Raslan was removed from all his positions. At that time repressive measures by the government against geologists became more intense. They usually happened in slow motion following two steps, first there was a public condemnation, then a court trial. In most of the cases the verdict called for an arrest and exile. As far as Raslan's case, after the public condemnation meeting when everybody was stunned, frightened and numb, he was dismissed from his job. The trial was scheduled almost a year later in April of 1953. Raslan was accused of many absurd things; but one accusation shocked him the most; the fact that he was brought up in the family of his relative who was a general. He was brought up? No, he lived on his relative's meager handouts when he, as a young boy, was sent from his village to study at a trade school. But who could know such details of his childhood, the details that he almost had forgotten himself? Not for a single moment did he suspect Googa. Their friendship, especially after Murat's untimely death, was a sacred thing for him, a temple of old traditions, memories of their youth and a bond to his beloved Caucasus.

Meanwhile his best friend and his secret enemy, inflamed by Zarema, decided to try again to knock Raslan down from his annoyingly high pedestal. And again in his little house surrounded by an apple orchard Googa wrote a libelous signal: "As a devoted citizen and a patriot I think it is my duty…" The notorious signal served as a powerful beginning to a whole host of absurd accusations, which then turned into a court case.

As if by a twist of fate on his way back home from work Raslan stopped by at the little house with the apple orchard. Googa met him like the very best friend, compassionate and understanding. He sadly nodded his round bald head. Now, when Raslan was cast down from his heights, Googa loved him. He was ready to forgive Raslan all the sufferings from jealousy and envy that he had gone through, all that pain he felt while writing his libelous letters. In his heart Googa always was aware of what a scoundrel he was betraying his friend and leading the dual life. He tried to find excuse for his action, but could not be fooled; and he suffered doubly, not only from the superiority of his friend, but also from the consciousness of his own meanness. In addition, he was always scary, playing with dark forces of the KGB that could crush him too. Now Googa was relieved. He was happy to show to Raslan what a good friend he was. Finally, Googa's dream came true; he could patronize his friend. And it felt great.

Raslan was touched by Googa's warmth. After the absurdity of all those senseless accusations he needed some friendly support and an opportunity to share what perplexed him the most. "Googa, listen, I cannot understand how they dug down to that crazy general story?"

Googa stuck out his fat low lip. "They know everything, Raslan. You should have written about it yourself."

"It never occured to me that it had any significance."

"Oh, everything is significant for them, especially your social background."

"But my father was a farmer. What could be better?"

"Your relative was a general and this causes suspicion."

"He was born a peasant; and he rose to the rank of general. This alone would be a reason to remove your hat in front of him to show the deepest respect for his achievement!"

"Had he lived until the revolution they would have removed his head with contempt!"

* * *

Raslan paced the floor in their empty apartment. Elena was at work, and the girls were in school. In the past, when he was sick and had to stay home, all kinds of people would usually come to see him. When he helplessly lay in bed it could be a doctor or a nurse. When he felt a little better he continued working, still staying in bed; and his colleagues and students would come. Now there was silence. When he became a social outcast, it was more dangerous to mingle with him than with a tubercular patient. He understood this and stopped any connections with the outside world.

Isolated from the whole wide world, feeling an outcast with no responsibilities, Raslan suddenly realized that for the first time in his life he had free time on his hands.

"In a way", he thought, not taking into account the possibility of impending imprisonment or exile, "this is an opportunity and I should take advantage of it".

He had the idea of writing a book, a big, all-embracing book that would put together all his thoughts, observations and experience of the past years. The familiar excitement of the anticipated work pushed away all other thoughts. He started the project with his usual enthusiasm and boundless energy. Life became full of meaning again. Their dining room turned into a big office; a desk in the bedroom was too small for this project, now a dining table overflowed with countless maps and drawings. Raslan was in a hurry knowing that time was running out. He forced himself not to think of the impending trial and its unavoidable gloomy consequences, writing page after page. His devoted Elena, the best possible helper, was always at his side.

Time was flying fast and Raslan begrudged spending time eating and sleeping. He never knew how to work at leisure, but this time he really had to rush, and he worked regardless of his own health. Elena knew that it was no use to try persuading him to slow down and she watched with fear as he continued working fourteen, sometimes sixteen hours a day. Understandably, it couldn't last long – such tremendous physical and nervous tension led to another tuberculosis relapse, and again he had to be admitted to a TB center. He continued working there too. His small room, the one to which he returned from time to time for many years, was filled with papers. He had to win this race; he had to finish the book before the trial, yet, March was almost here. It was the worst, rotten month for any T.B. patient, when this disease, as a rule, exacerbated.

"I must finish it before April, at least have a draft ready. Then, even when I am not there, Elena will finalize everything; of course if they don't arrest her too." He grew cold with terror at this thought. "Oh, no, let it be anything, but not this!"

A doctor who had long before become Raslan's friend didn't stop him from working. He understood that Raslan's book was more important for him than all his drugs. Only one rule was established, no light in the room after eleven o'clock. That is where the doctor was implacable.

The month of March came. On a wet and bleak afternoon Raslan's younger daughter ran into the hospital, all scared and looking lost.

"Papa, dear, did you hear the awful news? Stalin died. What will happen now?"

Raslan of course knew about it; they played funeral marches on the radio all the time since that morning.

"Let's go outside, we need to talk." he said.

They went down to a little hospital garden, which smelled of last year's moldy leaves. Raslan walked along a wet path, his arm around his daughter's shoulders. He watched the grayish spring skies and bare branches of apple trees with swollen buds deeply breathing in fresh air. He looked as if he had suddenly recovered after a long and serious illness. If not for the wheezing from his lungs one could have thought he had really miraculously become healthy and was happy about it.

"Papa, what will happen now?"

"Don't worry, baby; everything will be fine."

And then he added something that was so hard for her to understand: "Maybe now everything will fall into place."

Raslan was definitely born under a lucky star because his trial was scheduled for April and on March 5th Stalin died. It was the third time Raslan came out alive from the fire.

Life became happier; life became merrier. Two months later Raslan was restored to all his positions and got back all his awards. His book was published; reviews, especially from Moscow, were very enthusiastic, even ecstatic. A couple of years later something unthinkable happened; the iron curtain was lifted a bit and Raslan went to an International Geological Congress.

One day Raslan's daughter Maya opened the door upon returning home from school and stopped at the threshold surprised by her father's loud voice. Quietly she peeked into the room and saw one of her father's favorite students who were already a well-known geologist. He sat at the chair in blank despair.

"Shame on you", Raslan yelled at him. "It is an absolute shame; you are full of conceit. How could you have passed somebody's work over in silence, somebody's exceptionally good work? You used it, as it was your own. It is unacceptable! It is disgusting! Do you understand what it is? It is plagiarism! All of your works are not worth a pin if you are capable of this."

Raslan angrily paced the apartment. Maya cautiously entered the room.

"May, dear, give me some water, please", moaned the poor young genius. "No, no water for him; let him drink from his bitter cup!" yelled Raslan.

And the young man did drink from his bitter cup. He sent his apologies to the magazine, and he was forgiven. Raslan always loved and appreciated him.

His doctorate students, his musketeers, as they were called, did they understand they were almost as dear to Raslan as his own children? Did they realize that was the reason he was so strict? Of course they understood, but every once in a while they complained and resented those high standards that he set for them as well as for himself.

Years flew by and Raslan spent every summer in research expeditions. He didn't travel by car anymore. With help of a little plane, he flew to the numerous geological sites and camps of this big geological party. When boundless expanses of the steppes would open up before him, he felt as if he had come back home. Elena also looked forward to these field seasons. When they were out of the city Raslan was leaving behind responsibilities that were exhausting for him. It was very difficult for a man of his honest, direct and straightforward nature to work at the top where conflicts emerged all the time.

He had been raised in his native Ossetia as a "knight without fear and without reproach" (4). This spirit always lived in him and often had been the cause of worry for Elena.

---

(4) This expression was commonly used after the publication of the anonymous French novel (1527) entitled "The exploits of a good knight without fear and without reproach, glorious Sir Bayard"

Yes, he was always a knight. Elena especially liked this quality in him. He always stood up for people, for people close to him as well as for strangers.

A session of the Academy of Science started and Raslan had to fly back to Moscow. Elena followed him. She wanted to take advantage of this opportunity and visit the city of her youth. She loved Moscow, especially its old downtown alleyways and by-streets where everything breathes history, and where the sun shone on sidewalks along age-old buildings.

The day before the opening of the Academy Session, they sat in a café named Theatrical on Tverskaya Street. It was their rare leisure time, and they enjoyed it. The weather was warm and a fresh wind brought the smell of spring through open windows. Suddenly this peaceful atmosphere was disrupted by the tearful voice of a woman. A big young tipsy man was harassing her. Raslan frowned, his eyes flashed with anger. Elena froze. A long time ago Raslan's fearlessness fascinated her; but now he was neither young nor strong anymore. She wanted him to be more careful.

"Oh, my God", she thought, "I hope he won't start a fight! This guy is half his age!" Raslan got up suddenly, pushing the table aside, moved straight to the rowdy and pushed him out the window. Everybody around gasped in disbelief. The window was large; almost half of the wall of the first floor, and the man fell out directly on the sidewalk. At this point Elena was absolutely sure he would come back to fight with Raslan. But he got up, shook himself off and walked away without turning back.

* * *

On Raslan's desk, on top of his large scientific article which was just published there was another piece of paper, again a new threatening accusation which was as always absurd but distracting. This time he was summoned to a secretary of the Communist Party Central Committee to give an explanation for his discrimination against employees of native nationalities. "I am under the impression", Elena said one night, "that every time when something significant happens in your career somebody tries to get in your way. Look, right after your every success, every happy event some trouble or just an annoyance happens. What kind of discrimination are they talking about? Among your employees there are all kinds of nationalities!"

"Remember that stupid article with such a pompous title, "Earth as a Geological Crystal"? I showed it to you a couple of weeks ago."

"Oh, you're talking about that concoction you called "A Run of a Wild Horse Around a Green Meadow" in your review?"

"Yes. The writer of this absurd article is a native Kazakh, and my review is the reason for this new mess. You might be right. Somebody really wants to get me, and I can't understand who and why. Tomorrow I will have to go the Central Committee and give my explanation."

The day was gray and gloomy; understandably Raslan was also in a gray and dismal mood. He didn't like to visit that organization; and he didn't expect any pleasant conversation there. He stopped the car by the main entrance, and asked the driver to wait for him since he didn't think it would be a long procedure. It was over even sooner that he thought. Behind a heavy door "a party tsar" sprawled out in a chair; and he didn't even offer Raslan to sit down. Raslan couldn't take such

91

disrespect. His eyes sparkled with anger; he stepped towards the desk, grabbed an inkstand and with force put it back so the bronze covers jingled. Then he turned his back to the boss and with words, "I am not a petty boy for you!", he slammed the door and left. That was the end of his explanation.

Elena's heart sank with terror when Raslan came home and she saw his fiery eyes. She knew very well it was a sign of his readiness for a fight. She also knew that nothing good was to be expected. She turned out to be right. All kinds of threats and troubles followed right away. Elena was afraid Raslan would be imprisoned. The Central Committee was not to be trifled with; they didn't forgive such behavior. In her memory was still fresh Stalin's savage reprisal with outstanding scientists. But fortunately, times had now changed, "The Thaw" of Nikita Khrushchev initiated irreversible transformation of the entire Soviet society by opening up for some economic reforms and international trade, educational and cultural contacts, and to same small degree weakening of the dictatorship of Communist Party. Raslan was not arrested.

* * *

And again there was the steppes, another expedition, open expanses and a clear sky over their heads. Raslan breathed in deeply, filling his lungs with the familiar smells of hot soil and grasses. Everything was simple here; people's interactions were natural like the steppe itself. Local, steppe Kazakhs knew Raslan well and they respectfully called him comrade Raslan. He liked simple and sincere talks with them and he also knew how to honor elders talking with them in their nomad's tents.

Now the expedition was so huge that he had to fly from one site to another to coordinate their work.

On one sunny day Raslan's small plane made circles, soaring in the sky; and Raslan observed from the height of the flight the structure of rocks. The sky was clear; but dark heavy clouds gathered on the horizon as a sign of an approaching thunderstorm. As soon as the pilot found a landing spot, a heavy rain began and lightning crossed the sky.

The pilot impatiently watched the scary clouds while Raslan wrote in his notebook. They waited a long time until the storm was over; they were able to take off only later in the evening. The thunderstorm ended, but the sky was still covered with dark clouds, and a hilly steppe below was almost invisible. The pilot was nervous.

"I don't see anything! I cannot land in total darkness. We won't be able to see the campsite."

"There must be a light in their tents."

"This is not a reference point for me. The landing site is some distance away; it is very small and it's surrounded by hills."

"Don't panic. First we have to find the campsite. How much fuel do we have?"

"For about twenty minutes. We must burn it down to zero so as not to explode with a hard landing."

Raslan peered into darkness and he suddenly saw a weak little light. "This is a light coming through the tent. Try to descend as low as you can. We will be circling over the camp until they understand we need their help. Meanwhile we will burn down the fuel."

"Visibility is very bad; we can fly into a hill."

"Be careful not to fly into a tent!"

They were still making their first circle when they saw a small but bright spot of a flashlight. It was moving away from the tents; then it stopped and started waving from side to side. The plane made several circles, and began landing. It flopped down onto the ground, jumped up, and finally rolled shaking over the rough ground. Raslan's youngest daughter Nica came rushing to the plane's door. "Papa, I was so worried I almost lost my mind! Why didn't you come while it was still daylight?"

"We couldn't. Where are the rest of the people?"

"Everybody went in all directions searching for you! How did you fly in the dark? You could have crashed!"

"So we didn't!"

Raslan kissed her face; it was all wet from tears. "You were signaling and crying, my poor thing!"

* * *

A notification of a new denunciation was lying on Raslan's desk. This time it was neither life neither threatening nor created a danger of imprisonment; but just the same it was irritating and disgusting. It caused Raslan a pain. This denunciation was not directed against him, but his favorite daughter, his sweet, beautiful and talented daughter, May was the target. The accusation stated that the Ph.D. thesis she had defended recently was actually written not by her, but by her father, Raslan himself.

May was very nervous. She was summoned to the High Examination Board of the USSR Academy of Science. That was not a common event, and she was terrified by the thought that she would have to appear before well known and respected people as a defendant who had committed a crime.

The interview lasted more that three hours; it was like a second defense of the thesis and an extremely difficult examination. When finally it was over and the commission congratulated May on her success, the chairman of the commission took May aside. "I am happy for Raslan that he has such a wonderful daughter. I have to explain though why we had to be so strict with you. A geologist who insists that the thesis was written not by you but by your father is somebody who is very close to your family". He grinned sarcastically: "The closest."

May knew the closest person was Googa, "Uncle Googa" as she called him from her childhood. She didn't tell anybody. She felt sorry not for Googa, but for Raslan. Maya was sure this would be a terrible blow for her father.

Googa's son Alan was a failure, and the oldest and closest friend could not withstand another attack of envy. He congratulated May on her important achievement; and with his straight and neat handwriting put the poison words on a piece of paper. This time his denunciation could not be anonymous, but Googa knew very well that his name might not be disclosed.

About two or three months later Googa came to visit Raslan and Elena. After dinner Raslan sat on a sofa, put his arm over Googa's shoulder and said: "When I turned sixteen my Dad gave me a dagger as a gift. I kept it all these years; and I dreamed of handing it over to my son. But I don't have any sons; and now I want to give it as a gift to Alan, my friend."

Googa gratefully bowed his head. During these short solemn moments all his animosity died. His eyes moistened.

"Thank you, Raslan; you are like a dear brother to me."

* * *

Raslan died suddenly, the way it usually happens to people of irrepressible energy who spare no effort to do their best in everything they do. Still looking young and handsome he lay on a high pedestal in a big hall at the Academy; a long file of people flowed by.

Twenty years passed since that time. Many people died; many things were forgotten; but Googa, rocking his big round head, still shuffled his feet to the Institute of Mining. Where are they, all these pioneers, discoverers, and groundbreakers? They are all gone. But he, Googa, he is now treasured and respected as a relic; he is "the last of the Mohicans" though he has never been the first among them. He is well respected, he's been invited to a TV interview, and he was asked to talk about his brothers-in-arms geologists, about how it all started.

"Oh yes, I will tell them all, I will."

A sick and decrepit old man, Googa was full of emotions. At last he will have his revenge. Everything is gone, but Googa's jealousy, his malignant envy didn't die, it didn't get less intense. During all his life it was the sharpest, the strongest and the most powerful of his feelings. And it turned out to be the most lasting too. He prepared for that TV show very thoroughly while huffing and puffing, breathing heavily and taking heart pills. Now Raslan could not stop him; he could neither criticize nor correct him. For the first time in his long life he really enjoyed his revenge while doing it for everybody to hear. He kept talking and talking, striking out Raslan's name from every achievement, every event and every discovery that belonged to Raslan. Googa was triumphant over his own success; his breath was heavy but joyous as if he finally lanced a boil in his soul. He felt victorious.

Googa died a year later. He was buried with honors.

* * * * * *

I finished reading Leah's notes and put the last page back in the folder. In my memory I heard my father's words that he told me when I was a fourteen-year-old girl. "Envy is a low and disgusting feeling. Learn to respect yourself and you will never experience it. Learn to respect yourself," he repeated with a passionate and firm assurance, "and you will be above any meanness, any baseness. And you won't be afraid of anything".

Part II.

WATERCOLOR PICTURES

My childhood was full of adventures because both my parents were geologists. They lived in the big beautiful city Leningrad* on the riverside of the short, but wide Neva River, very close to the Baltic Sea. This gorgeous city was 3000 miles from the Kazakhstan steppes at the very south corner of the Soviet Union where my parents' geological exploration took place. I went with them to these wild steppes even before I was born. My brave mother, while waiting for my arrival, went every day on foot or horseback "to the root", as geologists call their investigation of the geological structure of the surrounding area.

---

* St. Petersburg was renamed Petrograd (during World War I), than Leningrad (after Revolution) and back to St. Petersburg (in 1991).

My parents were so carried away by their exploration into the geology of Kazakhstan they did not come back to Peterburg soon enough, and I was born on the train. This train was stopped in the middle of the wild steppe, and we were transferred to a small, obscure, godforsaken native village. There, in the tiny medical center, which two small rooms held hospital, maternity and emergency stations, an old midwife washed me, swaddled and wrote with an indelible pencil on my forehead the number 3 after moistening this pencil in her mouth. I was put in the cradle beside two other squawking babies having numbers on their foreheads made with the same indelible pencil.

I knew only by hearsay how and when we moved from Leningrad to Alma-Ata (or Almaty, as this City is called today), the capital of Kazakhstan close to the border of China. I began to remember everything around me after I was four years old. In 1941 Almaty looked very different from what it is now. Our new House of Professors, property of the just emerging Academy of Science, was one of the few multistory apartment buildings in the whole city, which was built-up from the small one-storied houses. Many streets were not paved, and their deep dust was soft and warm under our bare feet. Camels majestically stalked and little cheerful donkeys briskly trotted through the city. Our back yard looked at Red Army Street, which was crowned in the distance by the beautiful Opera House with the luxurious snowy mountains in the background. It seemed if the whole city was built directly inside the apple orchard and immersed in it. That was why the city was called Almaty, The Father of Apples in the native language. The apple trees grew along the streets, around every house and in the backyards. The huge magnificent mountains rose straight above Almaty giving this capital of Kazakhstan unique beauty and solemnity. Here my childhood was taking its course emerging in my memory now as some watercolor pictures.

The New Year's Surprise

Saipan was a piglet, but for ten children from a big apartment house he was never just a pig, he was their cheerful, playful companion, their true friend. He arrived at Nica's neighbors, professor Shlygin's family, in an old, but smart leather briefcase. The little piglet was given to the professor as a reward for some research to mark the occasion of a big holiday in the USSR, May First, International Proletarian Day. This way of recognition would most probably be taken as a bad joke or insult if not for the long years of World War Two, which depleted Russia's food supply and made people permanently hungry. The piglet became the most desirable present for anybody, even for a prominent professor.

For Nica and all the other children, it was a source of endless excitement. The World War ll had already changed their urban life and given it the flavor of a village. All of the flowerbeds in these children's big back yard of Professors House, a privileged dwelling for scientist, were long ago converted to vegetable gardens and divided among the inhabitants of the house. Amicably they all grew dills, cucumbers, tomatoes, potatoes, and even corn, which rendered a few sweet ears. The children already knew how to distinguish wanted seedlings from weeds, and they watched with happy curiosity the little red radish foreheads arising from the ground. But to see a live piglet, that was something new and amazing.

Six girls and four boys gathered together in Professor Shlygin's third floor apartment around the bathroom tub. The tub was not used for its intended purpose because the hot water, which was supposed to be distributed from the central boiler to all the tenants, was switched off at the beginning of the war. So the tub became a piglet house and the children crowded around it staring at the tiny pink creature lying on a thin layer of straw. There was no argument about the little piglet's name. From early that morning, everybody was excited about another step toward the end of the war. American forces had made progress through the Japanese island of Saipan. This new word, which sounded like a word of victory, was in the air; and this lovely piglet should be the one to commemorate the happy event. So he was named Saipan.

For the next three weeks, every one of the children from this house managed to find a thousand excuses to knock at the Professor's door in the hope of seeing the piglet. Finally, the' Shlygins gave up and granted them permission to take this tiny creature to the big backyard. It was the beginning of a summer vacation from school. All parents where busy from morning to evening, and the children were on their own, playing all day long in the big mutual backyard.

The games of their wartime childhood were always devoted to the most important events of their lives, to the War; and they indulged in them with rapture. They fired from stick guns, rushed to the attack, hid from the enemy, caught prisoners and sent scouts to the camp of the rivals. Naturally nobody wanted to be a fascist, so each of two fighting groups considered themselves "ours", and both sides felt like heroes of the Red Army.

Hunting spies was as exciting as battles on the fronts and a little scary, because these cunning Nazi werewolves lived in the attic, enormous, dark with sharp strips of light rushing through the slits and hot stuffy air smelling of fumes from a thick layer of slag paving on the floor for the prevention of fire. The children waded through the attic along wooden beams very quietly, but their hearts beat with such frenzy that their deafening knock would apparently shoo off all the spies.

The second attractive mysterious place was the semi–basement, a long corridor with a multitude of doors. This world was very different from their, towering over it by three spacious floors with tall ceilings, big windows and balconies. Wretchedness and sorrow lived there's, in the bottom of the house, in the twilight, in the stuffy air smelling of onions and poverty. Nica was always tormented by grief and pity together with a strange feeling of guilt for the residents of this semi–basement. She was afraid to walk along this long gloomy corridor because the severe one–eyed janitor Serafima, who lived behind one of these many doors, chased all children from there angrily. There were two entrances on opposite sides of this semi-basement corridor. Each entrance had two successive doors. One door was at ground level before the stairs, another downstairs. Two doors at one end were always open; but at the other end, the inner door was locked, and the second, on the ground level, was opened. There children of this house found their mysterious corner, crowding between the locked door to the basement and the open door to their backyard. In this cheerless gloom with the smell of dampness and mold they listened to horror stories that they made up themselves. Beside different cemetery narratives making six-year-old Nica cold with fear, there were endless tales about Hitler. "Oh, no", assured little Zina squatting and trying to pull down the hem of her dress which was too short for her over the sharp knees of her abnormally thin legs, "Oh, no, girls, don't try to wait. The War never ended. Hitler is sitting now in an armchair and he doesn't even move. He is fed white bread with butter and that is why he will never die. And the War will be forever." This Zina's prediction made Nica unbearably sad.

Saipan brought a peaceful mood to the children's endless backyard games, and from the very first minute he shared their games with his entire little piglet's heart. He was amazingly smart; and after a short while learned to run down and to climb up the seventy-two steps which separated the big mutual backyard from the Shlygin's apartment. The children's little pink friend willingly allowed them to hug and kiss him. His joyful oink-oink showed how much he loved to be loved. The children bathed him, decorated him with paper bows, and tried to save something for him from their more-than-meager meals. Every evening at exactly six o'clock, Saipan suddenly stopped playing and rapidly ran through the yard to the gate, twirling in impatient waiting. Professor Slygin usually arrived back home from the College of Mines a few minutes later. Saipan met him with happy oink–oinks, saw the Professor to the porch demonstrating his love and parted from the Professor. After this ritual the piglet ran back to the children to continue playing. How could Saipan guess time so exactly? It was inconceivable for everybody to figure out, but he never erred, as if a watch were implanted in his small head.

Like all of these children, Saipan was constantly hungry. When he reached the age of three months, he looked more like a lean dog than a piglet, and he ran with the speed of a greyhound. The small Saipan's tummy shank from hunger, but right here, at the edge of the yard, radishes rose from the ground with red crowns, and young carrots curled tufts of tender tops. It was impossible for the little piglet to understand why the children ran with empty tummies and did not fill them with deliciously sweet fruits of the earth growing right there. Saipan's seditious logic and constant preoccupation with food very soon led to a problem. He found out that the taste of a radish from one small garden was irresistible. As we expected, the owner of the radish patch did not take it as a flattering compliment. He was furious, and the children were warned. They knew that food, any food, was a very serious matter in those days. But the radishes were sweet and Sapian was smart. He pretended to be enthusiastic about the game, but the minute the children lost their vigilance, the little piglet grunting joyfully pushed out from the ground with his pink snout a little sweet red ball. The children watched the piglet carefully, but he always knew the right moment to escape to the tempting spot. Finally, Saipan was caught. In front all of the children, the radish patch owner grabbed the piglet and threw him across the tall fence which separated their yard from the busy street where trucks darted back and forth. The children froze with horror for a moment and dashed with howls to the fence trying to see through the cracks what happened to their unfortunate gourmet. Saipan was alive, but his somersault made him completely lost and disoriented. He floundered in the dense sagebrush growing along the fence, and goofily spun in all directions. The children knocked on the fence invitingly screaming and calling the piglet all possible affectionate names, but he, stunned and frightened, did not pay any attention. Finally he turned uncertainly right and left and stamped on his small hooves from the tall thick grass toward the street, which was more of a danger than he knew. The children tried to attack the fence, but it was too tall for them. Time was precious, and they decided to combine their effort. The friends pushed Nica up to the top of the fence because she was the smallest. Nica slid on the rough, splintery board and jumped down. But she did not reach the ground. She was caught on a big nail. Nica's skirt was pinned to the fence, and she was hanging three feet above the ground like a doll in a puppet show. Her impatient friends drummed on the fence and shouted, "Quick, quick!" But Nica dangled her feet helplessly while the nail slowly tore through her skirt, precious in wartime. Despite this desperate situation Nica thought, hearing the scary sound of bursting threads, "What am I going to get from my mom!?" There was a final rrrrrip, and she fell down. Too late! Saipan had reached the street already, and a big American Studebaker full of young Russian soldiers was racing toward him with fatal inevitability. Nica almost flew through the air and the next moment she was lying across the street grasping the piglet's hind legs. The quadruped thief of the private property was in good hands now, but he was still in imminent danger for the was a good chance that he and his loyal friend would be crushed by the truck.

The Studebaker stopped dead only five feet from Nica and Saipan. At this very moment an unbelievable cacophony exploded. The soldiers were whistling, laughing and loudly cheering Nica and the piglet from the truck. The driver yelled angrily. Agitated passersby were shouting from the street. Nica's friends were joyfully crying from the fence; and her horror-struck neighbors were roaring from the balconies. But the shriek of the piglet rose above all the din.

Fall came and with it abundant food for Saipan. A little park with spreading oak trees was just across from the Professor's House, and the children gathered many bags of acorns for their four-legged friend. Soon the fall's rain and cold stopped their backyard games. The children were busy in school, and Saipan was busy eating acorns. He grew bigger and was not now the same skinny, fast and cheerful piglet they had known in the summer. He turned into a serious and heavy hog and didn't feel like going up and down the seventy-two steps. The children saw less and less of him as time passed by. The cold November snow covered the ground; then the short dim days of December passed quickly and the New Year came.

The children of the Soviet Union did not know Christmas or Hanukkah. These holy days were abolished in the USSR. They put all their hearts in the New Year's celebrations for the children, the most welcome and happy days in the year. Adults celebrated the New Year only once, on the last night of December, as did all the rest of the world. But the children's parties began from January first and were often repeated several times at different locations during the next ten days of the winter school break. These parties were made around the Christmas tree, but it was called New Year's Tree or, in Russian, *Yolka*. They were the most anticipated celebrations of the year.

In the peaceful time before the War, the adults gathered on New Year's Eve at the table with cognac, vodka, and caviar, or they sat at the more modest tables with vodka and sausage. But most of the people celebrated the New Year sitting at the very poor table with boiled potatoes, herring, and absolutely necessary cheap vodka. In Wartime, the traditions remained the same. Tables also were very different, sometimes completely empty, but with *erimurus,* a wild cabbage that grows in abundance on the slopes of the nearby mountains and before the War was used for feeding cattle. Now it often replaced caviar, a sausage, a herring and boiled potatoes. The center of the treat was a moonshine with the vile smell but still very desirable.

In the House of Professors, the children's *Yolkas* celebration took place during school winter break as everywhere in the USSR. In the time of World War Two, there was neither electricity nor central heating. Food, or better to say pitiful semblance of food and fuel were distributed in the depressingly small rations. The toys disappeared from the sale because the factories were making hand grenades for the front lines instead of toys. But despite everything, the children from this big apartment house had the happiest holiday in the world. There were five *Yolkas* celebrations in five different families during ten days.

The heroic parents committed miracles of invention to let the children be as happy as if the horror of the War did not exist and nothing threatened their lives. There was heat from the homemade round tin stove, called for some peculiar reason bourgeois, consuming rationed fuel and much of the furniture. There was light from small kerosene lamps called smokers. There was music from an old piano and, more importantly, endless games which required nothing but imagination and energy. The most difficult task for the parents when arranging this celebration was providing food. But the children did not know or did not remember anything that was offered as a holiday meal in the time, which was always called *before-the-war* and remembered as Paradise Lost. For a long time they did not have even plain sugar and the only available sweetener was liquid saccharin. Everything their parents managed to save, to get by ration and to barter at market was immediately consumed by the children's' gaunt little tummies. Any food was a treat for them. The Christmas tree, *Yolka* was always standing in the middle of the room shining with *before-the-war* toys, which were saved with caution and complemented by garlands made from newspapers.

Nica and her sister May loved *Yolka* celebration at the Shlygins almost as much as at their own home. The mother of their blue–eyed, blond little friend Olga, was a great organizer of entertainments. Her name was Vera, Aunt Vera, as all children called her because Russian children address any adult as aunt or uncle. And in this particular time Shlygin's *Yolka* completely rewarded the impatient waiting of these girls.

Under Vera's strong fingers, tunes from the old tarnished piano announced the beginning of the festivities. The door flew open to the room where the *Yolka* shone with decorations. All the children went around the *Yolka*, making the dance moves of Sailor March with their hearts beating happily. A great joy began. They jumped and danced, played blind man's bluff, hide-and-seek, broken telephone and many other games that made them squeal happily and laugh to the point of tears. Only for a minute the entire din stopped when suddenly somebody asked,

"Aunt Vera , will you feed us?"

The hostess answered with a wide smile: "Of course, my dear children, and it will be something very good, something you never tried before."

The irrepressible gaiety began again, the children felt a little bit drunk from the premonition of eating. And finally, "Children, come to the table!" The door of the small adjacent room opened, and the smell from it was so wonderful that they became dizzy. They ran to their plates, and now something incredibly tasty filled the children's' mouths and poured delightful warmth all over their bodies. They were given full plates, so they could eat without worry that this bliss would be finished too soon. There was no need even to cut their food into the small pieces to prolong the pleasure. This time the children could fill their tummies completely.

"Aunt Vera, what is it?"

"This is a little sausage from the meat, from pork, and you deserved this meal. If it had not been for the acorns you gathered, our skinny piglet would never have grown into a big fat hog."

Skinny piglet? All the children froze with horror. This pink bliss... This is Saipan?! Sorrow, endless sorrow overcame them. Our little, beloved... They made sausage from him, and cooked him, and now we are eating him! Happy, merry Saipan no longer exists now, only these pink sausages on our plates. Of course they are pink; Saipan was so pink when we bathed him.

Tears flowed from the children's eyes and dropped on the plates. They cried and soon sobbed violently. They sobbed, but continued to eat because their hunger had grown so enormous during four years of the war it was impossible to manage it. They sobbed and ate and ate and ate.

"Monkey"

The word VICTORY became real in Russia in the fall of 1944, though the blood still poured like a river at the fronts. Battles moved to the West, closer to the German border, leaving smoldering ruins behind. The strained mood in the Soviet Union changed to eager expectation to an end to this massacre.

Meantime, life took its normal course in Almaty, the capital of Kazakhstan, and Nica went to the school, *"The first time into the first class,"* in the words of a very popular Russian children's song.

At the beginning of the Second World War the school building was transformed to a temporary military hospital until this autumn, when the school could function normally again because the hospital was moved closer to the front.

It should be noted that the whole population of this Kazakh capital spoke Russian, so the teaching in all schools was exclusively in Russian.

Nica's mother found an old but not too shabby sheet, saved from the blessed time which was always called *"before the war"*. She dyed it brown, and made a school uniform for her little daughter. She put a big white bow on Nica's head and solemnly handed her little first grader the last notebook with a blue cover and smooth white pages, saved from before-the-war time. The rest of the notebook was made from newspapers with parallel lines drawn in pencil. The father's old briefcase, too big for Nica, contained all the necessary things for a new schoolgirl. In the early morning of the first of September Nica and her older sister, May went to a school for girls. All Soviet Union's schools at that time were divided by gender. A very serious May, who was an excellent second grade pupil, tightly held the hand of small, thin Nica, taking complete responsibility for the little sister.

The whole school formed a straight line in front of the building. The poverty of wartime reached its limit, and many schoolgirls were barefooted, wearing old, tattered, too short dresses. However that was not an obstacle to the mutual festive mood and for their mothers' sweet tears of joy. The directress made a welcome speech, and a group of girls presented her with a bright bouquet of fall asters. The bell rang; notifying that school life for Nica had begun.

The young teacher, Zoya, led Nica and all her classmates into their assigned classroom, on the door of which was written 1 B. Zoya was a twenty-five-year-old war–widow, among millions of other women with the same fate. She kept calm and quiet; a weak smile lighted her face very rarely because she could not reconcile herself to widowhood after only one year of happy marriage. Of course, Zoya young students did not know anything about her private life, but her seriousness instilled authority, and as usual for little girls, they instantly fell in love with their first teacher.

It was almost impossible for the first grade students to be silent and quiet during the lesson, and every fifteen minutes Zoya gave them an order to stand and repeat a quatrain after her, shaking their small palms, *"We read, we wrote, our fingers got tired, we will have a little rest and begin to write again"*, though these little girls could yet neither write, nor read, but they were learning to draw lines in their homemade notebooks. When the teacher explained about something or read the book, the students were supposed to sit quietly, not fidget, and put their hands on the table one over the other, so these naughty, active little hands would not jerk the braids or, what would be much worse, would not pour ink on the dresses of the girls sitting in front of them.

The miracle happened just after the first lesson. Zoya entered the classroom carrying the big tray of *ponchiks*, small fried round pieces of dough. She distributed them among the girls, explaining that this was a "Present from our dear comrade Stalin"; a gift the students would receive every school day. These *ponchiks* seemed delicious to the girls famished through the long years of the War. They were glad that the dough was so tough because it took more time to chew the *ponchik* and prolonged the pleasure of eating. This, Stalin's Gift, was always met with joy. Many girls came to school without any crumbs in their mouths, and this was their only breakfast.

Nica was so tired after the third lesson that she fell asleep putting her head on her hand. She was awakened by a painful pinch from her neighbor, Manya, who could not miss this opportunity to fool around. Nica screamed unintentionally, and all the girls turned toward her, happy to have some amusement. The teacher pulled both girls to their feet and explained one more time how the students should behave themselves. But it was almost impossible for Manya to be quiet. Undersized, thin but very active, Manya was all hinges. She looked like a small funny monkey; and the name Monkey, sounding close to Manya, stuck to her.

Nobody knew what Monkey's father looked like. He was fighting at the front, but her small vivid mother, Muse Ivanovna looked like a monkey as well. She sold theatre tickets at the box-office, and in this way she was connected to The Great Art. Indeed, art was great in

Almaty at this time. There were actors from Moscow, Leningrad, Kiev, Minsk, and Odessa. They gave performances at all the theatres of this pretty small provincial, but now overpopulated city. One could meet on the streets many famous masters, very popular in the Soviet Union. The world-known directors Eisenstein, Pudovkin, Alexandrov moved there too, driven by the war. The actors and cinema workers were sent to the apple city, Almaty on a special mission from the government to shoot as many movies as they could, because these movies were a leading force of the political agitation. Except for Eisenstein's masterpiece, Ivan the Terrible, all the movies were devoted to the war. They showed the power, courage and invincibility of the Red Army. Stalin himself was informed of the productivity of the Almaty cinema studios. Eighty percent of all Soviet Union's movies were shot here during 1941-45 in studios hastily installed in the unsuitable buildings. The big parts of movies were shot in nature, far away from the city, often eighty kilometers and more up the mountains. All actors, cameramen, producers, and cinema workers walked long distances because the studios did not have any transportation. Now, it is hard to imagine what efforts were needed from the exhausted Representatives of the Great Art, especially from those only recently arrived from Leningrad (St. Petersburg) famine siege. They worked under unbearable stress; their rehearsals lasted until late at night. Conditions were horrible despite the national importance of their jobs. Some of the actors were tenants in crowded apartments of Almaty residents, but many of them just lived in the studios. The famous scenic artist, Zelzman, his wife and daughter were weak and undernourished after escaping from the Leningrad blockade, going over a frozen Lake Ladoga under the constant German cannons shooting. Now they had to sleep on the floor, under the grand piano with no privacy. The brilliant actor, Mordvinov earned his living by knitting sweaters, Ptushko made shoes out of wood. Throngs of girls hunted for the most popular actor, Olenikov. But he dreamed not about beauties; he longed for a bowl of hot thick soup.

At the Opera House, the most beautiful building in Almaty, with a magnificent ridge of mountain behind it, the famous ballerina, Galina Ulanova was dancing. Her glory was so great that monuments were erected honoring her in Leningrad and Stockholm during her lifetime.

She was evacuated to Almaty together with other dancers of the Bolshoi Theatre. The Opera House existed on government subsidy, so the price of tickets was nominal, and people waited in line the whole night to buy them. The popularity of Ulanova was so enormous that mounted police were needed to protect the theater during her performances.

The Monkey's mother, who changed her name from Maria to the more romantic Muse, dreamed about theatre from her youth; but her theatrical ability had not moved her any closer than a ticket office. Now her hope was her daughter. Though Manya did not show any talents, Muse made her take private piano lessons. Her music teacher was Julia Carlovna, who was, like all Germans, hastily exiled to Almaty from Saratov at the beginning of the war even though she was born in Russia and married to a Russian medical doctor. Before the Russian revolution in 1917 Julia had been abroad to give piano concerts. In Switzerland, young, beautiful and inspiring Julia met in the most romantic circumstances a Russian doctor who saved her from tuberculosis; and then became her devoted husband until his death one year before the war. For forty five years Julia had been a professor of Saratov conservatory and a concert pianist, but this did not help her to avoid deportation.

Julia was in a catastrophic situation after arriving in Alma-Ata. She did not have the right to work, and consequently, she could not get the ration tokens even for bread. The sixty-five-year-old musician huddled in one tiny room, almost a closet, the door of which was impossible to open in wintertime because ice permanently blocked the threshold. Every morning the scowling owner of this property had to come with a crowbar and break up this ice.

Fortunately, Julia's former pupil, Galina lived in Almaty at this time. She was utterly devoted to her music teacher and tried her best to help her. It was Galina who found a place for Julia Carlovna to live (this small closet) and gave her a piano, which was pushed in with tremendous difficult, taking half the tiny room space. A narrow bed, small night table and two simple chairs occupied the second half. It was easy to touch the window, the bed and the door while seated at the piano. Now Julia Carlovna was saved, she could earn her living by giving private music lessons.

Her first student was Monkey, because Muse was Galina's friend. Then Nica and May began to attend the lessons of the extraordinary music teacher. Later three more girls and a boy, their neighbors at their big apartment house, joined them. The students did not pay money to their teacher, instead they gave her a small part of foodstuffs, which their families got with their ration books.

Julia's lessons made a difference in the lives of her pupils. She taught them not only the music and its beauty but educated them in good manners and behavior. Mature but still beautiful, Julia was very impressive; noble, intelligent, tender, and kind. Despite the many blows of fate that she courageously withstood, Julia Carlovna never complained about her life or had any anger or bitter feelings. For Monkey the contact with her music teacher was a way to a new and beautiful world.

During one of the conversations after a lesson, she noticed that the little box where Julia kept her food was empty.

Monkey ran all the way home without stopping. She dashed to the kitchen and found her dinner for that day. She knew her mother had left her two potatoes and a piece of bread. She kept one potato for herself, but the other and the bread she hastily wrapped in the piece of a newspaper and flew back to Julia Carlovna. With her heart pounding with excitement Manya knocked on the door and blurted out hurriedly, "Here, my mother sent this to you, help yourself, please"

She did not wait for the answer, but bolted away. Little Monkey was very happy.

May and Nica did their music homework, using a keyboard drawn by their mother on cardboard. Monkey had a similar "piano". But these keyboards were very different. The sisters "piano" made sound, but Monkey's "piano" was silent. The explanation of these phenomena was very simple. Sister's mother had a very good musical education, and she sang the corresponding notes, when her daughters played their musical exercises on cardboard. But Muse Ivanovna was not able to do this, and poor Monkey drummed her fingers on the mute piece of cardboard. Not surprisingly, she dreamed about a real instrument, even if it would be quite small. Muse Ivanovna could not even think about buying a piano, but by pure luck she managed to get a little warm, fluffy rabbit fur coat for her daughter. Muse paid for this luxury with a loaf of bread. All Monkey's classmates envied this beautiful coat, and she allowed them to take turn trying on her treasure.

The winter of 1944 was very cold; and this fur coat was very useful along the quite lengthy way to the music lesson. Once a nice looking woman stopped Monkey. "To where do you hasten, my lovely girl?" the woman asked Monkey with a soft voice.

Monkey willingly answered, and a friendly conversation started. Very soon the woman learned that Monkey loved music, that she could play "The Butterfly" by Majkopar; but she did not have a piano at home, and therefore she was forced to play on the paper keyboard.

"You are such a nice pretty little girl, and I am moved by your love for music. I would like to help you, and I think, I can. How about having a very small piano at which you can play as if it were a real big one?" asked the woman.

A small piano!! Monkey dreamed about it all the time.

"I have one and because you are such a pretty smart girl and you love music so much, I, perhaps, will give you my small piano."

The girl's eyes lit up. "It is true? Will you give it to me? I can play on this small piano just as on a real one?"

"Of course. I will bring you this pretty tiny piano right now. Do you want it?"

"Very, very, very much!! But where is it?"

"It is in my apartment, in this house. I am living on the second floor. Wait for me for five minutes and the piano will be yours. Only, do you know, I am afraid that frost could damage it. Maybe you will give me your fur coat to wrap the piano?"

Poor, poor trustful Monkey! She took off her warm treasure and waited with impatience for the promised gift. The frost was strong, but Monkey waited and waited, till she became completely numb from the cold. Finally she went, shaking from her head to her feet, to look for this woman.

"What woman? What piano? Are you crazy?" a clerk from one of a long row of offices that occupied the whole second floor answered her roughly.

Small unfortunate Monkey got home almost unconscious. Her

mother would have whipped her in rage at the loss of this irretrievable beautiful little coat, but the poor girl was barely alive.

Monkey was ill for two weeks. She appeared in school depressed, pale and thin wearing her old shabby coat made from fish fur, as a Russian would say. But, is it possible that a seven- year- old girl would be sad for a long time? At the very first break Zoya wanted to punish Monkey, but she could not bring herself to do so. She said to her sternly, "Manya, our class is not a jungle and you shouldn't leap on desks like a monkey". Then the teacher sighed and handed Monkey one fried brown *ponchik.*

Crime, Punishment and Muse

Nica began to play with verses when she was a schoolgirl. The poetic mood would usually seize her during long hours of boring lessons. The very monotony of the voice of Maria Petrovna, their teacher of Russian language, provoked her poetic zeal. The rhymes scribbled on the last pages of almost every class work notebook were clear evidence of this. Sometimes, Nica became so absorbed in her underground activity that her face grew flushed with excitement. The teacher would then stop and look at her for few seconds much as a policeman who has caught a criminal. This silent scene usually excited the whole class, but Nica would fail to notice it until the teacher would bark, "Stand up! Stand like a post!" And she stood "like a post" beside the blackboard in front of the other students until the end of the lesson.

From her pillory Nica could see three rows of 20 black desks firmly attached to brown benches. Forty girls sat straight and stiff with their hands in a special position on the desk: palms to elbows. All the girls wore brown uniforms with white collars and black aprons. Their hair was neatly plaited back, which gave them the appearance of brown rabbits with ears pressed close to their heads. Forty rabbits looked obediently at the face of the python, their stern teacher, and made mischievous, grotesque and funny faces to Nica every time the teacher turned to the blackboard. When facing her mocking classmates, Nica always resolved never to write the verses again. But school days were so boring and the escape to fantasy so sweet those new scrawls with inevitable misspellings covered the last pages of her notebook again.

She never saved her little verses, and they went into the wood-stove together with the finished exercises in math and grammar. She forgot all of them; all but one.

Twenty years passed, and then one day Nica received from her friend and former schoolmate together with the usual letter an old and wrinkled page from a notebook with some of Nica's sad contemplation. It was a short verse, only eight lines. Like a flash, it drew from Nica's memory the dramatic details from of one mournful event in the past. *When I see no sunshine in the future at all, And I feel that some cat scratches and claws at my soul...*

This was written on the day of Nica's misfortune, on a gloomy day when the teacher, mad as a hornet, accused her, in front of all the students, of disrespect to their GREAT CHIEF, to their DEAR AND BELOVED COMRADE STALIN. To show disrespect TO HIM?! It was unacceptable, unthinkable! Nica was humiliated and frightened. Her classmates set up a boycott against her under the stern guidance of the furious teacher. Nica's friends, her devoted friends, stopped talking to her. Her mother was summoned to the school at once, and it was not Maria Petrovna, but the principal herself who talked with her in a low voice, almost in a whisper, as if someone could overhear. The face of Nica's dear mother was so sad and concerned that Nica was overcome with remorse. Life looked dreary after spending all afternoon in the principal's office. It was almost evening when Nica got home from school. The rooms were dim and made her melancholy even deeper. She climbed up on an old sofa, whose shabby gold trim was evidence of the long past better days of her ancestors who lived in the completely different world which was called "before revolution". With eternal sorrow, Nica thought about the recent events...

I am hiding myself in the dark of the room, I am grieving about my misfortune, my doom ...

The accusation was especially unbearable for Nica because her reverence and devotion to their GREAT CHIEF was absolute. From her kindergarten days HE embodied for Nica all the best in a human being. He was a saint without fault, constantly thinking about all Soviet Citizens, working day and night to lead them to a glorious future. Nica could not even imagine the cruel truth exposing and destroying her ideal, the horrifying truth that would come to light shaking and astounding her in another seven years. Nica did believe in the holiness of their DEAR COMRADE STALIN with all the passion of her small heart. And she was no different from her schoolmates in this unlimited devotion to the GREAT CHIEF. No, no, it is better to say, she would not have been different from them were it not for her inability to spell HIS name, without mistakes. Without three mistakes! Oh, what a shame, what a horror!

It was dictation (and Nica dreaded it) from the very popular political poem. This particular time, the teacher dictated with special feeling and expression. With complete adoration she read the verse, "We believe in you, dear comrade Stalin, more than in ourselves. Let me kneel humbly at the glory of your name." While dictating the teacher would promenade between the rows of the school desks, stopping sometimes to put with royal gesture her hand on the shoulder of a student. When it happened to be Nica's shoulder, she would freeze with fear and embarrassment, and all thoughts would leave her head in a rush. Fortunately, this patronizing gesture was not long lasting, and the royal hand moved further on to freeze and embarrass someone else. "Let me shake your almighty hand, bow to you to the ground!" continued the teacher. She almost sang with ecstasy. Nica tried to concentrate on the grammar, but she felt cold in her stomach. Spelling was never her strong point. The blow came with the culmination of dictation when the teacher pronounced sweetly, her eyes closed with great affection, the first and middle names of the GREAT MAN. All the citizens of the Soviet Union knew them as "dear to the heart of every Soviet person", Iosif Vissarionovich.

With her trembling hand, Nica wrote: *Iosi-v V-e-s-arionovich.*

When she handed her textbook to the' teacher, the Python looked over Nica's work and fixed her eyes on Nica as if she were going to reduce the girl to ashes. Nica's heart sank, and she thought, "This is the end!" But it was not the end - it was only the beginning. After this followed disgrace in front of the class, boycott, imprisonment in the director's study, the summons of Nica's parents, the anxious, unhappy face of her beloved mother and some unclear threats from school authority. The teachers and principal could hardly believe their eyes. Mistakes in the GREAT CHIEF's name! It would be a thousand times better if Nica had misspelled the name of her own father. After all, it was not repeated everywhere around her. But the name of their ILLUSTRIOUS LEADER, this name surrounded Soviet people from all sides, it was omnipresent, ubiquitous. It stared at their faces from the walls of official buildings, from the rooms of kindergartens and schools, offices and hospitals, theaters and concert halls. It was marching on the posters and slogans, rushing on railway engines, floating on boats, taking off to the sky on planes and descending from the heavens on balloons. No, Nica could not ask forgiveness.

I am seeking some penitence. I am filled with remorse, Gloomy day turns to night and I feel even worse...

Nobody was at home. Nica knew her parents, as usual, would be back when it got dark outside, they were too busy building the Splendid Communist Future, or in plain words, working late at night. Her sister was out somewhere too. Nica needed her, and she was sure her sister would never turn her away, even for the sake of DEAR COMRADE STALIN himself. She loved Nica more than him. Gray light from the windows did not help Nica's melancholy. She wanted to run from her dreary and ominous life, to escape from this room, from her gloom. She knew a place that could give her some relief, where she could hide from everything and everybody at least for a while. It was the roof of their four-story apartment house, her mystery island, where her fantasy bloomed. Nica had discovered it two years before. It had been a refuge for her when she wanted to escape from everyday life. Nica always climbed up there through an attic. Each time she dared to break the rules and, with trembling hand, opened the hatch of the attic, she stepped into another world. Here, the stuffy air and dim light were frightening and exciting. The complete silence could be broken suddenly by the quick staccato of invisible creatures rushing somewhere in the darkness. Nica prowled slowly almost breathless along the long and murky passage till she could see a narrow beam of light cutting as a razor the surrounding darkness. This light penetrated through a small, slanting door to the roof. Nica pushed it and was immediately dazzled by the bright light of immense blue sky. It was so blindingly bright, that she closed for a second her eyes, overcoming with happiness. The broad view from the roof made everything look and feel different. Up there Nica became disembodied, invisible and flew in the air. She could see everything and everybody clearly, but nobody could see her. Over the past summer, Nica had often climbed to her mystery island lost in the ocean of an ordinary life. She usually did it early in the morning, when the air was fresh and full of birds chirping, or in the evening, when she could watch the red sunset. But Nica had never been there in the winter. Today, the longing for escape from the misfortune fallen on her was so great that she did not hesitate. To the roof - closer to the sky and further from the people! To Nica's disappointment, the heavy hatch to the attic was locked. There was, however, one other option, to go up the fire-escape. It was of a very simple construction, two long iron bars with many cross ones. Their house was built in the shape of an L, and the fire-escape was in the corner, between two walls. Nica ran down to the back yard. Everything was white with fresh-fallen snow. The motionless air, an unusual quietness around her and snow reflecting the light of the dying day made the familiar place look a little bit unreal, and eternally sad. To reach the fire-escape, Nica needed to climb over the small, slanting roof above the entrance to the basement. It was not difficult, because bundles of iron sheets used in last summer for their house roof repair were standing edgewise right there; and she used them as a step. Nica felt their sharp edges through her boots. The snow had been accumulating on the basement roof for the whole winter making one huge snowdrift. After plowing through the deep snow, Nica finally reached the fire-escape. Fear squeezed her heart, icicles hung menacingly from every bar. She began to climb hastily as if trying to run away from her fright. The bright yellow squares of the light through the windows looked peaceful and happy in the twilight of the approaching night. A sharp, hurtful feeling of being a lonely outcast came over Nica. Higher and higher she climbed, her heart was pumping hard. The roof was very close now. With a bit more effort, Nica climbed from the fire-escape to the icy slope of the roof on her knees, then rose to her feet. The next moment she felt with horror that she began to slide along the sloping, icy, slippery surface toward the edge of the roof. In one instant, all her being concentrated on this terrifying slide.

"It cannot be! I should not die! Not me! Not me!"

She fell down.

To Nica's great fortune, before crashing to the ground, she hit the huge snowdrift on the slanting roof above the basement. She slid down to the ground together with this natural cushion. It saved her life. Nica had no idea how much time had passed before she came to her senses. She was lying in the heap of snow; it was stuck over her eyes and stuffed in her hair and under the collar of her winter coat. Nica's head was touching something hard. She rose to her feeble feet reaching for this hard thing. It was the bunch of iron sheets with the sharp edges. Nica's head would have been sliced open if she had fallen less than one inch closer to them. She remembered vaguely that this bundle helped her before to climb to the fire ladder.

Nica was shaking all over, her knees trembled violently, but she did not feel anything. A strange emptiness seized her. No fear, no happiness, no thoughts. It seemed as if she had looked into the eyes of death and it had made her half dead.

The door to Nica's home flung open and she was overwhelmed with light and warmth. Her sister May grabbed her, hugged her and pulled her inside. "You little fool, where have you been? You drove me nuts with worry!" May pressed Nica, cold and shivering as she was, to her chest. "Don't take this school business so hard. It will pass." Nica did not overcome the shock yet. Everything around her seemed unreal, uncertain, shaky. But May was warm, strong, loving and very real. It was so good to feel May close, as if she infuse life into Nica. May hugged her little sister until Nica's cold emptiness began to melt and stream out as sweet tears of relief.

I am crying and asking my dreams to revive, And my tears are washing the grief from my life.

It was the end of Nica's verse. A bit too melodramatic, but when you are thirteen years old, you can afford it.

"THE GERMAN"

Ludmila Pavlovna seemed to apologize with her shy demeanor for being so unattractive. Her wide, slightly flat face with small eyes was set in a frame of unskillfully formed yellowish curls. Red spots covered her face and neck when she got nervous or uneasy, making her even plainer. She was tall, thin and bony and would not look so awkward if she knew how to walk on high heels, but she did not, and her knees were slightly bent depriving her gait of any gracefulness. She was still young, but that only made her look even more insignificant.

All girls from the eighth grade were mischievously agitated when their new German Language teacher, or *German*, as girls called her between them, awkwardly reached the table struggling with her high heels. She looked at the class, blushed and greeted students with the unexpected and absurd, "Good morning, comrades". That determined the fate of the poor "German": nobody took her seriously.

By this time Nica's knowledge of German was quite poor, in spite of the fact she had began study this language six years earlier than all the other children. It happened because her parents were very rightfully convinced that a foreign language should be learned from childhood. So they had hired the kindest old *Povolzhsky* German as a teacher for Nica and for her sister May. The tribesmen of their new mentor had colonized a narrow strip of land along the Volga River since Catherine the Great. That way they gained their name *Povolzhsky* which means living along the Volga. These German people kept their identities, and spoke their native language for two hundred years till the Second World War, when they were dispersed by the power of Stalin in the majority of cases in Siberia or Kazakh villages. Only the decrepit elderly were resettled in the cities. Poor Karl Matveevich, Nica's and May's tutor, earned a modest source of income from his lessons with these girls; it was the only luck in his pitiful condition as an exiled person. He made a great effort to keep the girls happy. And happy they were, having more fun than serious study. The story of his long life, which the girls always asked him to tell them, had nothing to do with the German language, beside a very strong German accent. Any way, by the fifth grade when German Language appeared on these girls school schedule, the Karl Matveich's lessons had been discontinued. By this time both sister knew German well enough to skip their homework and pay little attention to the lessons. During the next three years the sisters were losing everything Karl Matveevich had taught them, and gaining nothing from the school. Appearance of the new teacher, who was afraid to raise her eyes at the class, gave them a wonderful chance to continue the same attitude without worry. These girls were busy with anything but German during forty-five minutes of German Lesson. And there was plenty for them to do! A book-devouring fever took over May and Nica in the last few years. They were reading with ecstasy the contents of their parent's big library packed with masterpieces of the world greatest writers, Balzac, Flaubert, Thackeray, Dreiser, Zola, Tolstoy and many others; you name it. There was no time for homework. Yet, the girls could not afford to have anything less than a grade of B. Their parents would never understand this; and the sister's pride did not allow them to fail. There was only one way out of this situation; during every lesson at school they managed to prepare homework for the next lesson. It was a difficult, feverish, tense and extremely nervous life. Miraculously the sisters did not go crazy from these mental acrobatics. Now, with Ludmila Pavlovna, their new *German,* they had forty five minutes of her lesson for preparation of Algebra or Chemistry, without any fear of being caught. It was great!

Meanwhile the school life went on without promising anything beyond everyday routine. Rumors reached the girls about incredible adventures in the School for Boys. The schools for girls and boys were separated, and they did not socialize much with creatures of the opposite sex. The boys' feats which were, of course, no more than hooliganism, terrified all schoolgirls and made them envious. Absolute discipline was the law in the School for Girls.

The more rumors they heard, the more inflamed were their imagination. The schoolgirls of Nica's class wanted to do something insolent to overturn the notion of obedient girls, which now, in eighth grade, seemed to them offensive.

The ill-fated *German,* Ludmila Pavlovna presented the girls the best opportunity for such a prank. It is difficult to tell in whose head this idea was born, but all of them were happily excited knowing that they were up to something very improper. The students spent the break on a special preparation for the German Lesson. Finally a broom, procured from a janitor's closet, was adjusted above the door just in time. The bell rang announcing the beginning of the lesson, and all of the girls stood stock-still in expectation. They heard in the unusual silence of the class the clicks of *German's* heels. Now she opened the door and made a step. A burst of laughter released the tension, when the broom brushed her head and fell down to her feet. The girls' hearts beat feverishly. They expected something exciting and terrible; the emergence of the furious Principal, summoning their parents, inquiries, interrogations, meetings, their proud silence, and of course, the rumors through all the schools of their city. But everything was entirely different. The face and neck of Ludmila Pavlovna were covered with red spots. She limped as usual to the desk, sat down silently and began to sort with trembling hands some papers without looking at the class. Suddenly it became clear, their *German* was afraid of the Principal even more then the girls were. She was apparently paralyzed by the very thought of the necessity to tell about the broom, the laughter and complete disrespect for her from the students. Thus they sat, thirty-four girls and the teacher terrified by what had happened and what would come of it. But nothing occurred. By the next lesson Ludmila Pavlovna explained for a long time something about the grammar, turning her face to the blackboard. As usual, nobody listened being busy with something much more interesting and important. The class was happily excited and felt heroic, convinced of their impunity. Yes, everything was just fine, but not for Nica. For the first time in her life she was dealing with a gnawing conscience. She looked at the blushing *German* and felt a simple and clear pity for her. Something strange happened to Nica. She began to listen the *German's* shy explanations of grammar instead of preparing algebra. She came to the point that at home she put away her favorite Jack London novel and opened a German textbook with the much hatred "Anna und Marta baden" at the first page. Every day she felt worse and worse. Nica could not even tell about the adventure to her sister May who had always been her confidant. It felt so rotten. Finally she came to her father for judgment and justice. He was very laconic. "If you want to live in peace with yourself you have to apologize to this poor thing, your teacher, openly and clearly, in front of everybody." "Oh, no! The girls will never understand this, and despise me!" "But you will respect yourself again, and that is hundred times more important!"

To apologize to *German* openly and clearly, in front of everybody? It sounded impossible to Nica. It would be a hundred times better simply to forget about this affair. Nobody expected an apology anyway. She struggled, but her conscience won. Next day Nica accused herself, bravely, but with melancholy, in plotting the infamous adventure with the broom, and profoundly apologize in front of the astonished girls and the teacher, who could not believe her ears. "Sit down." Those were the only words, softly pronounced by Ludmila Pavlovna, flushing to the roots of her hair. Than she quickly turned to the blackboard, rapping on it with he chalk for some reason. At the break the furious girls accused Nica of every possible sin. But she knew that she had gathered all her courage to apologize, so there was no point to accuse her of cowardice; and she took all blame for the broom adventure; so they should not call it treason. She deprived the girls of the excitement of being equal to the boys from the neighborhood school, it was the truth. But what could Nica do? It was saying that the teachers from the School for Boys were fierce, and maybe there was not reason to pity them. But it was different story with poor Ludmila Pavlovna.; she was so helpless!

At the next German lesson Nica felt so good, that she put away "Anna und Marta Baden" and began to prepare Algebra.

"MOLD"

At the beginning of this story, it is necessary to explain, that all the school children in Soviet Union from the age 14 were members of the "Communist Union of Youth". The Russian abbreviation of these three words was "Komsomol", and the children were called "Komsomolsky". Under no circumstances were they allowed to violate the Komsomol word given to someone.

In the year when Nica began her study at the ninth grade, the very last before graduation, a new regulation was installed in her "School for Girls". Beside the ordinary journal, where the student's grades were recorded every day, a little school notebook appeared on the table of the teacher to record the breach of student's discipline. If a girl had more then ten of these reprimands, her parents were notified. This notebook was thrown away after all the pages were filled, and a new one was begun. Lean and agile Anne could not sit still, and she had been receiving written notes of bad behavior very often. In this case Anne was severely punished by her parents, and that was why every time, when the number of Anne's reprimands were approaching ten, the notebook disappeared. Anne always got away by abduction of this notebook.

Once Nicka was in the classroom just when the Discipline book ducked into Ann's school bag. It was a break between lessons, and only these two girls were in the room. Anne glanced furtively at Nica:

"Please don't tell anybody."

"Come on, certainly I don't have a big mouth."

"But give me your Komsomol word!"

"Well, if you wish, here is my Komsomol word, I will not tell anybody"

The lesson began and the teacher looked for the notebook muttering something like, "You should be ashamed, girls, you did the same again." She wrote down a reprimand into a new notebook.

A week passed. During the literature lesson the door abruptly opened and the principal of the school, Vera Pavlovna, entered the class. The severe expression on her face did not promise good news. The girls automatically hunched their shoulders. With a stern look and harsh voice the Principal began to talk about some important State papers, which were stolen, about the necessity to find and punish the guilty students. The girls could not believe their ears, this important document turned out to be this notorious notebook. Then Vera Pavlovna called Anne and four other names. Nica's was among them. All four shared one feature, they belonged to the good families with highly educated parents. They were told to follow the Principal to her office at once. Nica went along the corridor, and she felt in her bones that something very bad was going to happen.

An unfamiliar man sat at the Principal's desk in the office. "Comrade Representative of the Komsomol Regional Committee is going to talk with you," announced Vera Pavlovna to the girls.

"Why is this Representative here? It is so strange. What is it all about?" Thought frightened Nica.

It seemed that he and Vera Pavlovna were least interested in Anne. The other four students were subjected to a real interrogation. When it was Nica's turn, she admitted she knew who stole the notebook, but she could not tell the name because she had given the Komsomol word not to reveal it. With the naive stupidity of her fifteen years, she was sure she gave quite an exhaustive explanation, because in all her nine years at school she was assured that she should not break this word under any condition, even of death pain.

Immediately after this interrogation a meeting of the entire school was announced. In front of a subdued audience of three hundred girls, the Principal read an article under the heading Mold from the main state newspaper, The True. The newspaper spat gross clichés such as plagues of society and parasites on the body of the working people. There were no hesitations in expressions. From the harsh words it was clear the children of professors were accused of the corruption of morals as a result of their isolation from the working class and contamination with gentility and aristocratic manners. "They even have their own rooms in their parents' apartments," the article choked with indignation. It finished as such directives from the top usually ended; by calling to fight and purify the ranks of the Soviet citizens.

Finally it came to the five offenders sadly facing all the students. After a short ominous pause the Principal announced with dramatic firmness in her voce,"Here, in our Soviet school we allowed the flowering of the mold; and as a result there is a decline in morality. A crime was committed. This corrupt group stole a State document, the Disciplinary Notebook. We have to confront this shameful phenomenon with all responsibility. I propose we exclude from the ranks of the Komsomol all the members of this group, all five persons.

Nicky's head spun. Her brain and her heart had been trained, programmed since her kindergarten years on absolute loyalty and inseparability of "the Komsomol, the Communist party, and the Soviet people". The words about expelling her and her friends from Komsomol sounded like a death penalty. Three hundred Komsomolets looked at the five accused schoolmates and thought the same thing. Before this minute nobody attached any importance to the Disciplinary Notebook. Five girls, who were announced guilty of State crime, were known as the best students, and this rapid transformation from "the best" to "the criminals" was absurd. Not one arm was raised voting for their exclusion from Komsomol. The mutual decision was to limit the punishment to a reproof.

After the meeting the Principal took the girls to the Chairman of Komsomol Regional Committee. Here Vera Pavlovna spoke with fervor about how actively the school combated the mold. "Today, only one hour ago, our three hundred members of Komsomol unanimously excluded these culprits from the Komsomol ranks."

Nica could not believe her ears. It was difficult to imagine that a blatant lie was possible, but it was absolutely unthinkable to hear it from the lips of the most authoritative person of the school.

"All five must come tomorrow, we will look into your case," the Chairman said dryly to the girls. He cordially shook hands with the Principal, "It was a good, quick response to the issue."

Next day the girls met at the appointed time in the entrance to the Komsomol Regional Committee. Nica looked at Anne with surprise. She had put on some old tattered clothing and tied a worn-out headscarf in the manner of an old village woman.

"What is this masquerade about?"

"You will see, these people from the Komsomol Committee will like it!"

All five of them were put in the center of a big room. The members of the Committee sat around them in a circle. The Chairman began to talk about the mold, how the children of scientists and especially professors were corrupted and contaminated with gentility and aristocratic manners, all the same stuff the girls had heard already from the Principal.

Anne was in a better position than the rest of girls, and Nica understood her masquerade now. Her tattered clothes announced clearly she had nothing to do with these spoiled-rotten children of the upper intellectuals. The members of the Committee talked with Anne in an almost benevolent manner, and she played along with them using the expressions of a simpleton, despite the fact she was not a numbskull at all.

Nica's situation was the worst. Her father combined all the vices. He was not only a professor, but he had reached the top of the scientific pyramid and was an academician. It was true, that for some unknown reason, he had been at home all the time for a half a year; and the family lived on Nica's mother's salary. She was told that her father was writing a book, bringing together all the results of his scientific work. It sounded strange that he should do it at home rather than in his office, but Nica did not think much about it.

The four girls, including the initiator Anne, were finally released. But Nica was subjected to a real cross–examination by all the rules of criminal science. She had no time to answer the questions raining down on her from her interrogators. Her head was spinning. She could not understand many questions, because her life was too far from the criminal world they had tried hard to cram her into.

Nica understood her life was over when she was finally told, "Put your Komsomol card on the table, you are expelled from the Komsomol."

"Better put me in jail, I can't live without Komsomol" she murmured with trembling lips. Mocking laughter rang out in the room. This cynical, derisive and insulting laughter shocked Nica, and shook her from the soft swaddling clothes of her trusting childhood. With a cold heart she suddenly understood the grotesque comedy of what was happening. She realized her life and true moral values meant nothing to these people around her. "I believed them, but they... They just want to respond quickly to the issue, to curry favor."

Something broke and bristled in her heart. She silently put her Komsomol card on the table.

Nica went along the street, not seeing anything around her. She felt a heavy load on her shoulders. In one hour her life had changed, she had become an outcast. Nica was tormented not only by the thought that her Komsomol card was taken from her. She was pursued by the offensive laugh over her childish ideals.

"Yes, they laugh at me", she thought, "but I am proud I did not break my Komsomol word. This word is inviolable to me even now when I have lost my right to give it. It doesn't matter if my conviction looks like a ridiculous farce, I am glad, and I am proud I kept my word."

At school she was immediately called to the Principal's office.

"You are not going to get a high school diploma. We'll give you a certificate of graduation. You can't be admitted to the university with this certificate. You'll go to work"

Nica's sister waited for her in the corridor by the principal's office. She hugged Nica and said, "I know you didn't do anything bad, and you never will. I believe you; I absolutely believe you."

At home the news that Nica had been expelled from Komsomol was met with silence. She expected that her father, who always was her protector, would intercede for her. He would win her rights and get to the truth. But he did not say anything; he only frowned. And it never occurred to her that trouble was looming over the whole family. She did not know that her father, her honest, noble father had been deprived of all his positions, titles, regalia; and that he waited for the court, which would sentence him to jail and exile according to the established order. A new wave of persecution of prominent scientists began, this time the prey were geologists.

The bleak winter months dragged on for a long time. At school Nica was an outsider. At night, the thought of being unable to enter the university tormented her dreams. She was afraid to think about the future. Her future without an education did not make any sense.

The lifesaver was books. Nica swallowed them one after another. Balzac, Flaubert, Dreiser, Emile Zola, Jack London and many others. There were bookcases from one wall to the other in the apartment of Nica's parents. She immersed herself in the books, as if in drugs. At the school she read through the slot in the desk and was oblivious to what was going on in the class. At home she began to read, barely crossing the threshold and forgetting about homework. She read even at night under the blanket with a small flashlight.

In March Stalin died. Nica was lost as was everyone around her. She wrote in her diary, "What is going to happen now? What will the country do? How do we live now?"

With these questions she rushed to her father. He surprised her again by his restraint. He answered, hugging Nica's shoulders: "Perhaps everything will fall into place. Everything will be fine." She did not see in him any signs of the grief that gripped the entire country, and this puzzled her even more.

In April, the sun shone with all its southern force. Nica wanted to believe in her father's words, that everything would be fine. And it seemed this "fine" began, because the Principal told Nica at the break, "Appeal to the Komsomol Regional Committee. In a year's time you need to receive a High School diploma."

With pounding heart, Nica handed her appeal to the receptionist of the Komsomol Regional Committee. She looked at Nica's paper, but did not put it into the file to deliver it to the Secretary of the Committee, as she usually did. Instead she opened the drawer of her office desk, and fumbling among pencils, paper clips and other rubbish found Nica's Komsomol card. "Is it yours, or not? Take it."

Nica was shocked. This Komsomol card had caused so much anxiety and suffering; but the receptionist gave it back to Nica with a negligence and carelessness as it was some trifle, but not a document from which so much was decided in Nica's life. The Komsomol Committee responded quickly to the issue, to curry favor to the power above, and after this neither Nica nor her Komsomol card interested them. But the more important was that everything changed after Stalin's death.

Soon another event brightened Nica's life. Her father with happy shining eyes hugged her, her mother and sister. He was rehabilitated and all his positions, titles, and awards were restored.

A Little Fool.

Finally Nica was at the Riga airport of the Latvia Republic. She made a jump from Asia to Europe on a small two motor plane, which in that time seemed to her enormous. Nica was giddy with happiness going on this long and, most important, totally independent journey. It was the eighteen hours bumpy flight with air pockets and five landings, each of which made Nica hide her face in the special issue vomit bag. The noise of engines shattering not only the aircraft, but every cell of her body. All of these resulted in a certain state of insanity, but it did not spoil Nica's mood.

In the Riga Airport Nica was supposed to meet with her older by twelve years sister, Gala and go with her to Liepaja . Gala lived with her husband and her little son in this city stretched on the Baltic seashore. But a poor telephone connection, which was in those years the subject of funny jokes, made Gala confuse the date; and she was late for her meeting with Nica by whole 24 hours.

Nica was totally unprepared to be alone in the airport terminal. She was sixteen, and while many girls of her age already sprouted wings of their femininity, she still was in the cocoon of her childhood. A pair of the thin stick-arms, a pair of the thin stick-legs, the freckled nose and unruly curly hair was her accurate portrait.

Nica worried about her sister's delay, but it did not frighten her much, she was sure Gala would appear sooner or later. She took a book, got comfortable in the armchair of a small cozy room for passengers, and tried to immerse in the adventures of Jack London's heroes. But it was difficult for Nica to concentrate on the book; she was too excited by the unusual surrounding. Everything was quite different from what Nica was used to in the Kazakhstan city of Alma-Ata, where she lived. Even a beggar behaved quite unexpectedly here. He came to Nica, elegantly bowed his head and asked politely, "Madam, lend me one ruble, please."

This Madam was never used in the USSR, it changed to comrade after the Revolution since it was despised as a bourgeois address. Besides if you were not older than 20, you were supposed to be called girl, not even comrade. So this "Madam" made Nica painfully confused, she blushed and answered in the same polite manner, "I am sorry, but I have only a ten ruble banknote."

"But we could change your money into smaller bills, couldn't we? Please, let me do it."

He took Nica's bill, her precious only one, because ten rubles was a lot of money at this time. The beggar bowed another time, went to the cashier booth, returned to Nica and honestly counted her nine rubles leaving one for him. At this point Nica realized she was in civilized Europe, because in her Asian city, such a respectable, honest and elegant beggar would be impossible.

The cleanliness, quietness and coziness of this place made Nica stop worrying about the failed meeting with her sister, and she began to investigate her new surroundings with pleasure and curiosity. In that before jets time the airport was situated in the city itself. A little park with neat flowerbeds, lawns and rounded tops of clipped trees began right at the door. Nica could see the street with four and five storied buildings under high roofs. The weather was perfect, the sun shone gently, the soft fresh breeze was invigorating, and Nica's mood was joyous. She wandered around the city with pleasure until evening, but upon returning to the airport she found the door was closed for the night.

Gala's train arrived from Liepaja to Riga at noon the next day, and Nica planned to spend the night in the airport waiting room. And now, after finding the door locked, she was confused and did not know what to do. But the air was warm, and she thought she could be quite comfortable sitting on the bench till morning. At sixteen, it did not occur to her to rent a hotel room.

Nica found a cozy corner under the spherical crown of a young linden, and felt perfect bliss. The ground was still a little shaky under her feet after she suffered eighteen hours in the plane. The thought that this bench stood firmly on the ground and did not threaten her with air pockets or thundering noise filled Nica with relief. She was surrounded by the floral paradise of a quiet little park.

The end of Nica's lyrical mood came very soon. Appearing from nowhere, a young man stopped in front of her and asked without any introduction, "Would you like to go with me?" Nica was astonished and politely refused. She noticed he looked strangely at her, but she did not have time to think about it because soon another promenade-lover asked her the same question. Then the third and fourth young man repeated it. Where this string of the Riga's residents came from, Nica could not imagine, and she could not grasp why it was necessary for them to go with her for a walk. All of them addressed Nica in a very polite manner with a slight Latvian accent, and being refused, they disappeared. She felt uncomfortable about these strange proposals; something was wrong here. Then a Russian middle-aged uncle flopped down on the Nica's bench, "Baby, how are we going to spend the night?"

"But... is it forbidden to sit on this bench?" distractedly mumbled Baby.

"Come on, let's go, I know a better place."

"I am not going to anywhere!" there were tears in Nica's eyes.

"What's wrong with me?" The man's question was viciously.

After this incomprehensible, frightening and somehow insulting question Nica jumped up and ran with such speed the uncle had no chance to catch her. An officer, who, she remembered, was one of the passengers on the same plane when she arrived at Riga, stopped her.

"Our noble Soviet officer, the saver and liberator of people! What a relief!" sighed Nica. She explained incoherently and excitedly the reason for her fright, and the officer comforted her, gently putting his arm around her shoulder. "I will take you to an absolutely safe place, where you, my little thing, can spend a quiet night."

They entered the back of the airport building and the officer led Nica through an empty corridor to a door, which he opened and turned a light. Inside the room a family slept comfortably on two soft couches. The picture was very peaceful, but at the moment when the light came on, Nica looked at her benefactor. His face was contorted with fury at the sight of the sleeping family. Nica's heart jumped with fear. The two of them sat on the hard wooden bench with a back. The officer muttered something in Nica's ear, and then he rested his head on her knees. This touch of his head was unbearably disgusting, insulting and scary for Nica. She jumped up; and the officer's head hit the bench with a loud thud. She rushed through the door, along the corridor, to the street and further, further, passing men walking in groups and alone. There were men and only men on every street. They looked at her and shouted something after her, sometimes even with compassion, maybe with desire to help. Nica did not try to find out; she ran with all her might.

She did not know how much time passed, but the streets became empty, and she felt nobody pursuing her. Nica stopped and looked around. It was already dead of night, but this Baltic's night was not velvet–black, as it was in Asia, but light–gray and transparent. A neat little park with benches was in front of her; she could have a good rest here. But almost immediately another young man popped up from nowhere with the same annoying and frightening question. Without answering him Nica begun to run again. The young man called after her, "I didn't mean to frighten you!" But she did not want any explanation, she ran and ran.

Finally Nica felt exhausted, but it was daylight already. The sun gilded the trees and the ancient medieval houses under the high roofs. This was the outskirts of the city, and the trams turned around with a loud creak. Nica stopped, unsure of what to do next. She was not in a hurry to go back to the airport. She shuddered at the thought of seeing again the terrible face of the uncle, or of hearing somebody ask her to go for a walk. It frightened her to run across her "savior", the officer.

But the new day and the bright sun changed everything. The streets were filled with hurrying women, and in their midst the men lost their predatory appearance. To Nica's relief, they did not pay any attention to her now. She stood for a while looking around and then she slowly trailed back knowing that the train from Liepaja would come by noon. Her legs trembled a little, she felt weak and dizzy because she had not slept the whole night and had not eaten in almost two days. In that time passengers were not fed in airplanes. meals came with jets, and Nica was ashamed to chew in front of strangers the delicious pirozhki baked by her mother.

The long marathon had taken all her strength, but she was so disgusted and so completely puzzled by what happened last night that she forgot about hunger and tiredness. She was tormented by questions. What had all these men wanted last night? Why did they not sleep peacefully, but instead wandered the streets? Why were there only men? Was it some kind of national holiday for the men? Why was the officer's face distorted by such an awful grimace?

When Nica finally returned to the airport, her sister was already looking nervously for her. After happy greetings Nica bombarded

Gala with questions, but Gala turned the conversation to another topic. It looked as if she did not want to hear Nica's story and the urgent request for an explanation of men's strange behavior last night, which puzzled and upset Nica.

After arriving at Liepaja, Nica immediately wrote a letter home. She did not describe all her adventures in Riga, because she did not want to make her dear mother worry. Instead Nica limited herself to a short sentence, "If you only knew, my darling Mommy, what happened to me at night in the airport!"

For some strange reason Nica's mother began to bombard Gala with telegrams in response to this simple phrase.

"Why did you drive our mother crazy with worry?" Gala gave Nica a good scolding with indignation, "You, little fool, at sixteen you should have a bit of brain and quicker wits!"

"A little fool without a bit of brain," it shamed Nica to tears.

Mark Belinki

The train picked up speed. Its wheels beat a merry rhythm on the tracks. Boom pa-boom, boom pa-boom was the magic sound, which carried one away from the mundane to the exciting world of travel with all of its surprises and adventures. However, this time the happy clicking of the wheels fulfilled an exactly opposite role; it returned Nica from two months of wanderings to the well-liked and warm routine of home. Home, about which she was already thinking of with love and impatience. Nica's first big voyage was coming to an end. She had been traveling for so long; first to Riga, then to the cold, northern Baltic seaside, and finally to Moscow. And here she was in the train that would rock her across Russia and Kazakhstan, to the green city, where streets babbled with clear mountain water streaming through roadside dikes. Five days in the trains separated Nica from her home. Sweet home where the balcony opened a magnificent view of the snowy Ala-Tau, a north part of the huge Tian-Shan Mountains to which Nica was so used to since childhood that she almost did not notice it. She was riding in a sleeping car, on the upper bunk. With her was the traditional traveling food, a boiled chicken, however it was not wrapped in a newspaper, as was the custom, but in clear wax paper. Nica put it on the table near the window, so that at the time of repast, she might share it with her neighbors. A simple old woman, clearly from the Caucuses, and a stout colonel with a flushed complexion were in the bunks below. The top bunk, opposite Nica's, remained empty till the very last signal, just before departure a fourth passenger came, a breathless young man, tall, lean, with a friendly, pleasant face. As soon as the train started moving, and the wheels began to click their merry tune, the colonel took out of his bag a bottle of vodka, and with a gesture invited the young man to join him. The young man answered him with an embarrassed smile, "I'm afraid I don't drink," he told the colonel. The colonel mockingly waved his arm, and removed a large bunch of grapes from his bag with the words, "This is for the young lady, and you can join her, but I, if you'll excuse me, will be in the next compartment." The three other passengers remained, and Nica's new companion cheerfully said to her, "If this is the way it is, climb down, and we will eat grapes." Nica really wanted to lie on her bunk, propping her head up with her hands, listening to the clicking of the wheels and watching the flowing away of Moscow. But she felt it would be impolite to refuse, and the grapes looked very tempting. She jumped down, and sat in the corner right by the window. The old peasant woman smiled at Nica kindly, and asked in her strong Caucasus accent, "How *yourn* name?" "Nica." "And *yourn?*" she asked the young man. "Mark. Mark Belinki." The old woman spoke Russian badly, but was very curious, and asked lots of questions. Nica soon found out much about the life of her new companion. Starting with the fact that he was 23 years old, that he just finished the medical college in Lvov, and that his specialty was phthisiology -- "It is a doctor who treats tuberculosis," he explained – that he was traveling to a Kazakh village, where they badly needed a doctor, and that he left his mom and dad in Lvov.

"No, I'm not married. Not planning on it now. Well, of course, some day there will be lots and lots of children". The old ingenuous woman was very nosy, and Mark laughed merrily. Next she began to give Nica a similarly detailed inquisition. She listened with such a good-natured interest, and commented on Nica's answers so kindly in her broken Russian, that it was impossible to be annoyed. So, whether Mark and Nica wanted to or not, even before the grapes ended, they knew everything about each other. This immediately removed the usual constraint between strangers, and made them almost friends.

Their little old inquisitor, constantly smiling amicably, finally satiated her curiosity and left them in peace. Mark led Nica to the very tail of the train, where from the rear glass door they saw miserable Moscow suburbs particularly squalid and dirty along the railway. Then a wide panorama of spacious green fields, birch and oak groves began to spin behind the train making Nica happy and giving her a keen sensation of flying away. It was easy and interesting for Nica to speak to her new companion. He addressed her as an equal, as an adult, and even used the *vows* form. In Russia all children and youth are addressed as *thou*. *You* is reserved only for adults. At sixteen, Nica was not used to this courtesy and was flattered. With that, he did not allow himself the least familiarity, neither by word, nor gesture, nor intonation. Nica felt at home with him and completely safe.

They spoke about all sorts of different things, starting with Nica's school, and ending with the just-announced Schmidt's theory of the origin of the cosmos. Her mother recently explained this theory to Nica; but of course, she did not admit that to Mark.

Still fresh from his college in civilized Lviv, and from the house of his loving mother and father, Mark hurried to the place where, in his own words, he was needed most. He sought to remote auls (Kazakh's villages with adobe houses) about which he had not the faintest idea. All he knew was that the *auls* were in the grip of a tuberculosis epidemic and eagerly awaited help. In spite of Nica's sixteen years, she had been in many such *auls by* riding across the boundless steppes with her geologist parents. It was hard for her to place this clean and well-groomed man from Lviv to these *auls*, which at that time knew nothing of even elementary hygiene. But he was enthusiastic about his profession and happy for the opportunity to exercise it in real life. For many years Nica kept the book he was reading at the time. The book had no relation to medicine, but the inscription that he wrote in it for her was "to a future doctor from a doctor," as if certain that Nica would follow in his footsteps. She did not become a doctor, but the book remained with her until confiscated as antique by humorless border guards more than thirty years later.

From the first minutes of the journey, Mark and Nica were inseparable for the entire five days. No, that is not true, they were separated once for five minutes but that did not lead to anything good. On one of the stops, Nica jumped down to the platform while

Mark remained on the train. Her attention was captured by the shrill cries of a street vendor, "Piroshki, hot fried piroshki with jam!" By the time she got to the door of the rail car, the peasant woman with her sweet merchandise had already disappeared. Nica could almost taste her favorite food, and she somewhat lost herself while searching for the vendor, when she suddenly heard Mark's voice. Nica looked around, her train had already started to move, and Mark was standing on the steps of the rail car, waving. Nica started running after the train, jumping over the rails, when suddenly, she heard a desperate "Stop! Stop!" She managed to stop, but so close to a barreling on-coming train, that it almost cut off her nose. When the cars finally moved past, she saw Mark standing exactly opposite herself on a neighboring platform. Their train was already beyond the station.

"How did you wind up here?" - asked Nica with amazement. Mark shrugged his shoulders "What else could I do? " Nica was ashamed, and glad, and scared. She could not look Mark in the eye, but he was already dragging her by the hand to a little booth, upon which was written, "Dispatcher." In a minute they were hurrying back to the platform to another departing train, which, by an amazing chance, was supposed to catch up with their train at the next stop. They caught this train just as it was starting to move. Nica jumped on the last slowly gaining speed car; but as her hand was still clutching the pirozhki, she was unable to hang on and began to fall. She felt Mark catching her, and pushing her up into the rail car. He then jumped in after Nica. They stood happily, breathing hard, on the rapidly accelerating train. Nica handed Marc a pirozhok. "No, thank you. I am afraid that this sweet which caused you to lose yourself, and then twice to almost wind up under the wheels of a train, might make me sick."

His chocolate-brown eyes smiled with kind sparks. The palm of his outstretched hand rested on the wall barring the door, as if to prevent Nica from again accidentally falling out of the rail car. Maybe from the extra excitement, maybe because the pirozhki really were delicious, she swallowed them both immediately. Two hours later, they caught up with their own train.

The wheels kept rhythmically knocking on the rails. Already the fourth day of their journey had flown by, and everything went now without any adventures. Boom pa-boom; boom pa-boom beat the train wheels on the rails. They were approaching Alma-Ata, and their travel was coming to an end. First from the seemingly endless plains emerged a thin ribbon of distant mountains that rose higher and higher with each minute soon turning to a chain of snowy ridges. Then small houses started to flash past the window, then larger and larger ones as they entered the city. Finally, the train station enveloped the train and it came to a stop. Marc and Nica somehow had not realized that their conversations would come to an end; and had not prepared themselves for the inevitable parting. As soon as the station appeared before their eyes, there rose an enormous confusion on the train. Everybody ran to the doors and windows. A dense crowd on the platform was waving and calling. Their little band suddenly lost its purpose and its intimacy. The old lady disappeared in the crowd of her noisy relatives, each distinguished by a typical Chechen hawk nose. The red-faced colonel, kind hearted but managing to stay completely soused throughout the journey, evaporated with a speed totally at odds with his solid bulk. Nica saw her beautiful sister May, happily waving to her, and lunged towards her, secretly proud to show off such a pretty sister in front of Marc. But the crowd was denser than Nica thought, and when she looked around, he had already disappeared from view. Of course, he was probably somewhere nearby trying to see the sisters through all the faces and backs of the crowd. But how to admit to your sister that you have to find someone; and this someone was a 23-year-old young man? That was impossible. Carried by the stream of people, Nica and May left the station without Nica saying goodbye to Mark. It seemed ridiculous to imagine that they parted forever. Nica was certain that they would meet very soon. As strange as it was, that is exactly what happened on the very next day.

They went to the theater, a flock of four girls. As soon as they stepped into the foyer, Nica's heart began to beat hard, and blood rushed to her head. She saw Mark. Unfortunately, May immediately noticed her discomfiture. Maybe if Nica was not so busy maintaining that absolutely nothing happened, she might have answered his joyous hail. But off-balanced and embarrassed, she... turned away. At the intermission, Nica secretly looked for Marc with her eyes, and she found him. He was sitting in the foyer on a chair, propping up his head with his hands with a discouraged, disappointed look on his face. Nica was afraid to attract his attention, and herself did not understand what was happening to her, what it was inside her that changed. Why was happiness mixed with panic? Nica's heart beat rapidly, and she was not able to overcome a paralyzing, incomprehensible shame. " Next time, next time when I meet him, I'll meet him without my friends. I will certainly tell him how happy I am to see him, and how I don't want to lose him again. Next time, but not now." There was no next time. Nica thought about Mark constantly, and with the hope of meeting him, she wandered the streets that led her to the theater, all in vein. She remembered that he must have stayed in the hotel, and at that time there was only one in the entire city. Nica had the idea that she could leave a note there with her address, so that he would know where he could find her. She spent many hours trying to write something that made sense, but her handwriting, which appeared to her then as such a childish scrawl, left Nica in tears of desperation. Finally, she decided to ask May to write for her in her beautiful, fully adult hand. To Nica's relief, May did not burst out laughing, though she was dying to, she admitted to Nica much later, but agreed immediately. Armed with her well-written note, Nica approached with her pounding heart the porter of the hotel. He looked at her with indifferent eyes, and opened up a grungy guest book. "Mark Belinki departed two weeks ago. Destination unknown."

"I'm only sixteen," Nica though, "we will certainly meet, somewhere, somehow. In front of me is such an endless, long life." She still hoped, and day after day, month after month, she imagined how they would meet. Years ran by so fast, and life turned out to be so short, that they never had a chance to find each other.

Where are you, Mark Belinki?

A Killer or A Courteous Knight?

It is necessary to give some explanation before beginning this and the next story.

Collective farming is the concept of Socialist ideas applied to agriculture.

In the USSR, this idea was exercised by forceful government expropriation of individual farmlands and combine them into one large collective farm. The advantage was that there would be more justice and more equality than capitalist farming. The transition from individual to collective farming was called collectivization.

In reality, due to unreasonably high government quotas, farmers

got far less for their labor than they did before collectivization. This led to the fact that the collective farmers worked without the slightest enthusiasm. The immediate effect was to lower grain output and reducing the quantity of livestock. The Soviet government sent every year for a month or two urban residents, especially students to collective farms to enhance their productivity.

* * *

It all began on the happiest day of Nica's life, the day she was admitted to the University. After the tension of eight brain-wracking exams, during which she lost the ability to sleep and eat, Nica looked over the list of the selected lucky entrants and could not tear her eyes away from her name on it. A student! It was something to rejoice. The contest was a huge, only one out of every ten could be taken to the University. Happy to the point of exaltation, Nica paid no attention to the little note below: "All admitted students must register for agricultural work. No exceptions."

A week later, a train took Nica, together with her new classmates to the distant sun-parched Uzbek cotton fields. They had to work there for two months. They were transported in a livestock boxcar as prisoners, with the important difference that they had no guards, except for their supervisor who was riding the same train, but in a normal passenger car. In her seventeen years Nica perceived this as an exciting adventure. Happiness from the fact that she was a student made he dizzy with joy. In light of this happy event, everything seemed wonderful.

Nica's parents had not returned yet from their geological expedition, and she prepared for her trip herself. This fact was easy identified, because her outfit was not consistent with the situation. Nica approached the railroad station dressed in her white silk gown for ceremonial occasions and high-heeled shoes. Her wild dark curls were hidden under a wide-brimmed hat with a bright red ribbon. However this party outfit turned out to be perfect for working in the cotton field, especially her fashionable hat. The high heels were conveniently broken quite soon.

Nica still did not know anyone by name, but they were all first timers, and that was enough to feel like she was among friends. Moms and Dads came to the station to see their dear new students off, and they looked with undisguised fear at the boxcar that was not adapted to carry people. Nica was the only one who was not surrounded by anxious relatives. Ecstatic cognizance of her adulthood and independence thrilled Nica.

The train whistled, creaked, jerked by convulsion, which ran over the long line of the cars. The wheels began to knock faster and faster. Nika and her classmates went to a new strange life.

The heat was unbearable. Too many young bodies crammed into the boxcar made it impossible to breathe. The students not only could not lie down, there was no room even to sit on the floor without bothering someone. Soon all the brave classmates climbed to the roof of the boxcar. Nica also climbed up, clinging to the cramp-irons. The society gathered on the roof was mostly male, or rather boyish, because everyone was not more than eighteen-year-old. Nica's appearance was greeted approvingly, with kind of patronizing attitudes. Here, on the slippery, rushing forward roof the feeling was great. Strong wind refreshed, blowing away hot; the wide view changed every minute, sailing away into the distance; and the consciousness of her mettle pleasantly tickled Nica's nerves. Her hat blew off immediately, and it fluttered behind her on the red ribbons. Nica was cheered by the novelty of adventure and by the attention of her new classmates.

The train dragged along slowly the whole week on the Asian open spaces, stopping at all large and small stations. The students slept in the boxcar, but on the queue due to lack of space. Uncouth boys behaved like clumsy gentlemen, and pestering the girls was out of the question in the train or, later in the collective farm. It seemed natural; traditional severity in the relationship between girls and boys had not yet undergone a sexual revolution and remained in full force, despite the fact that the overall morale of the population of this impoverished country after the war left much to be desired.

September sun burned in all its Asian power. The students became dingy from the wind and locomotive smoke after a week on the roof of the boxcar. They were tanned to blackness, became dirty and lost weight, eating only dry bread. But travel difficulty befriended them; and there were strong ties of comradeship between them now.

Finally, the students arrived at a small, completely baked by the sun station, where an old, shabby truck waited for them. They were pressed together in this truck like herring in a barrel. Surprisingly, none of them had fallen on potholes. Time after time this ancient rattletrap snorted and stopped. Then the driver got out, turned the crank handle, and speaking with set teeth the same short expletive, returned the decrepit motorto to life. The students jumped from the truck near the collective farm management, and walked another three miles along a dusty country road.

Nica felt quite happy in the wretchedly bleak collective farm, where she and her new friends had to work for two months. No wooden bunks with straw, where they slept; nor daily rice porridge on cottonseed oil, nor merciless sun, nor heavy bags, which they stuffed with cotton, could spoil her every moment of joy from the fact that she was a student. Her classmates completely shared these sentiments. They were seventeen or eighteen-year-old boys and girls; and they perceived student forced labor much as a hilarious adventure, rather than as a heavy duty. Jokes and laughter broke out on every occasion, and often without any provocation.

As happy as Nica was in her new, boisterous student life, she missed her long time friend, Natasha, future philologist, who began her road to high style literature working at the fields of a nearby collective farm. It was a big temptation for Nica to visit her and to share the joy and excitement of the new life, even while it was similar to the peculiar mixture of the Young Pioneer (something like Boy Scout) and concentration camps. Nica soon put a plan of action together with another girl, her friend Lena.

Both girls were highly complimentary. Lena had a well-balanced character and calming lazy movements in contrast to Nica's irrepressible enthusiasm and impulsiveness. Lena walked leaning slightly back and firmly set her foot on the ground. Nica's gait was hasty, and her feet barely keep up with her going forward light body. Difference in their temperaments were perfectly consistent with Lena's smooth blond hair, neatly and tightly braided, and Nica's mop of unruly dark curls. Two friends got along great.

Journey through the rural places of Uzbekistan was unsafe. The girls reckless daring was based on their light-headed stupidity and innocent ignorance. They did not think for one second that it put themselves at risk. Losing no time after finishing their workday in the field, the girls went out to the road to hitchhike to their destination.

The sun was setting already on the horizon, but the coming evening did not carry relief from daytime heat. The air, the land and even the wind were hot. Within ten minutes of waiting, they saw an old green truck approaching followed by a whirlwind of hot dust. The car stopped, covering the girls with a white cloud of dust. In response to the question where the truck was going, the driver waved his hand, "Come on, climb into the back!" Beside the driver sat his partner, who also invitingly waved his hand. The girls, wasting no time jumped into the back of the truck, and the dust began clubbing after them, like the smoke of a jet.

One hour passed, and the girls' excitement of the fast and well-implemented plan began fading. They expected to ride no more than twenty minutes, but the darkness already was coming. The girls had a sinking feeling they may not be heading in the right direction. Anxiety turned to panic. They banged on the cab of the truck; but the drivers looked at them through an open back window and laughed in an ugly and frightening way. The girls had no doubt that these two men were plotting something horrible. But what exactly, it was not clear to them.

Now, after the sexual revolution it is difficult to imagine the depth of these girls ignorance. Even a ten-year-old child would realize now, what kind of danger the girls were facing. But in 1954 the word "sex" was taboo, and a TV show "Law and Order", that could have enlightened them, appeared half a century later.

"What do they want from us? Rob us? But we have no money!", Nica asked.

"Maybe they want to kill us, make us into pirozhki and sell them at a bazaar." Lena replied.

This absurd assumption was not a joke. Crimes with pies remained firmly in their minds since the war, when there were persistent rumors, that some criminals sold *pirozhki*, tiny pies, filled with human flesh at a bazaar . It was such a poverty in the Uzbek cotton collective farms, which the girls knew only at war time. Not surprising that the idea of *pirozhki* came into their heads, as a terrible, but likely version.

After another half-hour had passed, the girls prepared for a drastic action, jumping from the moving truck. Just then, the truck turned off the road, slowed down and began to jiggle through the field. There was no time to waste.

"Jump! Jump! Quickly!" Nica cried.

"No! We will fall to our death!" Lena replied with horror.

And the girls jumped. The powerful force of inertia threw them to the ground. The soft, dusty soil spared their bones, but the shock from hitting the ground was so strong that a few seconds passed before they regained their senses. The girls saw with horror that the drivers had stopped the truck and were advancing upon them with repulsive grins. The girls were terror-stricken by now, their hearts were beating violently, and their lungs felt ready to burst. The feeling of helplessness and fear was overwhelming. Nica made a tremendous effort, jumped to her feet and pulled Lena up to make her stand too. The drivers were close now, and one of them squeezed a heavy wrench in his fist. They were obviously enjoying themselves.

In the next moment, something strange happened. To the girl's happy astonishment, the drivers stopped abruptly as if stricken by terror and ran back to the truck. It was hard to believe in such miracle. What was the reason? What were they so afraid of? The girl looked around. As if grown out of the ground, a male figure stood in a sinister stillness a few paces away. His appearance was frightening. His motionless body with broad shoulders radiated an evil force. His hooked nose, coal-black, uncombed hair and a red kerchief knotted at the temple· made him look like a pirate from "Treasure Island." But the most frightening were his big, black eyes that stared at the girls with a hard and stern glance. They were gloomy eyes, knowing neither joy nor fear.

"Who are you?" he asked without greeting. The girls answered obediently, with trembling voices, forgetting to brush dust from their faces and dresses.

"What are you doing here?" Again, they answered. He looked at the truck, now moving swiftly away, and cursed.

"Come with me."

The girls moved as two rabbits hypnotized by a python.

Night fell; the velvet black darkness surrounded the girls. They followed the dim figure of their silent guard without seeing the road; their feet in the soft, warm dust to their ankles. The blackness was like a wall around them. Only well above bright stars shone. When the pirate finally stopped, the girls could barely see an outline of a half-decayed shed. Two crossed boards were nailed over the window. The pirate knocked at the door and shouted something the girls could not understand. There was the sound of a bar taken from the door, and they stepped inside.

A small kerosene lamp dimly lighted the almost empty room. A rough table of unplaned boards and two benches along the opposite walls made up all of the furniture. The man, who opened the door, looked very much as the pirate, but his hair was red. He looked at the girls with an unfriendly, even angry perplexity, and said something quickly. The pirate answered him solemnly in Russian, "I am responsible for the lives of these innocent kids until morning." Then he pushed a bench to the corner, "You will sleep here, on this bench." After a while he asked Lena,

"Are you Russian?"

"Yes"

"Do you have parents?"

"Yes"

"Is your father communist?"

"Yes"

"Do you believe in God?"

"No"

Lena knew somehow instinctively that her answers were hostile to him for some reason, that they might hurt her and Nica, but she could not tell a lie. Yes, her father was a communist, but not out of conviction, but strictly out of duty. He was quite indifferent to any politics, but he had a passion for the plant which he led. By unretten but stringent law, only member of communist party could hold this position.

The pirate stood silently for a while. Nica dared to look into his eyes. They were big, black and not ferocious at all. There was some hardness in them, hardness and grief.

"Hungry?" He held out a piece of dry, flat bread.

Nica saw from the bench, which was given to them, their hosts, spreading on a clay floor across the small room. They talked quietly in an unfamiliar language. "Greeks!" she thought. Nica knew about them. They were evicted without warning within hours from Caucasus by order of Stalin and dumped here, three thousand miles from their homes. Nobody was spared. Children and women suffered the most. Many died. The survivors hated Russians indiscriminately, avenging them whenever possible.

"Back in his home" she thought" in the Caucasus, our guard likely had had a family, a wife and children. Greeks love children and usually have large families. Where is his family now? Are they alive? Maybe not. He must hate Russians, and I could not blame him", .

The voices in the opposite corner changed to snoring. Nica shoved her friend.

"Let's run!"

"Leave me alone, I want to sleep."

"They will kill us!"

"They haven't done it so far. Why should they now?" answered lie-abed Lena and fell asleep immediately. But in her words was undeniable truth; and Nica decided to be on the alert, wait until morning and prepare for any surprises. Without completing this thought she fell into a deep sleep.

It was still dark when the girls' host awoke them. "Let's go."

The girls dragged their feet again after this silent figure in the darkness that became much thinner now. The sky was changing from velvet black to dark gray, and the stars, now small, lost their magic diamond glitter and blinked faintly and wearily. In about an hour they crossed a narrow dusty road.

The pirate stopped. "Go along this road. It will bring you to a village. Go directly to the post office. Take a ride only and only from the post office car. It will take you to your collective farm. I am not responsible for your lives anymore."

He turned abruptly, went away hurriedly, without another word, and merged in a moment with the gray predawn shadows.

The sun was up high when the girls stepped inside a tiny post office. The first thing, which immediately attracted their attention, was a poster hanging from the wall with a picture of a man. Familiar eyes, that knew no fear, looked at the girls. They parted with this man less than one hour ago! It was their pirate, their guard, the man who saved their lives and maybe more than life... The man to whom they did not say thanks even once for all he did for them.

In disbelief, the girls read the words under the picture: "Most Wanted Murderer."

Margarita Borkaev

Candies From A Thug.

"All admitted students must register for agricultural work. No exceptions." This announcement meant that Nica and all the other students accepted by the University had to work for two months on some collective farm to help the unenthusiastic farmers with harvest.

The *aul*, a little Asian village, where a group of university students were to live while working in cotton fields, consisted of yellow-grayish clay-walled huts with flat roofs and two gloomy elm trees. There was not a single green bush or a flower, just a bare dry clay path between the little shabby adobe houses. On the outskirts the village, there were two wooden poles holding a handwritten announcement: Restaurant. This miraculous establishment was in a little shack with cracked adobe walls.

The most remarkable thing though was the five feet wide *aryk*, an irrigation canal, murmuring ravishing to the ear of the exosted by heat students. The water was dimmed a little with loess* but clean. All the boys were called to help arrange plank beds in an abandoned army barrack, a new dormitory; while the girls, excited and giggling, rushed to the *aryk*, casting off their shoes. They didn't splash happily in the cool water for long. Stones were thrown at the girls, and they realized right away they didn't know the local customs. Deeply tanned curious kids and Asian-looking angry old men wearing skull caps were staring at them. The girls were lucky it was hard to find big stones in the soft clay; otherwise their heads would have been smashed with no regrets by the elderly. The girls immediately jumped out of the water, running away from not-so-hospitable locals, and leaving behind their precious sandals. Their first encounter with eastern customs was not very encouraging.

The boys installed the bunk beds and divided the barrack in two halves; one for the girls, the other for the boys. A clapped-together rough wooden table with legs dug into the earthen floor in the middle of the barrack was for meals and a place for the night guard. The bedding was pretty simple, just a layer of straw. No pillows, of course; as for blankets, they did not really need them in those hot Asian nights.

In the evening the first hot meal in the whole week was given to the students. It consisted of some rice with cotton oil, instead of the real Uzbek pilaf they were promised. The students had not had anything to eat since morning, so they quickly

gobbled down the rice. From that moment on, this specialty of the house became an unfailing *plat du jour*, and after three weeks the students began to see in their night sleep pasta dreams. Then somebody remembered the so called Restaurant as a possible lifesaver. The inside of this parody of the restaurant fit perfectly with its outside. The ceiling was completely covered with flies, and the menu consisted of two items: the same infamous rice pilaf they were sick of and pastry. The fancy name pastry referred to small little squares made out of sweet sticky dough with a price tag almost the same as at a metropolitan bakery. The boys squeamishly turned the sweets down, but the girls' money pretty soon ended up in a dirty restaurant cash register. They were deeply saddened when their pockets were empty and they realized that now there was no alternative to the rise with cotton oil.

One evening a man, who was manager, cashier and waiter in one person, brought a skinny old mare to the restaurant. The animal could hardly move its legs. The girls felt sorry for a poor thing, but they could not find any grass to feed this horse, and it didn't want to eat their rice with its bitter cotton oil smell. The next morning on their way to work the students were passing the restaurant and they were stunned to see the poor mare's skinless carcass lying on the ground on its own stretched hide. The sullen restaurant manager himself was cutting the carcass. The girls surrounded him expressing their sympathy about the death of old *Rosinante*.** The manager waved his hand in annoyance as if saying, "Go away, it is none of your business".

That night the students saw a handwritten announcement on the door of this restaurant: *Fresh Lamb Shish-Kebab*. It was obvious; the poor old mare's sad demise made this amazing and incredible metamorphosis into a young lamb.

---

* Loess is a deposits of silt (fine sand with particles 0.002 millimetre in diameter) that have been laid down by wind.
** Rosinante is the name of Don Quixote's horse, taken as the type of a poor, worn-out, and elderly horse.

---

* * *

It was already getting dark when Nica's friend Lena came up to her and opened her fist showing some money and repeating a little verse

Gennady runs around,
A bow-legged, shorty-guy,
He's, happy, healthy, sound,
He's silly and he's shy!"

The teaser was not fair. Gennady was not short, his legs were fine and he was not running around. What was true – he liked Nica and always tried to take care of her from afar, and stoically substituted for her when it was her turn for a night-shift duty. Nica's intelligent fan seemed to her too ordinary. There was not anything mysterious or fateful about him. She appreciated him many years later, but at that time her criteria of being in love were based on ballads about knights and ladies, and she took for granted all signs of his affection and everything he did for her.

"Where did he get all this money?"

"Oh, it is simple! We vividly described to him how poor and hungry we were so he made all the guys give us their money!"

Nica's conscience remained untouched, she had absolutely no guilty feeling. The next day, each of the girls gobbled up three pieces of pastry and then told Gennady laughing nonchalantly about their feast. He got very upset. It was not easy for him to convince the boys to pitch in. By this heroic effort he hoped the girls would find a better way to satisfy their hunger. The girls were not sorry at all; just the opposite, they split their sides with laughter, "Did you really think we would buy another portion of rice, or this horrible *fresh lamb shish-kebab* made from poor old *Rosinante*?!"

The very first morning after arriving the students were broken into two teams. The boys were sent to do things requiring some physical strengths and technical abilities, and the girls were to work in the cotton fields, manually picking up whatever was still left after a special combine that harvested the cotton. With big bags tied around their waists the girls walked along rows of dry yellowish bushes picking soft white flocks out of cotton cups. By noon when they were burnt with heat and thirst, a shaggy little brown horse would show up pulling a cart full of wonderful Uzbek watermelons. The girls rushed to the cart taking out big heavy green balls. The girls broke open the ripe fruits and with the big spoons, they always had with them, scooped out the heavenly cold ambrosia. Only those who have ever been burnt by brutal sun in dry cotton fields can understand their bliss at those moments. Watermelons were food and drink for the girls; and they ate them until they couldn't move. Then they happily stretched on the hot and soft dust ground. Their elderly Uzbek supervisor walked among their motionless bodies repeating, "Hey, girls, come on, get up! Go back to work!"

Nobody paid any attention to him. They would be lying around until who knows when if not for their daily norm, the amount of cotton they were obliged to gather for the day to stay out of trouble with the University authorities.

After a whole month of this kind of life, the girls had not lost their optimism, but their meager diet was getting to them. In their imagination, they already saw a trip to the bread city of Tashkent where they would get some real food. There was another reason to go there. The girls' old sandals became unusable and very soon they would have to walk barefoot around the fields. The trip would take at least eight hours, but every one of the students had to work the "day norm". That rule was taken very seriously, because otherwise they would be expelled from the University. Finally the girls decided to send one person and the rest would contribute to that person's day norm. They cast lots and, to Nica's joy, it fell to her. The girls waited until they got their mail when, in addition to mom's and dad's love, they received some money with the letters. They put all their resources together and got a nice amount of cash. The girls' plan was simple. In the morning Nica had to walk three kilometers to the office. For a modest compensation, she would hitchhike to get to the train station and then take a three hour train ride to Tashkent. There Nica would buy some *boobliks* , kind of small dried bagels, sandals for those who needed them; and she would be back the same day. Nica was not afraid of getting lost in Tashkent because, everybody except the very elderly, in this old Asian city spoke Russian, and anyone would show her how to find the bazaar and the train station.

Nica dressed up for the trip very carefully, open-toe shoes with high heels and a white dress that she had just washed. She did not put on her hat, but she took a red ribbon from it and wrapped it around her waist that had become especially thin because of her recent pilaf diet. Nica's perfect look was a bit spoiled by a little pocket full of money fastened with a big safety pin. But, in general, everything looked just fine. She strolled around on her high heels making the boys whistle when she passed by them.

In the morning Nica enjoyed walking barefoot on a cool and soft dust road the three kilometers, carrying her shoes in her hands. She was lucky. When she reached the office there were many people there who needed to get to the train station, and a truck which was going that way was easily caught. In half an hour Nica was already on the train on her way to the Bread City Tashkent, as it was called in the Soviet Union for an obvious reason.

The infamous earthquake that led to the complete restructuring of Tashkent occurred eight years after the events described here. At the time of Nica's venture it was still an authentic old city. She walked through curved narrow streets resembling canals because of the high clay walls along both sides of them. She saw and heard a colorful Asian crowd bustling around with its unfamiliar Uzbek language. The air was saturated with captivating smells of Asian food. Right there on the streets one could buy unimaginably delicious *Belyashi,* a little round pie with minced meat sizzling in oil in huge frying pans, or heavenly steamy *Manti,* minced meat rolled in thin dough. Nica couldn't resist these temptations and pretty soon, instead of a pair of sandals that she needed badly, her own meager money turned into a Belyash and two Mantis. Later she did not regret it because she didn't find any sandals at the big and noisy bazaar anyway. All Nica bought were two bunches of *boobliks* strung on cords like beads which she put across her chest like a cartridge belt. After realizing that her searches for the sandals for her friends led nowhere she hurried back to the train station since the evening was approaching. The leftover money was still stuck in the small pocket closed with the safety pin.

* * *

In the south, dusk falls fast, the sun goes down and it gets dark. Sitting on the train, Nica stared out of a half-open window and saw nothing but complete darkness. The train passed shabby little stations. Passengers walked in and out, loaded with bags and bundles. All day long Nica felt fine, but now for the first time she became worried and uneasy. The strange world and strange people were around her. The thoughts about her parents and sister made her forget about reality. They were in Alma–Ata, far away from this hot and dusty place; they were probably worried about her. Nica's imagination took her home to a warm and loving atmosphere, to her world. Suddenly she was awakened from her sweet dreams. She felt that somebody was staring at her, and right away Nica saw a mean looking man, thirty or forty years old, with a grayish face and tousled red hair. He impudently plopped himself right by Nica, and she felt a knife thrusting in her side.

"Money. Now. And don't you dare to give a squeak!"

Feeling lost, Nica glanced around hoping to see somebody who could help her. There was not a single person in the car! How did other travelers recognize the danger? Why did all of them disappear so quickly? Nica couldn't understand, but one thing was clear – she was one on one with this bandit, and she couldn't count on any help from anybody. Nica undid the safety pin and pulled out the money. She probably did not yet grasp the gravity of the situation at that moment because she started explaining to the man that this money did not belong to her, and after she get off the train there would still be eighteen more kilometers for her to get to her place. "If I don't have any money I won't be able to get a ride". Nica's explanations were visibly entertaining to the thug. He chuckled, counted her money and gave her back some change.

"Here, hold it. And if it's not enough for the ride, tell'em that it is Mishka's order!"

He stuffed the crumpled bills in his pocket and waddled to the next car.

Petrified, with her heart pounding Nica sat there, with no thoughts; she didn't even feel any fear, she was just stunned. Fear came later, when after another stop Mishka came back. Nica had just began to recover from the shock when all of a sudden this stinker showed up again and headed directly towards her.

"Here, eat!" He stretched out his hand offering her some candies in a little bag made out of newspaper.

Nica turned away.

"Eat, I tell you!"

This rude barking made a candy fly into Nica's mouth. The bandit plopped by her side again. He was obviously in a very merry mood.

"Look at you, such a pretty curly girl! I like your kind so-o-o-o much! Today I take a break from my wet business. I am relaxing. Wanna relax with me?"

Mishka gave Nica a wink that made her heart sink. Was he really a wet business master, which in thieves' jargon meant a murderer, or was he just swaggering? She didn't know and froze with fear. It was not the first time when being a pretty curly girl caused Nica troubles. She recalled a moment when she came to St. Petersburg for the first time. She stood on the Kirovsky Bridge admiring the beauty of the city when a scary ugly mug peered right at her face, almost touching it. " You, pretty curly one, scared, ah?" Mishka got up. "Sit still! You move…" he made a cutting gesture running his fingers across his neck.

Nica was alone again, motionless, with the newspaper bag of candies in her hand. Now she knew for sure he would come back looking for her. She shuddered with a thought she was in the clutches of this filth.

"Oh no, this is not happening, no, this is just a nightmare; I should wake up!" Nica suddenly recalled her classmates and their innocent courtship. "Goodbye, boys, my life is over." she thought with horror.

The train slowed down and Nica's heart sank. "Where will I be ordered to get off? Maybe at the next stop. Or right now?!" This last thought made her jump off her seat. "It's better to be slaughtered with a knife than "relax" with this filthy animal!" Nica dashed to the door, jumped off the steps, glanced through an illuminated window of the train; and at this very moment she saw Mishka walking fast toward the door. She looked around in panic, where to hide?

Nica dove under the train and started crawling between the tracks. She heard Mishka's heavy steps on the train ladder and realized he was looking for her. Then he jumped off the train. Nica curled up hiding in the dark shadow of a wheel exactly at the right time because at that moment Mishka glanced under the car. He didn't see her. The thoughts raced through Nica's mind." What to do next? If I crawl from under the car on the opposite side he will catch me immediately. Should I wait until the train rolls over my head? Even if the terrible rumble doesn't give me a heart attack Mishka will still get me in his clutches when the train passes." He probably thought he could catch Nica like a little fish in a dried out pond, because he did not leave, she still could see his big ugly boots.

"If I can manage to slip away right at the moment the train starts moving…" Nica shuddered at this thought and realized this is what she would do. She also understood that since Mishka entered the car from the front door he would be watching the windows of cars at the tail end looking for her. "If the train doesn't run me over" she thought "I will be able to escape while the flashing cars will conceal me from Mishka." That was the only chance, but a horribly scary one for her.

A signal sounded announcing the departure; the wheels squeaked and Nica slipped over the rail waiting for her body, for her skin to feel the cutting blade of wheels. In one second she managed to get to the other side of the train. The danger was over, and Nica lay on the track, her knees up to her chin, feeling air from the deadly wheels. Then she pulled herself away from the train, once more, jumped up and ran as fast as she could. She didn't have much time because the train, which sheltered her from Mishka, began to pick up speed. A huge telltale sphere of the moon already rolled out at the black sky shining over the silver veins of diverging rails.

Nica noticed some dark spot ahead and she rushed there. It was a narrow ditch, probably for fixing train cars; she jumped in and fell down to the bottom. It smelt of tar. Nica lay there trying to catch her breath, with her heart pounding heavily. "It's a miracle that I am still alive," she thought, "but what do I do now?" She closed her eyes and vividly imagined home again. With plaintive feelings, completely new to her, she saw a light curtain flying in the wind at the wide-open balcony, a shiny black grand piano, and polished hardwood floors…. It was a different world, a different planet; it was a heaven where she had lived so recently. Only at that moment, in that dirty pit did she understand how pristine and beautiful that life was. "Oh, if my dear

Daddy knew what was happening to me!" With a gloating delight Nica imagined how he would punish this Mishka. But her Dad was far away, and the bandit was right here.

Nica jumped up and cautiously peeked out of her trench. And she saw him. He still stood by a light pole on the platform looking around as if in disbelief that she could utterly disappear. Then he crossed the track and slowly moved towards Nica's hole. He knew about it, he himself used it before, hiding there from police. Nica became all eyes, a bundle of nerves and muscles. "If he crosses one more railroad track I must run, even if he sees me. Otherwise he will trap me!"

He made a step, another one. Nica got ready to run, and at this very moment she heard a signal of an oncoming steam engine and saw a fast moving train. "Oh, I hope Mishka doesn't cross its track! Then I will be able to hide again behind the cars!"

It was a long-distance train; it didn't stop at this little station, but it slowed down. Nica jumped out of her trench and started running parallel to the train. She knew she had to jump up to the ladder of the train before it could accelerate, but she was terrified to do this. Again those scary wheels rattled so close. Nica ran and ran and then, almost unexpectedly for herself she grabbed a metal handrail and jumped up on a step of the ladder. The speedy train jerked her and her foot slipped off. Trying to hold on she pressed her body to the ladder, but her feet were dragged along the embankment. With tremendous effort Nica managed to pull herself up and to set one knee against the lower step, then the other knee; and then she froze motionless for a minute trying to catch her feverish breath. Holding firmly to the handrail she pulled herself up again one step; finally she reached the very top step and sat. The train sped up taking her she didn't know where. She didn't care, just away from that Mishka.

The door of the coach was locked, and Nica could not get in. She was completely exhausted; her whole body kept shaking. She leaned against the metal door and closed her eyes so as not to see the streaming railroad ties down below. Her hands clenched the handrails so tightly that they grew numb. Suddenly horror chilled Nica to the bone when she heard a rumbling of somebody walking over an iron flat connection between two cars. She did not know if it was Mishka or only her imagination; but she felt that his impudent eyes stared at her. Nica was so terrified that without thinking, without understanding what she was doing, she jumped off the train. She fell head over heels down the embankment. Everything spun around, unbearable pain ran through her whole body. The pebbles from the embankment slipped along with her, saving her life.

When Nica came to there was no sound of the train. She lay in the middle of some low shrubs smelling of better tarragon. A ceaseless shrill of the cicadas broke the silence of the night. The sky was velvet black, and the bright disk of moon rose high. Nica's body was hurting as if heavy sticks had beaten her, but her only thought was where is Mishka? That silence and calm all around seemed deceiving; Nica lay motionless, listening closely to the night until unexpectedly she fell asleep.

When she woke up it was already hot, and swarms of insects crawled all over her face, getting into her nose and ears. Nica sat up and shook her head in disgust brushing them off and moaned in pain. Her dress was all torn, a cheek-bone was cut, a huge bump hurt her head and both arms and legs were covered with dried bloody scratches. Moaning, about to cry, Nica got up. By sheer miracle she had no broken bones, but it was difficult to breathe because her ribs hurt. She looked around. Joy overcame her suddenly from the sharp, happy realization she had managed to run away from Mishka.

The day was sunny and beautiful. If not for her poor aching body it was hard to believe in all that happened so recently. It seemed like a nightmare. "It is great this filthy pig didn't catch me, but in a tattered dress, with no money, how can I get back to our farm?" Nica checked her little pocket. The change that the bandit gave her back was lost; but she found yesterday's train ticket. "Maybe they will let me use the old ticket. Then I have to walk for eighteen miles because nobody will give me a ride for free".

Nica had no idea where she was, where a railroad station was, where she needed to go. She could guess she was probably not too far from a station because last night events developed so fast. Overcoming the pain she climbed up a hill and looked around. An endless yellowish desert with poor prickly shrubs stretched on one side along the rails; on the other side she saw two posts or smokestacks on the horizon. It had to be a station.

The sun was high up in the sky, and everything around breathed hot. Nica didn't feel hungry, but her throat was parched. She was thirsty since the day before when she had eaten her *boobliks* with no drink. "Oh, the *boobliks!* I left both bunch on the train. Great! I'll come back with no sandals, no *booblicks*, and no money! I can imagine how disappointed everybody will be. And what a shame to tell them about Mishka with his candy!

First Nica walked, moaning at every step, then it became easier, but the scratches kept burning all over her arms and legs. She walked along the tracks. Everyone who has ever walked along railroad tracks knows that if you step on every railway sleeper you just mince along, but if you try to step on every other one then the steps are too broad, and you get tired faster. So, Nica had to step on one railway sleeper, then between two of them up and down. This required concentration and distracted her from the pain.

Now her immediate goal was not just to get to the collective farm, not even to reach the station, but to find a water pump. Nica licked her dry and cracked lips, imagined a stream of water, its murmuring sound and dreamed of drinking, drinking, drinking it. Only this thought, this maniacal desire get to water gave her energy to move ahead.

The first building of the station appeared, she was close to her goal, but her feet moved so slowly, she dragged them struggling. And finally, at last, there it was that heavenly bubbling sound. The stream of water splashed into Nica's face and she drank, drank, drank non-stop until her belly got heavy and pleasantly cold. Her head was getting clearer with every gulp, and she started washing beads of dry blood off her arms and legs. At first it caused a sharp pain but little by little the pain subsided and Nica enjoyed washing off all that dirt and dust. Cold water ran down her tangled hair, her neck and back. The water pump was right in the middle of the platform, so Nica could not take her dress off. That was good because it was washed right on her body, and under the hot sun it was dry in minutes. When this blissful ritual was over, Nica suddenly was paralyzed again with the same thought; what if Mishka is still here? She looked around the station, first with a quick glance, then studying every corner. Everything looked quiet and peaceful. Slowly limping she entered a small shack serving as a station house and checked a fly-bitten train schedule. A train was supposed to come in two hours.

In about an hour people started coming in. Nica sat on a stone behind a warehouse, to be able to see everybody, and at the same time not to be seen. She got tense every time she saw a man coming. Mishka did not show up. Finally Nica heard the whistle, and the train rumbled to the platform. She came up to a car and gave her day-old ticket to the ticket collector.

"Hey, get out of here. What do you think you're doing with your old ticket?" He pushed her off the door.

For a second Nica was lost, then suddenly she blurted out angrily, "That's Mishka's order" and darted in past the dumbfounded checker. The way she looked was probably a pretty convincing proof of her friendship with Mishka.

Luckily the car was pretty crowded. There were women with big bags, Russians and Uzbeks, sniveling kids and old men wearing skullcaps. They looked so peaceful with their tired hands resting on their knees that Nica suddenly felt almost cozy. She sat on a bench, leaned back and the moment the train started rolling she dozed off. She woke up from a sudden sharp pain. Somebody pushed hard on her shoulder. "Get up, go". Nica could not understand what was gong on and stared in complete amazement at two armed military men.

"You! Get up, go!"

"What is it? What do you want?"

"Go! We'll see."

A younger soldier pushed again on her aching shoulder. Everybody around got silent; they looked at Nica with fear and curiosity as if it was unexpected entertainment. "They look at me as I am a cobra in a Zoo", she thought. She had no choice but to move towards an exit, feeling those guns behind and gloating looks from all around.

The shabby station looked the same as the rest of them, maybe a little bigger. Nica was brought, not to a police station, but to a military commandant's office. An officer sat at the table leaning back in his chair. He glanced at her with surprise and amusement. Seventeen year old Nica looked like a homeless little girl in her torn and dirty dress, her tangled hair and shoes with their heels torn off. She was escorted by two armed soldiers and it made the whole picture quite comical.

"OK, make a clean breast of everything that's going on. And don't even dare to lie.

"I never tell a lie, comrade officer", Nica felt insulted and her voice trembled.

"I'm a Major! Don't you understand ranks?"

"I don't! And I don't know why I am brought here!"

The major frowned.

"Who are you? Where're you from? Where're you going?"

"I am a student, I am going to a collective farm where we work, " Nica said proudly, though she was ready to cry.

"How do you know Mishka? We are looking for him for a long time. Who is he to you?"

All last night events, all the feelings of being insulted, abused, so unjustly offended, the fact itself of being brought here, all these made Nica burst into tears despite how hard she tried to hold herself together.

"Now come on, spit it out. You can howl after it!"

Nica's story disappointed the major.

"Why did you threaten the ticket guy? Why did you use Mishka's name?"

"I needed to get to the farm. This bandit took all my money!"

"OK. We will check everything you said here. Now you wait. We will contact your superiors. Hey, comrade Sviridov, lock her up for now!"

The same young lieutenant with the automatic rifle brought Nica to a small room with gray walls, a guarded window, an old wooden table, and a bench. When she heard the sound of a huge padlock behind her back, she panicked and started hammering on the door.

"What do you want?"

"I want to call home, to my parents!"

"Ha! Give her mommy-daddy! Sit tight, the Major will sort things out!" They laughed behind the door.

It seemed everybody forgot about Nica. Hot sunbeams had already stretched across the room when the padlock sounded again, the door squeaked, and the young Sviridov showed up, this time without the gun.

"Come out", he waved his hand.

This time the major in the commandant's office was almost friendly.

"OK, you student, you can go to your farm now.

But then Nica stood for her rights as one who had been unjustly accused and abused.

"First, you held me here like a criminal all day long and didn't even give me a cup of prison gruel! And now I have to drag myself to the farm in the dark of night! Do you want some Mishka to get me in his clutches? Who will be responsible if he kills me?"

She asked this last question with some kind of a malicious joy.

The major looked at Nica very closely as if assessing her ability to resist and fight a bandit.

"Comrade Sviridov, take her to the kitchen for something to eat, then give her a ride to the collective farm and hand her over to her supervisor!"

Nica's escort, now with no gun, did not look stern anymore. He took her across the courtyard to a small house serving as a kitchen. A cook, with no surprise on his face, scraped inside a big pot and handed Nica an aluminum plate with the same rice and cotton oil. Sure, a sophisticated menu did not spoil the young soldiers here. Nica and Sviridov sat at a long clean table and she devoured this parody of pilaf with gusto as if she had never before eaten such a delicacy. The cook was apparently pleased seeing her appetite because he even served her a dessert. It was a huge piece of melon. It smelled wonderful and melted in her mouth like sugar.

Nica felt great when an old roaring and puffing motorcycle rolled along a bumpy road. Yes, she felt great despite the fact that her aching body was jolted in the sidecar. She was happy that all her troubles were coming to an end. Her friends certainly already knew how she escaped a thug, and they probably saw her as a hero. This thought made Nica smile.

Her classmates ran out of the barrack when the motorcycle sportily swung around by it. Ignoring the pain Nica swiftly jumped out of the sidecar and waved to Sviridov: "You can go now. Everything is OK". It was too bad he didn't have his Kalashnikov with him because it would have been an even more impressive spectacle. Nobody could see Nica's scratches, bruises, and scabs; even her shaggy hair was now looked like a wig of a 17-century marquise under the thick white powder of Asian dust. Her friends welcomed her as a true heroine. She was delighted.

* * *

Nica thought of Mishka frequently. His promises to kill her gave her no peace. It was so easy for him to find her. She gave him Ariadne's thread: "Eighteen kilometers from the station, a collective farm where students work." Some nights Nica would wake up and listen: what if he was sneaking up on her? But he never showed up. Was he too busy to waste his time on her or was he caught? She never knew.

"How strange things go in life" Nica thought one sleepless night. "What is in store for me?"

She dug in her bag, pulled out a pencil stub, and a little notebook. All the girls were sound asleep; and she started writing a little poem about randomness of events in our lives, and about a chance that may determine our destiny.

PART III.
Despair and Hope

TO THE BLESSED MEMORY.

Little seven-year-old Natasha, wearing a faded old dress climbed the stairs with uncertainty and fear following May pulling her arm. The difference in appearance of two girlfriends of the same age was striking. The one in front was pretty, large-eyed, cheerful, well groomed despite the difficult war times. She was the very embodiment of a happy child from a loving family. Behind her Natasha was a hunted, scared little animal, ready at any moment to run away and hide. This she did, when the door opened on the upper floor of the house and stately, beautiful May's mother came to meet the girls. Natasha rushed away knocking on the steps with her bare feet and, probably, she would have escaped, but May caught her, blocked her way and hugged her. The whole episode was repeated twice and the third time it was not May, but her mother who hugged Natasha, keeping firmly in her arms and saying something affectionate. That was how Natasha stepped over the scary threshold into her new family.

It initially appeared that except for her name, uttered with head bowed and eyes hooded, this girl did not know any other words. But nobody hurried her. May's father helped Natasha get on a high chair at the table and stroked her hair, while the little girl bent her head even lower.

What they ate in those difficult times of the Second World War could hardly be called dinner, but it was clear that even this scanty meal was a delicacy for Natasha. At the table children were supposed to keep quiet and speak only when parents asked questions. This was convenient for Natasha. With downcast eyes, she ate, picking the crumbs from the plate, as indeed did all the others, knowing that they could not ask for more.

Time went on, and Natasha visited this family every day after school, often staying for the night, but they all knew she lived with her grandmother who had given birth to 16 children and buried 14 of them. Stunted, skinny granny, like a penguin in an old, faded, but always-neat skirt and blouse, could neither read nor write, but was warmly loved by her granddaughter Natasha. It was not known who was more helpless, the little girl or the old woman.

That pair of small and old was supported by a strikingly attractive, if not beautiful, young woman, Natasha's aunt Anna, Anechka, Natasha called her tenderly, who worked anywhere and in any conditions to get a little money, and most importantly, the bread ration cards. All three of them survived on Anna's bread ration cards. Natasha could not claim the negligible state benefit for orphans. She was the daughter of so-called enemies of the people.

The shooting of her brother-in-law and the arrest of Anna's sister, with whom she had lived in Moscow, completely knocked Anna out of the normal track of life. She was immediately expelled from the Pedagogical Institute, where she studied; her fiancé disappeared; her sister and brother-in-law's apartment was sealed, and Anna had nowhere to live. A good friend advised her to run from Moscow for her life as far away as possible to avoid being arrested together with her sister.

Now all three of them, Anna, Natasha and the grandmother huddled together, taking a corner in a variety of disgusting and squalid garrets, in the so-called Shanghai, those scary areas just outside the city, where mud-brick huts clung one to the other like a beehive. Where it was possible people just dug into a hillside the caves, with doors made from whatever materials were available. The city was not able to accommodate a crowd of refugees, and these squalid Shanghais had grown around it. These areas existed even a decade after the war and were a ghastly and frightening skid rows. There was something to fear because besides helpless and unfortunate refugees, a ruthless criminal world found a habitable place at these Shanghais.

The events that led to Natasha's miserable existence began in an infamous 1937, when by the decision of higher authorities, and by order of Stalin himself a bloody purge started in the country and lasted almost two years. In historical literature it is referred to as the Great Terror, popularly known simply as Thirty-Seventh.

In people's memory Thirty-Seventh is an ominous symbol of mass killings, organized and conducted by the state's authority.

Thirty-Seventh was a gigantic scale repression covering all regions and all sectors of society, from the country's top leadership to the peasants and workers. More than two million were arrested for political reasons in these two years. Half of them were shot. Most of the political prisoners were men of working age and many of them were talented, of high social status. It is not difficult to imagine the disastrous consequences of the Great Terror for the fate of the country.

Natasha was born in Moscow two years before these terrible events in the family of a young, talented engineer, Alexander Miasnikov and his pretty wife, Tanya. Natasha was still a baby when her father was executed, and her grandmother took her, suddenly orphaned, to a village near Moscow where she lived.

Then another change followed in the life of the grandmother and her granddaughter. Anna took both of them to the outskirts of the Ural city of Perm. This city was chosen because here in the Permian prison Natasha's mother Tanya was kept in custody. A year later Anna, Natasha and her grandmother finally move to the outskirts of the Kazakh capital Alma-Ata, because Tanya was escorted to the concentration camp called ALGERIA, which was an abbreviation of the Russian words denoting Akmolinsk Camp for Wives of Traitors to the Motherland. This camp was located near the Kazakh town of Akmolinsk. Of course, the first two happiest years of her life with her parents left no trace in the memory of the little girl. Only one picture remained from this sunny time. From this photo Natasha's young, strong father and beside him her beautiful mother with a tender, cheerful smile always looked at her. Natasha knew that her mother was alive, and someday she would see her. She waited for her and dearly loved this happy and gentle face in the picture.

Whether May's parents guessed Natasha's fate is unknown, but one thing is clear, they did everything to cherish this frightened little creature. The warm atmosphere of family, which kindly accepted her, made a miracle. A swift and remarkable metamorphosis happened to Natasha. It was amazing how quickly her protective armor of distrust and fear melted. Natasha assimilated like a sponge the refined intelligence of May's family.

It was a real wonder that the four years of her life in so-called Shanghai left no trace in her speech or in her behavior. It was as if she had never heard any dirty swearing in her Shanghai environment and had not experienced its gross cruelty. She became merry, gentle and very friendly; and there was no mischievousness or childish capriciousness in her character. Kindness and an ever-present friendly smile involuntarily caused her to be liked.

Natasha's close friendship with May and frequent, prolonged visits to the family, who loved her, were a great relief to Anna; and the amazing changes in Natasha's character made her happy.

If it was debatable whether the inherited genes could protect Natasha from the harmful effects of Shanghai; there was no doubt her good genes were responsible for her flourishing abilities. She learned easily, studied with pleasure, had an excellent memory, and her school notebooks were filled with nothing but A. During the war she went to the school barefoot until November. Then she had to wait in her Shanghai den until the ground was frozen and dry, and Natasha could wear *valenki*, home made felt boots. They did not have any leather or rubber soles; and they immediately soaked in mud and rain. She had no other shoes, and she had no jacket to wear except the old gray-green one, which was shapeless and too big for her.

The war ended, and life was slowly becoming more humane. Anna found a permanent job in the cafe of a knitting-goods factory. However, this unfortunate family did not have enough money to break away from the Shanghai, but now they could live in a separate tiny room instead of a corner behind a curtain. This room was furnished not only poor but miserably. Nevertheless, every day reduced the duration of Tanya's imprisonment, and they lived in constant hope and expectation of her return.

Natasha was eleven years old, when the day she had dreamed about all her life finally came. Her mother was released from ALGERIA. Tanya was not allowed to go to Alma-Ata, and she now lived in exile a hundred kilometers from the city. Natasha and Anna looked forward to the long-awaited meeting with excitement and joy. The girl was preparing for this event with all diligence. The old dress was washed, ironed, and starched, her hair neatly braided, and shoes polished. Before leaving, Natasha studied the photograph of her beloved mother again, as she had innumerable times in the past. Her mother's face looked at her happily and gently as always. She examined this face so often that she knew it to the last wrinkle. A thousand times Natasha imagined all the details of their meeting. Her joy at the thought they finally would reunite, and, of course, never part, was so great that Natasha was filled with happiness. Now she would have her own mother too, a beautiful, cheerful mother. Such as May had. Anna often talked with Natasha about her with love, but always warned that the girl should not tell anyone anything about her yet. But now they both would go to visit May's parents, and everybody would see she had a wonderful mother.

It is easy to imagine the impatience with which Natasha waited for the coming happiness.

The long dreary gray barrack with peeling walls was at the edge of the village. They opened the creaking door and went through a dark corridor, which smelled of kerosene and dampness, until the last door.

"Tanya, open, please, it's us!" Anna knocked. Natasha's heart began to thump.

A strange woman opened the door. She was thin and bony; her stern and stiff face was a mask with protruding cheekbones, tight weather-beaten skin and sunken eyes. Anna hugged her, crying: "Tanya, my darling!"

Natasha stood petrified. There was nothing, absolutely nothing in this woman to remind her of the photograph, which she had lovingly studied all these years.

"Natasha, why do you not embrace your mother?" Anna fussed.

"Tanya, dear, do not worry, Natasha is just bewildered with joy!"

The mother took her daughter's shoulders, then pressed her to her chest for a second.

"Yes, finally, I see you, beyond all my expectation!" Her voice was hoarse and husky. Than she turned to Anna: "Have you brought something to gorge?"

"Surely, Tanya, dear, I brought everything that I could."

"Let's go to the table. These are my three companions; we live in this room together."

Only now Natasha noticed two other women. She looked around. There were three cots along the walls, a table covered with an old oilcloth in the middle of the room and four rickety chairs. This surrounding did not surprise her, it reflected the same dire poverty as in their own tiny room. The women came to them, and the older one told, "Well, what a joy for Tanya! To meet her daughter and sister! Let's go now to the table, to drink to this joy."

Anna, all her modest supplies of food on plates, sighed. "You are welcome to all we have. I even brought a bit of wine."

"Pour one for yourself, Anna, we have our own drink."- Tanya closely watched as one of the companions poured vodka in glasses.

They ate in silence, focused, as it seemed to Natasha, with avid veneration for what was on their plates.

"I will probably never be quite full after camp gruel." Tanya's voice sounded like an apology. "I've never eaten potatoes since my arrest."

When the meal had been eaten and the plates were removed from the table, Anna whispered to Natasha, "Please, say something to your mom!"

Natasha looked shyly at this strange woman with a mixture of fear and pity and said, "Mom, how have you lived?

"I, my daughter, did not live, I tried to survive."

Tanya stopped, and pictures that cut into her memory by red-hot iron came to life.

The ward was crammed with arrested wives, sisters, and mothers lying on the bunks, under the bunks and on the floor. Women howled with fear for the future of their children taken away from them; and Tanya's paralyzing thought was of Natasha. What happened to her? Where is she? Is she alive? When Tanya was arrested Natasha was only a two-year-old girl and left alone in the apartment.

She recalled all the horror of nights with interrogation 2-3 times, from which she barely crawled, beaten beyond recognition; incomprehensibility and absurdity of what was happening and the insane cruelty of all of it.

Then deportation; a boxcar where they were squashed to each other's bodies. After debarking from the train, a long walk to the camp numb from exhaustion, feet on the frozen ground. The cold, icy wind, thirst, hunger, utmost horrors when they, wives, sisters and mothers of political prisoners were kept during the night in one barrack together with the real unruly man criminals. On this horrible way to the concentration camp she learned, with hopeless despair, that her husband had been tortured and executed

And then the concentration camp: the rise at 4 am, lights out at 10 pm., all day exhausting work, rape and abuse by guards, hunger, cold, death. Could she tell this to her child? Tanya sighed.

"Yes, rare, but something good happened. Here, I shall never forget. We were led from one job to another. Somewhere in the middle of our way a group of white-bearded elders approached us with a bunch of boys. The old men babbled to the boys something in Kazakh, and they began to throw stones at us. Our guards laughed, encouraging the boys, but the stones flew so to catch them was not difficult. I caught one, and felt it was not a stone. The boy showed me imperceptibly that I should put it into my mouth. I licked a pebble and understood that it was a kurt - a piece of solid dried domestic cottage cheese. All the others prisoners understood what was going on. The boys ran away, but we managed to hide a stone or two. So, the elderly, these white-bearded Kazakhs were sorry for us, the hungry women, and wanted to help. Yes, the world is not without good people.

Or there was another incident I remember. We were 18 thousand prisoners suffer in ALGERIA. There were not only wives but also mothers, sisters and daughters of those so-called traitors executed by the KGB. Many died; they were buried in mass graves outside the camp. We also had infants, many, up to 500. They were dying first. Winters in Akmolinsk are harsh, the ground froze, and digging the graves was difficult. Babies' corpses were put in a large metal barrel, in order to bury them in the springtime when the ground thawed. One day a woman from the camp staff passed this barrel and saw a baby's hand moving. She pulled out a tiny little girl, hid her under coat, secretly took her home and nourished her. And then she found the girl's mother in the camp, told her what happened and promised to return the daughter to the mother after 8 years, when she would be released. All of us prisoners thanked this woman heartily and cried with joy, grief, and despair thinking about all the other babies and about our own children too.

On the way back, Natasha was silently crying. Sensitive Anna took her not to Shanghai, but to May's family. "Let her heart warm up a little bit!" And her heart was warmed. At night the girls, both in the same bed, whispered for a long time; and Natasha poured out to May her fear of her harsh, severe mother's stories and her infinite grief from the loss of that mom she had been waiting for and loved.

Five years later, Tanya's time in exile was over; and she was allowed to move to Alma-Ata. Anna was married; she finally found peace with a man older than she was, but kind and caring. From the holes of Shanghai she moved into his small house with an apple orchard. After fifteen years of struggle every passing day, a home with a quiet garden meant inexpressible happiness to Anna.

Tanya, Natasha, and the grandmother now lived in one room of a barrack, as dull and bare, as the one where Tanya had served her exile. There was striking poverty in their barrack room despite the feeble efforts of grandmother to decorate it with her hand-embroidered napkins. But Tanya did not notice the poverty around her; after years of disaster she was happy just to be out of the horror of captivity. And Natasha spent, as usual, much time in the warm house of May's family, coming sometimes to the barrack to see her mother and grandmother.

"We bathed our darling Granny today, and she shone like a Christmas toy" Natasha reported to May, and May understood the importance of the grandmother's happiness, and the wonder that all the trials did not change Natasha's heart of gold.

During these five years of her exile Tanya was slowly returning from prisoner of ALGERIA to what she was before the arrest. Her voice stopped wheezing, the rough chapped skin changed to normal and her revived face became warmer and kinder. Now she looked like that mother for whom Natasha had so eagerly awaited. Of course, Tanya could not be completely the same as before the arrest. The severity of her expression softened, but the bitterness of the past suffering was not forgotten. That remained forever.

And then came the real joy. The truth about the Stalin atrocities emerged; the country became a restless, irritating beehive. There were thousands and millions of petitions to revise the accusations, and the brand Enemy of People was exchanged for Innocent Victim.

In the summer of 1957, at the 20th anniversary of the execution of Alexander Miasnikov, the deafening news burst into the dismal barrack. It was the news that three women, Tania, Anna and Natasha had always known, "Innocent!"

This was a bitter joy, because no justification by the courts could give life back to 33-year-old Alexander Miasnikov, the talented engineer, beloved husband and father who was never known by his daughter. No justification could return Tanya her motherhood, which had been taken away so cruelly, or erase her suffering in the concentration camp. None of the courts could return her parents and normal, happy childhood to Natasha. But avowal admission of committed atrocities was needed, it was important.

In a few years Tania and Natasha moved from the terrible barrack into a small but quite human habitation. It was a studio near the Byelorussian Terminal in Moscow, given to them by the Soviet government in compensation for their flat, which was confiscated in 1937 during the arrest.

* * *

It is morning, the most ordinary morning in Moscow. Metro, trolleybuses, trams carry the inhabitants in different directions. Everybody is in a hurry at this hour, and Natasha is too. She is bringing her two-year-old twins to her mother before hastening to a publishing house where she works as an editor, and where she will plunge until evening into a pile of printed papers for which she, the editor, is responsible. Days filled to the brim fly fast. Life is trying to catch up with runaway time. Too many important and necessary businesses have to be done, and nothing can be stopped.

Would not be stopped the course of life? But what if someone again mixes by murderous hand everything into a pile of cruel absurdities?

One can only hope that people remember their tragic history longer than one generation.

Irma

May and Nica were deeply attached to their father, and it was not surprising, he was an example of all that is the best and noble in a human being. Also, he was for them a reliable protection from the vicissitudes of fate. When he passed away, the sisters felt the keen pain of loss. The woeful visit to the cemetery, to the white marble monument over the grave of their beloved father became a part of their lives. They spent time there in sorrow and memories. On the way back, they always stopped near another grave with a simple enclosure and a granite obelisk inside it with a portrait of a young woman. It was written on the tombstone that she died at twenty-one. The same portrait, only much bigger, hung on the wall in the living room of May's house. Her children were afraid of it because a tragic story was associated with this picture.

The word "death" was not part of the image of the portrait: round-faced, with two thick braids, she seemed to be too young, even with her strict eyes looking from the picture intelligently and seriously. Her name was Irma. The last time the sisters met her was the eve before the tragic day. Nothing predicted a sad farewell, even for Irma herself. However, Nica and Maya could not help blaming themselves, thinking that if they had looked more carefully into her heart, the fatal outcome might have been prevented.

The story that led to the premature and sad ending of this young woman's life began in Leningrad (now St. Petersburg), in the happy days when Irma was an excellent junior student at the Chemical Engineering College and her brother Cyril and his friends, Sasha and Julius, were the best senior students in the Leningrad College of Mines. Professors predicted a great future for all four of them, but several years later talented Sasha got tangled in some trifles because of his provincialism. Cyril, became a chief of a big geologist expedition, but did not advance in the science because of his stubbornness; Julius has not risen above the average geologist, having lost interest in everything in the world, and Irma's career was cut short, barely begun. But then, in the early sixties, life promised to be wonderful, and all four of them believed in the uncommonness and brightness of their fate.

Julius and Cyril were friends long before their arrival in Leningrad because their parents had been familiar with the early years. Sasha joined these two friends at the first level of the School of Mines. All three of them managed to fall in love with the same girl, a fellow student, and no wonder: she was very pretty and smart. She was very modest and never suspected the power of her charm, which made her even more attractive.

Julius followed at her heels, Sasha was thrilled with her at a distance, but Cyril acted decisively. He insisted, persuaded and almost dragged her to the Court to marry him, without giving her time to understand her feelings.

Sasha suffered silently when he learned about this marriage, unable to believe that his beloved girl would be happy with the gruff and impatient Cyril. Julius exploded with anger and despair, decided to commit suicide and that way to punish Cyril. This tragic gesture ended only with scratches of Julius' veins and a little lost blood, and he fell into a black melancholy. It was Irma, Cyril's younger sister, who pulled Julius out of his gloomy state. Julius remembered her as a child to whom he had not paid much attention, but now she had become a girl in full bloom, with an attractive oval face, plump lips, a slightly Mongolian shape to her mocking eyes and two long thick braids, which she continually tossed carelessly behind her back.

Irma's childhood, as well as her brother's, was not full of parental affection. Their mother, Elizabeth, raised her children in severity, cultivating strictness. Sometimes she did not hesitate to wind Irma's braids on her arm, smacking the girl with a belt for any fault. Cyril did not avoid the same penalties, especially when he was a small boy.

The children almost never saw their father, who spent all his days and often most of the night at a huge metallurgical plant. He managed the whole complex and was jokingly referred as "The King of Iron". Their mother worked at the same plant as a Personnel Manager. All the subordinate people of this plant related to "The King of Iron" with great respect and sympathy, but his wife was openly disliked and feared. Short, dense, with a village accent, Elizabeth kept throughout her life the old habits of those revolutionary women of 1917 who wore a triangular red kerchief and a revolver under a belt. In a very peculiar way she managed to combine this habit with the manners of the privileged Communist party mistress, taking for granted the status of the wife of a superior. As the head of the personnel department, she was connected directly with the KGB, and sometimes she enjoyed abusing her position to make the workers of the plant feel her power.

Eventually Elizabeth became addicted to deciding human destinies. Overbearing, rude, cruel, petty and insincere, she managed to ruin many lives, while she remained convinced of her public importance. Elizabeth did not stand on ceremony with her children either. She provided material benefits for them, but never cared about their emotions, moods or feelings because it was never occurred to her that her children had any inner life. According to her, the purpose of their existence was to strengthen the authority of the family: everyone should have been aware that their family was the best, exemplary and orderly, a subject of admiration and envy. The opinion of friends, acquaintances and even strangers was extremely important to Elizabeth. Her son and daughter were supposed to be absolutely obedient and excellent students, so the parents could be proud of them. Indeed, they were perfect students, since they had inherited their father's abilities, and they obeyed their mother unconditionally.

However, their psyches had been broken, with obvious signs of neurosis, which was manifested in a deep submergence of Irma inside herself and in Cyril's secret love of himself. It was not narcissisms, but an all-forgiving love, in virtue of which he called himself affectionately by the pet name *Cyril-chik* in his secret poems, which he wrote since his childhood. The siblings were attached to each other completely and painfully, with a tinge of tragedy.

Elizabeth announced proudly to everybody that their daughter after graduating from the high school as an honor student was admitted to the Leningrad's Chemical-Technological College. Irma did not share her mother's pride, believing that there was nothing unusual in this event, but she was happy to be a college student and studied with pleasure. A slightly sad reverie was her usual state. She maintained a good relationship with her classmates, but tried to avoid noisy and merry student parties.

Irma was a very pleasant and pretty girl: the seriousness of her intelligent eyes was softened by the oval of her face and the infant plumpness of her lips, usually composed in a slight smile. Long, silky thick braids, inherited from distant Kalmyk ancestors, suited her, and at the same time, gave her a subtle shade of tragedy. She was devoid of any trace of pride or vanity, but a dignity was clearly manifested, though unobtrusively. An ideal listener, she never confided to her girlfriends; the depth of her soul was closed to everybody. Irma never possessed any arrogance, rudeness or vulgarity, in direct contrast to her mother. Her naturalness and modesty could have won her many friends, but some slight chill emanated from her, and she has always shied away quietly from friendship.

After the first term, which Irma passed with all "excellent" marks, she fell seriously ill. The cold and wet weather of Leningrad was too different from her native hot and dry climate. She was hospitalized with acute pleurisy. The disease lasted, Irma waned, and doctors recommended taking a break for a year. She wanted to return home to recover, but her parents strongly opposed this. Her mother told her by telephone there should be no breaks in school and that both her parents would not tolerate the interruption of Irma's study. Their daughter must finish college on time and as an honor student. There should not be any disruptions or failures in the family of the Chief Engineer.

Irma continued to study, receiving "A" in all subjects, but making up the lost time with difficulty and tension. A weakness overcame her, joy faded, and the long cold winter guided her to the saddest thoughts. Her only consolation was her brother. He was a little gruff, sometimes even vulgar, but always gentle to his younger sister. He worried about her state, and tried to cheer her.

Shy northern spring lifted Irma's mood; her studies went easier, becoming more interesting for her. Then the summer came, and Leningrad appeared before her in all its glory. She did not hurry home for summer vacation, spending long hours walking along the streets of the gorgeous northern capital.

The second term was quite successful. Irma became closer to her classmates. She still was not taking part in the noisy parties and skits, but she worked with pleasure on the students' newspaper, because she could draw well. Teachers praised her not only for her ability, but also for a diligence rare for her age.

The love between Irma and Julius began with an unusual and dramatic event, clearly indicating the affinity of their souls. Both of them took the news of Cyril's marriage as a misfortune. But if the cause for Irma's despair was the same as that for Julius, the reason for this was quite different: she thought she has lost her brother, the only person close and dear to her, and she felt betrayed and intolerably lonely.

Irma was so upset and miserable, she could not go to the newlyweds for a few days, wandering through the gloomy city cemetery and trying to commit suicide by cutting her wrist. When she appeared finally in a dormitory of the College of Mines, the sleeve of her winter coat was saturated with blood; she was deathly pale and could hardly stand. Her brother was absent, and Julius, who lived in the same room, met Irma kindly. He bandaged Irma's wounded wrist with all sympathy, and put her on Cyril's bed to rest.

By a strange coincidence, or because of the similarity of their psyches, both of them, Irma and Julius, decided to part life almost at the same time, and at the same occasion, and both were unable to complete it. The burning pain of the razor blade cut frightened Irma and sobered her. It seemed the same thing was happening with Julius, and now, looking at Irma, he was painfully aware of her suffering.

Irma was lying on the bed lifeless. Her full lips were slightly parted and created the impression of childish helplessness. Her long thick braids were rolled up on her chest on top of the blanket like two snakes. It gave her a mystical charm. Julius was afraid to breathe from awe, and at the same time he was scared that Irma would never open her eyes.

Fortunately, she did open them when Cyril and his wife May came back. The young couple was terrified seeing bloodstained clothes and Irma's bloodless face. They caressed her, surrounded her with warmth and comfort, demonstrating that her despair was only the fruit of a sick imagination. She had not lost her brother and would never lose him.

The gloomy thoughts in Irma's head dissipated, and Julius finished her recovery by falling his ardent love upon her. The traces of the recent suicide attempt had not yet healed, but Julius fell in love with Irma with the same passionate desperation as he had with May. Fortunately this time he was more successful and happy. Irma had dreamed of him since she wore her schoolgirl uniform. The mere fact that he was a close friend of her beloved brother set him apart from all others. In addition, Julius' excellent ability and pleasant intelligent appearance made him irresistible to Irma.

Julius' last year at the College of Mine was filled with intensive studies and passionate love. However, the relationship between the young lovers was not always cloudless: their fervent meetings after the lectures were often followed by short arguments when Irma's eyes became dark with suffering, and Julius' expression changed to desperation. Then the lost paradise returned by the magic of reconciliation, and the partings of the two lovers were long and made with assurances of eternal devotion and hot kisses.

They registered their marriage without any pomp, because they wanted to stay in the nirvana of happiness, and any diversion from this heavenly state by earthly vanity was unbearable to them. Only one thing seemed strange: when May sincerely and warmly congratulated Julius on his happy marriage, he fell into a strange, frightening nervousness not responding, looking aside, and his hands began to tremble. May hastened to say goodbye, startled by this strange reaction.

Julius and Irma rented a small apartment and they lived there as a happy young couple. Within three months Irma was pregnant. The future father was thrilled.

Cyril and May went to the far southern city, to Almaty, after their graduation from the College of Mines to begin their life as geologists. Julius and Irma decided to visit Irma's parents, so Julius could meet his father and mother-in-law. The young husband spent only a few hours in the house of his new relatives: he hurried to fly farther, to join Cyril and Maya. Luckily Julius' parents and sister lived in Almaty, where he would begin his career. They were happy to see Julius and looked forward to meeting his young wife.

The city where Irma and her brother Cyril grew up was located in the middle of a desert, on the edge of a big lake feeding a huge metallurgic plant, which belched flames and clouds day and night.

After returning from cold and wet Leningrad, Irma was happy to feel the dry desert air so familiar to her. Hot and sleepy summer and the spacious house surrounded by a garden promised peace and rest to Irma so needed by her. When the ceremony of introducing her parents to their son-in-law accompanied by a plentiful dinner ended, and Julius left for the airport, Irma was alone in her room. She stretched out happily on warm sheets, engrossed by her thoughts of the recent events and smiling at them. She did not want to tell her parents about her pregnancy, it was a sweet secret, warming her heart and inextricably connecting her with Julius.

The next morning the dazzling sun greeted Irma, and she recalled a pleasant feeling of carefree school holidays. She jumped happily out of her bed and was overcome suddenly by an irresistible wave of nausea: the little creature inside of her announced his presence. Irma thought with terror of greasy fried eggs, sizzling on the stove in the kitchen where the family usually ate breakfast. She went back to bed to rest a little more and than went to the kitchen managing a cheerful smile. No matter how Irma tried to overcome nausea, when fat yolk touched her lips, a spasm stopped up her throat, and she jumped in time to run to the bathroom. Her mother frowned comprehensively:

"Pregnant?" Irma nodded.

"Look here, my dear, I'll tell you: until you've finished college - no children!"

"But Julius wants a baby..."

"Wha-a-at?"

This vulgar " Wha-a-at ", which mother always used as an expression of extreme contempt and anger, made Irma shiver.

"He is not able to stand on his own feet, but he dictates already?! You think we strained ourselves to make it possible for you to study in college in order to become a housekeeper for Julius? Do you know how much we have invested in your staying in Leningrad during these four years? And now all this is for nothing?! How long are you pregnant?"

"Two and a half months."

"Just the time. Tomorrow you will have an abortion. Here all the doctors are our friends or acquaintances. At first, you get a diploma, and then you can bear children!"

The next morning Elizabeth took Irma's hand firmly and

authoritatively and led her to the doctor, with whom everything had been arranged.

Irma felt a strange emptiness, as if she had lost a part of her soul along with a tiny fetus. How could she tell Julius? Would he be angry or calmly accept the news that she ended the pregnancy against his wishes? Logic dictated that at the last and most important year in the University it would be wise not to burden herself with a baby.

It was difficult in those days to phone to other cities, but Irma knew Julius would certainly call. When the telephone rang, she experienced mixed feelings: the joy of forthcoming talk with her husband mingled with anxiety of how she would tell him what had happened.

Julius was happy to hear Irma's voice. He started to describe to her how the relatives here in Almaty were waiting for her. It calmed her, and his obvious love warmed her. That was why Irma confessed simply and directly that she had had an abortion when Julius asked her about her state. Silence fell at the other end of the line, and Irma heard a short buzzing. She started to dial again thinking there was the problem with the phone line. No one responded for a long time. Finally Irma heard the voice of Anna, Julius' mother: "Irma, dear, I do not know what happened, but Julius locked himself in his room, and he is not answering my knock." Irma's heart fell.

No letters, or phone call came during the next week. Irma could not calm her anxiety. Her mother reassured her that Julius "has sown his wild oats and settled down", but those assurances did not help her. Irma sent a letter to Julius with long explanations, so uncharacteristic for her discreet nature. She assured Julius of her love, asking him to forgive her and to write. Julius was stubbornly silent. The time came to visit Julius and his family at Almaty, as they had arranged. Irma was packing her suitcase when Anna, Julius' mother, called. She advised Irma with an apologizing and gentle voice not to come to their house now, but wait until the conflict exhausted itself. As Irma understood, Julius did not want to see her. Stunned by his sudden cruelty and hostility, she went to Leningrad to finish her studies and wait.

The months passed but Julius remained silent. Irma was a very good student as usual, but neither the strenuous schooling nor the college's routine distracted her from thinking about Julius and their former enormous love, and how their happiness suddenly snapped.

Now it was complete rejection instead of love. Irma could not understand and accept this.

She was alone in cold Leningrad, without the usual support of her brother and, more important, without the love to which she had devoted her whole heart. She sent Julius letters in desperation and waited, and waited. He was silent.

The autumn and winter passed, and spring came. Leningrad thawed after the severe cold; big slabs of ice floated down the Neva River. The northern, rain-washed blue sky appeared through gray clouds, and May fever swept through the college dormitory life. Only Irma could not wake up from the icy paralysis of spirit and depression. The whole year had not brought any relief nor broken Julius' stubbornness. She was never a social person, but after the summer conflict, she shrank into a shell of gloom. Thoughts about Julius and her misfortune became her constant and only companions.

Irma was one of five Honor graduate students who were awarded a diploma in a solemn ceremony in the big college hall. She received a congratulatory telegram from her parents, but nothing from Julius. Nothing! One could go mad from this. The heavy stone, which lay at her heart, became harder, and her depression deepened. However, Irma still believed that in one wonderful day, the most joyous day, Julius would say, as before, that he could not live without her, and this time of painful experience would pass like a nightmare.

The coming summer required an answer to the confusing question, what to do next? Since Irma was married, she was given a free diploma, without specifying the location of future work. Irma had to seek a job by herself. She could not join Julius. It was clear that he did not want to see her. She took the only possible solution, to return to her parents, live with them, work at the Metallurgical plant and wait for Julius.

Her mother met her not too affably. "You're a married woman. Why are you going to live with your parents and work here? What will people think about that? Your father is a very popular person here. Everybody knows our family, and what will people say? Well, you can stay here for a couple of days and then you should go to your rightful place. Your father himself will take you to your husband! ".

And he did. When father and daughter came out of the station in Almaty, they saw a wide sun-drenched straight street before them. Two rows of tall, slender poplars and two narrow irrigation ditches, which gurgled with clear water, decorated this street. Just behind the verdant city, snowy sky-high mountain peaks rose so beautifully in their unexpected nearness that Irma involuntarily stopped in amazement. Her father impatiently called her, and they hurried to the trolley bus.

Anna opened the door. Irma's father put her suitcases on the doorstep. "This is your daughter-in -law." Then he turned angrily and walked away, not adding a single word of greeting or farewell.

Julius' parents were extremely tactful people, intelligent and kind. They tried their best to make Irma feel welcome in the new house. It was not easy. Julius reacted to Irma's arrival as if it was not his business. He was not at home, already working at the geological expedition along with Cyril and May, and not planning to go back home till November. All geologists had the right to take a break for a few days and go to the city if they wanted to. Cyril and May went to Almaty two times during the summer, but Julius did not use this opportunity even once.

Djungarian Ala-Tau at the border with China, where the geologists worked, was magnificent with snow-capped mountains, slopes covered with dense forests, cliffs and waterfalls. The geological routes through these uninhabited, inaccessible places were difficult. They climbed ridges, cliffs and went dizzyingly downhill, but Julius enjoyed this. He went back to his tent, tired but content. There could be nothing better for his unbalanced, nervous nature than the constant physical exertion, the primal nature, fresh air and relative independence.

When he learned about Irma's pregnancy last spring, the prospect of becoming a father thrilled him and raised his importance in his own eyes. The news about the termination infuriated him not because of the loss of a child for whom he felt nothing, but because this was done against his wishes and will. His pride was deeply wounded; and he could not forgive the insult. Now he enjoyed the opportunity to avenge his in-laws and all the family who did not take him seriously. He knew very well, what a powerful weapon he chose - to ignore their existence completely. It was difficult to say whether this was the result of his psychological disorder, or his extreme selfishness. It is impossible to understand how this sadistic mentality arose in Julius, who was brought up in a kind, intelligent and tactful family. This handsome and slender young man, who did not show cruelty outwardly, had found the way to keep three families in maddening suspense. His love, which until recently could reach ecstasy, changed to cold pleasure in torturing his former subject of worship. And he continued this policy of silence, holding Irma on a short leash.

Cyril never spoke to Julius about the conflict with his sister, believing it was impossible to intervene in the affairs of newly married couples. May did not agree with him. She knew in her heart it was an unhealthy, abnormal situation, and she pleaded with Cyril to talk to Julius. Cyril refused to do this even when another person appeared on the stage. It became clear that Julius often visited the tent of a young and pretty draftswoman, Olga. Julius did it with a challenge, almost bragging, openly spending all his spare time with his new passion. May was horrified at the thought of what would happen to Irma, when rumors about Julius' affair reached her. She decided to intervene. The conversation turned out to be a strange and discouraging monologue. Julius was silent and in response to all May's accusations and warnings about possible tragic consequences, he gazed blindly at her; only his hands were nervously shivering. "Cyril," May admonished her husband, "Julius is just crazy, you need to save Irma from him somehow!" Cyril's answer was the same as before. "I have no right to interfere with their private lives, let them solve this situation by themselves."

Julius' parents tried to mitigate the cruelty of their son, but the fact remained apparent, any attempt to reach him failed, he ignored their letters where they begged him to bring certainty in this unbearable situation. Irma continued to live with her in–laws, but she suffered, knowing that her whole world had been destroyed, that she ceased to be loved. Her parents did not want her to stay at their house and she become totally dependent on her husband's family in such an ambiguous situation. Depression converted to disease, her friendliness transformed into dull politeness. Anna and her husband, Victor, were increasingly oppressed by their daughter-in-law's condition. Irma was tight-lipped, immersed in the darkness of her sorrow. They pleaded with Julius to do something, but in his rare letters, he simply ignored the existence of his young wife.

In mid-summer Cyril and May went home for a few days from the geological expedition, and by that time Elizabeth arrived to meet her children. She visited Irma and had a conversation with Anna, as if there were no problems for the young family, and everything was fine. With her farewell, Elisabeth ordered her daughter, "Be part of the family, settle down. No foolishness, no thoughts about divorces, I don't want to hear about it!"

In September, Irma found work as a junior scientist at the laboratory of the Research Institute of Chemistry. The interesting new job somehow diminished the pain of Julius' silence. Soon Irma, together with her young colleagues, was sent to the nearest collective farm for two weeks to help the peasants gather the apple harvest. This helped Irma. She was in the midst of her fellows, with the comradeship between all of them and with the vivacity, proper to youth. Irma came back refreshed and, to some extent, thawed from her protracted depression. By this time Cyril and May returned from the expedition. They brought news, which stung Irma. Julius had decided to remain with the expedition until January as a chief of the drilling team. Despite the dashed hope of ending the long and tormented wait for Julius, the arrival of Cyril and May brought in Irma's life a kinship of love and warm care. She often visited them; usually the brother and sister went for a walk and a long talk. There was a good and friendly relationship between May and Irma, but Irma was never frank and open and frank with her sister-in-law, who was too shy to ask questions or talk about the young family's problem.

In the laboratory, Irma won praise as a talented, orderly worker with a sense of responsibility. She was too serious for her age, and this contributed to the benevolent and respectful attitude towards her. Maybe it would be better if Julius never came back to Almaty, would leave Irma forever, just disappeared. But he returned to his family from the expedition around New Year's Day.

The meeting was tense and grim. Under the guise of calmness Irma hid her disturbance; her heart pounding so strong that she felt dizzy. Julius behaved as if he returned not to his family, where he was so impatiently expected, but to slightly bored neighbors. Everybody was disappointed, upset, but none of the members of the family displayed or discussed their sentiments. Julius left to rest immediately after his arrival and came back only for the family dinner. At the table, he supported meaningless conversation without engaging in it. Anna felt her nerves and heart had begun to fail. She took a pill before going to bed, deciding not to intervene into the life of the young couple and hoping that everything would settle somehow.

That night Julius slept apart, turning away from Irma. She was lying with her eyes wide open; the tears rolling down slowly to her pillow. Early in the morning she got up and went to her laboratory.

Anna was right. The relationship between Julius and Irma had been established in some way, but happiness did not return to them, giving way to a dull, inexpressive everyday life, with small talks and brief quarrels, which passed without reconciliation to the same unemotional routine. Outwardly, at least, it looked decent, and the parents were satisfied.

Spring came in March, and the sun shone brighter and longer. At that time, Julius declared that he was going to leave for ten days on a business trip to the mine. There was nothing strange or unusual in that, but Irma felt uncomfortable. Perhaps the departure of Julius reminded of the her recent painful waiting for him. However Julius came back just in time, and it seemed he even missed his wife. It was enough for Irma to believe in the return of good fortune; she revived, and Julius parents saw her friendly and affectionate smile for the first time.

The next day Irma and Julius went to their work together: Julius headed to the Geological Survey, Irma hurried to the Research Institute of Chemistry. Both buildings were located on the same street separated only by two small blocks. The morning was wonderful with fresh, fragrant air, clear blue skies and cheerful spring drippings, in which the sun shimmered. The trolley was crowded, Irma and Julius stood almost pressed to each other. Irma was smiling at her inner thoughts when she heard a loud voice from nearby. "Hello, Julius! How was your time with Olga at the resort? I am sure you had ten sweet days!" Julius replied in a sluggish voice: "Yes, I did."

Irma was shocked. "This could not be!" She searched for Julius' eyes with her inquiring glance, but he turned away, suddenly becoming infinitely distant from her. At the first stop, he got off the trolley and walked away. Blood pounded in Irma's temples, her mouth was dry. At that moment, she forgot where she was. The sun, sky, people, all were gone; there remained only her breaking heart, a terrible feeling of loneliness, misery and humiliation. And then the whole last year appeared before her mind in all its pitiless clarity. Lie! Dirty, banal, trivial lie! Proud and puritanical-clean, Irma has been the victim of a vulgar vaudeville all this time. There were some vile scenes behind her back, and now nothing remained for her but to meet pitying and ambiguous glances, and pretend that everything was right.

Irma gasped, "No! No and no! All this was filth and lie! Filth and lie! It is better to disappear forever. Yes! This is the way! To disappear, not to be a nuisance to anyone, and to stop this torture!"

Irma jumped off the trolley and hurried toward the institute with one thought, "Quickly! Quickly!" Stairs, offices, laboratory..., she rushed into the closet where the chemicals were kept. Then she opened a strongbox with her key. Hurry! Hurry to stop this unbearable pain.

She was given one moment, only one moment, to realize how life was huge and beautiful and how this little sadist was insignificant. She had only a second to shout, "What have I done!" And darkness fell.

Bright sun! Put out your light,
And let the rain shed tears,
The falling star, cross out the night,
The young life disappears.

I WILL NEVER FORGET

Nica stood at the window leaning her forehead against the cold glass. She was hypnotized by the faded spot in the streetlight where snow flows swept; circling, rising and falling. Wind tore them and threw them in the darkness. The commotion outside the window was a match for what she felt. It seemed that the snowstorm would be forever, and forever she would be anxious and lonely. Nica lost track of time, benumbed by this gloomy picture outside when a sharp ringing of the telephone broke the complete silence of the room and returned her to reality. She looked at the clock; it was almost midnight. Nica picked up the phone with a pounding heart, and in the same instance, the snowstorm and all worlds around her ceased to exist. A painfully familiar voice was telling Nica something in the receiver. She had not heard this voice for a long time and thought she would never hear it again. The words were difficult for her to comprehend through an overcoming excitement.

"Yes, yes, it is me, Nica. Where are you?

"I am very close to you, only three floors above, at your neighbor's apartment. They are out of town and left me the key, so I am all alone here waiting for you. I know it is late, but I just arrived; and it is too long to wait until morning. Could you come up here?"

"You... it is... you? Or yes, yes, of course! I am coming. I am coming right now!"

"Don't run, take the elevator. I will have the door open for you."

It was unbelievable. Nica was confused and enormously happy. "How could it be? How could it be? He is here, so close?" She waited for him many years, knowing that she should not wait. She hoped, knowing there was no hope. And now she was going to see him.

The elevator was slow. It would be too long to wait, so happy as a lark, Nica ran up passing one floor, another. She remembered involuntarily that long-long ago when she was only twelve, the steps were flashing under her feet the same way. How easily and effortless she ran up the staircase in those long past days, how lighthearted and carefree she was!

It happened in late autumn, yet the bright Asian sun streamed through the big dusty windows of the doorway of the four-story apartment house. Merry noises came from the backyard full of children.

"Geese, geese, ga–ga-ga.

Do you want to eat?"

"Yea, yea, yea".

On the third floor of the House of Professors in the bright apartment of Nica's happy childhood, her family and the family of her uncle waited for her. Nica did not guess that she was running to the first meeting with Cherdar.

Their fathers, Raslan and Bulat, were cousins connected not only by kinship, but also by close friendship and mutual affection. As adults, they chose different professions and went separate ways. Raslan became a geologist and Bulat was an actor and producer; but throughout their lives they maintained their fraternal feelings. It was not surprising because family ties were always strong and important in Caucasian Osetia, the tiny republic of the enormous Soviet Union where both of them were born. And right now the family of Bulat came from a faraway city to the sunny capital of Kazakhstan with green lines of tall slender poplars and murmuring irrigation ditches, *aryks,* along the streets.

Both families gathered around a festive table, but Nica was late. She flew up the stairs, opened the door and immediately found herself in the arms of her cheerful, merrymaking and extremely handsome uncle Bulat, or Bibo, as he was lovingly called by his friends and relatives. He whirled her, laughing, joking, and Nica fell in love with him in the same instance, as did her sister May and all who ever met him. Two boys rose from the table to get acquainted with her. A thin, small, funny and awkward one came close to Nica and told her in sarcastic voice. "Here she is, a still unknown celebrity, making everyone wait for a look, as befits a real prima donna". Nica felt at a loss from this confusing verbiage and forgot to greet the older boy, who did not say anything, but smiled pleasantly.

Bibo was invited as a producer at the local Theater of Young Spectator, and all his artistic family became frequent and welcome guests in Nica's parent's house. Usually there were only three of them, the uncle and both boys. Their strict, stiff and a bit standoffish mother rarely appeared. Nica and May eagerly waited for their uncle and the boys; and their impatience was always fully rewarded by Bibo's witty, amusing and funny inventions. No one could resist his charm, even the girls' serious and always busy father, Raslan broke away from his desk to be included in the merriment. Uncle's jokes were funny, but always good-humored and kind because kindness was something as natural for him as his laughter and gaiety. Bibo mastered the secret of happiness remaining his entire lifetime a big, kind and loving child.

Nica and May were reluctant to let Bibo and the boys go home when the time was approaching ten o'clock. Nica secretly admired the boys, especially Cherdar, and no wonder. Both brothers were very gifted, always busy inventing something and their school grades consisted of A, while Nica's grades were quite diverse.

Fourteen-year-old Cherdar and twelve-year-old Muraz inherited a sense of humor and artistry from their father and took seriousness from their dried–up and strict mother. For all their love for fun, they could not match their irrepressibly gay father.

Cherdar was much taller and stronger than his younger brother. He resembled his Russian mother, who was far less beautiful than Bibo, but she had a visage of utter intelligence characteristic of hereditary noble families. Cherdar's appearance was pleasant but undistinguished except for the clarity and purity of his eyes. His Ossetian name sounded funny in the absence of any Caucasian features.

It was impossible to tell whom his younger brother, Muras resembled, certainly not his mother or father. He was too small, thin and frail for his age. And definitely ugly. This Ugly Duckling shared the fate of his prototype from the famous fairy tale. He grew up to be a tall and handsome well-known physicist. His Caucasian appearance became pronounced and mixed with his Russian features made his face look romantic and noble. At the time when Nica met him she did not know he would be her soul–brother for life.

From the very first day, there was a warm and sincere affection between all four cousins.

At this time the Theatre of Young Spectator resembled a Magic Box, thanks to the diligence of the famous producer, Natalia Satz. The Soviet Government exiled her from Moscow to Almaty for her views on art that diverged from the establishment. She managed to convert an old miserable theatre building into a wonderful impersonation of the fairy tale. The young audience went with delight through the Wonder Rooms made for them by her bright talent in this impoverished post–war time of 1949. Natalia Satz's wonderful innovations brought so much joy to children that the evil people who were envious accused her of formality, which in that time was quite a crime. It is difficult to understand now what they meant by this term, and why it was a crime. But anyway, she was exiled to a region even more remote than Almaty. Natalia Satz disappeared, but the fruits of her labors were not so easily destroyed by a frightened Administration of the theatre, and magic corners persisted for a long time.

Bibo was invited to the Theatre of Young Spectator about two years after this. He and his family lodged inside the theatre. Two screens in one of the "Wonder Rooms" enclosed a corner with enormous colorful butterflies on the walls and a ceiling painted as a bright blue sky with white clouds. All the family was located in the small space of this tiny corner. These eternal nomads who went from one city to another did not have any possessions beside the very necessities, but the concept of poverty did not exist for them. Their lives were completely filled with the theatre.

Nica and May loved to go to this very unusual apartment to visit the Bibo family. In the evening, the young actors gathered in the hall with the bright butterflies on the walls, and different games began. The most popular was Sheep Head, the repetition of words with constant addition. It required a good memory. The very first time Nica repeated a set of these random words; but she missed the last one that she failed to hear because of excitement. Nica lost the game, remaining on the sideline. It was very embarrassing for her and she looked at May and Cherdar waiting for their encouragement, but they were too busy to notice it. The merry and noisy game was going on, and suddenly Nica felt sad and lonely in the middle of all the excitement. At this moment uncle Bibo purposely mixed up all the words, making them sound funny and in rhyme, then hugged Nica and announced a beginning of a new game, charades.

After two years, this restless family left Almaty. Bibo received an invitation from another theatre at the big city of Rostov. The cousins parted in tears.

The years were passing by. The two families corresponded, but not often. Nica and May spent long, boring days at school waiting for summer when they would go with their parents on the geological expedition. They knew Cherdar also spent summers with his aunt–geologist and dreamed of meeting him somewhere on the abundant steppe. Strange enough, it actually happened. On one pitch-dark night, a Moscow geological party was leaving a small Academy base, when a big caravan of cars headed by Raslan entered it. The departing and arriving parties stopped to greet each other, as was the custom among geologists. Suddenly Nica heard Cherdar's voice calling her father's name. She jumped out of the jeep happy to meet him. They barely could see each other in the pitch darkness of the night. They had time only to exchange a few goofy words, but before parting Cherdar told Nica almost in the whisper, "I would like you to promise me something"

"What is it?"

"Never-never forget me."

"I will never forget you!" Nica put all her heart in these words.

Cherdar lightly embraced her for a brief moment.

This meeting and its happiness warmed Nica for long time.

* * *

The school graduation party did not at all resemble the beauty of the same event in the movies Nica had seen. It began with a solemn, long, boring speech by the Principal, and then the schoolgirl–graduates danced to the ill–played music of a small orchestra. They danced *la cherie with la ma cherie* as they called it on defacing French when a girl danced with a girl. Boys from the neighboring school stood huddled in the corner feeling like fish out of water. It was understandable. Schooling was in this time separate for girls and boys. Clumsy guests, who hardly heard of something too *bourgeois* as gentleman manners, shunned girls. The girls were not much better. It was a dull and awkward atmosphere at the party. Jokes, laughter and brilliant wit were, it seemed, only in the movies.

"It looks like Cherdar came from another world," Nica mused watching the guests. It was true; he was so different from these clumsy boys who shifted from one foot to the other, to hide their awkwardness. Everything would be different for Nica if only Cherdar were there. She thought about it and involuntarily a New Year's masquerade party four years ago came to her mind. The Principal of her school invited boys from Boys School to this masquerade party, and it happened to be one where her cousins studied. The girls prepared for this unusual event beforehand with great emotion, each excelling on devising costumes. Nica was wearing a skirt in black and white cells sewn by her mother from starched gauze, and a magnificent Chess Knight made by her father from whatman paper decorated her head. The boys also tried their best. Cherdar wore a stunning Corsair costume converted from old theatrical rags.

It was forbidden for sixth grade girls and boys to dance together, so the games began after some traditional performance on the school stage. The party would have been fine had the Principal not taken notes during the Post Office game. The next day's investigation and trial caused a lot of tears. Among confiscated notes was one which written for Nica. It was in rhymes in Russian.

If you threw the gauntlet
Down in the arena of wild lions,
I would rush to pick it up
Without second thought.
I would die for you gladly!

Nica recognized immediately the author of this note. Cherdar loved the Russian poet, Jukovsky and, of course, his poem Gauntlet. The Principal had never heard about this poem, and the note struck her as immoral. Nica was given severe censure for provoking the wild imagination of a boy. In the office of the principal she felt awful. But back at home Cherdar made a funny performance depicting the formidable Principal, Nica trembling with fear, the Corsair fighting with this lion, and even the roaring lion itself. He was so good in these parodies that all the family laughed to tears.

But it happened long ago, and now the Rubicon had been crossed, and the school with Nica's childhood remained on the other side. She received a School–Leaving Certificate, and this was of major importance. It allowed her to enter university. Her sister May was already a Leningrad, St. Petersburg now, University student, but Nica dreamed about the Capital. She knew Cherdar studied in this huge Moscow University.

It was very difficult for Nica to part from her parents; they always were the most important persons in her life. In spite of the strong desire to meet Cherdar, she hesitated to leave her warm and loving home; but her father wanted her to have a good education, and Moscow University was the best.

Eight strict exams were passed with the necessary A in July; and in September Nica was in a whirlwind of student life. It was difficult, but exciting and interesting. Lectures, parties, visits with the student group to the movie, and long hours of study in the library, everything made Nica happy.

Cherdar was close and that was the main reason for joy. Often when Nica hurried along the street to meet him, she looked at unfamiliar faces of pedestrians streaming toward her and thought, "If you only knew who is waiting for me! Yes, he is waiting and maybe worried that I am not there yet. Could such happiness be?" She was overwhelmed with emotions and almost flying, tapping easily and quickly with the high heels of her shoes. "Could such a joy be?" Nica thought at the party with Cherdar and his friends, listening to Cherdar's soft and wonderfully pleasant voice. She was afraid to believe in the miracle that she was here with him, and he, so remarkable and unique, loved her. Yes, he loved her; she could see it in every one of his affectionate glances, in every note of his voice. His friends noticed it too. "They look at me with interest and benevolence because I am connected to Cherdar, to their wonderful and remarkable friend, "Nica thought with a thrill of joy again.

Cherdar lived in a university dormitory, but Nica moved to her aunt's, her father's cousin Kosha, whom Nica had adored since childhood. Her caring parents feared the bohemian atmosphere of the University dormitory, but they had no idea that Nica lived in classic "La Bohem" now. Her kindest aunt, Kosha and her husband, Emil were circus actors; and the circus filled their home completely. Uncle Emil Kio was a very famous magician with a distinguished appearance and the manners of an important diplomat. Announcements about his performances were all over Moscow. The Soviet Government liked him and gave him some privileges; a much higher than other actor's salary, a good apartment with three big rooms and a spacious kitchen, a luxury by Soviet standards in this time. And last, but not least, his family had permission to buy food in a special, privileged, closed-to-the-ordinary-people store.

Lilliputians scattered from Nica like peas when she opened the door of the apartment. They were also actors of the circus, and they acted, worked, as they always the Uncle Emil corrected Nica. From the beginning Nica felt awkward in the presence of the Uncle Emil's tiny partners. She pitied them and was taken aback by their Lilliputians figures. After a while this creepy feeling passed, but she still felt embarrassed and uncomfortable when the peewee coquettes flirted with a huge heavy juggler-heavy athlete.

The house of Nica's dear relatives began to fill with guests at noon. There was no end of jokes, anecdotes and all sorts of actor's inventions. Grand Magus Emil Kio usually looked at this commotion, sitting in his big armchair and from time to time giving leisurely replicas. Cherdar had often visited this incredible house, entering the mutual merriment as a duck takes to water. Uncle Emil liked Cherdar and

Nica, he asked about their studies in the University and treated them with chocolate candies from a gorgeous box. Sometimes he took them to the circus, and they watched his performance, which always began with his driving a luxury car into the arena. Back then it produced a far greater impression than something like that would now. A car was a special privilege and luxury. The glossy varnished automobile made a circle around the arena, then a servant with absolute respect opened the door for Emil. He came out with all the magnificence of Magus in a black tuxedo with a shining white shirt–front. Large gold–rimmed spectacles decorated his handsome, significant face. He acted as a conductor performing miracles on the stage, and never revealed his secrets even to his closest relatives. Nica got to know about only one trick. Emil told her how this magic worked because he tried to persuade her to be a main figure in the trick. The scenario was as follows: a young houri, Nica dressed in something shiny was to be carried in a cage to the very center of the arena. She had to do a graceful curtsey in all directions. Then Emil waved a magic wand. The light would wink, and the houri, Nica was to turn into a roaring lion. No one should notice that in a split second of darkness she had to be swallowed in one manhole; and the lion had to be catapulted out from another one. "Don't be afraid of the lion," Emil told Nica. It looks fierce but it is so old we feed it from a baby bottle." It was not the lion that Nica feared; she knew for this trick she could expect from her dear father a scolding far more fearful than a roar from an actor with a mane.

After the performance all the actors always went to a restaurant for a good party; and Grand Magus Emil paid for everybody with the careless gesture of a king. No libations were allowed. Emil could not stand drunkenness, which was quite unusual for Russian actors.

The night events were not finished yet. The real merriment began at the apartment of the magician and continued till 2–3 in the morning when everything went quiet and calm till noon. This was the everyday life of circus actors, a shift from the schedule of ordinary mortals by about 5–6 hours.

* * *

The specialization at the University began in the third year, and

189

Nica chose microbiology. Great Men looked at her from the walls of a big laboratory, Pasteur, Koch, Metchnikoff, and Bering. She liked to stay there studying till late. In the winter, darkness came early, and Nica saw through the windows the ocean of city lights and in the pane her own reflection, dressed in a white lab coat. It was so tempting for her to imagine that she reveals together with Koch the secret of tuberculosis, or saving children from diphtheria with Emil Behring. And sure enough, Nica dreamed of one day making her own discovery. With excitement she put a drop from the flask on the microscope slide and touched her eye to the cold surface of the ocular. And one day... it was difficult to believe! Koch toiled in his lab almost all his life before making his discovery. Impatient Pasteur worked for long years; but she, Nica, just a student, was already making a discovery. But it was so obvious. She saw on the slide a new type of microbe, totally different from all described in textbooks. Choked with emotion, she broke away from the microscope to calm down. A minute later Nica looked again. No, it was not a delusion, she saw them clearly, and she was absolutely sure this elongated form of microbes with a characteristic curve had never been demonstrated to them as students. But she did not want to believe so easily in her discovery. She took calmly and professionally a full pipette from the turbid liquid in the flask and put it to the fresh nutrient medium, like the great Koch himself would do.

Nica did not sleep well that night. She could not bring herself to swallow breakfast. The way to the University was painfully slow, but finally she was there. Her heart skipped a beat. The liquid in the flask was visibly turbid. With trembling hand Nica put a drop onto the microscope slide. The microbes were here and all the same with elongated form and characteristic curve.

"What are you doing here so early in the morning?" It was a professor's assistant. Overly excited Nica could not talk; she silently pointed to the slide. Neatly arranged assistant's curls bent over the microscope, her right hand slightly corrected a tip–off. "This is the most common type of bacteria Escherichia coli". The assistant continued to talk explaining something, but Nica could not hear her. She almost pushed the assistant from the microscope and stared at the image swimming in front of her eyes. It was a well known bacterium to her. Nica touched the fine adjustment on the microscope, and her face became red from embarrassment. She realized painfully clearly:

the cause of all excitement was an incorrect leveling. Her discovery was the tiny cracks in the glass of the slide.

In the evening, Nica told with chagrin and embarrassment the whole story to Cherdar. He laughed, but so kindly and lovingly that it made Nica happy again. They felt wonderfully good holding hands and going together along the crowded street of flamboyant Moscow. Nica laughed now too, remembering dramatic details of her scientific research. She thought she would never exchange the joy filling her heart for a sparkling fame. Her happiness was absolute in these minutes.

"It is important to make discoveries", Cherdar told her, "but it is a hundred times more important not to kill existing ones, as your colleague Lysenko has been doing"

"Oh, I didn't tell you the most important news. Professor Kukuev found me today and gave me the manuscript of Medvedev that is prohibited to read by censorship. This scientist wrote about it, about the atrocities of Lysenko."

"How do you know professor Kukuev, and why would he trust you? It is so dangerous to distribute banned literature. He could be put in prison for this!"

"Oh, yes, he was in prison already. Do you know why? Only because of he wrote an article about chromosomes. He is a geneticist. My father helped him a lot after he was released from exile; that is why he trusts me. And you are right, it is dangerous to distribute banned literature; but he is determined to let young biologists know what genetic really is. The Professor is eager to reveal the whole truth about Lysenko, his criminal activity and his false postulates. This manuscript is very dear to him. He asked me to read it carefully, and return it to him as soon as possible."

They began to read the precious pages from the manuscript by Jores Medvedev that same evening. There was the brutal and terrible truth of the persecution of the most prominent geneticists of the Soviet Union. There were shocking and heartbreaking revelations of injustice and cruelty in the Soviet system killing the best and the most talented. It was painful to read about this truth and impossible to hide herself from it.

The manuscript was big and it took three evenings to finish. During the night Nica turned in her bed from side to side. Gruesome pictures of the brilliant geneticist, Vavilov's humiliation and torture in prison prevented her from sleeping. Her heart was pounding with pain for him and for all who suffered and were persecuted.

The most disturbing thought was his realization that this cruel injustice continued. Lysenko still prospered despite all his atrocities and crimes. Every holiday his huge portrait was set in a number of Great Figures of the State along the Lenin prospect, where columns of people marched in a festive demonstration. Lysenko still terrorized geneticists; and genetics remained suppressed despite tremendous progress and achievements in this science abroad. Now, two years after Watson and Crick's brilliant discovery of DNA structure, which initiated an intellectual revolution all over the world, here, in the Soviet Union genetics was replaced in every University by the false and primitive Lysenko science. And this so called science was proclaimed as a State law.

Nica and Cherdar put aside the pages they had read, stacking them in a neat pile. It was completely incomprehensible how three pages could have disappeared. They were overcome by fear, not only from the possibility of exposing secret readings of the underground book; but mostly from need to confess loss of these pages to the professor who trusted them, and to whom this manuscript was so dear. Only one solution remained. Whatever it took they must find duplicates. It was easier to do for Nica than for Cherdar. In this time she was an intern in the Research Microbiological Institute and was hoping to find Jores Medvedev himself. And she was lucky. The head of the her lab, professor Maisel with his coworkers were going in three days to present some of their new research at the Obninsk Institute of Medical Science where Jores Medvedev worked. Nica begged them to take her along, and to her delight, he granted her permission.

The way to Obninsk took three hours. Professor Meisel's group entered the big meeting hall when it was already crowded with scientists. Nica looked round, trying to guess who from all these people was Jores.

"Do you see over there, close to the wall a group of three? The one on the right side is Jores."

"But he is very young!"

"Oh no, he is not so young, he is in his thirties. But why do you think of him as an old man?"

Nica was reluctant to answer, but she had always imagined him with gray hair, white beard and a wrinkled, courageous, brave face.

She did not listen much to the reports, all the time looking at Jores. She was agitated by the thought of meeting him. In the first break between sessions Nica approached her hero together with professor Maisel.

"Here is your big fan, Jores. She is eager to talk with you."

Nica was embarrassed by this introduction and by the fact that Jores himself looked at her carefully. She expected his gaze would be a one of a rigorous sparkling with heroic fortitude, but a pair of very peaceful blue eyes looked at her smiling shyly. She was confused and began to explain quite incoherently the reason for needing to see him. She talked about professor Kukuev and his, Jores's manuscript, which she read secretly, about mysteriously, disappeared pages and the absolute necessity to find them. Jores shrugged regretfully:

"I am sorry, but here at my lab I don't have any part of my manuscript. I will try to find the pages you need at home. Tomorrow is Sunday; could you come to my house to pick them up?"

Oh, of course, Nica was happy to do this, and they agreed to meet at eleven o'clock in the morning.

The next day in a pleasant hurry, Nica took an electric train to Obninsk. It was the beginning of fall; and the town looked quite attractive with all the yellow and red maple leaves. She found her way without any problem. But it was not Jores who opened the door, but one of his colleagues. He and Jores were working on a scientific article on this Sunday. They met Nica with friendly smiles and a pleasant welcome, treated her with tea and *bubliki,* something like bagels, but she did not receive the pages she needed so urgently.

"I looked through everything and did not find anything," explained Jores. "My colleagues wrested the manuscript copy from my hands the minute I finished printing it! I am so sorry you came in vain this far. But I still think I can help you; and you will not have to come to Obninsk another time. I will give you the address of my brother's office in Moscow. I am sure he has these pages. I will call him today."

Nica was not sorry at all; she had come so far. Jores was her hero who had no fear of the dangerous and ruthless KGB (the successor to the NKVD, the state secret police). He wrote openly the truth, which ordinarily people were afraid to talk about even in a whisper. She was happy to make his acquaintance and was filled with pride when he spoke with her as a friend on various topics with evident interest. He definitely liked her.

Nica said good-bye after a pleasant time with Jores and went happily skipping along toward the train, feeling great. It is never occurred to her that even if Jores had had the manuscript at home, he should not give it to her. If she were not the one she claimed to be, but a KGB provocateur, Jores would be immediately arrested. Nica admired Jores' courage but never thought and never conceived that he dealt with the KGB on an everyday basis. A sharpened Sword of Damocles was hanging directly above his head by single horsehair. One wrong step and he would be completely at the mercy of the KGB. After finishing his manuscript Jores sent a copy of it to the Kremlin's highest hierarchy. He wanted them to know the contents of his book. It was very risky because the patron of Lysenko was Khrushchev himself. In Stalin's time, Jores would have been arrested and prosecuted immediately, but Khrushchev wanted to appear just concerned about justice. Formally, the KGB could not arrest Jores if he did not participate in the distribution of his manuscript. But people, especially employees of scientific institutions, read it avidly and reprinted hundreds of copies. The KGB tried in every possible way to catch Jores at a missteps. It would be most convenient for them if he would have handed his manuscript or any part of it to someone could confirm this.

Nica was happily not aware of all those complications, and next day she sought Jores' brother Roy in Moscow's back streets and alleys. Finally a building appeared in front of her with the sign Labor Education in Schools, an innovation of irrepressible Khrushchev, where Roy, philosopher by trade, was employed because he was forbidden to work in his specialty. Nica entered the building and knocked at the door, opened it and stopped bewildered. It was the same Jores who got up from the desk to greet her. He looked at her with his blue, slightly embarrassed eyes and threw back hair from his forehead with a familiar gesture.

"Jores Alexandrovich."

"No, my name is Roy, Roy Alexandrovich. Jores is my brother, but we are often confused because we are twins. Jores called me and told about your request. To my regret, I do not have the pages you need right now, but tomorrow I will receive a new copy of Jores manuscript. If you would like go with me to the typist she will gladly type the pages for you." Nica agreed with pleasure, and Roy explained to her where they would meet tomorrow night.

It was already dark when Nica approached the appointed subway. She was afraid she would not be able to find Roy in the dense crowd of outgoing and incoming people, but he was tall and his height enabled him to see her in the subway commotion. He called her name, and they began to descend by the long elevator.

"I must confess you are my cover. Who would dream that at a meeting with a young pretty girl, I carry in my briefcase underground literature?"

They really looked like one of the many couples for which the subway was a common rendezvous. Roy took Nica's arm and began to speak the words, which did not fit with the impression they probably produced. He explained to her how to get rid of a possible the KGB tail. They boarded the subway train, continuing to talk as if nothing had happened, but in the very last second when the door began to close they jumped off the train, ran across the platform and managed to take the train departing in the opposite direction. And all this time Roy observed whether or not someone was behind them. This trick was repeated twice.

"Roy, you fight like Don Quixote tilting at windmills without any hope for success. Why do you run the risk knowing that it is all in vain?"

"The ashes of my father are knocking at my heart" – Roy paraphrased the words of Till Eulenspiegel with a sad smile.

Nica knew that his forty-year-old father was arrested in 1938 and died soon after in one of Stalin's concentration camps.

They traveled quite a long time by subway train and then walked even longer along the unfamiliar streets and down some alley, till they reached a small two story dilapidated apartment house. A gray-haired woman opened the door. She apparently knew Roy very well, because she was obviously pleased to see him. They walked into a hall of a communal apartment populated by many families. This woman escorted them to her small cramped room with the typewriter in the corner and bookshelf with neat stacks of papers. From the old woman's conversation with Roy, Nica understood she was a widow of one of the old Bolsheviks, the idealist–communists cruelly destroyed by Stalin in the late nineteen thirties.

When everybody started to say goodbye, Roy put in his briefcase a thick bundle of papers, and Nica finally received the pages she have been hunting for.

"Roy" asked Nica many years later. "You did not know me well, if I happened to be an agent provocateur, I would ruin you and the typist. Weren't you afraid?"

"It was a big risk, of course, but the danger was there always, and the old typist was well aware of it. Formally she would not have been responsible for the contents of the printing material. The typists do not have to delve into the text. But this is only formally; the KGB has its own rules. As for me, I am a very good physiognomist, but to tell the truth, I wanted so much to believe you, which is really a bad excuse for a conspirator."

* * *

Spring break was near, and Nica longed to see her parents and planned to spend a week at their Almaty home. Chedar phoned her in the late evening, as usual.

"I am going to your house right now, but I would like to talk with you alone about something very important. There is a little bench close to the flower bed in the backyard. Please, wait for me there."

They met in half an hour, embraced and sat on the bench. The air smelled of spring, but it was still cold. Nica leaned against Chedar to warm up, and he put his arm around her shoulders.

"I am going to have my diploma in a month, my darling Nica. What is next? What are our plans for the future?"

"We are going to marry!"

"But you have not even told me you love me."

"First of all, it is you, who should tell me this; and then, you know very well I am crazy about you."

"We should marry now, before I finish at the University, but the thought of your father and how he will react to our decision to marry, makes me very concerned and even frightened."

"Why are you concerned about it? You know he loves you!"

"Raslan loves me as a nephew, here what's scary. I talked today with my father; and he thinks our marriage is impossible for Raslan because of our kinship."

"But you are my second cousin!"

"In Osetia we would be called brother and sister. They do not allow marriage within the family of one line regardless of distance in the relationship."

"It was like this long before, but not now."

"Yes, I am sure right now such rigor is long forgotten, but your father left Osetia when he was young, and when this tradition existed in full force. I am afraid all customs of Osetia live in Raslan intact and preserved, because he was not a witness to their disappearance. My father thinks so, and it frightens me."

"I could not imagine my daddy is so orthodox. It simply impossible! He is so bright and civilized, and he loves me very much!"

"I told the same to my father, but I am tormented by anxiety."

"I will write a letter home today, and I am sure, my mother and father will be happy for us."

"Please do that, I would like to believe you are not mistaken."

They sat silently arm in arm feeling their happiness fade. A heavy cloud of uncertainty hung over their heads.

Nica did not sleep much that night. She finished her letter very late, feeling it was not persuasive enough and went to bed, turning from side to side till dawn. The gray morning came without much comfort. A week later she received a telegram with a request to fly home immediately.

A storm of anger burst out over the heads of Nica and Chedar. Raslan was infuriated, enraged. He accused them of breaking the most sacred law of the ancestors, of violating the law of nature itself.

"If you marry him, I could not bear such a disgrace, you will kill me by your own hands!"

Nica knew her father never threw his words to the wind, never used them as a mere threat. She was seized by endless despair. No, she could not kill him by her own hands. She loved him too much. All her life Raslan was her model of honesty and nobility, an example for emulation. Anything but to kill him! It would be better to her to die. But she could not imagine her life without Cherdar, without his love. The very thought of parting with him was unbearable.

Entreating and tears were useless; Nica was unable to break the age–old traditions that grew into the soul of her father with all their roots. She could not persuade Raslan that this custom was a thing of the past. Now she came across his iron will and unshakable principals. There were two and only two possibilities for her, stop being his daughter and kill him by this, or to obey. And she obeyed.

All were in mourning at home. Her mother did not know which one, Nica or Raslan she should worry about more. May took Nica's misfortune as her own, but how could she help? And Nica, she was deaf and dumb with grief.

Her spring break was not yet over when Raslan went to Moscow to the big meeting. Cherdar tried to see him, but Raslan simply banished the boy from his presence, and Cherdar's pride was deeply hurt. Sweet, kind and unusually sad Bibo tried to reason with his second cousin, but he received such an angry rebuke from Raslan that he stopped arguing.

Nica returned to Moscow as if after a funeral. Cherdar met her at the airport. His soft eyes did not sparkle any more, and his mouth was compressed in an unusual bitter line. "What can we do? You will not be able to live after breaking with your family, you attachment to your parents is too strong."

Nica was silent, her tears flowed without stopping.

"I am going on a geological expedition in two weeks. I was invited to enter a Postgraduate course at Novosibirsk Academic City. I will go there straight from the expedition. It will be better this way."

"But what about the exams and thesis?"

"The thesis I finished already, and I have permission to take preliminary exams, I am taking them right now. Are you going to come to the railroad station to see me off?"

At the station Nica still could not believe they were to be parted. Cherdar was in the bustle of loading equipment. At the last whistle of the train before departure he embraced Nica.

"Don't be so sad, we are alive, I will write to you and love you, my darling little sister."

Then he smiled and added, "I would like you to promise me something."

"What is it?"

"Never-never forget me"
"I will never forget you, never!"
He touched her lips with a light brotherly kiss.

* * *

Nica moved to a little cell in the University dormitory to be alone in her grief. Her joy died, it seemed life itself was gone from her soul giving way to a constant sting. She lived as if in a fog, all colors of nature were lost; the sky was gray, even on a sunny day. The faces of the people around seemed expressionless masks. Sometimes in her sleep she dreamed of Cherdar and felt happiness wakening with a cry of despair. "It cannot be, it cannot be," she repeated to herself trying to hide from the horror of reality somewhere under her pillow. "If only I could shoot straight in my heart, straight into this pain to stop it!"She thought pressing her hand to her aching chest.

Nica spent long hours in the laboratory, as before, but not to study. She was there to be alone, not to exert her efforts to understand questions, or to talk. Just to be alone, not to think, not to move. She stared into nowhere with unseeing eyes caressing her heart to make it hurt less.

A tightly closed black flask on the shelf with red letters Poison looked so tempting. "How well it would be to cease to feel, to die. To die to stop this sting, to die... to die..." Nica's hand reached the flask with eagerness. One sip, another, and another. She stopped terrified. "What have I done?" She realized in panic she would die in a moment, she would vanish completely, forever. "NO! NO! NO!" Before her eyes came the forest with a warm scent of pin pitch, a sunny meadow. Life! A terrible burden fell suddenly off her soul. She wanted desperately to live.

And life returned.

Fortunately after lectures the lab assistant had poured the poisonous reagent into a special container and locked it into the safe, substituting the poison in the flask with tap water.

The bad smelling water made Nica endure the strong shock of awaiting imminent death. This shock did not return her joy of life, but it returned her joy that she was alive. The pain had not disappeared, but it was not so overwhelming now. It did not obscure the blue sky; it did not make Nica deaf and dumb to everything around her. The dark night changed to a gray dawn.

* * *

One evening Nica had an unexpected call. It was Roy Medvedev. Their conversation was very brief.

"Could you do me a favor and meet me tomorrow at four o'clock at the Mayakovsky Square?"

Nica agreed without asking any questions or even mentioning on the telephone Roy's name, just as he warned her to do when they first met. She came a little earlier and looked around waiting for Roy. They had not met since their trip to the typist, and she tried to guess what made him call her. She saw his tall figure from the distance and hurried toward him.

"Thank you for coming. If you don't mind, let's go for a little walk."

Nica waited for the explanation, but there was none. Roy asked her questions which had no political meaning and listened very carefully as it had some big value. After about one hour he thanked her. "I am so grateful to you, you helped me a lot."

"But, Roy, I did not help you in any way, talking about student's small events and nonsense!"

"You cannot even imagine how I needed to listen to you. I deliberately steered the conversation to what you call nonsense. This is the best medicine for my nerves to recover after meeting with the KGB."

Roy saw her off on the subway, but before they parted she asked him to give her some underground literature Samizdat, self published, forbidden typewritten literature directed against the political power.

From this time on Nica began to read avidly Samizdat in the late evenings and nights, including 400 pages of To the Court of History written by Roy himself. Inhuman sufferings on every page of Samizdat did not let her sleep. Now she understood the people who put themselves on fire. She also wanted to participated the fire of protest; she was in a rage about the secret crimes of the Soviet State government. Her own pain passed now into quiet aching, and did not peek out from her eyes so openly as before.

Friendship with Roy became more and more important to Nica. His calm courage brought her admiration. His deep conviction of necessity to tell the truth did not allow him to retreat from his principles and purposes under any circumstances. Roy preserved his outward calm even during the time when the KGB strained his nerves to the limit. Many years later when the power and the regime itself changed, and when everybody suddenly became bold because it was no longer dangerous criticizing everything and everyone, Roy included, he remained the same with the same calmness, with the same principles and with the same vision of the world.

But in the nineteen sixties, when Roy risked his life daily, Nica liked to meet him and go for a walk around the center of Moscow, or in the hills of Gorky Park listening to his quiet responses to her impatient questions which only he could answer. Sometimes Roy took her to meetings with well-known people, with writers, producers and scientists, and life became remarkably interesting. At such events Nica got close to him quietly and in silence, embarrassed and amused by the curiosity aroused by her presence. Roy made her realize there were important purposes and big ideas beyond her personal pain, and that was the best cure for her.

A few years passed, and one day Nica took an elevator in the big, prestigious house where a family of general, old friends of her mother lived. On the third floor the elevator stopped, and a tall stout man in his fifties came in. Nica looked at him with curiosity. The new passenger seemed to have been waiting for this glance. He was so excited he had to share with somebody at least a little bit of the secret, which burst his chest, to let off steam.

"Wait for an event! Wait for a big event which has to happen this very evening!"

He sighed with his whole chest and stepped off in a hurry from the elevator on the first floor. That evening the radio announced the end of Khrushchev's reign because he ostensible cannot cope with his health. It was a coup at the upper level of the government and Brezhnev was brought to power.

Next day the scientific world of the Soviet Union was excited. With the change of the power and the end of Khrushchev's reign the, withdrawal of the veto on genetics was expected. The works of geneticists, which were kept underground before, now were urgently prepared for publication, so urgently that some of them appeared in the bookstores in a few days. All scientists sighed with tremendous relief.

Nica came to the bookstore at five in the morning to find big line there already, so thirsty were scientists for genetics books. She held Micro-genetic by Rappoport with reverence and the understanding she must study before reading it. She should begin with the not yet published textbooks. There was much for her to learn, so she was eager to do this.

At the big scientific meeting the most prominent academician, Astaurov made a speech which boiled down to the quite sober realization. The fruit of labor of all Soviet geneticists for the last thirty years was one big event, opening the door of a prison where genetics languished for so long. "Thirty of our creative years we spent not for discovery in genetics, but for the right to be a geneticist. In the 1934 we were ahead of the entire scientific world on advances in genetics; now in 1964 we are thirty years behind."

At last genetics was rehabilitated, but not fully. It was sad that the official authorities, after allowing the Genetics to exist, did not banish the killer of the Genetics and geneticist: nor did they diminish his power. Lysenko still thrived, however. Liberalization in the politics of the State did not happen either. The books of both Medvedev brothers were still banned.

* * *

Genetics, its discovery and its logic enraptured Nica. Sitting inside the hall of the newly opened Institute of Genetics she felt the excitement and stimulation, which was comparable with the exultation of Catholics inside St. Paul's Cathedral. Reports were due to begin in a few minutes when a tall, thin man on the stage began to write on the blackboard. Big white letters announced that here in this Conference Hall Academician Sakharov collected signatures of those who were outraged by the forced political confinement in a psychiatric asylum of the prominent scientist Jores Medvedev. The whole auditorium roared like a beehive, everybody jumped from the seats. Jores was well known here. "He is arrested! How it is terrible" thought Nica. "But who is this man writing about this? I know him, it is Sakharov himself!" She had seen him only once but remembered his face very well. "If it is true, Jores is in terrible danger!" Nica rushed to the phone. Roy answered and confirmed Sakharov's announcement.

"I fear they will begin to treat him forcibly with strong drugs to unbalance his mental ability. This is the most awful revenge they can come up with. I've already called many friends, writers, scientists, and doctors." Roy's voice was very tense.

"Do you want me to come?"

"Please do; only be aware, my apartment is under constant surveillance by the KGB now.

Roy lived quite a way from the Institute of Microbiology. Nica almost ran along the street to a subway. A Moscow crowd flowed with her and toward her like a river. The sun shone warmly and tenderly in this last day of May, and the streets looked beautiful and festive. "So gorgeous a day does not match what is happening now. This day is made for joy and happiness, and not for this gloomy reality!" Nica thought, crossing the Manege Square and hurrying to the entrance of the subway. A voice of a stranger stopped her. "Do me a favor, pretty!"

She looked with surprise at the young man barring her way,

"Could you, please, lend me five kopeks?"

Nica took a coin from her pocket, gave it to the young man and hurried on.

"Wait a minute, please, I didn't ask you to give me money, I asked you to lend it to me. I need your address to return it!"

Nica looked at the young man more carefully. No, he could not be with the KGB, his nice merry face smiled from ear to ear. This witty way of courtship fit perfectly with the wonderful spring day, and the generous sun pouring the bright light all over Manege Square. Nica felt sorry she could not be frivolous, have fun and flirt. She smiled.

"You addressed a wrong person. I have a fierce husband and a bunch of terrible children." The young man laughed, tried to object and followed Nica; but she plunged in to the crowd and soon he lost her.

"Maybe he is from the KGB. But it really doesn't matter; I am going straight to their arms anyway. One of them has watched Roy's door for two days already, it is meaningless to confuse traces, as Roy taught me"

Nica tried not to look around coming up to the fourth floor of an old blockhouse where Roy lived without an elevator. She knew she was watched. A man went down the staircase, and Nica glanced at him and stopped. She had seen this man only three hours ago, when he was writing on the black board in the Conference Hall.

"Hello, Andrei Dmitrievich!" Her voice was full of admiration. Academician Sakharov waved a friendly hand and hurried to the entrance.

The flat Nica came looked like a military headquarters. Phones rang all the time. Roy was collected, purposeful and calm; but she could feel his strained nerves. He always suffered from insomnia, and now he had not slept for almost two nights. But there was not any trace of tiredness in his face. The tension was too strong. He concentrated on one desire, as soon as possible to free Jores from this dangerous imprisonment and prevent the murderous treatment. A spiritual link between the two brothers was absolute; the twins syndrome demonstrated in full force these wonderful properties.

"Roy, why did they arrest Jores now? Why did they choose this awful confinement, a psychiatric asylum?"

"It would be the best gift for Lysenko and all his men if Jores would be declared a lunatic. Just think, Lysenko still has all his political and scientific power, he keeps all his titles. But the earth is burning under his feet, and he goes to the most extreme measures feeling collapse is close. Recently Jores book exposing Lysenko, his crimes and his ridiculous "science" was published in the USA, and Lysenko decided to act. He needs to prove that this book was written by a madman. This way he hopes to preserve his reputation and power. This killer of genetics and geneticists has many supporters in the government, and that is why it is so difficult to fight with him.

"I know you collect the signatures of protest, I would like to add my name too."

"Oh, no! No way! I am asking only the known all over the world people to sign my letter to Brezhnev. It is difficult for the government to arrest them; but if you sign it, you would vanish, and I wouldn't even know where to look for you."

What had been impossible in the time of Stalin happened now. The prominent people protested against outrageous injustice. The letters of remonstration from the most eminent scientists, artists and writers came every day. It seemed the supreme government power and Lysenko were dumbfounded by the powerful wave of indignation and protest of almost all intellectuals of the USSR, but they tried to hold their ground. The desperate struggle continued twenty days. Twenty days and nights Roy did not have rest until finally Jores was released. The battle was won.

* * *

A green and fragrant coniferous forest was all around the newly built Academic Town. Eleven narrow nine-story towers houses and five research institutes were hidden deep in the woods. On a gray rainy day, Nica could barely see a small black village drenched under the recurrent downpour. Twelve black wooden huts stretching along the horizon served as a kind of calendar. She watched as the sun crept closer and closer with each passing month to the first hut in the East, and it set closer and closer to the last hut in the West in the evening. The day's arc of the bright heavenly body became shorter and lower. In December the dim yellow sun rose just above the first hut and set above the last one. Nica was full of sadness every time she had to say goodbye to the warm summer. The winter in Moscow had been harsh.

The life in Academic Town was very different from nearby Moscow. The Town was newly built by a special project. The government spared neither strength nor resources to give the best to this place, which was supposed to be the center of the world's best science. One of these Research Institutes worked on developing a solid fuel for rockets, which the Soviet State eagerly needed.

Almost all the population here consisted of young scientists who had just received their PhD's. Even the Laboratory Heads were barely past thirty. They lived in the small forest clearing 25 miles from Moscow, so that could concentrate on their research. They worked at the cutting edge of science; and it filled their lives with meaning and joyful enthusiasm. At the seminars, the discussions were fierce, and hides had been taken from the speakers with sophistication and daring of the young and talented. It gave the young scientists' lives passion and excitement. Merriment flashed at every occasion, youthful joy gave special flavor to this Academic Town.

Seven years passed since Chepdar left for Novosibirsk, and four years since Nica married Vlad, a young scientist. Nica finished her PhD, and the young family received the keys to a brand new two-room apartment with a balcony. It was an unimaginable luxury in any other city. All apartments in the USSR belonged to the state. They were given to the citizens free of charge, but there was a shortage of lodging all over the country. In many cases 3-4 families, sometimes more crowded into the separate rooms of the communal apartments at the rate of six square meters, 6.6 square yards, per person.

In this new and exciting settlement, Nica and Vlad had very many friends and acquaintances. Vlad got along with everybody quite easily. Women adored him and not surprisingly, he was tall and handsome with masculine charm. His scientific ability would provide him an excellent career. Other women quite understandably envied Nica, but she and her husband glided through life without the spiritual closeness that had been the basis of her relation with Chepdar. Nica was too busy, too captured by the novelty of life to think about it. And could she complain? She and Vlad were delightfully young and cheerful. Only sometimes in the middle of a merry party, Nica felt suddenly a frightening emptiness in her soul, and she wanted desperately to wake up from this delusion, to have Cherdar close to her, to have real happiness rather than playing at it. But Cherdar lived in the other Academic Town far away in Siberia. All of Europe and Asia lay between them. Nica met his beautiful wife who was and focused on her career. Was she too businesslike? Nica heard they did not have a good relationship. "Cherdar has the fragile delicate soul of an artist, but she wants him to be a scientific bureaucrat."Nica thought" It could ruin him." She remembered that they had once come out from a Moscow concert hall to the already hushed street and hugged in some sort of outburst elated by the beauty of the music. They wandered about for a long time in silence, still listening to the music inside of them and knowing what the other felt.

But life was boiling around Nica, and she swam in it eagerly. Her PhD thesis was accepted to be reported at the Ninth International Microbiological Congress. Nica was happy and waited for this event with impatience and some kind of fearful chill. She not only rehearsed the report many times but also thought over what to wear. Her father's gift, a pair of high stiletto-heel shoes was very useful.

On the day of her debut Nica went to the University early and climbed to the very last and highest row in the Conference Hall. Too late she realized the length of the hall separated her from the stage too late. The chairman of the Congress, a French professor Lvov called her name, and Nica ran along the steep gangway. Halfway her wonderful high stiletto-heel pierced the carpet, and she somersaulted the remaining distance to the stage. Two gallant foreigners caught her, and she took to the stage in only one shoe, the other one was ceremoniously handed to her to the complete delight of the audience. Nica was enthusiastically applauded after finishing her report, but it remained unclear whether her success was due to her achievement in science or due to her wonderful acrobatic performance.

* * *

It took fifteen minutes to go from the houses to the Research Institutes through the forest. The woods were thick, green and smelling of fragrant resin in the summer, dropping clear tears in the fall and glittering with sparkles in the winter. Nica liked to go along this aromatic wood path, enjoying the friendly views and feeling young and pretty. Laboratories, library, and seminars - new methods required new knowledge. Nica hardly had time to breathe, and she loved it. Every member of the lab was her friend, and she liked to spend long hours in late evenings listening to the rumble of the new glittering chrome ultracentrifuge. It was so pleasant to have an unexpected little feast in the lab, when one of her colleagues received a parcel from concerned parents with all sort of goodies. New witty, talented friends gathered in Nica's and Vlad's home on the holidays, and they also received invitations for different celebrations. Life was vibrant.

While Nica went from the Institute to take her little son from the kindergarten, she gathered a full basket of mushrooms making the supper much nicer. It was so heartwarming to listen to the sweet talk of her little son. Gen adored all kind of animals, and they liked to discuss and admire the length of whales, the speed of tigers, et cetera. Time after time the whole family went to the Moscow zoo. When they heard of two newcomers from Africa, two elephants, they decided to see them to make Gen happy.

The enormous large–eared animals were housed in a temporary enclosure. They blew sand from trunks and looked at the viewers with small canny eyes. "Daddy, Daddy I cannot see well! Lift me, lift me quickly, please!" cried Gen in excitement. Vlad put him on the concrete barrier. In the same moment a long thick trunk entwined the little boy's body like a huge python and lifted him up in the air. Nica seized the hard-as-iron trunk in complete panic, but the elephant shook her away casually. The lovely baby with blue eyes and long blond curls was far above the barrier. Through her horror Nica heard heart–rending cries around her. She jumped and jumped trying to grab the iron trunk swinging her little son up and down. Then a girl threw a sweet bun across the barrier. The huge wild African put Gen down. He did not toss the little boy, did not drop him, but put him back on the barrier as carefully as a caring nanny. But the smaller she–elephant had already managed to grab and push the roll into her mouth. The giant was seized by rage. He stood on his forelegs and began to beat with all force the barrier with his hind legs. The spectacle was frightening. All viewers jumped back to safety, but Nica, Vlad and little Gen were away from the enclosure. The parents sat exhausted on the bench, but Gen was surprised by the panic surrounding this episode with Jumbo. He had read a few sugary children's books about elephants' kindness.

"Mommy. Why didn't you want the elephant would give me a ride on his back?" Gen asked. Nica could not answer, she was almost fainting.

"His back was dirty" – squeaked Vlad in an unnaturally hoarse voice and turned to Nica. "Just imagine, if this beast squeezed his trunk a little bit." Nica shook her head fending off a horrible vision.

She could not sleep that night and came into the little room of her son. He snuffled serenely, and Nica looked with affection at his lovely little face. She was sobbing quietly and thinking she did not want anything else in this world, only to see her baby in the lunar twilight and to be sure he was safe.

* * *

A tragedy struck unexpectedly. Nica's father was dying. It was impossible to believe as he was has always been the embodiment of energy and vitality. At sixty-eight he still looked young and strong. Nica forgot her bitter reproaches to her father for a lost happiness and deep pain. There was only love for him. The next day when Nica flew to Almaty, Cherdar's airplane headed to the same city from Novosibirsk.

Those days were gone as in a fog. Her mother's grief and her whisper, "Quiet, quiet" as she was afraid to upset or disturb Raslan by their cries. High Academy staircases, when the coffin was carried down from the big hall. Long lines of people mourning Raslan's last journey. Speeches, wreaths, and the terrifying sound of earth dropping on the coffin, all filled her with sadness.

Vlad arrived too late; he caught up with the procession close to the cemetery. Nica called him and stretched out her arms to him, but his presence did not comfort her. Vlad was as usual, handsome, elegant, and distant. She took her hands from his shoulders.

In the evening Nica sat with her mother and sister in the darkened room, where Raslan's voice was heard not so long ago. Cherdar came in and sat beside them. Vlad's conversation with two of his buddies was heard from the veranda. All three talked loudly and animatedly at the time when silence was so badly needed. Nica shut the door and took her mother's hand in her own. Everybody was silent and deep in their thoughts. Too much had happened. Cherdar turned to Nica and said almost soundlessly, "You father died and all the obstacles which separated us are gone. But we could not change anything now." Nica answered him with a sad look. They still understood each other so well they could talk almost without words. Cherdar left the next day.

Very soon Nica learned that some of their acquaintances and even friends dramatically changed their attitude toward her mother, sister and herself. The friendliness, attentiveness and courtesy disappeared. The modest requests, which previously would have been satisfied immediately, were not carried out now. Those who formerly fawned before them now did not even greet Nica, May or their mother. It seemed the halo of an academician family was extinguished with Raslan's death. It was unpleasant, disgusting, but easy to ignore and forget. Much more serious was the fact that the relationship between Nica and Vlad went from bad to worse in this very year when Nica's grief was so fresh. Vlad now had his own friends somewhere in Moscow where he went very often and stayed till late hours saying there were Academy meetings. Once, Nica called over there worrying. The sleepy and grouchy voice of the night watchman answered her:

"Don't bother, nobody was here after four o'clock" Nica looked at her watch. It was close to midnight.

One year later Nica was jolting about in an old dilapidated bus with torn leatherette seats going to the Municipal Court, which was in the Center of this region, in the town called Noginsk. This God-forsaken Noginsk was like the unwieldy bus Nica was riding, dilapidated, miserable and dreary. The Court was in the gray and dirty building with old shabby floors and a musty smell. Here Nica found quite unexpectedly a kind of female united front from the women– receptionists "Divorce, you say? Give your papers right here. I see, consenting. Yes, we know him, we've seen him, didn't we, girls? A dandy in a beaver hat as cool as a cucumber! Ha! All blame you take on yourself. Very clever for him! It is clear as day, he persuaded you to do this for him to make the divorce easier. And what is this? A power of attorney, so without him to divorce him! Where is he by the way? What? Went abroad! Could we ask why? To ski! It is re-al-ly something! He is skiing and having fun, and you, poor thing, drag your legs to us. Just marvelous! Did he give one little thought to what kind of a wretched life you would lead all alone with a child? Divorce he wants! Oh yes! We know very well this kind of dandy!"

Nica was stunned by this fast investigation and trial, by these waves of emotion from these poor and simple clerks and by such a demonstration of female solidarity.

She was torn by the contradiction. On one hand she realized divorce was the best solution for her and Vlad, but the threat of a single mother's wretched life made her uneasy, even afraid. And Nica felt pain for her little son and pity for him. How could she admit his father left him? Nica remembered a favorite Vlad joke when he was sitting at the big festive table full of their friends. "Tell me, dear sonny, who is the head here?" Repeatedly trained Gen answered his father in his high baby voice, "The head here is daddy!" for Vlad's great pleasure and the general merriment of the guests. Now this "head" would live with another family in Moscow, 25 miles away. How to explain this to Gen?

Mother and son sat embracing on the couch. Nica read to Gen a funny children's book when he unexpectedly interrupted her, "Mommy, where is our daddy?"

Nica was confused. She thought a hundred times how to answer this inevitable question, and yet it caught her by surprise.

"Your daddy is very busy, Gen. He is writing his doctoral thesis, and he can't live with us."

Gen slowly got off the couch and silently went to another room with his head down as if from an excessive burden loaded on him by adults. All her life Nica would not forget this small mournful figure going to the dark room as if trying to hide from the frightening truth.

Loneliness scared Nica too. She was brought on Turgenev's romanticism and did not want to think about frivolous affairs, but where one could find Turgenev's noble hero in this pragmatic world? Chepdar lived in an unreachable, far away world. Nica felt lonely now in her beloved Academic Town, where it seemed everybody lived as happy couples. No, it was not exactly like this, Nica knew a few divorcees and always was sorry for these deserted wives. Now her friends and acquaintances would pity her. This thought insulted her. She he did not want to be pitied; she wanted to be happy and loved. But where in whole world is there one unmarried or married woman who has not dreamed about this?

To Nica's surprise she was not the only one who was concerned about the change in her status. Some agitation began around her, steered by unmarried and married acquaintances. This did not smooth her existence, just the opposite, it brought embarrassment and inconvenience.

Once, Nica was invited to a newly-opened restaurant rotating around its axis at the top of a television tower. The invitation came from a very pleasant and highly respectable, and... married scientist. He always showed his liking for Nica and sincere sympathy after her divorce. She found it awkward to refuse and decided to make a bold change in her life. "Enough of these romantic follies" she tried to persuade herself. "I will begin a new life, a luxury one!" But nothing came from this luxury life. The evening was pleasant: the restaurant rotated, the conversation was interesting and the food was great, but all Nica's bravado vanished when this highly respectable scientist tried to kiss her in the taxi on their way back. She pushed him aside in panic. "No, no, I am sorry, I can not... I cannot be a chocolate dessert after dinner for you!"

He pleaded and tried to explain something, but Nica shook her head feeling disgust and shame. "Please forgive me, I shouldn't go with you, it is my fault, I misled you." He paused trying to calm himself down and asked after a while, "Could we at least remain on good terms?" She agreed with relief.

Friendship with Roy was a great comfort to Nica. All her personal troubles faded into the background when she talked with him, as if she peered into another world where there was an ongoing struggle with the ills of all the Soviet Union. But between them was more than thirty miles. It took too much time to go back and forth by the bus, tram and subway. So Nica saw Roy much less often than she would like. She plunged into her research, knowing that the best medicine for all misfortunes is work. She had dreamed since the time she was a student about becoming a geneticist. The head of the Institute of Physical Chemistry, where Nica was working, the famous Academician Semenov gave shelter to a group of young geneticists even before the ban on genetics was withdrawn. It had grown into a large laboratory now, and Nica was eager to work there. A young and friendly manager of this lab, Dr. Grekov, encouraged her every way, and nothing could have pleased her more. Now Nica spent long evenings in the library extending her knowledge of genetics and getting ready for the interview. From time to time she tore her eyes from the books and gazed through the huge window, enjoying the view of the lavish forest in the soft light of the late north summer sunset.

Finally the day for the interview was scheduled, and Nica spent a sleepless night, looking the last time through the books and concentrating all her thoughts on the coming presentation.

The Genetic Laboratory was surrounded by a thick forest on all sides and stood away from the main building of the Institute of Physical Chemistry. Nica went along a corridor and knocked at the door of Grekov's study. It was just six thirty, the appointed time. The workday was over, so there should not be any interruption of the interview. Grekov himself opened the door. To Nica's surprise he was alone and very nervous. "He could be in trouble again with his boss," she thought seeing he was strangely agitated. Grekov paced up and down the room, as if pondering something. Then he turned the key in the lock, stepped quickly to Nica and with a powerful hug pressed his lips to hers. She pushed him without thinking, absent-mindedly, as she would brush away a disgusting spider. Then all the absurdity of what had happened struck Nica, and she began to laugh loudly, almost hysterically. Grekov expected anything but this. He did not know what to do and stood reddened, bewildered, wishing the ground would cut out from under him. Nica opened the door continuing to laugh and dashed along the corridor, not paying attention to some scientific worker showing himself from the lab to investigate such an unusual noise.

"Why am I laughing?" thought Nica going along the path through the warm evening forest. "I should be crying! All my dreams now are stupidly, unexpectedly over, and finished forever."

But she could not restrain herself, she laughed over the red face of Grekov and over her own foolishness, over all these seminars where she strained every cell of her brain. She could not help but laugh at her admiration for this researcher "thinking only about science." "And what was he thinking about? Ha-ha-ha! I was sure he saw in me a serious future geneticist. But, what he actually saw in me? Ha-ha-ha!"

After that she could not hold her laugh every time she ran across Grekov. She laughed and Grekov blushed looking away. Nica laughed, and then she wanted to cry.

Winter came with a cold and sharp wind. It seemed the first gleam of daylight appeared only to fade in the nearing dusk. In the course of past five years, Academic Town became aged, lost its initial excitement. Tension arose between the titled scientists. Conflicts emerged more and more often. Sometimes the whole town trembled with tragedy. One of the scientists committed suicide inside of the Theoretical Physics building; another one hung himself in his lab at Chemical Physics. The Japanese published a long article surpassing Nica's group and spoiling everyone's mood. There was general disappointment, and in addition, the long cold winter nights began, blizzards raged. Nica felt sick at heart.

She put little Eugine to sleep and sat at her desk to finish reading some article. The snowstorm had begun in the morning and was still in full power. Nica listened to the eerie howling wind. It seemed the windows were ready to burst under the pressure of the blizzard, and winter would rush into the house. She could not concentrate on her reading, put it aside and went to the window, leaning her forehead against the cold glass. The pale spot from the streetlight, where snow flurries where circling, rising and falling, hypnotized her. It seemed that the storm would last forever, and forever she would be sad and lonely. Nica lost her sense of time when a sharp ringing of the telephone in the complete silence of the room returned her to reality. She looked at the clock; it was almost midnight. She picked up the phone with a pounding heart, and in the same instant the snowstorm and the entire world around her ceased to exist. A painfully familiar voice was telling Nica something in the receiver. She had not heard this voice for a long time and thought she would never hear it again. It was Chepdar; he was here, only three floors from her. "How could it be, how could it be, he is here, so close?" She had waited for him for so many years, knowing that she should not wait. She had hoped, knowing there was no hope. And now she was going to see him.

The elevator was slow, it would be too long to wait, so Nica ran up full of happy impatience. She passed one floor, another. Chepdar stood in front of the opened door when she reached the last flight of stairs. He hurried to meet her, embraced and kissed her with love, as if he had found her again after ten years of longing. Nica felt she had traveled a difficult, painful path and finally she was at home. All her suffering and torment were erased by the happiness of this meeting. She did not want anything in the world, only to prolong this moment.

They could not remember how long they embraced. Finally Chepdar began to speak:

"I learned about your divorce only three days ago, and I came here to tell you there are no obstacles now for us to be together. I separated from Irma a month ago. I have to fly to Irkutsk for a meeting, and I hope so much you will go with me. It will be only five days, then you will return home, and I will go to Novosibirsk to prepare everything for your and Gen's arrival. And Nica, you only think about it. We will never part again! Could you go with me now to Irkutsk?"

"Yes, of course, I will go with you. I am so, so happy! Gen can stay for a while with my friends, who love him. I will take five days leave from my job. How could anything stop me now?"

The five days in snowy Irkutsk were a fairy tale. Never before had they been so close and so absolutely happy. But the time flew by quickly, and sooner than Nica would have liked, the plane carried her back. It was difficult and fearful for Nica to leave Cherdar. Her heart ached with pain. Was it a premonition?

Before the departure Cherdar took his watch and put it in Nica's hand.

"You can see now how minutes running make closer our meeting."

He raised the watch to her ear smiling: "Can you hear the beating of my heart?"

He hugged Nica, kissed her, and she reluctantly forced herself to break away from him. Through the small round window she tried to see Cherdar one more time; but he disappeared in the white haze of snow.

At the beginning a fabulous happiness remained with Nica all the time. Then there was anxious, and finally she was gripped by panic. Ten days passed, and she did not hear anything from Cherdar. Nica knew he would not be silent without a reason. Something bad had happened. She was literally sick from anxiety. Long distance calls were not possible yet from the Academic Town; so Nica went to Moscow Central Telegraph. She tried desperately to reach the Research Institute where Cherdar was working, but a secretary growled she did not know where Cherdar was and immediately hang up without further explanation. It seemed the white blizzard of Irkutsk or Novosibirsk devoured him. Nica's imagination painted the worst pictures; and she could not bear to be tormented by uncertainty any longer. She left her son with friends again, took leave from her job and went to the airport to fly to Novosibirsk on the first available plane.

As the bus rumbled on the long road to the airport, the blizzard began. The airport froze under the snow. Nica spent the night in a hard armchair in a state of feverish expectation. Sleep was out of the question, but it still was better than doing nothing at home. In the morning the storm had subsided and the plane took off. Already in flight Nica realized she had no idea what to do next, where and how to find Cherdar in the big city where she did not know anybody.

Novosibirsk greeted Nica with bitter cold. The sun hung like a pale yellow spot and could not pierce its rays through an icy glass of the frozen air. Nica's legs were weak because of the sleepless night and heavy foreboding. She tried to ask the way to the Novosibirsk Academic Town, but her lips barely moved, and anxiety did not let her understand the explanations. It took a long time for Nica to find the right bus station, and then she was jolted in the frozen bus for what seemed forever. Finally it stopped in front of a wide pine alley covered with snow. Nica walked along that alley until she saw the building of the Geological Institute.

A secretary looked at her with surprise and told her drily she did not know where Chedar was. Nica stood motionless, completely lost. After a while the secretary realized this visitor was not going to leave and called to somebody. Soon a young man appeared.

"Are you looking for Cherdar? I could explain how to find him, but it is far away, in the City, about twenty kilometers."

Nica looked so feverishly sick that he unexpectedly offered help.

"Let me see you off. I am going in this direction anyway."

And again it was a long way in the same frozen bus. Nica's companion tried to start a conversation and asked her about something, but she could not comprehend his question. One and the same thought made her unable to listen to him. "What happened to Cherdar, what was she going to learn now?"

They got off the bus and went a long way through the City until the young man finally stopped in front of a four-story house.

"Here, second floor, apartment twenty. The bell does not work, so, knock loud."

Nica extended her hand and made an effort to smile. She couldn't.

The hallway smelled of cats and dampness. Nica climbed up the stairs holding the railing, trying to overcome the weakness and pounding of her heart. She knocked quietly, the door opened at once. Cherdar stood in front of her. He was pale with dimmed eyes, lips compressed with a mournful line like at their first separation ten years ago. He embraced Nica hard, and held her for a long time.

"I felt you were going to come, I wanted to fly to you first. The ticket to Moscow is in my pocket."

"But... what happened?

"Yes, something happened. I could not write about it. I am totally baffled and don't know what to do, what we have to do?"

"But what is it? Tell me!"

"Irma is with child, already four months... I learned about it only when I came back from Irkutsk. She pleaded with me not to leave her now. I did not tell her about my decision. I don't have any, I am lost and feel miserable. Nica, darling, what should we do?"

She did not die in this moment; but she could not stand any more. And then uncontrollable bitter tears flowed. Cherdar held her in his arms, not comforting. He also cried. In Nica's memory her son arose going silently from her to a dark room with his head drowned in his little shoulders as if from an excessive burden loaded on him by adults.

"You will be a good father, Cherdar."

"But what will be with you and me?"

"What will happen with you and me? We will be brother and sister again..."

Rachel.

Nica's life did not work out, did not go as she had dreamed. However, how many can say that the life turns out well for them? Not many, of course, but Nica were not cheered by the fact that somebody else's life went topsy-turvy too. She wanted to pity herself and complain to someone about her evil fate."It is foolish to set love in the center of the life and to measure happiness by the categories of feelings" Nica tried to persuade herself. "It is an artifact, left to us by our grandmothers. I want to, and I can become a modern woman. The most important things are logic and reason, leaving emotion behind. I have loved and suffered enough, now I should dedicate my life to work, the laboratory and articles."

Nica believed her longing for the past and fear of loneliness was the manifestation of philistinism and mental primitiveness. But contrary to reason, of which she was a strong advocate, Nica was confined to the thoughts already endured. Again and again, awake or asleep, she immersed herself in those past experiences. Nothing came out of her desire to be free, strong and independent. She was sad and lonely.

Isn't it amazing how sometimes we form plans in accordance with our understanding and purpose, but often the most important events in our life we leave to chance? There are lots of examples and they are right here. The husband of Nica's friend, a well-known pianist, while still a bachelor, gave concerts in the most prestigious concert halls. One day by chance, absolutely by chance, he went into a rotten-potato-smelling greengrocery cellar and there he found the one who turned his life plans completely on end. Surprise knocked on Nica's door too.

One early morning a colleague came to Nica's house warning her he would be absent that day at the lab. By chance, just by chance, he was accompanied by his cousin, an artist not at all interested in neither scientific problems, nor in the people working on them. He came from Moscow to draw, inspired by the thick, green, resin-scented woods surrounding this small academic town.

Nica opened the door, but looked past her colleague to the man standing beside him. Blue light shone on her from the eyes of this stranger. She felt neither surprise, nor curiosity but was instantly hypnotized. Her unexpected guests stayed two or three minutes and left, but Nica was unable to overcome the strange obsession. She moved agitatedly through her apartment, absent-mindedly rearranging the books on the shelves, sorting pens and collecting some papers in a pile on the writing desk, unable to forget those dazzling blue eyes.

In the evening when it was dark, the doorbell rang again, and now the owner of those extraordinary blue eyes was there alone. They talked late into the night until he had to leave for the last bus to Moscow. The next day, coming back home from her job, Nica thought about yesterday's guest and about their next date, scheduled for Sunday. However, this meeting happened much earlier. When Nica turned from the forest path to the street leading to her house, she saw her future husband sitting on the bench at the entrance. He had waited for her all day long.

Gersh was handsome, with a well–built, muscular figure, an inspired face with a stubborn lip fold, soft straight hair over a high forehead, and those large blue eyes, constantly floating away thoughtfully into the distance, into another world. He and Nica were both dumbfounded by the fact that they so unexpectedly found each other. They were married three days later, afraid something might destroy the charm of their meeting.

The Moscow apartment, to which Nica and her seven-year-old son Gene came, and where they were supposed to live now, consisted of one nearly empty room, a bathroom and a kitchen. A narrow, sagging couch stood in the corner of this single room, and the walls were covered from the floor to the ceiling with large and small watercolor paintings. They were not hung, but attached to the walls with adhesive tape without any kind of order. A tall, unpainted, homemade bookcase, constructed of plywood boxes, stood in the kitchen and was filled with the kind of books Nica herself would have chosen.

Gersh awaited the arrival of Nica and Gene, and worried. A kettle was already boiling; bread and cheese were laid out on a small wobbly table pressed against the electric stove. Gersh gave a glance at Gene and slapped his forehead. "A cake! I forgot to buy a cake! Wait a minute; the store is on the first floor of this house." He began to open and close small bottom drawers of the bookcase, where, apparently some food was kept. After fumbling in several of them, he pulled money out of onion flakes and rushed to the elevator.

The whole atmosphere in the house, including the small drawers with the onions flakes where money was kept, spoke of a very modest lifestyle. But the studio was on the eleventh floor of a new and, at the time, expensive cooperative house, built not by the Government, but with the money of the occupants of this house. It was a new regulation, and not many could afford to take advantage of it. Later, after Nica and her son moved into Gersh's home and hopelessly spoiled its wonderful emptiness with their stylish furniture, Nica learned that this apartment was a gift to Gersh from his mother. Before that, he had lived near Moscow in the attic of a small house of his uncle.

"Mother married three years ago, moved in with her husband, sold her house and bought me this apartment."

"You say it in a tone as if you are dissatisfied that she pulled you out of your uncle's attic".

"No, of course I am grateful to her. I feel pity for my father."

"But where is he?"

"He was killed during the Second World War at the Kursk battle in 1943."

"Was your mother alone all these thirty years?"

"Of course she was, she had enough troubles with us, with my brother and me. It seemed to me she never even thought about marriage. I couldn't understand why she decided to change everything now in her old age."

"More likely your mother married for the same reason that we did."

Gersh did not answer and Nica did not continue; the subject was obviously unpleasant for him.

Married life was a whole new world for Nica. She wanted to know more about the people who had suddenly, quite unexpectedly, become her relatives. Soon she had an opportunity. Two weeks after their marriage, Nica and Gersh were invited for dinner by Gersh's uncle Naum, the same uncle whose attic Gersh had once occupied. Naum was witty, colorful and merry, and his wife Klaudia met the new couple with hospitality and friendliness. Nica felt immediately that they were her relatives too.

The next day, Nica called Uncle Naum and asked him to tell her more about the people who were her family now. "Come to us again next Sunday in the daytime," answered the uncle. "Gersh will be happy to go to our woods to make watercolors, and I promise to tell you everything I remember, everything I know about Rachel, Gersh's mother and my cousin. We were friends from childhood."

A few days later, Nica sat comfortably on the couch next to Naum, ready to listen.

"You know, of course, the Second World War in the summer of 1941 was rolling through the country as quickly as fire," Naum began his story, and pictures of those remote times came to life before Nica's eyes.

Thunder from exploding shells sounded very close. The war front approached the city. Twenty-six-year old Rachel stood at the open window and listened with strained attention as if the sound hypnotized her. She was thin, of less than average stature, with a heavy dark braid laid around her head as a wreath. Her big, black eyes looked hard at the flashes of fire. Two little boys, Gersh and Osik, five and three years old, puttered about behind her with a wooden truck made for them by their father. They were frightened, knowing something was wrong and time after time cried plaintively. "Ma-a, ma-a..." But Rachel did not answer. Who would have predicted that the front would advance so far and so rapidly? She felt helpless, caught in a trap; her fear for the boys was paralyzing.

Suddenly the door slammed, and Rachel rushed to meet her husband. She had not seen David for two weeks, since his mobilization to the army. David did not hug Rachel; in a mad rush, he picked up the boys in his arms, shouting, "Hurry, hurry, the train departs in a minute, don't collect any clothes, we don't have time for this. Run after me!" He dashed to the street. In a panic, Rachel grabbed her passport, a completely useless key for the door which was left wide open, and rushed after David as she was, in a light summer dress because it was hot July. She barely could keep up with David, who crossed the Station Square and fled, jumping, through the rails to the long departure chain of freight cars.

All the cars were overcrowded, but the soldiers, who tried to make some order in this mess, pushed Rachel and the children through the open doorway into one of these boxcars crammed with people. David jumped in after them, and here in the uproar and hubbub of the train and crush of human bodies, he hugged her tightly. In a desperate whisper he told her hurriedly, "Here is money, hide it, no, not in your purse, it would be stolen there. Write to this number of my battalion. Write, please write, so I know where you are. Take care of the children, do everything to save them!" Then he lifted both his boys, kissed them hastily, and jumped to the platform, as the train started moving. The door of the train car rolled closed, shielding the desperately waving David, the city, trees, and sky, as they seemed to float away. The train was carrying Rachel and children nowhere, but now only one thing was important, the front and the guns' cannonade were left behind.

They ran away, but the war front caught up with them. The bombing began only an hour after they escaped. As the train grated to a stop, people poured out of the open doors and, under the roar of Messerschmitt planes, ran into the field and fell to the ground. Rachel pushed the children into the first ditch, trying to cover them with her body. The boys were frightened, stunned and obeyed unquestioningly, despite little Osik's constant high-pitched wailing. The Messerschmitt flew low, and Rachel tried to press the children into the ground, still hot from the burning sun. The deafening roar of the planes drowned Osik's squeaks out. A bomb exploded somewhere close, nearly deafening them and covering them with earth.

Finally the rumbling of the airplane motors subsided, and they heard the whistle of the train. Rachel brushed the dirt off the children and pulled them to the train, trying not to look at the terrible sights all around. There were many dead. Osik obediently trotted after his mother, but Gersh pulled her hand and asked in a frightened voice, "Why they are lying down? Mom, why are they lying down? Tell them that they should be up and running, tell them, Mom, tell them!"

The locomotive puffed and began to move slowly, hurrying people, but giving them time to climb back into the cars. When all who could get back, the train began to speed, leaving behind the dark bodies stretched on the land.

There was much more space in the train now. It was unbearably painful to realize that the dead once lay on the field, unburied, and among them were the still living, wounded, dying. Rachel pressed her children to her chest as an apology to those who were thrown to the earth, furrowed by the bombs. Shaken and tired people sat in silence; only children cried.

A new bombing could begin any minute. It seemed more dangerous on the train than in the city. Rachel listened intently, fearing the roar of Messerschmitt would again interrupt the peaceful tapping of the train's wheels. "Maybe we should have stayed home," she thought. "Maybe my father was right that Germans are civilized people and not going to harm civilians. He did not leave his home, he did not run away. But I. Where am I taking my children without food, without any belongings? Even if we survive now, in this train, who would pity us, the homeless, the poor, far away in an unfamiliar and maybe hostile part of Russia?"

But the train's rattling wheels, carrying its passengers to their destinations. Soon Rachel's fellow travelers, before had mingled into one common mass of faces, regained their traits and character. People began to talk. From a young woman with a little baby in her arms, Rachel learned that the train was going to Irkutsk, at the East of Siberia, and had to cross Ural Mountains. This was good news, because there, not far from the railroad, in Sukhareva village, Rachel's sister Rosa lived. Rosa had been evacuated with the plant in which she worked, and Rachel would find her now. It was a big relief, it was salvation.

A lonely elderly woman, with a simple plain face and the hands of a worker, sat at the right of Rachel on a large seat. She sighed, and quietly lamented, "I have three of them fighting, my husband and our two sons." She sighed again. "I pity children, the little ones. It grieves me to look at them. Yours, I suppose, are weary and hungry. But here is a bag. An old man sat here next to me, and he didn't return after the bombing." She untied the small bag. "Here is bread and bacon. Give it to the children, and you eat too. These goods shouldn't be wasted. There is a kettle too. I have my own, but you, I see, with the children, have empty hands. Take it to collect hot water. And, look, there is an old jacket. You can put it under your children, I see, your poor things lie on the bare floor."

The bread and bacon and old man's worn jacket were, to Rachel, salvation. It was terrible to think she had all these treasures only because the old man was left lying there on the blood-blackened earth, but Rachel only gratefully murmured, taking the bag. This was the first time she experienced such a hasty and unexpected evacuation, but soon it would become part of everyday life. And she must at all costs adapt to it, to save her children. They were tired and scared, sleeping, cuddling her from two sides. What awaited them in the future; she would learn later, but right now she could only cover the boys with this dead man's old coat, feed them bread and give them drinks from an inherited kettle.

* * *

Life did not spoil Rachel. The first seven years of her childhood were quiet and happy, spent in the house of her grandfather and grandmother, the parents of her mother whom she could not remember. Rachel was only two years old when her mother had been abandoned by her husband, Rachel's father, and went to her relatives in far-away Vienna. In a photograph, sent from this legendary city, Rachel's unknown mother leaned on the arm of a swarthy man with a thin mustache above plump lips. Her mother wore a light dress and a little white hat with a feather, and Rachel felt guilty because she possessed no love for this woman. She gave to her grandparents all the quiet warmth of her heart. They loved her, cared for her and pitied her. Rachel saw her father only on rare occasions. During those infrequent meetings, he always averted his eyes in annoyance, as if she were the reason for some trouble. Her father lived in the same city with his second beautiful wife and a daughter from his first marriage, Rachel's older sister, Rosa.

Vinnitsa, the city where they lived, was small and cozy. Single-story houses in the midst of cherry orchards ran from the hill to the wide quiet river Southern Burg. In the center of the city stood an ancient castle, built of red granite and covered over with ivy. It had been built by a rich Polish Duke in the time of the Polish dominion, and was used now as a City Hall. The people spoke mostly Russian, but one could hear Ukraine *mova* and Yiddish, which was common in the Jewish house of Rachel's family.

Rachel's grandfather enjoyed a certain respect from his neighbors; he owned a mill, and the family was considered prosperous. They had enough to send money to Vienna, and to provide for the family in Vinnitsa. Life was quiet and slow, and even the war of 1914 did not bring major changes. But the revolution of 1917 sowed discord, and the city was overtaken in turn by several armies and bandits. Anarchists, monarchists, Greens, Whites, Reds, and even Symon Petliura, leader of Ukraine's fight for independence, had their turns.

Rachel had turned seven by this time. She had big brown eyes in a narrow swarthy face, always looking too thin, too pale, and too fragile. She spoke rarely and quietly, as if she was embarrassed to be heard. Her shyness and quietness made her almost invisible at home, in sharp contrast to her pert, green–eyed and redheaded older sister Rosa, who had been admired by men since turning fifteen.

On her birthday, Rachel received the last present from her grandfather, small golden earrings. He then put her on his knee, stroking her hair, and said, quietly as if to himself, "What would happen to all of you without me?" His hand froze on Rachel's little head, and his eyes became detached as if he saw something frightening that no one had yet guessed.

From that day on, their lives changed. Grandfather did not go anywhere and spent all his time in a small room, praying. The city stopped being cozy and clean. Soldiers marched along its streets and heavy guns rolled and crashed. The noise from the agitated city was heard through the closed shutters even at night.

Grandfather's prayers did not help. One gloomy winter day,

anarchists, who were particularly virulent anti–Semites, raided the house. Grandmother pressed Rachel to her chest and they froze in the corner of the kitchen, while the dough grandmother had been kneading slowly rose on the table. They heard loud coarse voices outside, and Grandfather's words in frightened tones, as if he were trying to explain something. And then there was a shot.

The rest Rachel remembered as a nightmare: Grandfather, motionless and covered in blood; Grandmother moaning over him; and the ruined room with ransacked cabinets, broken dishes and clothes scattered on the floor.

The poverty began with hunger and cold. After everything was sold, they lived on charity. Neighbors and friends pitied them, but helped rarely. They were not the only ones who had lost a breadwinner; they were not the only ones who had nothing to eat. Strangers settled in their house, and Grandmother and Rachel nestled in the small room where Grandfather had prayed only recently. In only two years, the cold and hunger took their toll, and Grandmother died. Seventeen-year-old Rosa, already married, agreed to take Rachel in.

Rosa was kind, merry, careless and disorderly. The changes in her life seemed to not bother her at all. She worked as a secretary at some strange institution whose purpose was unclear. When she came home late, which was quite often, scandal was raised in the house. Rosa's husband, who was twice her age, began to lament and complain, pathetically raising his eyes and hands to the heavens, as if asking God himself to be witness of his indignation. This lofty tone did not stop him from adorning his dramatic accusation with the lowest sort of swearing and cursing. Rosa never repented and never expressed any regret or remorse. She looked as she had eaten well and heartily, and was now bored with the bother and nonsense of her husband's lament.

Rachel hid from these fights in her room, a former closet, the only space for her narrow hard cot. Usually Rosa appeared at the closet after a while, locking the door and announcing she would sleep with Rachel till the fool is done with his madness. The next morning "the fool" knocked softly and asked Rosa plaintively to be a decent woman and worthy wife. Young, beautiful and shameless Rosa flung the door open and, hands on her hips, expressed to him all that she thought. And she thought the slavery for women was over, and her husband could go to hell if he didn't like it. After this, "the fool" retreated to the kitchen to make for his dear little sweet Rosa acorn coffee, the only coffee of this time.

Rachel pitied him, but the light–hearted gaiety of her sister in the midst of starvation and a difficult, monotonous life roused in Rachel amazement and the most sincere admiration. Rosa's ability to bring with her a festive mood in spite of anything was a wonderful gift, which warmed Rachel too. She also wanted to be happy, merry and pert, but the most she could afford was a shy smile. Her shyness over the years developed into self-control, and attractive features of her face acquired an icon restraint.

The greatest pleasure for Rachel was school. The teachers noticed her ability and zeal. But right after the lessons she was obliged to go to the furrier shop where she worked till the end of the day doing a variety of assignments. Rachel's hands were always stained by the corrosive dyes she had to deal with in this shop, and she tried in vain to hide them.

When Rachel turned sixteen she became possessed by a passionate dream in which there was no place for finery, successful marriage or amusement. She wanted to be a doctor and her heart ached with the realization that it was an unattainable dream. Her brother-in-law did not want to support her any longer. He had an agreement with the owner of the furrier shop that she would work there the whole day after she finished school.

Rosa came to her rescue again. She emerged victorious from the scandals, which Rachel listened to with bated breath hidden in her closet. Of course, five years at Medical School was out of the question; but Rosa's husband agreed to support Rachel during the two-years-courses of midwife and nurse.

Rachel studied with gusto, incomprehensible to Rosa. During workshops Rachel went on medical calls together with an experienced paramedic. They made their trips in any weather, and, as a rule, far away from the city.

In this particular time an old horse dragged through the mud uncomfortable and unstable flat cart called a ruler. The mud road was soaked and the wheels of the ruler stuck in the clay swamps. The village was close, when the wheels slid crossing the small bridge, and the ruler bent sharply. Everybody jumped to the ground. Light as a feather, Rachel landed quite safely, and only old Rosa's boots, which Rachel wore for such travel, were muddy. The paramedic was not so adroit and not so light; his knees at sixty-five no longer sprang. He fell heavily on his right hand and dislocated his joint. It was difficult for him to get up, and he said to Rachel wincing from the pain, "I hope the childbirth will be easy and you will manage yourself with my prompts."

Their patient was an exhausted, disheveled, pregnant woman with wandering eyes: due to her swollen face, her age was hard to determine. It was difficult case. A quick exam proved their premonition. A child was cross-lying. The obstetrician was disappointed and perplexed. "We cannot take her to the city hospital in time. It is necessary to turn the child right now. Oh, the damn hand!" He shook his head and asked Rachel, "Did you study how to turn a cross-lying fetus?" She, as if spellbound, recited the entire passage from the textbook. "You remember the theory well, only here." He looked dubiously at his small, skinny assistant and muttered, "You need to eat more to gain strength!" And then, as if realizing his words were not proper in this situation, he added cheerfully, "Please, we need hot water and soap. Scrub your hands and act!"

Rachel's thin, deft hand easily entered into the woman's womb. Her fingers touched the baby, and here it was the tiny buttock. Now she needed to turn a little body in one strong movement. Everything became strained inside Rachel, some amazing confidence, almost ecstasy seized her, and the movement was just right. The baby came into a normal position to enter safely this unsafe world. Now everything was easy. "Breathe, strain yourself. Now relax. Again, push…harder, harder! Well, darling, with all your might, come on!" And there was a long-awaited croaking, pathetic cry bringing joy and immediate relief. The softened obstetrician could not restrain his feelings: "So small and weak but so deftly, just to think, ah! And without any experience! Have you ever seen something like that? Well, well done, well done!" Rachel was happy.

She finished her nursing school with praises and awards, and began working at a city hospital. She liked her job at once, but her dream of further education was never realized. It seemed it was her eternal destiny to fight poverty and hunger forever.

Rachel met her future husband thanks to a fire at the factory where he worked as a turner. As David later said, it would not be a good luck if a bad luck would help. The fire was put out safely, but several workers were burned, including David. Rachel and another nurse were sent from the hospital to the scene of the accident.

Smoke still poured upright, thick and greasy, when two young nurses came to the plant. The hands and face of the injured were covered with a thick layer of soot. The bright blue eyes looked at her through a black mask with a soft focus, almost caress. The effect was so surprising that Rachel could not help smiling. In response the black mask smiled back with a white even row of teeth.

Three months later their marriage was registered without any signs of the solemnity in a shabby office. Then David moved to the flat of woeful Rosa's husband. Rosa had a strong argument. This young couple had nowhere to live. The poor fellow put up with it, though he grumbled that wherever he turned in the apartment he would run across Rosa's relatives.

In general, it was true. It was more than enough for him that Rosa and Rachel's mother Mahri drove up from Vienna in 1920 and suddenly appeared in his house. Her Viennese smart and dandy boyfriend with his trendy mustache disappeared when the cash benefit stopped after Mahri's father was killed. After knocking around Vienna and realizing that to live in this beautiful city without money was impossible, Mahri decided to join to her eldest daughter's family. Rosa's husband did not show the slightest joy; on the contrary, he boiled with indignation. Mahri was quite smartly dressed in those miserable days and behaved, as if she were the Viennese lady. These high-society habits led her son-in-law into a rage, but he had to restrain his temper because of Rosa.

Mahri began her life in this modest home with pursed lips. However after a while she became a hostess in the kitchen because Rosa preferred to never appear there, not liking to cook. And Rachel was still small and spent all day long at school or in the furrier shop. Mahri did not limit herself to the "kitchen kingdom". After a month or two all members of family took for granted their mother's commanding voice, and her way of poking her nose into all family matters.

A few months after Rachel's marriage, an unexpected visitor appeared in this small, miserable and overcrowded apartment. It was the father of the two sisters. Throughout his life he never helped her younger daughter in any way, and it seemed, did not think about her. The elder daughter was also cut off since she got married. No wonder he was met without cordiality. Anyway, they sat at a table with more than a modest dinner, exchanging customary phrases. When the plates were empty, the father protruded his lips, in annoyance or irritation, and without any preliminaries stated unequivocally, "All of you, collect your junk and move into my house. I give it to you. My woman old man died, and we moved to his place." Then he stood up. "Well, so be it!" He shouted and slammed the door behind him.

Now they had their own home, small and old, but their own. The very next day the families placed their simple belongings there; Rosa with her husband took one half of the house, Rachel with David and Mahri another. Now when Rosa and Rachel began the life as individual families, their mother preferred to live with Rachel. The company of the silent and never arguing youngest daughter suited Mahri much more than the company of sharp tongued Rosa. In addition, Mahri disliked Rosa's husband, who tried to snub his imperious mother-in-law with evil hisses. David, to the contrary, never opposed Maher's comments, often toxic, but at the same time, he never sought a filial communion.

David was quietly immersed in his special world, strange and incomprehensible to Mahri. He evenly and truly loved Rachel; however, his real passion was their son, Misha. The boy became the center of David's life. He was happy to play with his son endlessly, make toys for him, and carry him on his shoulders on long walks. David had worked at the factory since he was fifteen, but with the advent of his son, the need to leave his baby every morning for the whole day became a torment for him. He never took overtime, to the disappointment of his mother-in-law, who grumbled that David brought home less money than he could.

Great Famine, instigated by Soviet leader Joseph Stalin, raged through Ukraine in 1932-33. Guarded by military troops and the NKVD (KGB), 44% of the Ukrainian crops were dispatched to Moscow while Ukrainians were starving. The main goal of this artificial famine was to crush all vestiges of Ukrainian nationalism and to force the Ukrainian farmer–peasant into collectivization. The death toll from the 1932-33 famines in Ukraine has been estimated between six million and seven million. Yet one of Stalin's lieutenants in Ukraine stated in 1933 that the famine was a great success. It showed the Ukrainian who was the master here. It cost millions of lives, but the collective farm system was here to stay.

During this Great Famine David became a skeleton, saving every crumb for the adored son. Alas, his desperate efforts were in vain. When the boy got measles, his weakened body could not fight, and he died. David was distraught with grief. He spent all day at the cemetery, sitting next to the grave and stroking the small knoll. At night, Rachel tried bringing him home by force, but he refused to go to bed when his beloved baby was sleeping in the cold November ground. David lay down next to the knoll, hugging the frozen earth. As expected, he fell ill with a cold, which turned into pneumonia. Rachel brought him, unconscious, to the hospital, where she worked. David was seriously ill for a long time, with all sorts of complications, but when he finally returned home, he was indifferent to everything. Rachel knew only one way to return him to life, to give birth again and certainly to a boy. But David became indifferent to her, and she herself could hardly stand from hunger and misery.

A son was born four years later. When Rachel gave David a small warm bundle of new life, David's large blue eyes became almost insane, his strong hands were trembling. He pressed the baby to his chest and buried his face in swaddling clothes, muttering with broken voice, "Misha, Misha, you returned to me! You're back, you are back!" The boy, indeed, grew up looking very similar to Misha for the simple reason; both brothers were their father's exact image.

Two years later the next son was born, this time swarthy and dark-eyed like his mother. Life seemed to be normal; the children grew up healthy and happy. Rachel became stronger and prettier. David was happy spending all his spare time with their children.

And then World War II broke out. Murder became the main occupation of people. The large mass of Europeans, who proudly called themselves civilized, crossed the Russian border and poured across the country as lava burning all on their way. They killed and killed as much as possible, hundreds, thousands, millions of people.

The war tore David from his children. He was drafted shortly after it beginning. Now Rachel was the only one who could save their boys from all afflictions. How? How long would they ride on this train with a stranger's old jacket and with bread and hard lard inherited from the dead? "If only we can manage to get to some safe place," Rachel tried to persuade herself. "I have my hands, midwives and nurses are needed everywhere. Everything would work out somehow."

The bread and hard lard were gone three days later, though Rachel did her best to be economical. Food at the stations was terribly expensive and the money quickly melted, but the train dragged along very slowly. A week passed, and another. After twenty fifth days they reached the Ural Mountains. The village Sukhareva was about fifteen miles from the station; and they arrived to it by a horse-drawn cart. It was autumn already in the Ural, the sky was gray and low; but all three of them were dressed for summer. The money ran out, Rachel could not buy food, or clothes. The children were hungry and cold. The younger one whimpered quietly, but an elder son tugged her hand, "Mama, I am hungry, I am hungry!"

Rachel saw no signs of the factory that had been evacuated from Vinnica where Rosa worked; the locals had not even heard about it. Rachel's heart sank from fear. "Perhaps, it is a different village with the similar name? Perhaps there is one more Sukhareva in Ural?" Somebody pointed Rachel to the Village Soviet. There the clerks surely must know about the factory. And they knew. The plant had not reached Suckharevo; halfway to this place it turned to Kazakhstan by an order of some authorities. Rachel asked for help, "The children are hungry, frozen". But the clerks just shrugged their shoulders. There were more refugees in the village than indigenous people. "Go, and ask around, maybe someone will help you," was the answer.

Rachel was knocking at the doors, but the locals did not want to take the refugees into their houses with the simple argument, "Who knows, what kind of people they are. You will take them inside and then you won't be able to push them out even by force. They could be thieves, and we could get typhoid infection from them."

Almost every house was burdened with refugees. Local authorities placed them in the houses without asking the owner's permission, especially if the newcomers had Russian government warrants. For Rachel's pleas of temporary shelter for her and the children the response was approximately the same, "Get away from here, there is no place available for all of you beggars." Rachel could not scrounge even a piece of bread for the boys. The local people exclaimed, "We have nothing for ourselves. There are too many of you who are hungry. We cannot feed all of you!"

Horror and despair drove Rachel from door to door. The hungry, tired and cold children were howling without stopping. Finally, when hope was lost, one door opened before them. Rachel put all her heart in her plea. "Let me in, dear old man, at least for a couple of days. I'm a nurse, a midwife. When I get a job, I'll pay you for everything. Help me, please, my children are dying."

"Come in. Just looks how your boys are bawling! I see, you are from far away, eh? You are not dressed for our weather."

"We are refugees from the Ukraine; we are just from the train."

The shanty looked very shabby; there was one small room, and a small inner porch. But it was salvation. The old man brought some warm rags into the corner of the room.

"Make yourself a little bit more comfortable. You are welcome to all I have, and you will return the debt to me later. Here there is bread, a bit of sunflower oil and onions. Give it to the little ones and eat yourself. I see, you are all skin and bones."

At night, they were bitten mercilessly by bed bugs, but the house was warm, and the rags seemed remarkably comfortable, especially after the bare wooden floor of the train's boxcar. Rachel and the children broke down in a dream, hardly bowing their heads.

Early in the morning, Rachel scraped and cleaned their current habitation and with kerosene lubricated all the places where bed bugs could be. Behind the shanty was a self-made tiny but easy to heat bathhouse. She washed herself and the children vigorously, with enormous pleasure and relief. Then she left the boys at home, strictly ordering them not to stick the noses on the street, and went to look for a job.

Fortunately, the Medical Center desperately needed midwives and nurses because almost all the medical staff had been sent to the front. That same day Rachel had her job, and she also received bread ration cards.

This Medical Center served not only the village, but also the entire area around, and Rachel's endless traveling started. She went from one village to another, from one hamlet to the next, to every place where people were sick or dying, and children came into the world despite global catastrophes and disasters.

This young woman was always in a hurry to bring into this world one more life, to treat ill people or close the eyes of those who ceased to suffer. She jolted in the horse-cart from spring to fall. In winter she slipped on the crisp snow in a sledge pulled by the same old horse. Small, thin, almost weightless Rachel was wrapped in a huge old fur coat from the Village Soviet. She drowned in this coat; but it saved her from the severe cold and frost. The sledge carried her into a white haze at any time and in any weather.

Joy and hope came to Rachel from the military triangular envelopes with David's letters. It was the second year of the war; but he was not even wounded yet. Rachel started to hope for a miracle of his safe return. Letters overflowed with questions and concern about their children. And it was worth worry. No one watched the boys while Rachel traveled. The old man, the hut-holder, worked as a night watchman at the state-farm storage. During the day he slept on a sleeping nook called *lezhanka*, which gained plenty of warm air because it was arranged between the Russian stove and a wall, just beneath the ceiling. The old man slept soundly, and the children spent their days without any supervision. They were often alone all night.

The shanty was situated on the outskirts of the village, with a thistle wasteland and state farm fields behind it. The elder boy, Gersh, was a great explorer, and to putter around near the house was a bore for him, whereas the world around the village attracted him by its novelty. He explored it with curiosity and always dragged with him his younger brother. Since Osik was still small and could not go too far, the boys usually returned home safely.

Nevertheless Gersh's fantasies often caused Rachel to worry. Once, a very strange idea came to this boy's mind. He burned with the desire to find a forest, but no forest existed around Sukhareva. The children's search expedition began on that rare day when Rachel remained in the village and worked at the Medical Centre from early morning. After she left for her job, the boys tramped briskly through thistle wasteland to a mysterious forest, where, in their imagination, the wind shook mighty branches.

The brothers were very different. Five-year-old, tall for his age, sturdily built, blue-eyed Gersh always lived in a fantasy world. Three-year-old black-eyed Osik was small, fragile, with thin legs and hands, and was far more agreeable and affectionate than his brother. Osik did not live in fairy tales, as Gersh did, but he unconditionally followed his elder brother wherever Gersh had been lured by his imagination. And this time Osik trotted behind his older brother until tired. He began to whimper, asking to go home; however, Gersh was so anxious to find the wood that he pulled his brother ahead.

Finally, they found, not a forest, of course, but a small grove, with a deafeningly noisy bird rookery. There were more rooks' nests than branches on the trees. They stuck everywhere like gray shaggy clumps among the wretched sparse foliage. It seemed the birds had a lack of housing just like in the boy's village. The hubbub of black birds gave this place an ominously frightening mystery. Osik did not like this ugly grove at all, and was scared by the hue-and-cry around. He was exhausted and wanted to go back home.

The field stretched before the children; and it was not clear in which direction to go. They went at random, and soon came upon a group of women returning from fieldwork. This could have been the end of their adventure; but Gersh's imagination painted witches, the mistresses of black birds, instead of weary women. The boys ran, forgetting fatigue in such a speed that the women could not stop them. "Witches, witches," repeated Gersh chokingly. "If they catch us they would grill us!" And the boys fled until they could not breathe. When they finally stopped and looked around it became clear that they were lost. It was unknown what would have happened to them if their mother, warned by "the witches", had not rushed looking for her two sons using the Medical Center horse-cart. She found them, completely exhausted, a mile away from home.

Another six months went well, the military in form of triangles came infrequently but more or less regularly; and Rachel's weak hope that David would come home alive from this hell became stronger. Now she did not feel like a stranger among the villagers; they showed sympathy and respect for this thin but very skillful *doctoress*. The old master of their house became very kind to Rachel, and trying to help her, he agreed to buy bread with their ration cards while she traveled around farms and villages.

It looked as if Rachel's life normalized more or less, but during one of her night trip in the sleigh she felt beaten by chills. The fur coat did not warm her; and her thoughts became confused. "Typhus" she diagnosed herself with horror. "What will happen now with the children?"

The driver felt something was wrong.

"What is it? Are you sick or what?"

"Take me to the Medical Center, go straight to it, plies, be hurry!"

There were many more patients in the Center's infirmary than the space could hold and all the beds stood close to each other. Even the corridor was full of ill people lying on mattresses on the floor. The air was heavy and stinky from helpless human bodies; and the atmosphere was completely devoid of oxygen, which patients tried to catch in their wheezing and whistling lungs. Here, Rachel changed from a nurse to a patient. She sank into the darkness of unconsciousness, and then it seemed to her she floated out from a muddy pool at the surface agonizing, gasping for a breath, and in the gray mist of her dim consciousness the same thought aroused, "Children! Children, what happened to them?" And again everything became blurred and confused, and Rachel plunged into darkness. She flounced and tossed from life to near-death for a month until the disease had retreated finally, and the same question, "What happened to the children?" arose in her mind clearly and with frightening reality.

"Do not panic, do not flounce. Your children have a place," her nurse tried to calm her. "The elder one is with the old master of your house, the youngest was sent to an orphanage."

Such news did not bring consolation. Rachel wrapped her shaved head with a shawl that covered now a short fluff instead of her heavy dark braid, and went home on weak and staggering feet. Gersh rushed toward her joyfully. She hugged his thin, emaciated dirty body. The old man did not wash Gersh and did not change his clothes during all that time; but he kept the boy alive, and Rachel was grateful to him. However, Osik had disappeared without a trace. The orphanage was far away, in a neighboring town, and the name of her son simply was not listed there. Rachel was allowed to meet all the children, but Osik was not with them. "We have a lot of children here, and we do not remember all the names. Maybe he is over there, in the outbuilding, where the sick kids are "suggested one of the nurses.

He was there. He lay next to the window, dying, unconscious. His scattered hairs were frozen to the pillow due to the ice cold air. Rachel did not scream or cry, she took off her shawl, wrapped Osik in it, took him in her arms and hugged him, feeling a weakly beating little heart.

When Rachel was leaving with Osik, the head of the orphanage tried to stop her. It was not permitted to take away a child without registration papers, but glancing at Rachel's face, she waved to her, "Go now!"

The old man, the master of their hut was deeply moved by the pitiful condition of the little boy and gave him his warm place on the top of the Russian Stove, his *lezhanka*. He even managed to get milk and a little bit of honey for Osik; and Rachel nursed her little son until life returned to him again.

The endless traveling of the young woman began again. She became so thin during her illness that it seemed the first breath of wind might carry her away. It was incomprehensible where and how she gained her strength. But Rachel had not thought about whether she could or could not withstand this entire ordeal. She just knew she had to do. It was the war, many people were dying; her husband was at the front in the trenches, and he could be killed any minute. But here was the rear, and she had to do what seemed impossible. She slept mostly on the move, when the sledge carried her to the next village to save every hour and minute for her children, cleaning, cooking, sewing, all that was necessary, all that one cannot do without

In February 1943 the Germans surrounded at Stalingrad. It was the strategic turning point of the Second World War. After Stalingrad, Hitler had no hope of winning on the eastern front and that meant inevitable defeat in the wider conflict. The Soviets lost a million soldiers in this battle, more than the British and Americans during the whole war. Such sacrifices, as Churchill said, tore the guts out of the German war machine.

The hope of the victory emerged after the victory at Stalingrad, Life seemed easier, lighter, although famine in the rear became harsher; and the battles on the front got bloodier.

The terrible news of the Nazi's atrocities came from the liberated areas; but Rachel did not know yet that her father, who believed so much in the progressive Europeans, was no longer alive. He was killed in the cruelest way. His legs were tied to a horse that set off at a gallop, smashing the man's head to the delight of the Nazi soldiers. Mercifully, she also did not know that none of her relatives survived in the occupation zones, no one, not a single soul was left alive.

Rachel strained internally when she heard the word Kursk Bulge on the radio. David was right there at Kursk, in the tank unit, in the heart of the long and bitter battle. It was here the Germans centered their attack in what was called Operation Citadel. Hitler ordered, "This offensive is of decisive importance. It must end in swift and decisive success. Every commander, every private soldier, must be indoctrinated with awareness of the decisive importance of this offensive. Victory at Kursk will be a beacon for the whole world. There must be no failure."

For the attack on Kursk, Germany had grouped 900,000 soldiers in the region, 10,000 artillery guns, 2,700 tanks and 2,000 aircraft. Elite Luftwaffe units took part at Operation Citadel. About 1/3rd of all Germany's military strength was concentrated in this area. No offensive was ever prepared as carefully as this one.

The Russians had also placed vast numbers of men and equipment in the Kursk bulge. 1.3 million Soldiers were based there, 20,000 artillery pieces, 3,600 tanks and 2,400 planes.

The greatest tank battle of World War Two took place on July 12th. In total, 1,500 tanks were involved at Kursk.

By July 19th, the Russians had pushed forward 45 miles. General Model warned Hitler that the Wehrmacht faced another Stalingrad. The German Army pulled back 60 miles in an effort to regroup. However, by the time the withdrawal had occurred, German troops were exhausted. The material damage done to the German Army was massive - 500,000 men were killed, wounded or missing; vast amounts of armor had been lost.

"The immense battles of Kursk heralded the downfall of the German army on the Eastern Front," tolled Winston Churchill.

The military triangles stopped coming. Rachel was calm outwardly, doing everything what that needed, but her heart ached, when the postal worker promised her to bring a letter next time. She had not received a death notification yet, and it gave her hope. Finally the envelope came, but it was signed by someone else's hand. Alive! He was alive, but wounded, could not write; he told her not to worry, asked about the children. For the first time she burst into tears of relief and fear. "He's alive, but how badly is he wounded? Will he survive?" Rachel wiped away her tears with her palm, but they still flowed. The address of the hospital was on the envelope, Tambov. Rachel understood, not by her mind, but with all her heart, with all her being. She must go to David, and not alone, but with her children. David would see them and survive, no matter how severe the wound was. She herself would nurse him in the hospital.

At the Medical Center Rachel was called crazy. They persuaded her to stay and refused to let her go. She begged, implored, and then went away, taking the children on trains, freight cars trying to reach Tambov hospital in time. She did not. David died the day before Rachel arrived.

The voice of the surgeon came to her as from a fog. One word sounded stunning in her mind. He is dead, dead, dead. Rachel did not want to live now, but she could not afford to allow herself to be absorbed by grief. She held her children by the hands. Her little sons did not understand yet all the depth of the tragedy. Now they were two orphans, for whom only she was responsible. Rachel was given David's military greatcoat. She held it and pressed it to her chest. Something solid was in the pocket. She pulled it out. It was a little book; David bought it for his children before the war. The three little pigs laughed on the cover. They looked happy as if the war had never been.

* * *

The sun lit up the edge of the curtain and disappeared. Nica sat in silence at nightfall, absorbed in her thoughts. Suddenly the electric light flashed, and it made Nica return to the present day. "It is enough to sit in the gloom and melancholy!" Claudia Ivanovna smiled broadly. "What happened then passed, nothing will come back and nothing can be fixed. Let sleeping dogs lie. Go to the table, my pie is ready!"

The Telegram

Nica looked tensely at the telegram and could not make anything out of it. Even the fact that she received it in Rome seemed impossible. The first reaction was fear. Something awful had happened to her mother, left behind in the Soviet Union when Nica and her family had emigrated from this country.

Her worry was heightened by the fact she could not read the telegram. It was not written in Russian or Italian or English. Looking at the strange words, Nica finally figured out that it was in German. The meaning of this telegram came with difficulty from the depth of her long-forgotten German. "Hope to meet you. Call me. Kiss. Eugene Muller".

Nica could not believe her own eyes. Only one person could be Eugene Muller. He was her first cousin, who died in childhood during the Second World War. He and his mother, Nica's Aunt Nina, stayed behind in the city occupied by the Germans. Nica was only four years old when they disappeared, gone in the flame of war. It seemed that Nina and Eugene had vanished forever, and now here was this telegram.

Nica recollected the portrait of a two-year-old boy in a velvet suit with large white collar. He was skinny, big-eyed, looking at the world with seriousness and slight fear. Nica and her sister, May often examined this picture with sadness, thinking their little cousin perished. Their mother's multi-year search for the lost family came to nothing; and it was considered a family tragedy. In secret the girls fantasized that the little boy and Aunt Nina somehow survived, despite the impossibility of it. They imagined the most incredible pictures of an unexpected and happy meeting with the lost family.

Truth appeared to be even more fantastic than the children's imagination, and the proof was this telegram from Eugene that Nica was holding in her hands.

The picture of the boy in the velvet suit was kept in the old leather-bound family album with a huge silver buckle. There were other old photos on the thick, smooth pages. One of them portrayed the noble Baron Eugene von Muller, May's and Nica's grandfather. He wore pince-nez, and his aristocratic face was framed with a small beard *a'la Chekhov*. The picture of their beautiful grandmother Mary was placed next to the grandfather. She was remarkably similar to Nica's and May's mother Elena; she had the same big lively and bright blue eyes, expressive mouth and high forehead. Two girls, Nina and Elena in white dresses, fashionable in the beginning of the twentieth century, looked from the photograph happily, not suspecting cataclysms in the near future.

Nina was four years older than Elena, but it never prevented intimacy and love between the sisters. Their childhood and adolescence could be part of some romantic nineteenth century novel. They grew up in Baltic Livonia, now Estonia, in the ancient city of Dorpat, now – Tartu, in an aristocratic family, which had lost its luster and richness but was well-provided and highly cultured. The house was surrounded by a blooming garden, nicely kept by a gardener. There were eleven spacious rooms, among them the vast library and a music hall with the big concert piano and soft armchairs. Besides this, there was a small apartment in the mezzanine where their old, beloved nanny lived who became decades ago a member of the family. The housemaid, cook, and gardener, who helped in the kitchen too, formed the small servant staff.

The head of the family, Baron von Muller, a well-educated man with advanced views, was history professor at the famous Dorpat University founded in 1632 by King Gustav II of Sweden.

Everybody in this household adored the lady of the house, Mary. Family members spoke to her in German and French because she was not very comfortable with her Russian.

Aunt Lily, who ran a private girls' school, was another personage in this family. She had remarkable beauty despite her mature age, but in the past she had rejected the possibility of marriage and spurned her suitors only in order to dedicate her life to her beloved brother. She was convinced it was unreasonable to entrust his care to Mary. Lily considered her brother's marriage a misalliance. Mary was just a teacher, the daughter of poor Protestant priest of no noble lineage. This marriage according to Aunt Lily crossed out all brilliant possibilities for her brother and thus broke her heart.

Eugene with his soft character never contradicted Lily, but looked at life differently and acted according to his high moral beliefs. Mary and Eugene were tender, loving spouses and parents, and with amazing patience, tolerated the jealous tyranny of Lily.

The Muller's house was always opened to highly intellectual and cultured people. The book Napoleon written by their friend Eugene Tarle is still read not only by historians. The paintings of Igor Grabar, another close friend of Eugene Muller, are exhibited in the Tretyakov Gallery in Moscow. In this happy and refined family atmosphere, Nina and Elena were absorbing culture and knowledge as naturally as breathing. All this luxury and delicate upbringing led to sad circumstances. The sisters grew up idealists, romantic, and vulnerable to the severity of future events.

The happiness of their childhood and adolescence was broken by the drama, which corresponds to the cynical cruelty of the twentieth century.

The First World War brought the anxious foreboding of threatening changes. For people who thought ahead, it was clear that Russia would not be able to build an army equivalent to the very well organized German forces. Russia had an enormous population but it was mostly illiterate peasants, who knew nothing farther than their villages. They heard something about Moscow, but were unaware of the existence of Germany or France and the meaning of war on a foreign territory was unclear to them.

Nevertheless, at the beginning of the war, the hope of a quick victory overcame Russia, and patriotism spread everywhere, Derpt included. Livonia in those times belonged to Russia; although it was ruled by upper class of Baltic Germans, and most of the population of this city spoke German. Since the beginning of the war all German sign boards were changed to Russian, often with funny grammatical mistakes.

Masses of the badly trained and poorly armed Russian peasants were killed at the front. This infuriated progressive intellectuals who opposed the czar's power, and the Bourgeois Revolution in February 1917 was accepted with elation. Derpt University boiled with enthusiasm. However, after the October Twenty-Fifth coup, when the Bolsheviks became the city authorities, there was a hostile split of opinions among professors and students. The Bolsheviks, derived from majority ultimately became the Communist Party of the Soviet Union.

The peasant–soldiers accepted with readiness the Bolsheviks call to throw down their arms and go home. They killed their officers and left fronts open for the German armies, which went on with victorious attacks and in 1918 captured Derpt.

Now the Muller family was ordered to give up part of their house to German officers, who, by the way, behaved as civilized people. The difficulties appeared because of Lily, who was grasped by Russian patriotism despite her German origin. She could not endure the presence of the enemies of her Motherland in her house and she moaned loudly and with drama about having to give shelter to the foes. This greatly confused her close relatives, and finally, under the influence of the sister's rage and because of famine Eugene decided to move away. However, where to go? At this time many of Muller's friends went with their families west to Czechoslovakia, Poland, and France. German did not prohibit this; actually they helped the emigrants. Lily did not want to hear about going to the West. Only Russia had appealed to her patriotic spirit. But all she knew about Russia was from the pages of literature, and reality was quite different.

At that time, a letter from Eugene's pupil was received. He persuaded his teacher to move with all the family to Novozybkov, the small city at the border between Russia and Belarus, where he was a principal of a new Soviet school and trying to gather good scholars for it. He promised an immediate job, attention, and help.

"Do you know where are you going, Eugene, my dear?" one of his intimate friends was horrified. "They are savage people with savage customs!" Later Eugene recalled this phrase many times.

There was a party on the eve of departure when many close old friends of the Mullers came to say goodbye. Eugene, who was an excellent reciter, was asked, as usual, to read some ballad or a poem. He chose for some reason "The Raven" by Edgar Poe. Nobody applauded when he finished reciting, and a gloomy silence of foreboding hung in the air. The friends parted with heavy hearts, they foresaw it right. The departure, which was planned as a temporary measure against hunger and German occupation, was irreversible.

An empty room with the smell of fresh lime replaced the warm, comfortable and beautiful Derpt home. It was one of the schoolrooms prepared as living quarters for a new teacher and his family. Starvation found them very soon here too. Inhabitants of this small city got provisions from their kitchen gardens. The farmer's market here was poor, and food was expensive. Nobody in the Muller's family complained but Mary's health deteriorated. It was too difficult for her to endure the cold, the miserable meals and the lack of the basic condition for normal life. She was unaccustomed to cooking, and the stove refused to burn under her clumsy hands.

Before long Mary passed away from pneumonia. Her premature death was a horrible blow to Eugene and the girls. But nevertheless, this miserable city Novozybkov, where Mary died so tragically, saved the lives of all other members of the family.

At the end of 1920 the political persecution of KGB, NKVD at that time, was rampant. The title of "Baron" meant a death sentence, but this small city allowed the Muller to hide their noble origin. Nobody knew them there and no one was interested in them. Besides, the humble position of a schoolteacher was a good coverage.

But the bitterness of pain and loss found the Muller again and again. Three of Eugene's nephews, three White Guard officers, were lost forever. He learned that after the White Army was defeated, one of his nephews shot himself in the temple with the words "Russia lost". What happened to the other two young men was unknown. Eugene dearly loved his three wonderful nephews, and mourned their death till the end of his days. The Bolsheviks executed his brother-in law, the general Geimovsky, immediately after the overthrow of the bourgeois government. He hoped his sister, Anna, the wife of the general and the mother of those three boys, managed to immigrate to France, but his hope was slim.

Eugene tried to oversee their poor and miserable life, and did not allow himself to lose his spirit. He was the one who supported positive moods in the family and showed his enjoyment of simple pleasures, such as a gift of a pencil, which was hard to get at that time. Eugene's kindness and deep knowledge made him the most popular teacher in the school where he taught history and literature. No doubt, he deeply missed the circle of his Dorpat's highly educated and enlightened friends. In secret moments of weakness, it seemed to him that he, like Robinson Crusoe, was thrown on a desert island to be surrounded only by the savage Fridays *.

But he had as compensation two loving, beautiful and intelligent daughters. It was a great comfort for Eugene and at the same time a source of great unrest. What was the future for his girls in this new grotesque and cruel life?

The sisters could not continue their education after graduating from the Soviet public school. The colleges and universities were limited to the children of the intelligentsia and formerly wealthy people. The oldest, Nina, found a job as secretary in a newspaper office. She soon married a young talented journalist. The marriage looked happy, and it was a source of joy for Eugene.

In a couple of years, Elena left for Moscow, where at first she found work as a maid in the house of a well-known medical doctor, and later became a nanny in the child care center. It was a very important step in her life. This job granted her permission to be a student at the school of Working Youth. The diploma from this school was a passport to any college and university. As a result, three years later, she was admitted to Moscow State University. Elena chose the geological department without any clear realization of the hardship of this profession, but she was genuinely influenced by romantic and heroic images of explorers. She was very happy to be a student, studying was a joy, but hunger tormented her constantly. The student cantinas saved her. In these years it was possible to get free bread and mustard. Very often it was the only meal for Elena. Before graduating from the University she married the head of the geological expeditions, a very decent and brilliant person. Eugene was still alive when his first granddaughter with the cheerful name May was born.

It looked as if family life was reaching some level of normality and happiness. Alas, this superficial prosperity did not last for long. Nina was the first to become a victim of the Great Stalin's Purge of 1937 –1938 (**). She, who knew several foreign languages and had a German last name, was accused of spying for foreign countries and arrested. Eugene was not able to tolerate another cruelty from the

Bolsheviks; he became an old man overnight and soon died from a stroke

---

* Friday is one of the main characters of Daniel Defoe's novel Robinson Crusoe. Robinson Crusoe names the savage, with whom he cannot at first communicate, "Friday" because they first meet on that day.
**At 1937-1938 there was a gigantic scale repression covering all regions and all sectors of society. More than two millions were arrested for political reasons in these two years. Half of them were shot.

In 1937-1938 the Soviet people were full of enthusiasm for building a new world, socialist country. And at the same time, they were paralyzed by fear of the NKVD, abbreviation for The People's Commissariat for Internal Affairs, which in later years was called KGB. Nobody knew the truth about the Great Stalin's Purge; nobody could comprehend what was going on. More than two million people disappeared in these two horrible years. Innocent victims were interrogated by use of torture. Half of them received the death sentence without any public trials, and were executed almost immediately. The NKVD hunt for the "traitors" rolled through the Soviet Union like a plague.

Nina's arrest ended the existence of a young family. Her husband publicly denounced her and signed the special affidavit annulling their marriage. Elena called him scumbag, not realizing that any refusal to sign this paper could mean immediate death for him but would not help Nina. Nobody knew what happened to him later. He was probably arrested and sent to one of the Soviet concentration camps.

Once during the Second World War he showed up unexpectedly as a beggar in Almaty at Elena's house. When Elena's daughter May opened the door, she saw the homeless penniless person clothed in rags. It had been a common sight at this time, but something shocked May in the appearance of this desperate man. She called for her mother. When Elena saw him her expression hardened; and she said in a flat stony voice, "Go away and don't come back ever."

May was terrified by this event especially by the stern gaze of her mother. She did not dare question her, but the scene May witnessed was imprinted forever in her memory. As she found out much later, it was he, Nina's husband. Every time she recalled the image of this poor man, her heart ached with pain.

Nina was pregnant when she was arrested. In September 1938 she gave birth to a son named Eugene in honor of her late father. Conditions in the Soviet jail were impossible to describe. Nina could not sleep from fear that lice and bed bugs would eat her newborn son. Compassion did not exist toward the Peoples Enemies. Despite all the rules, Nina's baby son was not taken away from her. Probably it happened because the current chief of NKVD, KGB,

Ezhov was arrested and shot. Now Lavrentiy Beria came to the power. Those in charge of the jails were disoriented and did not know what to do with the people arrested by Ezhov's orders. Indeed, a short wave of amnesty rolled across the country; and a small part of prisoners, including Nina, was dismissed in 1939.

Almost all people released by Beria were soon rearrested again. Nina managed to avoid arrest only because the Second World War engulfed the region where they lived.

In the summer of 1941, the threat of war hung in the air like a black cloud. Elena's husband left her for a geological expedition and made her promise to be home all the time with their little children. But fears for Nina, Aunt Lily and the little boy, who lived close to the border, were stronger than her promises. Elena went to Novozybkov by train with the aim of bringing all Nina's family to her home in the safe city Almaty, Kazakhstan. Next day after arriving, Elena played with her two-year-old nephew. Little Eugene ran toward her from the small green hill, Elena caught him, and both laughed joyfully. Nina watched them with a happy smile. The day was warm, the sky was blue, and the sun was so bright... when sirens began to howl hysterically. The Second World War had begun.

Nina and her son were not able to join Elena because Aunt Lily lay motionless after her stroke.

"Nina, my darling, let me take Eugene with me. He would be safe with us in Almaty." Elena begged her sister desperately.

Nina embraced her firmly and said, "No, if we are fated to perish, let it be all of us together."

They parted with dry eyes. Horror of the coming future dried their tears. Would they see each other again? They did not know, and they feared to unclasp their last embrace, sensing that they were losing each other forever.

It was the last information about Nina and her son.

Elena was leaving Novozybkov that very day. She barely managed to get onto the train, overcrowded with refugees. Nina, Lily and little Eugene had disappeared in the flame of War.

* * *

Nica almost ran down along the Rome streets to the Post office, to make a return telephone call. Hurriedly she dialed the number, and what a disappointment! She was answered by a female voice speaking German. Nica understood nothing; she repeated her name distinctly a few times and then hung up the phone. Next day she received a second telegram. "Please, call me at six p.m. I will be waiting. Eugene."

Nica could hardly wait for the appointed hour. But this time she heard the voice of her unknown cousin. He spoke in broken Russian, but so warmly and heartily with such a genuine joy that tears rolled from Nica's eyes.

Nica and Eugene agreed to meet in two days in a small city at the border between Italy and Austria. "Eugene, how will you recognize me?" Nica asked. "Don't worry, I will sense you," Eugene laughed.

The train stopped at the small clean station. Mixing with the crowd of passengers, Nica came out anxiously from the train and saw a slender blue-eyed gentlemen running toward her. He immediately hugged and kissed her.

"How did you guess that it was me?" Nica asked.

"Just by your eyes. Everybody who came recently from the Soviet Union has a frightened glance," he replied laughing.

The small, quiet, cozy hotel with a family restaurant was placed high in the Alps. Nobody disturbed them during their long conversation. The night flew by as if just an hour, but the two cousins could not stop talking to each other. It was necessary for them to fill the gap of thirty-five years of separation, which was almost, all their whole lives. Here at the small table, lighted by the dim lamp with a multicolored shade Nica heard the continuation of the story, which had stopped for her in July 1941.

"I was too small to understand and remember anything," said Eugene. "Mother told me that German soldiers came to Novozybkov a few days after the beginning of the War. They were absolutely different Germans than those who occupied Derpt in 1918. It seemed that some awful metamorphosis occurred with that nation. A civil attitude to citizens changed to the cynical cruelty of the supermen, who had completely lost their humanity. Mama recalled the big crowd of civilians who were led to be shot. On the chests of the forefront was written, "We are Jews. We have no right to live." Among these people were our friends and acquaintances, the schoolteachers, medical doctors and mother's colleagues. It seemed that misdeeds had become a way of life for the whole world. My mother had hated her jailers and the soviet power, now she hated these German invaders. It looked as if a normal person was not able to live in this encirclement of overall evil."

"It is painful for me to talk about it because I know the people of the present Germany. They are very different. They are friendly, kind and highly civilized. I feel myself among them as a fish in the water. I lost my Russian ethnicity a long time ago, and now I am a German. I cannot understand why the whole world became crazy in the first half of the twentieth century. Was it like some epidemic of atrocity?"

"Let me continue. Fascists sent us to Germany, to the labor camps. Was that accidental or did it happen because my mother's last name was German and she spoke German fluently? We were allocated to a farm in a small village without any guards. In her past, she was taught to play Chopin and Beethoven and recite Goethe's poems, but she was never taught how to work with a pitchfork. The farmer wasn't a cruel person, but he required good work with minimum expenses. Mother overstrained herself and she didn't have time for me. I grew up like a weed among the horde of village boys, and I was their leader. Certainly, our grandfather would be horrified by my wild behavior. But it was most important that we survived those terrible years. We never had enough food. By the end of the war, starvation became more and more severe. I was hungry during all my childhood and adolescence."

"When the war ended we remained in Germany. Mother managed to prove that she was persecuted in the Soviet Union due to political reasons. She received a pension and a special
apartment in Bonn as a victim of fascism. From that day, she never

worked, because the pension was bigger than any salary accessible to her. I went to school and then – to college. Afterwards a job and the family followed, as usual."

Eugene pulled photographs from his pocket, "There are your nephews." Nica looked at these pictures. It never occurred to her that she would find not only her cousin but also new shots of young relatives. They looked at her with smiling faces, and in some way they were quite different from Russian children. Maybe because Russians did not smile in photographs and their faces were always tense.

It was dawn when Eugene took Nica's hand and said, "Good morning, my dear sister. Now we will never lose each other again!"

TO NOW

"Nostalgia? No, I have never experienced it, but I often have nightmares of Moscow. My dreams vary, but the essence of them is always the same. The Soviet authorities forbid me to emigrate from the Soviet Union, and I should stay there forever. I am seized with infinite despair. When I wake up, I feel joy and relief knowing that it was just a bad dream."

Two young women, Nika and Olga, walked along beautiful Via dei Condotti toward the Spanish Plaza, Piacca di Spania, as it is called here in Rome. Nica was a refugee from the Soviet Union who arrived in Rome only a week ago, and Olga was an American tourist traveling to Italy. They met by chance on the steps of the ancient Pantheon. This was their second meeting; the first one was twenty years ago at Moscow University. Olga and Nica have not seen each other since, but now they met as old friends. "I have lived in America for 16 years," said Olga," but I see these dreams constantly. I suspect that all who managed to escape from the Soviet Union will tremble from the same nightmares the rest of their life."

Fantastic Rome surrounded the two friends, and they felt happy. The famous Spanish Staircase, this lovely monument made of travertine towered in front of them, and both women stood fascinated by this beautiful view. Broad steps raised high above the Spanish Plaza and crowned by light, skyward church Trinita dei Monti.

Spanish Plaza was already filled with cheerful crowds. Tourists mingled with souvenir sellers, artists, magicians and jugglers.

Somewhere a clear voice poured sweet Naples Romances. Nica thought that this celebration whirled her around and she took to the carefree joy.

A huge white amphitheater of the staircase was filled with sitting tourists and Romans. She and Olga climbed the steps to the middle and sat down.

"We are so lucky that we managed to run away from Russia," said Nica. "One shudders to think about those who were and who will be the victims of this regime."

"I would like to tell you about the amazing destiny of a remarkable woman, who also ran away from the Soviet Union immediately after the Second World War," replied Olga

"Please, do," answered Nica, "I love to listening this kind of story."

Olga thought for a moment and then began to talk:

"Among many people I noticed her at once. The expressive profile of Dante, female version, framed by slightly wavy short hair gave her face surprising significance. The intelligent vivid eyes sparkled with humor, and an infectious laugh provoked instant sympathy. She was about seventy. I knew that she had moved to Sarasota from New York recently after the death of her husband and her retirement from the University. She was introduced to me as Doctor Fedukovich, but she objected to this formal title. "Call me just Elena in the wonderful American tradition."

At the end of the party, which was held in the hospitable house of the Sarasota University's president and his pleasant, slim Russian wife Irina, I invited Elena for a dinner party. She laughed and replied, "It would be better for you to visit me. I don't make dinners, but I guarantee you hot rolls with cheese and a cup of coffee."

These rolls, warmed in the small electric oven, became a favorite delicacy for me for years because this simple treatment was always accompanied by lively conversation. I admired Elena's humor and erudition. Her constant excursions to her beloved ancient Helladic gave our conversations special flavor.

From the early years of my childhood I read and reread the Ancient Greek Myths in the big book with the colorful pictures, belonging to my grandfather, and this enhanced my reputation in Elena's eyes. It was pleasant and a little bit funny for me to discover that I had found the way to Elena's heart remembering the names of mythic heroes engraved on my memory. Once more my trump card was the novelty regarding the tiny and enigmatic subjects of my research, viruses. I brought fresh articles on this topic or retold them to Elena. In response I got constant enjoyment from our conversation, unexpected questions, no less unexpected answers, and witty explanations of past and present events. Sometimes we argued heatedly, but we never quarreled. The voice of Elena, lapsed into silence for others, but still lived for me. "The man is in a cage, the beast is free. The cage is our civilization, and if the man is released from this cage of civilization he becomes a beast."

Elena's quiet one-story house, surrounded by a green lawn and hidden under the tall flowers-blazing jacaranda tree, was for me my Ionic School.

Elena and her husband Gabriel, the young professors of Kiev University, escaped to America just after the Second World War. The reason was the story, which almost cost Elena her life. It began with the innocent passion for mountain climbing to which this couple devoted their summer vacations.

This time they decided to attack the main peak of the Caucasian mountain Elbrus. It was not possible to make it without a guide. It was suggested to them to hire the best guide, one-hundred-three year old Ger-Aka, who was the father of many children, the youngest one not yet four years old. The guide's address was very peculiar, the Republic of Karachi, the village nearest the peak, Elbrus. However, it was sufficient. They found Ger-Aka instantly after showing his picture, which they received from the Moscow Alpine Club to the folk at the village bazaar. The famous guide himself was there at the bazaar, enthusiastically discussing the late political news with his countrymen. He was short, friendly, good-natured and extraordinarily mobile. It seemed he did not walk, but only ran. As soon as Ger-Aka saw his portrait, he became greatly excited, but when he understood the same picture was kept in Moscow, his joy changed to irrepressible pride. The curious countrymen made a long line to see the photo of the respected old man.

In the Ger-Aka's house Elena and Gabriel were met with honor, and treated with shish kebab and wines. The one-hundred-three year-old man agreed to be the guide. After two nights of wonderful rest on high soft feather beds and pillows, the three travelers, not counting the donkey, started their way to the Shelter of Eleven which was located at the foot of the peak Elbrus. They climbed all day, in the evening, reaching the mount Hotty Tau, covered with glaciers. Alas, here Ger-Aka started to feel his age: "I can't go anymore, my poor head is quite ill."

Saddened, he turned his donkey around, leaving Elena and Gabriel in total frustration. To go back was not the way of this couple. They went farther without map and guide. They crawled up the slope, slid on their bellies on the ice, flopping into snow, got up and repeated all this again. In few hours they lost their strength, but they could not rest on blocks of ice. They continued to move all night until they reached solid ground, where they fell down, utterly exhausted. The next evening they got to the Alpine camp The Shelter of Eleven's. Here they found thirty mountain-climbers, contrary to the name of the shelter resting in a big wooden barn. Elena and Gabriel got two folding cots and after eating cold soup from a tin, they went to sleep.

Elena returned to this part of the story many times. She narrated with a laugh about the bazaar-forum, where half of the residents of Karachaevo so easily solved all international problems that Chamberlain, who tried but did not manage to bring peace to the world, could be envious.

I felt that behind this story something more important was concealed. Elena always avoided my questions by changing the topic. Once, when Sarasota's golden sunset faded out and the patio was plunged into soft shade, I dared to repeat the question. I immediately regretted it, seeing that this caused Elena great agitation. She rose to her feet impetuously and began to pace across the patio. I realized Elena was far away from the imperturbable beauty of seaside Sarasota and the comfortable life of prosperous America. I thought with embarrassment that I didn't have a right to rush into Elena's past and began to apologize, but at this moment Elena began to talk.

"Imagine the closing dusk of night and the enormous bulk of the black mountain hiding the star-filled sky. We are in the Shelter, hardly moving due to fatigue, still hungry and almost falling asleep. Suddenly the door opened wide and two men entered the shelter. One of them is young, wearing a military uniform. He makes his way directly toward the table, and pulls out of a suitcase with all kinds of delicious food from which comes a dizzying aroma. The second man of medium stature wearing the Russian national shirt kosovorotka greets everybody in the Shelter with a loud confident voice and causes bursts of laughter with his jolly jokes. This reaction whips him up, and he continues to spout jokes to the right and left.

I am bad-tempered and hungry, glad of the opportunity to fend off his jokes and my answers provoked loud laugher too. Gabriel gave me a sign, which I didn't understand, and then he closed my mouth with his arm and is whispering, "Be silent, please. This is Bukharin, the closest companion-in-arm of Stalin!" Nikolai Bukharin was at that time the outstanding figure in Soviet government. He was close to Stalin and very popular among the Soviet people. The man in the Russian style shirt came directly to me. "Well, you have sharp teeth!" And I cannot leave it without an answer. "I am supposed to have sharp teeth; I am a woman and must protect myself from you men." "I see in your eyes you are hungry. Let's go to the table!"

"What about my husband?"

"Bring him too."

What a table it was! How many delicacies there were! I don't think we ever ate anything so fantastic."

The next morning Bukharin invited Elena and Gabriel for a walk. Elena and Bukharin continued to compete with witty jokes, and this Party theoretician took an obvious pleasure in it. Gabriel was silent almost all the time. He only smiled sadly and ironically expecting nothing good from this friendship developing so fast. Elena argued with him when they were in private, "What kind of friendship could there be between us? You know my opinion about the communists. They shot my father and sent my brothers to Siberia to assured death! But it is strange. Nikolai Ivanovich is not like that narrow-minded tyrant. He seemed to be quite a different person, very vivid, interesting, and talented. It is difficult to resist his intellect and charm. Did you see his watercolors? They look as if a professional made them. There is a lot of feeling in them. In different circumstances and in another life, we could be close friends, but not now."

The walking and exchanging wits went on for three more days. Elena tried not to speak about politics, but for once she could not suppress her curiosity.

"Nikolai Ivanovich, what do you think about Stalin?

"Caucasian donkey", he growled through his teeth. Elena was astounded by the disrespect and sharpness of this dangerous answer. She remembered the recent surprisingly rude Bukharin's article about the much beloved Russians poet, Esenin. What did this refer to? Maybe it was adapted among Party bosses parlance?

When their meetings ended, Bukharin asked the young couple to go down with him and his adjutant to the valley where his limousine was ready to take him to the Commissar's Resort. On their way to the valley they passed the Inn for foreign journalists who instantly ran toward Bukharin and his companions to interview the famous Party leader. Questions in different languages poured out, and Bukharin answered all of them without any interpreter. Elena wasn't surprised, she knew, that Nikolai Ivanovich could speak twelve languages, but she felt respect for him. Every reporter tried to take a picture. Bukharin embraced Elena by her shoulders. Click, click, and click. She smiled, not suspecting that these short flashes sentenced her to death.

Reaching the limousine, Bukharin offered to give Elena and Gabriel a lift to the closest tourist camp. His driver looked at the weather-bitten clothes of young couple with evident displeasure. With contempt he threw away Elena's rough stick, which she used since her alpenstock was lost.

"Promise to visit me in the Commissar's Resort!" shouted Bukharin departing.

Elena and Gabriel didn't make use of Bukharin's hospitality, but Elena met the theoretician of communism one more time before returning to Kiev.

The young couple decided to spend the rest of their holiday in the tourist camp where there were very nice horses. Elena was a wonderful rider. She grew up in the family of the village priest, who kept horses in his backyard among the other domestic animals. Elena was a tomboy, and the riding was an act of freedom and independence for the girl. Now she didn't want to miss out on the opportunity of indulging in her favorite sport. Elena rode at full speed when her horse suddenly reared in front of a car, unexpected in these places.

"Hey, crazy doctor!" Elena heard Bukharin's voice. "Why didn't you visit me?"

"It is better to be a little bit farther from you, commissar!" cried

Elena laughing. She could not imagine how right she was.

In February, 1937, Bukharin was arrested. He was accused of counter revolutionary activity. The real reason for his arrest was Stalin's fear of the growing popularity of Bukharin in the Soviet Union. Stalin could not tolerate any rivalry.

Shortly, Elena was arrested too. She and Gabriel had burned all the compromising pictures remaining from the Caucasian meeting with Bukharin, but the KGB had the same photos. During the rude interrogations, these pictures were used as proof of political bonds with the betrayer. They were hurled at Elena's face. She wasn't allowed to sleep at nights, and during the days she was interrogated until she fainted. Then she was doused with cold water and the interrogation continued. Clenching her teeth Elena rejected all accusations. She spent one year in prison and received the death sentence. Suddenly without any explanations she was released and even allowed to return to her job.

Elena began to hope that all her troubles were over, but half a year later she was arrested again. This time she was accused of poisoning the city wells with cholera germs. She was kept in prison for five months. Then they let her go again without any explanation. This sadistic cat-and-mouse play went on until the Second World War enveloped almost all Ukraine.

One disaster had been replaced by another, and Elena and Gabriel were sent to a German labor camp. Now this couple lived among five million people whom Germans called "Ostarbeiters" - workers from the East. The official statement from German authorities announced: "All workers have to get food and habitations sufficient for their maximum exploitation with minimum spending."

Elena didn't tell me about the horror of these years. "I cannot. I don't want to." By a miracle they survived, and finally came to America after the liberation of the labor camp by the American Army.

But it was not so simple. There was an agreement between Stalin and Truman that all repatriates should be returned to the Soviet Union. To get permission for emigration to America was almost impossible, but to go back to the Ukraine meant inevitable death.

It is difficult to imagine now and explain this inhumanly cruel Stalin order, but all the Soviet citizens who were captured by Germans and kept in the labor camps as Ostarbeiters had been sent to Soviet

Concentration Camps.

Elena, with her previous prosecution and imprisonment in USSR had no chance to survive. With big difficulty they managed by a miracle to persuade American representatives not to send them back to USSR. Gabriel was Polish by birth, and it helped.

America! Exhausted, nearly beggars but extremely happy, Elena and Gabriel greeted the statue of Liberty. Nobody was waiting for them. The young couple had no place to stay, but it was not difficult to find work; very simple jobs meant survival. The first living space they were able to rent for a small amount of money was a tiny, unfurnished room. The windowsill served as a chair and the hard floor was their bed. The meager life never depressed them. Any small purchase was a reason for celebration. Two chairs, then a table, followed a narrow bed. After they bought proper clothes, they began hunting for professional jobs.

In December, New York was in a fever of anticipation of the coming holidays. The streets looked like a flowing river of people with gift boxes and packages. In this happy stream of people only Elena's hands were empty. Overcome by the general mood she allowed herself be carried away in a gleaming splendid store. All the tempting things on its shelves were far beyond her buying capacity. Everything was dizzyingly wonderful there and dizzyingly unapproachable. However, she could buy the beautiful empty gift boxes! Each of them cost only one cent. Elena chose two of them and asked the salesmen to tie these boxes with red and green ribbons. This service was free. Now happy Elena flittered out to the street and continued her way home, proudly carrying her gifts. She was no different now than all the people around her. Elena opened wide the door of their apartment with jolly excitement. "Elena!" screamed Gabriel with horror. "Are you crazy? How much did you pay for this stuff? What is it?"

"I bought the Air of Festivity," Elena announced smiling widely. "I paid only two cents for cheers!"

She solemnly set her trophy up on the windowsill.

* * *

Gabriel noticed in the backyard of their house an old broken car.

He asked their landlord permission to use this car to learn to drive. "I give this carriage to you, it is yours," said the landlord with a laugh.

Gabriel was as happy as a child. "I have my own car! This is the first car in my life!" he announced gleefully to Elena as if it was not a heap of ruins but a new shining Ford. He was busy with this iron invalid every evening, disassembling and reassembling all its parts. Finally the old car came to life with terrible growling to the astonishment of all witnesses. Gabriel's first car moved!

This 44 years old man was a physicist by education. He knew English pretty well from his school years, and it helped him a lot now. He sent resumes to every possible place. In two months Gabriel was invited for an interview with the Oceanography Survey. Everything was going smoothly while he talked about his previous job in Kiev, his many articles and lectures, but then an inevitable question followed. "Well, but what do you know about the ocean?"

Gabriel sighed, "I know that the water in the ocean is salty."

The interviewer laughed. "It is not much! But I see, you are a strong physicist and I am sure that soon enough the ocean would be more than salty for you." This prediction was correct: Gabriel became the leading scientist there for the rest of his life.

Elena was sending her resumes to all possible medical institutions, but it was quite difficult for her because her English was very poor. She worked hard all the time to study it, but without much success.

At last, she was employed by the University of New York as a junior research assistant. She knew she needed only to start; it was important for her to show what she was capable of. Her great abilities moved her up quickly. In two years she got a position as a research-microbiologist; then she was invited to give lectures to the young doctors. Elena resolutely refused. Her English left much to be desired. The rector comforted her, "Don't panic, I am sure you will cope with it." She coped with this job too, but not without some funny incidents.

Of all immigrants, who had not experienced a joke perpetrated by English grammar, when changing one letter led to a stylistic catastrophe? For Elena it was compounded by the fact she faced an auditorium of young physicians. One day she wrote the long medical term on the black board. In a minute she understood that she had made mistake in this word. She fixed it and underlined. In the next five minutes Elena realized, that there was another mistake in the same word. She turned to the black board, changed "o" to "u" and underlined this mistake again. After the end of the lecture one of her student asked Elena politely, "Doctor Fedukovich, could you let me correct one more mistake in this word?"

Humor always saved Elena. She never turned red or pale, or cold in such situations, but made jokes. This time she asked laughing, "Does somebody know why English vowels have several sounds that are confusing to the poor foreigners and even English people themselves?" Nobody knew it, and Elena was a victor again. "I will give you a small linguistic lesson. When the Romans subdued the British islands, the aborigines, the Celts, didn't have the written language, but they had fifteen vowels in their spoken language. They borrowed their written language from the Romans and pushed their fifteen vowels into six Roman ones. It created a real mess, which I pay for now."

The students loved Elena for her knowledge and for her humor and helped her with English. Her lectures were unbelievably popular. For the rest of her life Elena received letters of gratitude from her former students who lived and worked in many different countries.

Elena taught and learned. Any new knowledge was her joy, she absorbed it like a sponge. She did not have time for everything she longed to know and to do. "If only twenty-four hours would be redoubled!" she thought.

Her first book was presented successfully at the crowded University's meeting. "Professor Fedukovich," addressed the Rector to Elena after her speech, "What is your best wish?"

"To have a slave!" responded Elena without a moment's hesitation.

Slave?! The audience was shocked. "Yes," confirmed Elena not being confused, "a small domestic slave, who would make me free from slave labor for my household." "Wonderful!" The rector parried resourcefully. "The University will present you with the pressure-cooker." All the people burst out laughing.

* * *

Elena's ninetieth year's birthday was celebrated with splendor. Guests arrived from different parts of America as well as from many other countries to participate in the jubilee meeting honoring Elena Fedukovich. Her books, which were the standard instruction for young physicians for forty years, were placed on the anniversary stand. From the waves of ovation, she rose upon the stage in order to give once again wisdom and vitality of her mind to her pupils and the colleagues. She looked rejuvenated among the ocean of flowers, the warm words and greetings. She was beautiful at this festival of the victory of her spirit. Her joyful eyes and sharp humor obliterated age. I looked at her with adoration remembering involuntarily Elena's favorite parable.

Socrates on the eve of his execution heard a boy playing a reed pipe.

" Teach me", he appealed to the young musician.

"Tomorrow you must drink the cup of poison and die, but today you want to learn to play. Why?"

"Why? The philosopher repeated. "Just, to know!"

Across the Border

The huge plane landed at last in the JFK airport in New York. Nica's throat was squeezed by a spasm. The leap from the accustomed absurdities of Soviet life to the USA, The Country of Yellow Devil, to some people or, The Country of Great Opportunities, to others, seemed to Nica impetuous, despite the four month halt in Rome. There was a long trip for Nica's family of four before the wheels of the double-deck Boeing hit the American ground. They had with them a small part of the native life, because twenty-five compatriots-refugees accompanied this family all the way to America. Among them were good and bad, pleasant and unpleasant, acceptable and absolutely intolerable persons. And now Nica, Gersh, their eight-year-son Dima and Gersh's mother, Rachel prepared to step into a completely new and unfamiliar life. The country where they were born, grew up, lived and worked was left behind as well as their battle for the right to emigrate and their long journey that scared them by uncertainty and excited them by novelty and hope.

America. How had it started? Why had Nica and her family come here with only three small suitcases forsaking everything else at home? There were several reasons. First of all Gersh was Jewish and the word "Jew" was printed in bold letters on his USSR passport, causing constant troubles and insults. Gersh craved "to die as a free man in the free land" and dreamed about America. Then it was Nica's horror that her little son with his black shining eyes and a constant gullible smile would too be "Dmitri-the-jew" for all his life in USSR with all the inevitable consequences in this anti-Semitic country. "Dimka-the-jew" (Dimka - offensive diminutive of Dmitri) was already announced in children's scrawl with misspelling on the white wall of their house. Besides, Nica's freethinking and critical attitude toward the Soviet regime urged her on. However, there was one more reason about which Nica have never told anyone. She felt dizzies from the burning desire for freedom, irresistible thirst to escape from the stuffy atmosphere of the "Iron curtain" and break out of the ubiquitous in the USSR grip of KGB. She dreamed of adventures, her soul was longing for something unknown, exceptional.

The path to the new life has been painful and unpleasant. Needless to say Nica and Gersh were exhausted passing through multitudinous bureaucratic offices. This created a feeling of walking through a maze, which had no exit. Up to the last moment, they did not know what direction they would move, to the West or to the opposite side, to Siberia where dissidents were often sent. Nica stared for a long time when she recalled these trials. Nevertheless, in this chain of constant stresses there were some funny moments.

As it was authorized in the Soviet Union, Nica had to endure the "Court of disgrace",at the Research Institute where she worked. Of course it was not a happy event. It meant that at a general meeting the head of the Institute (with whom Nica always was on the best terms) was forced to find something bad in her character and unmercifully criticize her for betraying socialism and the Motherland. All the employees had to support him and stigmatize Nica trying to say the worst thing they would invent about her. It was the only way to prove to the ruling authority of the Soviet Union that the Institute and its employees were patriots and were not betrayers themselves. It would keep them from political troubles. Nothing honorable was in this Court of Honor, and everybody knew that. The head of the Institute had a private conversation with Nica and asked her not to come to this meeting where he and all the employees had no choice but to smear her in front of a big Communist Party boss.

After this notorious meeting, three posters were given to Nica's subordinates: "Forward to the triumph of Communism!", "Be on guard: the enemy never sleeps!" and "Love your Motherland, the best country in the world!" These posters were a kind of punishment for the failure of the members of the lab to foster their leader in a spirit of devotion to socialism.

And here it was that Nica and her colleagues had fun. Nica herself nailed these three posters on the wall of the lab, and they all laughed heartily telling their favorite anecdotes about Soviet life and making sarcastic jokes about the stupidity and absurdity of the Court of Honor. Then a Goodbye Party followed, and Nica cut the cake on the laboratory's desk for the last time in her life. After this party she left the Research Institute as a person without definite occupation. She had been fired, and as a betrayer lost any possibility to be employed anywhere.

Nica and Gersh eagerly waited for the moment they could leave the Soviet Union for another three years, but when it happened, they were not prepared. Flabbergasted, stunned and entirely ignorant about their future, they looked at the thick clouds the plane went through. Then the sun appeared in the boundless blue sky, and their past life was cut away by the gray clouds below. They were hanging in the air outside of any country and border, not belonging to any scrap of the earth, cosmopolitans in the literal meaning of this word.

The plane landed in Vienna and was immediately surrounded by a brigade of armed soldiers. All emigrants were guided to a big and beautiful chateau, where the Red Cross quartered them, separating men and women and putting 12 people in every room. It was not clear if the armed guards protected emigrants from Arabian terrorists or shielded their country from the strange Soviets. Three days had passed, and Nica and her family were put on a train. Motionless inaccessible soldiers with machine guns stood in front of every door while the train slipped fluently through beautiful neat Austria. Next morning, when Nica woke, there were no Austrian soldiers, nobody guarded the emigrants, and unique landscapes of Italy stretched outside the train windows.

Rome! Nica dreamed of seeing this fabulous city, which absorbed two and half millenniums of human passions. She walked across

Rome far and wide during the four months of their stay there. By then she knew this city better than many of its inhabitants. Rome turned out to be much more glorious than Nica imagined, and people were just as Italians should be, friendly, joyful and noisy.

Emigrants were quartered in a small old inn with squeaking wooden staircases and domestic coziness. However there was a rule. Six persons in each room was the minimum, and it was not cozy at all. Because Nica's family consisted only of four members, they shared their room with two more people, a Moldavian cellist and a comely twenty-year- old girl with the short name Lina. The Moldavian spent only nights in this room, and nobody saw him during the daytime, but Lina became a friend of Nica's. Beside being a pleasant companion, Lina knew Italian and was helpful for everybody around.

Entering the room, Nica immediately zoomed to the heavy curtains and leaned out the window to examine the surrounding street. The inn was almost in the center of the city, and Nica enjoyed the gorgeous view from the window. In about five minutes, she heard a loud voice from below. A nice looking young Italian tried to explain something to Nica, helping himself with gesticulation. Nica was in a wonderful mood and she wanted to help this nice gentleman, but she did not know Italian. The stranger changed to English, which was of no help. Their reciprocal misunderstanding went on too long. Nica smiled and helplessly spread her hands and suddenly understood with clearness the essence of the matter. She started back from the window coming down from the blissful heaven, the hot flush on her face. Nica learned in a painful way that her curiosity was a trap, because in this country it was the custom. If some woman opened the curtains and showed herself from the window, it meant, "Here I am. Give me your price".

Three weeks later all the emigrants were moved to Ostia, which was only twenty minutes, by train from Rome. There they waited till their papers could be checked by American's Immigration office. Here, in Ostia, Nica's family lived in an excellent four-story house with a glassy foyer, decorated by bronze ornamentation. Their apartment had huge windows and a balcony with delicate railings. Nica had never seen such luxurious quarters. It went without saying that they could not afford to rent this place; so three families united together to occupy three rooms of this apartment with one bathroom for all the inhabitants. The apartment was designed for only a young couple with one child and not for eight adults plus four children. But this small problem did not bother Nica. Emigrating from Moscow she did not expect a first class voyage.

Every morning Nica got up trying not to step on her son, Dima, sleeping on the floor next to her bed. She made her way through the small cramped room to the window, and, oh, miracle! Fabulous view of Ostia smiled to her with the sea shining at the sunrise. After a few minutes of quiet pleasure at the window she woke Dima, and they went to buy fresh Italian brioches with a crisp crust for breakfast, or they walked to the market to get the cheap turkey wings for dinner. The fried turkey wings together with fresh sweet tomatoes were absolutely delicious.

For four months HIAS, The Hebrew Immigration Aid Society, provided benefits not only for Gersh's mother and Gersh, but also for Nica and their son, although both of them were not Jewish. They received enough money to get the most needed things but not enough to exhaust themselves for any shopping temptations. Nica felt a delightful sense of freedom not having any obligation or responsibilities. It was like a long, amazing holiday, which happened for the first time in her adult life. Almost every day she wandered around Rome feeling like a student embarking on an adventure permitted only to youth.

Nica could afford to stroll around Rome due to the generosity of the same HIAS, which organized the all-day camp-school for emigrants' children. Her son, Dima attended this school every day. The children were taught, fed, entertained and made acquainted with religion. Besides the Synagogue there was the Baptist church that was trying to convert the emigrants. Eight-year-old Dima joined the new life with a curiosity, enthusiasm, and an inexhaustible optimism, his greatest gift from birth. He perceived religious dogmas skimming the cream off very literally .

"Mommy, he declared decisively, today we will go to the Baptist church. It will be very interesting for you, I assure you."

Indeed, it was interesting for Nica for a good reason. Religious knowledge was only theoretical for her before coming to Ostia, and she was glad for the opportunity to learn more about it firsthand. After all, civilization gave birth to religions almost at its own beginning.

While Nica carefully and attentively listened the long preaching in Russian expressly for Soviet emigrants, her son escaped to the nearby room where tables were set with all kind of sweets. Nice women in black dresses kindly smiled of Dima and allowed him to fill his mouth with these luxuries. When after the sermon all parishioners were invited to the tables, it seemed that sweetness ran out of Dima's happy, trustful, black eyes. This was repeated in the Synagogue. After the sermon, Nica always found her son at the tables with delicious cookies and candies, which she could not afford to buy. Thus, Dima's religious experience was very sweet.

Nica and Gersh were lucky that Dima always got along with the people around him and was happy in any situations. This made their life much easier. The secret was simple. He sincerely believed that all people around loved him. And he loved them back. He was ready to love even villains. This unique ability of little Dima to love even scoundrels could be a good illustration to the bible stories. To Nica's amazement he performed true miracles taming hyenas, although still anthropoids. This ability of his began long ago when he was a baby, and the family lived in Moscow in a huge multi-story apartment building. There were benches at the entrance to all doorways, which served as the observation posts for old women. Suspicious, gloomy and condemning looks pierced Nica every time she entered the building or went out of it. But everything changed if Nica appeared with Dima. "Aunt Dasha, Aunt Pasha, Aunt Masha" he exclaimed as he rushed from one fury to another with exhilaration and rapture. And the gloomy old women became miraculously kind grandmothers for few minutes. They pulled hard candies from their pockets and tried to embrace and caress the little boy. But if Nica or anyone else came home without this tiny magician, they were pierced again by looks of hatred and suspicion.

However the most impressive story was the domestication of the former KGB officer Valentina, the next-door neighbor of Nica's family. She hated Nica, the wife of a Jew and a suspiciously intelligent white-collar worker. She hated this young woman openly with unaccountable and overpowering odium. It was nothing less than class antagonism.

One evening, when Nica was going home after picking up her three-year-old son from daycare, she saw Valentina approaching them slowly, burning ominously with blue flame. Nica's heart jump in her mouth. She expected with horror that Valentina would eat her guts. Suddenly Dima rushed to this monster with his small wide-open hands, "Aunt Valya!"

He was so happy to see her as if this "Aunt Valya" was going to give him as a present, an elephant, he had dreamed about for a long time.

Valentina lost herself for a moment, and then a very clumsy, weak, uncertain smile started to stretch her mouth. When Dima embraced her knees with all his vigor, Valentina, shining already, lifted him and kissed his cheek. The enemy died at once and forever. Beginning from that moment a loving and attentive friend lived next door.

Five years later, when Nica and her family emigrated for the USA, the KGB officer cried. Possible, Dima with his rare gift to love even villains was the only one soul in the whole world who loved her.

But Moscow and Rome were left behind becoming only memory. Now this family of four stepped off the plane into their new Promised Land.